THE FLASH™

CLIMATE
CHANGELING

ALSO AVAILABLE FROM TITAN BOOKS:

FLASH: THE HAUNTING OF BARRY ALLEN
by Clay and Susan Griffith

ARROW: GENERATION OF VIPERS
by Clay and Susan Griffith

ARROW: VENGEANCE
by Oscar Balderrama and Lauren Certo

ARROW: FATAL LEGACIES
by Marc Guggenheim and James R. Tuck

GOTHAM: DAWN OF DARKNESS
by Jason Starr

GOTHAM: CITY OF MONSTERS
by Jason Starr

CLIMATE
CHANGELING

RICHARD KNAAK

SERIES DEVELOPED BY GREG BERLANTI,
ANDREW KREISBERG, AND GEOFF JOHNS

TITAN BOOKS

THE FLASH: CLIMATE CHANGELING
Print edition ISBN: 9781785651434
E-book edition ISBN: 9781785651441

Published by Titan Books
A division of Titan Publishing Group Ltd
144 Southwark St, London SE1 0UP

First edition: August 2018
10 9 8 7 6 5 4 3 2 1

TIBO40872

Visit our website: www.titanbooks.com

A CIP catalogue record for this title is available from the British Library

Printed and bound in the United States.

THE FLASH™

CLIMATE
CHANGELING

Thunder rolled, shaking S.T.A.R. Labs and making Cisco Ramon tightly grip the arms of his chair. The lights flickered and the screen he had been staring at for the better part of an hour dimmed. Cisco swore under his breath in Spanish, then relaxed when the weather settled down for the moment. Rubbing his hands through his dark, shoulder-length hair, he began looking over the system.

"How are we looking, Cisco?" came Barry's voice over the com link. "Just give me a location and I'll force his hand!"

"All systems are go," Cisco replied in a much more confident voice. "Got every city Wi-Fi hotspot monitored, all 4G and 5G tapped, and I've even hooked into Photogram in case he tries to pass things through there!" He leaned back, put his hands behind his head and grinned. "All we need to do now is wait for you to drive Snapshot into using his phone! Rigged or not, it'll run through one of those!" Cisco looked back. "Where's Caitlin, H.R.? She won't want to miss this! It was her who caught on to him using his phone to pass on an imprint of his mind so he could control his victims!"

"She mentioned something about a headache; said she'd be right back."

"Good! She'll want to be here, especially after what he tried to do to her friend Darla."

As Cisco momentarily shut off communications, thunder shook the building again. Cisco let out another quiet oath.

"I wasn't aware you were afraid of storms," H.R. commented companionably from the table to Cisco's left. The thin, middle-aged man grinned sympathetically then took a sip from his coffee mug before adding, "You know, they say it does wonders to talk these things out. Now, I'm no psychiatrist—at least not on this world or the one I came from—but I'm definitely a good listener and could maybe still give you some suggestions—"

Leaning forward again, Cisco double-checked the system to make certain everything was running properly. Without glancing at H.R., he replied, "Not the storm, not exactly. Usually, they don't bother me. Just when they get a little wild like this one." Cisco tapped another button. "Yep. All systems perfect. Sometimes I even impress myself, which I have to tell you is getting harder and harder with all my illustrious achievements!"

"'Sometimes'?" H.R. returned, with a look of

false shock. Setting the mug down, he tried to look knowledgeable, something from which his very casual shirt and jeans detracted. Despite the twenty-plus-year age difference, it was Cisco who was in charge when the pair were alone: it was Cisco who knew S.T.A.R. Labs as if he had built it himself, not H.R., who merely wore the identical face—and body—to the man who had actually created the futuristic facility.

They were joined by a smartly dressed attractive young African-American woman with long dark hair who currently had her cell phone pressed against her ear. She nodded, then said, "Great, Dad. I'll let them know." Hanging up, she told the others, "Dad's got the truck set up. He's given me the coordinates. If Barry gets Snapshot, the truck's ready to secure him, thanks in part to the equipment we provided."

"Cool! Great, Iris!" Cisco replied. "That's the last piece. We're ready."

"How's Barry doing?"

"All set. Grab some popcorn and take a seat!"

"Let me see," H.R. murmured, still caught up in his conversation with Cisco. "A storm. Lightning. Thunder. Rain. It was a dark and stormy night—"

Cisco gave him a look. "Really?"

"Sorry. As a writer I couldn't pass that up." H.R.'s brow furrowed. "Damn it! I *am* dense. Now I know what's bothering you! Mark Mardon! The Weather Wizard!"

As if in response, yet another round of thunder nearly deafened the pair. The power remained constant but Cisco's brief scowl did not go unnoticed.

"It *is* Mardon. He's still safely locked up in Iron Heights, isn't he?"

Iris suddenly looked anxious. "He's still there, right?"

"Of course he is… I think he is… Let me check… Just to be sure." Cisco tapped a finger on the desk, then returned to the console. Typing in a few words, he waited. With a bit more relief in his voice than he realized—but that H.R. noted with a frown—he replied, "Yep! Still safe and secure! Guess it paid to make sure the prison got some of that marvelous tech I used to create the Wizard's Wand. Right now Prisoner Mark Mardon is slumbering away the storm. Hmph! Figures he could sleep through this."

"Thank goodness!" Iris smiled as she relaxed.

H.R. took up his mug again. "So, that's that fear dealt with! Maybe I missed my calling! I *must* be a psychiatrist or psychologist or maybe a talk show host on *some* Earth!"

"Or just plain nosy on most," Cisco quipped. Dismissing the prison directory, which he did not mention he had broken through top-level security in a matter of seconds to breach, Cisco returned to the task of updating the lab's systems. "Considering what we've faced over the last few years, we should all be basket cases. Each time I think we've seen every power a metahuman could possibly have, a new one pops up!" He typed in a few brief corrections to the program he had been studying. "'Course, if not new ones, the worst ones seem to repeat. Like Mardon and his brother. Never seems to end."

H.R. saluted him with his mug. "You guys deserve a medal for remaining as calm as you have! I've only been here a short time and I'm already frayed at the edges half the time!"

"If anyone deserves a medal, it's Iris," Cisco countered. "Or maybe Caitlin. She's—"

"She's *what*?" asked a feminine voice from the doorway.

Both men looked up at the pretty brunette woman entering the room. Roughly the same age as Cisco, Caitlin Snow was every bit his match in intellect and Cisco was more than happy to say so. Even *more* than a match in some ways. Caitlin was very much the clinical scientist. She was dressed neatly and fashionably, only the odd bracelet on her wrist seeming out of place. As Cisco watched, Caitlin instinctively adjusted the sleeve of her thin leather jacket so that it covered the bracelet. She smiled at him, then at H.R. and Iris before eyeing the nearest window. "Wow! It's pouring out there… and getting worse by the moment."

"Yeah." Cisco swung back to the console. After a moment's perusal, he hit the ENTER key. "The lab central system program is fully updated, by the way. Had time to do that too, genius that I am!"

"Gosh. So sorry I missed *that* fun—" Suddenly wincing, Caitlin put a hand to her temple.

"Are you all right?" H.R. asked, rising.

"It's just that migraine. It'll pass. Since this storm started, my head's been pounding!"

"Thought you were going to get some aspirin."

"I got distracted. Kept looking forward to teaching Snapshot what it's like to play with people's minds. I didn't miss that pleasure, did I?"

Cisco chuckled. "No, that game is about to commence!"

H.R. rose. "Let me get you some aspirin anyway. I'm little use as it is here and you deserve a ringside seat."

"That's sweet of you. Thanks!"

"I'll go with you, H.R.," Iris interjected. "I guess I'm a little too antsy to sit just yet."

"Happy to have the company."

As they left, Caitlin sat down next to Cisco.

He took a close look at her. "Your eyes are a little bloodshot. Maybe you should've gone home."

"And miss this? I know I shouldn't feel this way, but I'm looking forward to the payback. Darla deserves that." She smiled. "My migraine will be nothing compared to the headache he's got coming."

At that moment a new round of thunder shook the building. Once more the lights flickered.

But Cisco paid little attention to all that, more concerned with how Caitlin had reacted to the latest crash of weather.

Exhaling, Caitlin noticed him staring at her. "What?"

"Let me see the bracelet." Without waiting for her,

Cisco took her wrist and pulled it close. He touched the top.

"Cisco—"

"Readings normal. Good. No power manifestations?"

"Cisco—"

"Caitlin? Don't lie to me." He tapped the bracelet. "Just answer."

"No. No manifestations." Caitlin smiled. "Thanks for the concern. And thanks for the bracelet."

"Just so long as it keeps doing its job—"

Once more it thundered harshly and once more Caitlin rubbed her temple.

Cisco rubbed his chin. "This storm is really touching you. That's odd. Ever have that happen with a storm before?"

"No. Never."

"Never. Of course, never. Let me check something else." He swung around to the computer and brought up another program. Cisco typed in the information he had and waited.

"What are you doing? Is there something about the storm and me?"

"These readings don't make any sense." He input the data again. "The storm shouldn't have these levels. These look more like…"

She slid next to him. "Look like *what*? Don't leave me asking questions!"

"Here's your aspirin, Caitlin—and we've got a metahuman problem, don't we?" H.R. asked, clutching the aspirin as if it had suddenly become a badly needed weapon.

"Something go wrong with the setup for Snapshot?" Iris asked.

"No, that's all good to go still! I don't know *what* we have here." Cisco studied the readings for the dozenth time.

Caitlin picked up on his growing concern. She bent toward the nearest console and started typing. "Anything we should warn Barry about?"

"About what? Let me try to make sense of this first. He's got enough going on helping out people caught up in this storm." Cisco tapped a button, updating the readings. If anything, they looked even more peculiar… and yet familiar. "Reminds me of something—"

The system began beeping.

Cisco returned to the computer. "Looks like it's show time! Smile, Snapshot! You're on Capture Camera!"

"Cisco!" Despite her initial reproving tone, Caitlin smiled. Turning to her own console, she grabbed a headset.

Still grinning, he switched on his own microphone. "Got 'em, Barry! Here you go!"

The Flash raced through the city, purposely avoiding the address Cisco had given him. He needed Snapshot to commit himself. Once that happened, the plan would fall into place.

"He just hit SEND!" Cisco called.

"Get him, Barry!" Caitlin added.

"I won't let you down, Caitlin!" The Flash braced himself. In a moment he would have to be virtually in the same place—or rather *ten* places—at the same time.

Cisco's voice came over the link. "They're answering! Ready for all coordinates!"

"Ready, guys!" the speedster responded.

Cisco and Caitlin fed him the addresses. Barry picked up speed. Suddenly, he was on the north side, in a bank that had just closed. A well-dressed businessman—the bank president, in fact—had his cell just out of his pocket.

The Flash seized the phone and raced out of the bank. Not even a second later, he was on the west side, where a young woman in military garb was just pausing by a bus to grab her mobile. Barry snatched it and moved on. The Flash darted back and forth across Central City, gathering phones before the users could actually see what they had been sent.

Except for the last one.

The figure leaned against a wall protected by a wide overhang. As the Flash neared, he got a good look at what was apparently just a teenage boy... providing one paid no attention to the silver eyes.

Gritting his teeth, Barry seized his cell phone. Up close, he could see that the boy's normal eyes were still in part there. Snapshot had not yet taken control.

The Flash had no need to see what each of the

metahuman's victims had been sent. Snapshot's "selfie," along with its hypnotic eyes. Snapshot's images were a variation of the old superstition that a photo captured a person's soul. In this case, though, the electronic image sent a bit of Snapshot's mind to each of his victims. Anyone who opened the attachment and stared at the image became his puppet for several hours. Snapshot had used his abilities for revenge and then profit, stealing secrets and other things of value through his victims.

Caitlin's friend had been one of those victims, later accused of theft and more. Thanks to the crew, she had eventually been cleared, but Snapshot had remained at large.

That was about to end.

Cisco and Caitlin sent Flash the final coordinates. They had had trouble tracking him thanks to Snapshot rerouting all his calls, but Cisco had finally set up a program to counter that measure. This time they knew exactly where Snapshot was.

The tall, gaunt metahuman with the shock of silver hair stood inside a decorative gazebo in the middle of the city park, wraparound sunglasses on despite the darkness. Other than the hair and sunglasses, Snapshot was dressed fairly normally, in a leather jacket, jeans, and boots.

The Flash had made the mistake of looking into those actual eyes once and had barely shaken off their hypnotic effects. This time he knew exactly what to do.

He tore off Snapshot's sunglasses and tossed them aside. Before the spectacles could even drop, the speedster began circling his foe. As he did, he set the open cell phones at eye level.

The Flash slowed just enough to be able to see the reaction.

"What the—?" Snapshot's silver eyes widened. He gaped and tried to look away. Unfortunately for him, he looked right into another phone with his image staring back.

Snapshot froze.

"It worked like a charm, guys!" Barry called as he slowed to a halt. He caught all of the phones, making sure to keep the one Snapshot had ended up staring at in front of the metahuman's gaze. "He had as strong a stare as we thought, much to his bad luck right now."

"That should keep him good long enough to bring him in and have something more permanent done to keep his eyes under control," Cisco cheerfully replied. "Here's the coordinates for the truck. Joe and the police will take over for you as soon as you get our friend secured in the vehicle."

"Got it! Hang on!"

Hefting his prisoner, the speedster raced Snapshot to where Joe waited. The journey was so quick that the captured metahuman didn't even have time to register that the phone was no longer in front of his gaze.

"One in the bag?" asked Iris's father. Detective Joe West might have been twice as old as Barry, but as a veteran lawman with an earnest desire to keep justice in Central City, he had stayed as fit as most of the younger officers around. Coat pulled tight to fight against the weather, he pulled out a pair of the cuffs developed to hold those with meta powers, and snapped them on.

Snapshot shook his head. "This—what?"

The Flash took a visored helmet from the truck and set it on the villain's head. The opaque visor entirely obscured Snapshot's eyes.

"All yours," he told Joe and the officers.

"Thank you!" Joe turned Snapshot over to two men in the truck. "You have the right to remain silent. Anything you say…"

Grinning, the Flash raced off.

Cisco leaned back. "We *are* good, aren't we?"

"Try not to get a swollen head," Caitlin answered, standing. "But yeah, we did good."

"Ha! The storm's going to be dull compared to this!" Cisco stretched a hand to the keyboard, typed, then waited. "Well… maybe not dull… but more straightforward at least…"

Iris sighed. "Thank goodness."

H.R. looked at her. "Are you all right?"

"Yes… I'm just glad it went so well."

"How could it not with a crew like this?" Cisco asked with a grin.

"I hope I get a little of that credit."

The others stood up to greet Barry. Pulling back his cowl, he raced over to the coffee machine, poured a cup, and joined the others while they were still rising.

"Definitely a great job, dude," Cisco replied with a wide smile.

"Thank you, Barry," Caitlin added.

"Not at all. Wish they all went this easy."

"Hey!" Cisco interjected. "It wasn't easy; we're just that good! First Plunder just a few days ago and now Snapshot! We are on a roll!"

Iris joined Barry. The others surreptitiously pulled back from the conversation. "I'm so glad you're back. Are you all right?"

"He didn't even touch me. I told you not to worry. Joe's perfectly fine too."

"Thank you." Iris kissed him. "I am really glad you're back safe and sound."

A guilty look crossed his face. "Yeah… Iris. I have to get back out there. On my way back, I already had to help people twice. The storm's causing all sorts of problems."

"Must you? No, never mind. I know." She touched him on the cheek. "Go out there, but please be careful."

"I always am." Thunder rolled as Barry slipped his cowl back on. "Hey, Cisco! I'm going back out there! When you're through celebrating, do me a favor and switch on the police and emergency bands. Alert me to anything I can help with!"

"Will do! Nice job again, Barry! Can't wait to add Snapshot's mugshot to our collection!"

The Flash grinned. To Iris, he said more quietly, "I swear I'll be careful, all right? We've had this conversation a lot lately. I don't know what else to say."

"Just… Oh, never mind. Go!"

This time he kissed her. Then the Flash called out, "Thanks, everyone!"

Cisco positioned himself at the console. "All set for you, Barry!"

With a wave to all and one last look at Iris, the Flash raced off.

"Please be careful," she murmured.

He had to do something. His brother was about to die again. Despite all Mardon's vaunted power over the weather, history was about to repeat itself.

"Keep away from him, Clyde!" he shouted through the tempest in which they both hovered untouched like gods. "Let me take him! Not you!"

But as had been his younger brother's way throughout his life, Clyde Mardon lunged forward. As he did, the tempest roared to life and followed him.

"I've got him, Mark!" Clyde shouted. "Just watch what I can do!"

In the distance, a blurry form raced toward them. Mardon tried to strike at it, but Clyde somehow got in the path, forcing the older brother to abort his attack.

"Fastest man alive?" Clyde mocked at the blurry figure. "You can't outrun what's all around you!"

Thunder crashed. A dozen jagged lightning bolts struck the area surrounding the oncoming form. Mardon cheered his brother's efforts… until it became clear that none of the bolts had come even close to their enemy.

"Not too shabby," Clyde snarled. "Try this!"

A hailstorm erupted. Thousands of diamond-hard stones poured down on the racing figure.

None of which even touched it, the crimson attacker easily dodging every single one.

"Let me handle him, Clyde," Mardon shouted. "Let me!"

Clyde glanced back at him. The brothers didn't look much alike save in general build. Clyde had a wild, rough-hewn aspect that fit his personality well; Mark Mardon was thinner in the face—in part the product of the strain he had been through since the accident— and where Clyde's eyes flashed like the lightning, the older sibling's were dark and steady. Mark had always guided his brother, always kept Clyde from his own impetuousness… until fate had kept the two apart and the so-called hero of Central City had tricked the younger Mardon.

Tricked… A sense of dismay filled Mark Mardon. How could he have forgotten the other player in this game, the one the Flash had used to be the actual executioner? Couldn't have the city's squeaky-clean champion actually be the killer. No, better to let the cop do that and pretend it was self-defense…

"Clyde!" Mardon had to strain to be heard, so violent had the storm—Clyde's storm—grown.

A single short crack of thunder resounded throughout the city—

"No!" Mardon realized that it was not thunder he had heard, but rather a lone *gunshot*. "No!"

"Bullseye!" mocked a deep voice just behind him. "Never takes more than one shot to down a rat."

Mardon spun around. Where a moment ago he had been floating high above the soaked ground, now he stood in the middle of a street. Behind him, the speaker chuckled.

"West! Damn you! No!" Mardon tried to grab the imposing detective, but with a triumphant smile the law officer replaced his smoking service revolver in his overcoat, then dissipated like mist.

"M-Mark?" Clyde called in a weakening voice.

"Clyde!" Boosted by a strong gust of wind he himself created, Mardon flew toward his brother. Head bent down, Clyde hovered awkwardly. Then, just as the older brother neared, Clyde turned in the air to face him.

Blood poured from a gunshot wound directly where his heart was. The blood spilled out, coloring the torrential rain a deep red.

"M-Mark?" gasped Clyde, face as pale as the hail. "You were supposed to be th-there for me! You were *always* supposed to be there for me—"

"Clyde! No!" Mardon tried to grab his brother, but at that moment Clyde dropped like a rock.

Screaming, Mardon dove after Clyde, but without warning the river of blood became the same damned crimson figure the brothers had been fighting. The speeding form of the Flash rushed to a spot just below Clyde, and he caught the falling figure with ease.

Mark Mardon's momentary relief turned to renewed rage as the Flash briefly paused to smirk at his remaining adversary. Mardon's gaze went from the masked speedster's smirk to the lightning bolt insignia on the Flash's chest.

Gritting his teeth, Mardon used the insignia's influence to send a barrage of bolts at the speedster from all directions.

Still carrying Clyde's limp body, the Flash gave Mardon a mocking salute, then seemingly vanished.

"Come back, damn you! Come back—"

Without warning, the storm seized Mardon, tossing him high into it. He watched as the Flash stole his brother from him again and roared his bitterness and fury. The storm echoed his emotions, growing wild. Tornadic winds tore entire buildings from their foundations. Monsoon rain washed streets away. Yet the Flash raced on unaffected, he and Clyde dwindling in the distance.

Mardon unleashed another anguished cry. The storm reacted with an explosion of ear-shattering thunder—

And woke Mardon up to the harsh reality of Iron Heights and the true fate of his brother.

"Flash…" he whispered as he stared up at the thick stone and steel ceiling of his cell. "Flash…"

The actual storm outside chose that moment to rumble ominously, fueling Mardon's dark thoughts concerning the speedster. Detective Joe West would be dead by now if not for the Flash. At least there would have been that satisfaction.

"Unngh!" Another of the headaches struck him. He yearned to tear the metal cap off his head, but thus far his bleeding-heart lawyers had not managed to get Iron Heights' latest attempt at keeping his metahuman abilities dampened removed. Mardon didn't know if the headaches were part of the treatment, but they were certainly proving capable of keeping his concentration from lasting more than a couple of minutes.

But even the worst headaches, the worst pain, couldn't keep him from thinking about Clyde and his killers.

That was enough for him to try again. Mardon did only three things. Sleep, eat, and try to overcome the machines Iron Heights threw at him. Someday one of those machines would fail. They had to.

For the moment managing to force the headache pain back, Mardon concentrated his will. He was no mere prisoner. He was no mere metahuman, even. They had called him the "Weather Wizard" and he liked that name. The elements were his to command. No device, however clever, should be able to hold him!

Thunder shook the sturdy penitentiary. Mardon grinned, imagining that thunder an acknowledgement by the weather of just who its master was: Mark Mardon. The Weather Wizard!

Now who's the cocky one? a voice in his head suddenly joked. *I'm supposed to be the one with the big ego, bro!*

"Clyde?" Mardon paused, but the only sounds were the thunder and the pouring rain.

Frustration growing, he again poured his will into overcoming the machine. Mardon couldn't shake the feeling that this latest device shared ties with the wand one of the Flash's allies had created. Of course that had proven a double-edged sword for the speedster; Mardon had discovered that not only could he manipulate the mechanism himself, but the wand actually enabled him to focus his powers even better. With the wand, Mardon felt certain that he could have easily overcome the prison's mechanisms and escaped.

Awful lot of "maybes" and "ifs", Mark... thought you were the leader type. Show some spine! Make them pay for what they did to me!

"Clyde?" Mardon shot up to a sitting position, an act he immediately regretted. The headache intensified, making his head feel as if it were about to explode. He growled as he clutched the thin plastic and metal helmet he had to wear twenty-four hours a day. The warden had said the scientists were working on a more mobile version that they'd have ready in about a week, but that hardly cheered him. The current helmet was locked on tight and until his lawyers got that court order, it looked like he was going to have to wear the new version as well.

You're not gonna just roll over like that again, are you, Mark? Come on! Those two are out there savoring my blood and you're whining about headaches!

"Shut up…" Mardon pictured the Flash and Detective West going about their lives while Clyde lay dead and he struggled just to keep his thoughts straight. "They're not going to get away with anything… anything."

As if to punctuate his oath, lightning struck Iron Heights. For a moment the lights all died. They returned before Mardon could react, but the knowledge of the system's fallibility stirred him on. Still seated, he took a deep breath and once more imagined Clyde's death.

Clyde's death.

Clyde's death…

"I swore they'd pay," Mardon said to his brother. "I swore they'd pay and soon."

Prove it, Mark! Prove it to me!

"Stop shouting!" Mardon shut his eyes, the better to concentrate.

Another bolt struck Iron Heights. The lights faltered. For just a second the Weather Wizard felt utter clarity and utter control of his powers. And once again, the systems came back on before he could react. Still, Mardon felt a flush of hope. The storm was on his side almost as if he had summoned it himself. Thanks to the helmet that was impossible, of course, but Mardon still clung to the thought that if lightning could disrupt things twice this night, why not a third time?

He adjusted his position and waited. He could be

this patient. He had endured months in this hell; he could bide his time a little longer. All he had to do was pay strict attention—

"Mardon!"

The Weather Wizard scowled. He had no idea which guard had called his name. They were inconsequential to him and therefore not worthy of being remembered... except for the fact that right now this guard was distracting him.

"Mardon!" the faceless figure on the other side of the massive metal door shouted angrily. "It's lights out! No sitting up!"

"Storm's keeping me awake," he replied sarcastically.

"Down! Now!"

Mardon refused to move. He had himself set exactly the way he wanted to and worried that any movement would undo his focus. "I'm doing nothing. Go away."

"Mardon!"

You never let people step over you before, came his brother's voice again. *You'll never be able to stand up to the Flash and West if you can't stand up to a damned guard!*

"Shut up!" Mardon told the voice.

"That's enough out of you!" the guard commanded, mistaking the Weather Wizard's shout for one aimed at him. The guard called something to someone in the hall. Reinforcements, Mardon knew. They would never confront him alone, not even with his powers dampened.

They fear you, Mark, his brother said. *Show them they've got reason! Show me!*

A burst of thunder shook the prison. Mardon glared at the door, glared at the unseen guards gathering outside. If he had had his powers, they would have been fleeing in terror.

The wind howled. Lightning struck nearby. Mardon continued staring at the door, waiting, calculating. It had to happen again. It had to.

The door swung open.

Lightning battered Iron Heights.

The electricity—and the security system keeping Mardon from using his metahuman abilities—ever so briefly failed.

With an evil grin, the Weather Wizard struck his surroundings. A powerful whirlwind barreled into the guards just beginning to enter, sending them crashing into the hall. Lightning assailed the roof above his cell, battering it. Thunder pounded continuously, matching Mardon's racing heart as he reveled in his godhood.

That's it, brother! he heard Clyde urge triumphantly. *Show them what a Mardon is made of! Tear down these walls!*

"Tear down these walls…" the Weather Wizard repeated in the same tone. "Tear down these walls…"

The whirlwind with which he had so contemptuously tossed the guards back into the hall now swelled around him. The thick cell walls groaned as the incredible forces relentlessly pushed at them.

But Mardon was not satisfied with that. Even as severe cracks began to spread across the cell, the Weather Wizard summoned lightning. Bolt after bolt wracked the room. Mardon heard faint voices crying out in fear, but whether they were guards or other prisoners meant nothing to him. All that mattered was proving that he would not fail his brother.

The constant barrage proved too much for the cell. First the ceiling collapsed in. Any other prisoner would have been buried under tons of cement, steel, and more. Not so Mardon. The same winds that ravaged the cracking walls also kept anything from hitting him.

The outer wall finally shattered, spilling more debris beyond his ruined cell. Rain poured in, as with the debris just missing Mardon.

Breath coming rapidly, the Weather Wizard stood. The thunder continued to pound in a beat identical to that of Mardon's heart.

"I'll show all of them, Clyde!" he shouted as the storm enveloped the ruined interior. "I'll show them what happens to anyone who crosses us!"

Teach them, Mark... Teach them to shake in fear at the very mention of our name!

Arms outstretched, Mardon brought rain, hail, wind, lightning, thunder, and more down on what was left of his surroundings. Shouts continued from every direction.

The Weather Wizard smiled more widely.

The walls shattered, massive pieces of concrete flung far by the incessant wind.

"There you go, Clyde," he murmured. "Just the beginning..."

"Mardon! Halt!"

Three armed guards aimed at him from what was left of the corridor. The Weather Wizard gave them a scornful smile.

Hail pelted the men. They scattered like the ants they were to him. He had not let the three live out of any humanity. Mardon wanted witnesses to his power, witnesses that would make certain to remind the Flash and West just what they could expect.

It vaguely surprised him that the speedster had not shown up yet. "You're late, Flash!" He laughed manically. "Slowest man alive tonight!"

Stumbling back to what remained of his bed, the Weather Wizard reached underneath the mattress. He pocketed a few small bits of newspaper stuffed there, then stepped back.

The thunder intensified. The rain poured down harder, still spilling over everything but him. Mardon panted as he took more and more control of—nay, *became*—the storm. He felt as if it had been years since his confinement. The Weather Wizard struck out left and right, leaving ruin in his wake.

That's more than enough! Clyde's voice interrupted. *You want the Flash to come when you're all worn out? You always told me to pick my fights when the odds were best for me! One more night… We can wait one more night now, right?*

"One more night," Mardon gasped, only now feeling the effects of using the storm to ravage Iron Heights. Around him, alarms went off as the prison tried to deal with the havoc. "Yeah, one more night, Clyde…"

Rubble surrounded the Weather Wizard, blocking all exits. Anyone wanting to reach him on the ground would have to climb over tons of broken concrete and twisted metal. If Mardon wanted to leave by normal methods, he would have to take the same challenging course.

Inhaling, Mardon spread his hands. The wind gathered tightly around him, then below.

The Weather Wizard rose into the air. The wind carried him up above Iron Heights, where he momentarily admired his handiwork. The damage he had inflicted had affected other parts of the prison. There were probably other escaped convicts, including perhaps some metahumans. Mardon really didn't care save that it might mean more trouble for the Flash. Anything that kept the speedster distracted helped the Weather Wizard.

The wind carrying him briefly faltered. Mardon refocused his concentration. For the first time, he realized he still wore the damned helmet. Now bereft of any power, the helmet proved very simple to remove. Mardon watched with pleasure as it plummeted from sight, but then the wind faltered once more, dropping him several feet before he recovered.

Easy, Mark! came Clyde's voice. *You don't want to splatter all over the prison!*

He had to get to safety and rest. Once rested, he could concentrate on taking out the Flash and the detective. Clyde would understand...

Memory more than consciousness guided the Weather Wizard through the storm toward where he knew he could hide until he regained his strength. Mardon barely heard the thunderous din as he neared the old house that he and Clyde had used during their careers as bank robbers. It was actually one of three they had used and one he knew the cops had never located.

Below, Central City had become a murky shadow of itself. Sirens blared everywhere. Through his exhaustion the Weather Wizard grinned. Small wonder the Flash had not shown up. The storm had served Mardon well even when he had not been in control of it. It was almost as if his brother had sent it to watch over him—

The wind faltered and this time didn't immediately recover. Mardon dropped several yards before a weaker version of the wind managed to at least slow his descent. Rain that had previously avoided him thanks to his ability to bend its path away suddenly drenched the escaped rogue. Mardon knew that he had reached his end quicker than he had imagined. Between fighting the device and destroying his cell and part of the prison, the Weather Wizard had burned himself out.

He could see the outline of the old house, but now he was descending too fast again. Mardon tried his best to concentrate as the ground rushed up at him.

He hit it standing up, but his legs immediately buckled. Mardon collapsed, falling face first onto a drenched street.

The great Weather Wizard! Clyde's voice echoed. *Geez, Mark! Pull yourself together! You can't lie there!*

"You—you could at least give me a hand," Mardon growled as he fought to push himself up. "Easy—easy to—to bitch when you're dead!"

"You want a hand," responded someone behind him. "All you got to do is ask, Mark." Strong hands pulled him up not only from the street, but into the air again.

The Weather Wizard shook his head in a failed attempt to clear it. He knew he couldn't have heard what he heard... and yet... "Clyde?"

As he drifted through the air to a broken window on the second floor, the voice added, "We're home, brother. Time to get some rest. Time to plan revenge, eh?"

2

Sometimes, being the fastest man alive still did not seem fast enough to Barry. Each time he thought he'd finished rescuing those trapped in some manner by the wild storm, another crisis arose. Sometimes it felt as if the storm itself battled against him, foolish as that sounded. Even though it had been merely hours ago, the Flash had already begun to miss battling Snapshot. Fighting another metahuman was a task far more straightforward than dealing with nature. Of course, nature really had nothing against him nor had some nefarious plan in mind. It just was.

He raced along the overflowing river, piling sandbag after sandbag at the breach until the raging water was forced back. From there, he rescued a woman whose car had gone skidding off a bridge. The Flash left her with some grateful if startled firemen working on a warehouse set ablaze by lightning, then raced around and around the flames, using his speed to create a wind in his wake that drew the pouring rain behind him. The constant drench of water put out the fire in seconds.

The same forces that had granted him his super speed had also enhanced his stamina, but there were still limits. The Flash paused under an overhang from a building, perfectly dry despite the hours in the rain. His crimson suit had been designed to eliminate drag in all its forms as much as possible. The material was not only water resistant, but with his swiftness what few drops managed to touch it quickly slid away.

"I hope Iris will understand why I'm not back just yet," he muttered, seemingly to himself. In point of fact, someone at the lab generally monitored him at all times, but communication was kept to quieter times, not the madness through which he had raced for the past hour. When no one answered, the Flash asked, "Hey, Cisco! Are you on break?"

"Sorry!" came Cisco's weary voice. "Guess there's only so much ten gallons of coffee and a case of energy drinks can do! What'd you say?"

"Iris! Has she called since she left the lab a couple of hours ago?"

"No, she's not called. She'll understand. Listen, I—hold on!" Cisco's voice faded away, only to return a moment later. "Barry, Joe's just called in! You need to get over to Iron Heights fast! There's been a power outage and a lot of damage! Looks like lightning hit the system—"

"On my way!" By the time he answered, the Flash

had already covered more than half the distance to the prison, despite being on the other side of the city. Of all the possible disasters the storm could have offered, damage to Iron Heights was one of the worst he could imagine. More than a few of those incarcerated there had the Flash to thank for their prison terms, especially among the metahumans.

The streets became a blur as he picked up the pace. The Flash bypassed cars as if they were standing still. He paused long enough to grab a jaywalker more concerned about the rain than looking both ways and set the man back on the sidewalk just in time to avoid being hit by the emergency truck racing in the very direction the speedster headed. Barry took a deep breath and finished the last few miles in just over a heartbeat.

Fire raged from further inside the massive structure as the Flash entered the grounds. Several policemen and prison guards ran toward the nearest building as a fire crew got ready to douse a burning guardhouse.

Detective Joe West leaned on a squad car, talking into the radio and gesturing at the main facility.

"I'm here, Joe."

The detective flinched. Generally, Joe was one of the few so used to Barry that he was now rarely startled by the Flash's abrupt appearances, which revealed to the speedster just how frantic the situation overtaking the prison had to be.

"We've got fire, an explosion, and several loose

prisoners," Joe snarled. "You can see which wing got the worst of it."

The Flash nodded. "Is that where—"

Gunshots cut through the din from the storm. Barry didn't even hesitate, racing toward the sounds.

Two policemen hid behind the side of another car, weapons directed at the nearest building. The Flash caught a glimpse of a pair of convicts secreted by a damaged metal door. He could also make out a third figure next to one of the convicts: a guard whose arms had been bound.

One of the convicts raised a gun the Flash could only assume had been taken from the guard. The convict looked very comfortable with the weapon, which Barry believed meant he was probably an expert shot.

Of course, it hardly mattered. Barely had the convict acted than the Flash seized both the gun and the guard and carried them back to the police. After handing the weapon to one officer and the stunned but relieved guard to the second, the Flash eyed an item on the belt of each lawman.

"Mind if I use those?"

They had hardly even started to nod before he took what he needed and raced back to the two escapees. The Flash seized the still raised arm of the would-be shooter, pulled it and the other arm behind the convict, and bound the limbs with a restraint. He then did the same to the second convict, who had just begun to notice that the hostage had vanished.

Leaving both prisoners bound and seated, the Flash returned to the policemen.

"They're all set for you!" With a slight salute and a grin, Barry headed back to Joe.

"Sorry for the brief interruption," he said.

"I've got an idea what you just did, so don't apologize. Besides, you've got troubles enough coming. There's been a breach in the metahuman section all right. One prisoner escaped."

"That's better than I feared."

Joe West made a sour face. "No it isn't. It's Mark Mardon... and they say a lot of this damage is all from him."

"You didn't tell him about the change you noticed inthe storm over the past couple hours," H.R. pointed out as Cisco cut off communications with the Flash. The news about Mardon had put a slight damper on their celebration after dealing with Snapshot. Mardon was a metahuman of another level.

"It's not important right now. Barry's got enough going on. Besides, it may or may not have anything to do with Mardon. It doesn't fit the data we have on him. I mean, there are similarities in the readings, but also enough anomalies that you could argue either way—"

"I guess I got more excited about catching Snapshot than I thought."

Caitlin put a hand to her head. "I need an aspirin."

"I already gave you two," H.R. reminded her.

Caitlin picked up the cup of water he had also grabbed for her after handing over the aspirin. She swallowed what was left, then cleared her throat. "He's probably correct, H.R. This storm has been raging for a while. Cisco, you said you got into the Iron Heights system and everything was fine at the time, right?"

"Yeah. Running perfectly."

"Then the storm's probably just a normal if violent one. Not everything has to do with dangerous metahumans," she added. "Sometimes rain is just rain."

H.R. nodded. "Now if we could just make it go away and come back some other day, like next time it reaches a hundred degrees."

Cisco put a hand to the earpiece connected to the police reports and Barry's communications. "Updates coming in about the escape. Sounds like Iron Heights has some heavy damage, but it's confined to one area." He swiveled away from Caitlin. "Hey, Barry. Can you get close to Mardon's cell? Is there a chance yet?"

H.R. leaned down to try to hear Barry's response. As he did, he glanced one last time at Caitlin, who seemed to be mesmerized by her empty cup. H.R. frowned, then focused on the Flash.

Why could they have not just listened to her and moved on right away, Caitlin thought with sudden bitterness. H.R. could be maddening at times and Cisco was maybe one of the densest people she knew. Sometimes Caitlin wondered how she even put up with them—

What are you thinking? she reprimanded herself. *H.R. is always trying his best to be nice and helpful to you, and Cisco… and without Cisco where would you be right now?*

Where would *you* be?

Caitlin reached down and gently touched the odd, thick bracelet on her other wrist. She remembered when Cisco had first given it to her. *Wear it always,* he had quietly told her. *Wear it always and be safe.*

At the time, she had been pretty skeptical. However, since she had been wearing the bracelet, she had not had any bouts. Not, that is, until this storm had begun.

"Caitlin?" Cisco called. "Can you monitor that?"

She realized that he had been talking for several seconds. "I'm sorry. What did you want?"

He looked apologetic. "I need you to watch Barry's readings while I try to match them with the storm's fluctuations. I want to make certain that there's no connection between him and this weather."

"Why would there be?"

"I'm sorry. I know we just discussed it, but something's tied to this storm, something I can't help feeling is metahuman. I'm sure of that."

"But wouldn't Mardon make more sense?" interjected H.R. "I mean, being the Weather Wizard and all that… and escaping just now too." He cocked his head. "Just saying."

Cisco tapped his screen. "That would make sense,

but the pattern doesn't fit his readings at all."

Caitlin felt her irrational irritation stirring again. Fighting it, she straightened. "All right. I don't think you'll find anything, but let's try." She suddenly hesitated. "Does Barry know we're doing this?"

"I don't think there's reason to mention anything yet. Barry's a little busy at the moment." Cisco checked his earpiece. "Yeah, just a little... We'll tell him when things calm down... and if we even find anything."

Speed was not everything. Barry had learned that early on. If speed alone had controlled his life, for instance, the Flash would have already been well into his search for Mardon. Of course, even then, all the speed in the world didn't matter if he had no idea where to look. Clyde Mardon had been a creature of the moment; his brother Mark was far more of a planner. Mark Mardon would not be found anywhere obvious.

Meanwhile, what the storm and the Weather Wizard had wrought also demanded more from the Flash than simply speed. He had managed to douse more than a dozen fires and capture nearly twice that many escapees, but now the remaining convicts unaccounted for had secreted themselves away. Of course, Barry had the advantage in that the escaped prisoners had not had time to get very far. As the Flash, all he had to do was race repeatedly around the vicinity of the prison, trying to measure out the greatest distance any of the felons could have gotten before he arrived. Then, one by one, he narrowed down the places the escapees could hide and dragged each back to Iron Heights.

All the while the storm continued its relentless attack. The Flash kept to a run, the better to evade its effects. He circled Iron Heights for the two-hundredth time before stopping by Joe again. Unfortunately, it was to discover the detective on his personal phone. That meant only two people calling... and Barry doubted he could be so lucky as for it to be Wally on the other end.

"Now just relax, honey," Joe said in his most fatherly voice. "Yes, it was the metahuman section, but that's not important. I'm all right. We're all right. Barry's with me even now—"

The Flash made a warning sign, but it was already too late.

"You want to talk with him?" The detective looked relieved to find any excuse to end the conversation. "Great! Here you go!"

"Joe..." Barry began.

"Take it!" Joe whispered desperately. "She may listen to you!"

The Flash reluctantly took the phone. The moment he put it to his ear, he regretted it.

"Barry? Barry! I heard from a friend in the department about Iron Heights and the Weather Wizard! The Weather Wizard! I told my father he can't just stand out there! Mardon nearly killed him once before and swore he'd do so next time he ever had another chance. I don't want him to get another chance. *You* promised me my father would be utterly safe—"

"Easy, Iris…" the Flash began.

"Did you or did you not promise me more than once that my father would be safe from the likes of Mardon? Didn't you promise me that Mardon could never escape Iron Heights?"

"Well, I did, but—"

"No. Listen to me! I've had too much time to think about this! If it isn't Mardon, it's one of those other monsters. There's a metahuman around every corner. I just won't stand for it anymore."

A siren went off. With a tremendous look of guilt, Barry said into the phone, "I've got to go, Iris! We'll talk, I promise. Here's your father again."

"No! What're you doing—" Joe West had no choice but to take the cell phone thrust at him. "Iris, dear! Listen—"

By that time, the Flash had long raced off. He headed toward the siren, both relieved and concerned about the call. Barry *had* promised her that her father would be safe from all these metahuman threats, and yet the threats kept coming in worse and worse forms.

And then there was always Mark Mardon. He had come too close to killing Joe once before, and he had made it very clear after his capture that her father's death remained one of his greatest desires. It had taken Joe and Barry weeks to convince Iris that the Weather Wizard would be going nowhere, that Iron

Heights prison had him properly secured.

The siren turned out not to have anything to do with the escaped prisoners, but rather with the damage the storm and Mardon had caused the facility. Already overtaxed by lightning strikes, both natural and not, the power grid for the penitentiary had finally begun to collapse completely. All around the speedster, the power flickered madly. The Flash realized that if the system ceased functioning a new round of dangers would be unleashed, including more potential escapes by metahuman convicts.

Barry halted in front of a fire captain. "How bad is it?"

After gaping for a moment at the figure who had seemingly materialized out of thin air, the senior firefighter answered. "It's very bad! They need to transfer over to the auxiliary system, but the damage means we need to get the wiring between the two reconfigured."

"Do you know how it needs to be set?"

"We've got a call in to the engineers. We're waiting back."

The Flash thought for a moment. "Excuse me."

He darted over to a spot far enough away for no one to hear. "Cisco, did you hear that?" Silence. "Cisco?"

"Go ahead!"

Barry quickly explained, then added, "It needs to be done quick! Can you call up the—"

"Already have! I may not be the fastest man alive, but I'm pretty damned quick, if I do say so myself!" Cisco quipped. "Just had to dig through a few security walls. These people really need to upgrade… although I'm glad they didn't do it just yet."

"So tell me what you can do."

"Lemme see. Lemme see." A pause. "Got it. This looks familiar… Yeah… this is based on S.T.A.R. Labs work! Some of mine, in fact. You know—"

The Flash heard a crackle of electricity from the prison electrical system. "Cisco! I think we just ran out of time!"

"Okay, ready when you are… but be careful: there's enough power there to fry you to ash!"

Barry braced himself. "Yeah, I kind of figured that."

The Flash raced into the madness. He dodged random bursts of electricity as he neared the system. Ahead stood the arrays.

"Give it to me, Cisco!"

"Here you go!" Cisco gave him the first five steps. The Flash darted in and adjusted or replaced things accordingly. Power bursts highlighted more than one of his actions, power bursts that would have killed anyone slower than him. As it was Barry was usually on the next move before the electricity even had time to shoot out.

The only delay was for Cisco's instructions. Each time it became necessary to listen, the Flash rushed back out. Once he had what he needed, he raced back.

And then it was done. Barry eyed the adjusted system dubiously. It *looked* under control, but it also looked as if Girder or King Shark had gone through it. "That's it, then? No more?"

"That'll work better than the original," Cisco

assured him. "And be safe enough for them to come in and make the needed replacements."

"All right. I'm heading back to Joe. In the meantime, I need you to try to see if you can figure out where Mardon headed."

"We're already on it, but if you can find any personal effects from Mardon, maybe I can also use my Vibe powers to help track him."

"Will do." Cutting the connection, the Flash raced around what was left of the cell. In the end, he found a toothbrush the Weather Wizard had been issued. Tucking it away, Barry returned to Joe West.

He saw with relief that Joe was off the phone and instead directing the efforts of the police. The detective looked slightly exasperated when he saw the Flash.

"She wasn't happy," Joe said when they were alone. "She's not been happy for a while. Not with either of us."

"She's always known you as a policeman, though. She's your biggest fan, Joe!"

"Yeah, she had concerns enough, though, but she was able to cope with those before. Apparently it's gotten a lot worse since the first time she realized I'd be facing metahumans on a regular basis... and that revenge where they're concerned reaches a whole new level of danger."

"Listen, Joe, I've got Cisco and the others trying to trace Mardon. If anyone can locate him—"

"Got a trace!" Cisco called in the Flash's ear. "It's a scant one—the storm's still wreaking havoc on readings. Better follow it now: Head south to 44th and we'll take it from there."

"Got a line on him, Joe. Gotta go!"

"Yeah, well, you better—"

But the Flash was already a mile away. He hated having just left Joe like that. There had been no choice though. If Cisco thought the trace a weak one, it had to be nearly imperceptible.

"Go ahead, Cisco! I'm listening!"

"Turn on 44th! Head toward the stadium—"

A massive explosion of thunder drowned out what else Cisco had said. More importantly, the thunder was accompanied by a new barrage of lightning.

The Flash dodged one bolt, a second, and a third. By the fourth, he felt certain that the Weather Wizard had to be involved... and yet there was no sign of Mardon.

"Where is he?" Barry demanded as he shifted to evade another bolt. "This is getting a lot closer than the prison electrical system!"

"These readings don't make any sense now! It's like Mardon just faded away—but there's something else stirring. It kind of reminds me of Mardon's readings, but—"

"But none of that matters, Cisco," the Flash reminded him as he dodged yet another strike. "These things are shooting down in every direction. I can outrun them, but I might also run right into one!"

"I'm double-checking something—hang on!"

"Hang on, he says," Barry muttered. He skirted

another strike—and as he had feared raced right into the next. Gritting his teeth, the Flash tried to change his path. He knew it would be close. *Very* close.

It was even closer than *that*.

The strike shook everything. The Flash evaded the actual bolt, but not its effects on its surroundings. He was thrown hard.

Twisting in midair saved him. He landed not on his head, but his shoulder. The suit took some of the force, but Barry still felt as if someone had taken a hammer to every bone in his body.

"God! I don't want to cut it that close again!" When there was no response, the Flash said, "Hey! I'm toasty and bruised but okay!'

Still nothing. Barry frowned. The near miss had still been enough to ruin his communications system.

Temporarily drenched by the rain, he stumbled to his feet and looked around. Without Cisco to give him directions, he had no idea where Mardon might be.

"Damn!" Barry glanced up at the heavens, where more lightning raged. The storm had stopped him as thoroughly as if the Weather Wizard had actually been controlling it. Barry could almost imagine Mardon laughing at him. Tonight's failure meant that Joe was in very real danger. Mardon was not to be taken for granted.

"Damn," he repeated, wincing as he rubbed his shoulder, "Iris is *not* going to be happy."

* * *

High above and obscured by the storm, the Weather Wizard hovered over where the Flash had just stood. Mark Mardon stared down at the area, his eyes never blinking. The huge gust of wind he had created kept him perfectly in position despite the elements.

The Weather Wizard continued to stare for several seconds after the Flash had departed. Had anyone else been close enough to see, they would have noticed his eyes had a slightly glazed look to them.

Mardon's mouth abruptly shifted into a severe frown. The Weather Wizard rose several feet higher... then, eyes still glazed, swiftly floated away from the vicinity.

"Barry? Barry?" Cisco made a face. "The link's dead. Lightning must've shorted things out."

"So long as it didn't short *him* out," H.R. said. "Just how close was that strike?"

"Too close. I'm definitely not getting anything here. Caitlin?"

When there was no answer, both men looked to her. Caitlin sat hunched forward, her unblinking gaze on the screen.

"Caitlin?" H.R. called tentatively.

She started.

"Barry," Cisco offered. "Do you have a definitive reading on him? This part of the system's fried."

Caitlin studied her screen, and finally spoke. "He's all right. His readings are a little on the high end, but he's been even more active than usual."

"Not too bad for a guy who had a run-in with lightning—" Cisco's phone rang. He plucked it up. "Ah! The man himself! Hey, there! We had a little fright. Couldn't get an immediate reading on you…"

As Cisco talked with the Flash, H.R. slipped over to Caitlin. "Why don't you go home?" he said in a low voice. "Cisco and I—well, Cisco anyway—has this in hand for now. You could—"

He hesitated as he eyed where her right hand gripped her chair. There were hints of frost under her fingers, frost that had no obvious source but one.

"Caitlin?"

She looked up… and H.R. found himself staring into eyes colder than any ice.

Then Caitlin's eyes returned to their normal vibrant selves. She looked at him with a pleading expression.

"Don't say anything!" Caitlin whispered. "I'm fine now."

"I thought those powers were under control."

"They are. It was just a momentary lapse. Promise you won't bother Cisco with it?"

H.R. had made some questionable decisions in his life, most especially choosing to cross over to an Earth in order to escape his past mistakes. He knew that the proper thing to do would have been to tell Cisco immediately, but Caitlin continued to plead silently with him.

"I'm a damned fool," he muttered under his breath.

Slightly louder, he replied, "All right. If you're sure you know what you're doing."

"I do." She held up her right hand. "See? Normal."

There was not even any hint of ice on the chair. Still, a part of H.R. screamed that he should warn someone. He knew very well the risk he was taking. Caitlin had her own metahuman powers, ones that she supposedly kept suppressed with the device Cisco had given her. Even as small a reaction as he had just witnessed indicated the device was certainly not doing its job.

"If it happens again I have to tell everyone," he warned.

"I understand. Don't worry. I've got everything under control. I've got *her* under control."

3

Thunder shook Mark Mardon awake. The Weather Wizard's first impulse was to call out his brother's name.

The only response was more thunder, followed by a renewed gush of rain on the roof of Mardon's unlit surroundings.

Bits and pieces of his escape returned: he relived his destruction of his cell and the surrounding area, but after that things became foggy again.

Take a deep breath, he heard Clyde say. *You always told me to do that after I got my head whacked or had an all-night binge! Take a deep breath—and swear you'll learn to pace yourself better next time!*

This was followed by Clyde's brash laugh.

"Don't find that funny at all," muttered the Weather Wizard.

"You did when it was *me* who was the one all banged up! Guess when the shoe's on the other foot, it isn't so good a joke!"

"I never earned being the butt of it, unlike you," Mardon retorted. "You had a hard time learning a lesson, Clyde—" He looked up in shock. "Clyde…"

There was no response save the thunder and rain.

The Weather Wizard stumbled to his feet. After battling for his equilibrium for several seconds, he stared at his surroundings. Even though he couldn't make out much, there was a familiarity to them.

"Let's have a little illumination," Mardon growled as he raised his left hand.

A tiny bolt of lightning burst above his palm. It lasted long enough for Mardon to get a better idea of just where he was.

He smiled, recognizing the safe house. Even battered and drained, he had managed to get himself here without anyone apparently seeing him. It was a testament to his power and control.

"Yeah, you always had better control over things. Maybe if I had had your control, he'd have never have had the chance to shoot."

Mark Mardon spun around. This time he was certain that he had heard the voice… and yet…

"Who is it? Who's there?" The Weather Wizard created a series of short lightning bolts. He had no desire to truly light up the room—that would attract some busybody's attention—but he needed to see the entire room clearly for a change.

The bolts enabled him to do just that. Mardon surveyed everything… and found nothing.

Letting the last bolt fade, the Weather Wizard stood motionless. He waited and waited, but no one spoke, no one materialized.

The exertion was too much. His legs gave out under him. The Weather Wizard barely managed to keep himself from falling face first onto the floor. As it was he ended up on his knees with his nose only inches from the wood.

"Can't let that happen when we go after them, Mark! Maybe the detective won't be a problem, but you know that the Flash'll take advantage of any mistake or hesitation! You can't make a mistake if you're going to avenge me, brother!"

"Clyde? *Clyde?*" The Weather Wizard shook his head in disbelief. "No... Clyde's dead... The Flash and that detective did him in!"

"Revenge is something that can keep on going even after the last breath!" came his brother's unmistakable voice. "That's all you really need. Revenge... I want revenge, Mark... And you've got to get it for me."

"This isn't possible!"

At that moment, in a part of the room the Weather Wizard knew had been perfectly empty a moment ago, a vague shape formed. He stepped back in shock as the shape took on a more and more human appearance.

And he had no trouble recognizing the slightly shorter figure now only a couple of yards beyond.

"Clyde? No... You can't be. You're dead..."

Clyde rewarded him with that same wide

mischievous smile Mark Mardon had lived with nearly all his life. "You're one to talk. You were supposed to be dead after that crash." His expression darkened. "You were supposed be or otherwise you'd have been there for me when that damned cop shot me!"

Mark winced. Clyde's words expressed exactly how he himself always thought of the situation. It didn't matter that the air crash had left the older brother with nearly every bone broken and in a coma for several weeks. All that mattered was that during that time Clyde had evidently discovered the same powers that his sibling had and had decided to use them. In typical Clyde fashion, he had made a grand spectacle of himself, drawing the attention of the police and the damned Flash.

"I couldn't help it," Mark rasped. "I really couldn't, Clyde! I had nightmares the whole time I was in the hospital, nightmares of the plane, that weird explosion, and you! Always you! If I could've been there to protect you, I would've been!"

His brother smiled again. "Yeah. You would've. Well, you're here now. You can teach 'em both. First the cop, then the Flash…"

Clyde reached out a hand to his sibling, and without thinking Mark took it… or tried to.

His hand went through Clyde's.

Reality finally overtook the Weather Wizard again. His last comment echoed in his head. "You're dead… Clyde… you're dead…"

"Yeah, you said that before. You know, that can change too… if you really want it."

Desperate curiosity overcame the Weather Wizard's shock. His greatest failure had been not being able to save his brother. If he could change that, nothing else mattered. But once more, common sense fought to take over. "No… You're dead. That can't be changed."

"What? You want me to stay that way? When you hold the key? I thought you'd do everything to have me back! You've been saying that since you woke up and found out! You still want that more than anything, don't you? To have your little brother back?"

Guilt finally conquered. "Yeah—yeah, of course I do! Damn it, you should know that! But how?"

Clyde drifted around him. The younger brother shook his head. "Look at you! The great and powerful Weather Wizard! Maybe I *am* the smarter one! Mark… look at the storm last night! Look at the tidal wave you created the first time you came here! You would've destroyed the city if the Flash hadn't interfered! Think of the power at our fingertips—the power you still have! You're a damned god, Mark! You just need to harness your abilities even better…"

The Weather Wizard had to admit that Clyde wasn't saying anything that he had not thought about before. That was why it had burned him so much to have been outwitted by the Flash.

"You just weren't aware enough of your abilities yet," his brother went on as he drifted back and forth.

"Look what you did to Iron Heights! Man, I bet they never saw that coming!"

"I could've used that to bring you back? That's all?" The Weather Wizard immediately summoned a miniature storm in front of him. He made the storm rise, drop, then grow to twice its original size. "Yeah…"

"That's it, Mark! You've got it in you… Compress it all together, then stir it up! Go past what you've done before…"

The Weather Wizard focused. He'd summoned tidal waves and huge storms, but those couldn't be used to bring his brother back. No, he needed to concentrate all that energy together just as Clyde had explained, then create such a primal force that surely it had to be enough to resurrect his brother.

"Keep at it, bro! Keep at it!"

Sweat already covered the Weather Wizard. His heart pounded faster and faster. He molded the energies he had gathered into a smaller and smaller volume. The strain of doing so quickly began to tell, but all Mark had to do was glance at his brother.

"Yeah, you're doing it! You're doing it!"

The Weather Wizard sensed that he could not hold the energies together much longer. He had already accomplished something he had not even thought himself capable of doing; now he had to use it before he lost control.

Without a word, the Weather Wizard directed the energies toward Clyde. As he did, a wind stirred from that direction, a wind that swelled in strength as Mark fed the power into his brother.

An explosion of energy filled the room. The Weather Wizard ignored the pain with which both it and his efforts assailed him. All that mattered was to keep his gathered power circulating around Clyde.

"Yeah! Yeah!" Clyde roared.

The intense wind radiating from his brother's location pushed the Weather Wizard back several inches. Mark gritted his teeth and pushed forward again.

Clyde howled with glee as the energies engulfed him. He faded into them, leaving only the condensed storm. Yet his triumphant howl continued.

The Weather Wizard fell to one knee. He gasped. Try as he might, he could find no more strength. Desperate, he let everything he had left fuel the storm a few precious seconds longer—

Mark collapsed. As he did, lightning crackled where Clyde had stood.

The Weather Wizard blacked out. He knew it was only for a moment, but still a new wave of guilt overtook him as he came round again. At some point during his unconsciousness, the tremendous wind had faded. Now there was only a tense stillness. Taking in several quick, deep gulps of air, Mark managed to push himself to a kneeling position. He tried to make out his brother, but between his blurred vision and a thick smoke covering that part of the room, he could see nothing.

Rubbing his face, Mark croaked out his brother's name.

A figure coalesced in the smoke. The Weather Wizard blinked, clearing his gaze.

Clyde stepped out of the smoke. He did not look happy. Mark swore as Clyde *rippled*.

"You've let me down, Mark. You've let me down…"

"No!" The Weather Wizard spread his hands in apology. "No!" He looked back and forth as he tried to think. "No… it just… It just wasn't enough. That's it. Not enough…"

Clyde cocked his head. A slight chill breeze wafted over the Weather Wizard as his brother finally said, "Yeah, not enough… But how are you going to make it enough, Mark? How are you going to make up for everything?"

"I'm thinking…"

"Come on, bro! You're the man who nearly drowned Central City! You're not just a wizard of weather, you're a god! Show it!"

"A god…" That was how it had felt the first time Mark had discovered his powers. That was how he had felt last night after devastating Iron Heights.

"Just look what you did to the prison!" Clyde gleefully remarked, once more mirroring his brother in thought. "That's what we need!"

"That's what we need, yeah." The Weather Wizard considered the event. "Maybe a way to magnify what I just tried… but that still might not be enough."

"Maybe I'm the smarter one after all…" Clyde

jested, leaning close. "Maybe instead you could take some other powerful natural source and *magnify* that. A ready-made source already pretty damned powerful... like a river, you know?"

"Like a river," the Weather Wizard repeated. "A river, a storm, *anything* huge..."

"Now you're thinking! There should be plenty of places in this fancy city that could generate such power! The river, though! You could stir that up pretty good, build up some strong raw power! Think what you could do with that!"

Mark nodded, his gaze already toward the unseen body of water. "Yeah. Think what I could do..." After a moment, though, he frowned. "But I still don't know how to turn it all to bringing you back. Something's just not right. I don't know—"

Clyde growled. "You're not letting me down *again*, are you?"

The Weather Wizard was quick to placate him. Hands spread in apology, he answered, "No, Clyde! Never again!"

"The river'll work... and it'll also bring out the Flash. You thought of that, Mark?"

"Yeah. I thought of that."

Clyde suddenly stood beside him, whispering in his ear. "And there's something else. Look at the power you have. The Flash, he's got some power too. There wasn't any Flash until that same night we changed! We got control of the weather; he got to be quick on his feet! You know what that means?" Clyde's smile resumed. "He's a source of power for us too, Mark! We could use the Flash to help bring me back! Kill two birds with one stone—hell, three, counting getting rid of Detective West! You know wherever the Flash is, West eventually turns up!"

The Weather Wizard shook his head in an attempt to clear it. Clyde's words kept echoing though. The river. The Flash as a source of energy just like the river. Killing the speedster and the detective.

Clyde alive again.

Clyde alive *again.*

That last thought was all Mark needed to shove aside his misgivings about the logic. Clyde would live. He would be able to wipe out his greatest failure. His brother would live.

Thunder roared again. Rain continued to come down hard.

"Looks like a nice night for a stroll on the river walk," the Weather Wizard remarked.

"So, here you are," Iris declared in a frosty voice. "You've been avoiding me, Barry."

Barry sat at an empty desk on the far side of the lab, a coffee in one hand, a screen with the local news in front of him. He looked up sheepishly at Iris. "I haven't been hiding. Cisco needed to run a bunch of tests after last night and they went on so long I just crashed here! Honest!"

"You couldn't call, at least?" she asked with tremendous skepticism.

The dark-brown eyes that Barry usually enjoyed staring into now proved too stern for him to meet. He finally had to look away. "The storm fried both my communications with the lab and my cell."

"And all the phones here weren't working either?"

He stood up. "Listen, Iris. It was late and I'd been running all over Central City. I was more exhausted than I thought, I guess. I think I searched through every hole I could find trying to—trying to—"

The frown on her face grew stronger. She knew what he had been about to say and why he'd held back from actually saying it. "You didn't find him. You didn't find Mardon! He's still out there, waiting to kill my father!"

A tear plummeted down her cheek. Aware of just how strong a woman Iris was and how badly this was affecting her, Barry reddened in shame. "Iris, listen. I'll find Mardon. I won't let anything happen to Joe. He's been there for me so much of my life. You *know* how I feel about him… and how I would never want to fail you! I'd give my life for him!"

If Barry thought that would make her feel better, he discovered immediately that he was very, very wrong. Iris eyed him as if he had just stabbed her through the heart.

"You really don't get it, do you, Barry? Do you think I just worry about—"

The lab shook from another round of thunder. Barry

and Iris instinctively grabbed one another for support. The thunder was followed by an intense wind howling so loud that it sounded to Barry like a huge pack of wolves just outside the door.

"Something's happening!" Cisco shouted.

They hurried over to him. The screen before Cisco danced with constantly shifting numbers and coursing wave lines. Barry was not well versed in the data Cisco was studying, but he knew that the fact that everything on the screen mirrored the havoc now going on outside did not bode well.

"It just started," Cisco added. "Off the charts on several scales!"

"Mardon?" Barry asked.

"If it isn't, we've got a whole new problem to deal with! It still doesn't read like him... but there are similarities at times. I know I've seen something like it, but—"

Emergency sirens went off outside.

Barry turned to Iris. "I've got to go! I promise we'll talk."

"Barry, I wanted to tell you that—"

But he was already gone.

As the Flash, Barry covered the distance between S.T.A.R. Labs and the nearest siren in the blink of an eye. He paused under a store overhang and contacted Cisco.

"What've you got for me? So far it's just a really bad storm. No specific danger."

"Getting reports now! The Mayor's office has declared a State of Emergency! Hills collapsing! The river is pouring over its banks! Get down to Second Avenue—"

"Already there!" responded the Flash, having left the overhang as soon as Cisco had mentioned the street by name. "I see it!"

"It" was a ten-story building listing badly to the north. Worse, he could see that despite the terrible weather, several people had actually insisted on going to work. Now those same industrious souls found themselves in terrible danger.

The reason for the listing had to do with the ground, where a sinkhole had abruptly developed. The sinkhole's presence seemed odd to the Flash, not something he would've expected. "Cisco, you getting a visual of this?"

"Yeah! That doesn't look right! According to the data I'm calling up, the ground there shouldn't be susceptible to that!"

"Mardon?"

"Him or another meta."

Barry grunted. "Let's at least hope we're sticking with Mardon."

The doorway stood at a precarious angle. The Flash saw that no one inside would dare step through. Already, several chunks of decorative stone and twisted pieces of steel decorated the entrance. Barry considered clearing the way out first, but determined that the rubble was in fact keeping the rest of that side of the building from completely collapsing.

With that choice unavailable to him, the Flash went with what was left. He sped through the entrance quickly but so carefully that nothing was disturbed, raced up to the top floor and began checking office after office. Whenever he located a trapped worker, he took hold of them and raced them outside to safety. At first the Flash took a moment to question each about other possible victims, but soon realized he could search the building faster and more efficiently.

As he worked to clear the third floor, the Flash felt the building rock. Whoever or whatever had created the sinkhole had done so with the intention of the building not taking too long to collapse. To the Flash, that sounded just like Mardon.

One after another, he carried the workers from the building. Barry knew that each time he paused to set a victim safely down, precious seconds passed.

With the building starting to rip from its foundations, the Flash doubled his speed. Finally, he had the last one out.

A heartbeat later, the office building collapsed into the sinkhole, the upper floors breaking off and spilling into an empty parking garage across the street.

A terrible wrenching sound made the Flash immediately turn east. There a fearsome wind ripped out the nearest trees from the nearby city park by their roots and tossed them into the air.

As he shooed the workers to safety, Barry contacted Cisco again. "We've got a tornado here! Mardon's got to be close by!"

"Still can't get a good reading—" Whatever Cisco wanted to say beyond that was lost in a crackle of lightning that left only static in the Flash's earpiece.

More trees were torn from the ground. Barry watched them warily. For a moment, they spun madly around the vicinity of the park, but then suddenly they flew toward him.

"Got to be trickier than that, Mardon," the speedster remarked. The Flash easily dodged one tree after another. Still, he knew there had to be more to come. The Weather Wizard would not waste time on frivolous threats. Mardon had to have something bigger in mind—

Caitlin's voice crackled in his ear. "—overflowing along the entire walk! Do you hear me?"

"Overflowing? The river?"

"Yes, it started just a minute ago! Cisco's calculating the extent of it now!"

Barry grimaced. The trees had been a violent distraction. Once again, the Weather Wizard had turned to water for his true threat. This time, though, he had not turned the ocean against the city, but rather just the river.

Not just, the Flash corrected himself. The river ran through the heart of the city. While compared to the devastation the tidal wave would have wrought, the river would still be capable of enough destruction and chaos to leave the middle of Central City in ruins, at an additional cost of hundreds of lives. By the time he reached the public walk, the water was already pouring into the nearest buildings.

Picking up his speed, the Flash ran along the edge of the overflow, back and forth, creating a counter wave of wind that began pushing the river back into its proper channel. As it did, Barry narrowed his path, keeping the turbulent waters from returning. When he reached the end of the flooding, he crossed at the nearest possible point and repeated his efforts on the other side. Racing back and forth from one bank to the other, he soon had the river flowing as it should.

Gasping, Barry came to a halt.

"You okay, man?" Cisco called. "Your readings are showing you pretty burned out! Haven't seen you this exhausted in a long time!"

"I just need—I just need a moment to—catch my—"

More sirens went off.

The Flash quickly looked around. "What is it?"

"The hills along the main highway! Report says they're all collapsing due to the rain and wind!"

"On my way!" Barry raced to the highway. Despite the storm, there were several cars on the highway attempting to go in either direction. Several had already had to bypass two lanes buried in dirt and rock from one collapsed slope, but as the Flash neared, he saw that an entire section large enough to crush dozens of vehicles had begun to break loose.

I can't let the slide reach the highway! Eyeing the already collapsed area, the Flash had an idea. He raced over to the rock and earth and began taking armfuls over to where the other section was falling apart. Again and again and again, the scarlet speedster carried a load to the area before the collapsing hills. There, he packed the earth and rock together until it was hard, then went for more.

When he had exhausted what there was from the initial slide, the Flash raced up to the current collapse itself and took what he needed. That served him twofold; not only did he gather what he needed for his earthworks, but he lessened part of the collapse.

And then he had a barrier so large and so thick that when the collapse finally reached it, the earthworks cracked and crumbled somewhat... but held.

The Flash stared at his work then, fighting his intense exhaustion, stiffened. "Cisco! Caitlin! Either of you hear me?"

"Go... head," Caitlin responded.

"Where's Joe? Does Iris know?"

There was another crackle from the communicator... and then, "...duty... quarters..."

Barry ran as fast as he could, only the physical barriers in his path slowing him at all. Despite his incredible swiftness, he prayed he was not already too late.

Now at last he felt he knew the Weather Wizard's plan. Mardon had set not one but a series of distractions. None of these destructive incidents had been his true intention.

The Weather Wizard had wanted to keep the Flash occupied long enough to avoid being there to protect Joe West.

"Barry!" Cisco shouted in his ear. "We should have a better connection now!"

"Joe's in police headquarters?"

"Yeah, but there's something else! I'm getting some worrying readings from you! It's like you're suddenly burning out! You need to get back here so we can see what's going on!"

Barry couldn't argue with Cisco's analysis of him. He wanted desperately to curl up right where he was and sleep for a month, but knew that he dared not stop tonight until he at least made certain Joe was safe.

As if some power heard his thoughts, Joe West chose that moment to exit police headquarters. He had his coat tight around him and glanced from side to side as he hurried through the storm. The Flash noted that Joe kept one hand near where his gun would have been located.

Lightning turned the area as bright as day.

The Flash spotted a figure standing on the headquarters roof.

"Joe!" The Flash darted over to him, plucking him up and carrying him to a safe location—a police substation—more than a mile away. He paused only long enough to let the detective see him, then raced back.

The lightning had just begun to fade when the Flash returned. He picked up his pace, then leaped. His feet had just enough traction to give him time to make the next step up. In the blink of an eye, the speedster ran up the wall to the roof.

There, a strong wind nearly threw him back off. The Flash struggled against the wind as he tried to focus on the figure ahead. Try as he might, he could not make out the man distinctly. Yet there was something familiar in the stance.

As if realizing the Flash was there, the figure started to turn.

At the same time the wind's ferocity magnified tenfold. Barry dropped to one knee as he struggled to keep from being blown away. Shielding his gaze with his hand, he tried to keep the turning figure in sight.

The shadowy man dissipated just before he would have faced the Flash.

Barry gasped.

4

"I swear he was up there," Barry muttered, "and then the next second, he wasn't!"

"Wouldn't be the first metahuman we faced that had some crazy power like that," Cisco said. "Teleport from one spot to another—"

"No, he didn't do that. If he had, I might not have paid it much attention. No, this guy broke up as if the wind scattered every little piece of him like dust."

"That doesn't sound like a very comfortable way of traveling," H.R. offered from the desk he had his feet up on. "Breaking up each time."

"Creepy all right." Cisco typed. "Nothing even close on Dustman yet—"

"*Dustman?*" Barry and H.R. uttered in unison.

Cisco made a face at his own suggestion. "Yeah... maybe I'll wait until we know more about him before I try to give him a name..." His expression changed to one of exaggerated pride. "But I promise you that when

I do, it'll definitely be another Cisco Ramon masterpiece, right up there with Captain Cold and Prism!"

"I'll bet it will be," Barry replied with a grin.

"You scoff, but I've been thinking about a full set of trading cards and everything... Think of the market..."

"Providing there's a city left," H.R. pointed out.

"Yeah. Getting back to which... our mysterious new meta. Funny how he was there just where you'd expect Mardon to have been."

"I was wondering about that too," Barry returned. He still wore his suit, but had pulled the cowl back. It should not have been a bother to change quickly, but he was still suffering after-effects from his earlier intense exhaustion. Cisco had already had him run a few times for some tests and while those runs had not been especially grueling, simply having added them to his already wearying night once more had Barry thinking wistfully of a bed... or at least a flat surface he could trust.

H.R. scratched his chin in thought. "One would assume that maybe he's *working* with the Weather Wizard?"

"Wouldn't be the first team-up," Cisco agreed. He frowned. "Maybe he's the source of those odd readings... although if so he barely even registers as alive!"

"Yeah, that wouldn't be a first, would it?" Barry countered. "Some of our previous adversaries didn't exactly fit the description of 'alive'."

"No, suppose not. Did Joe see him?"

"Nope. I got him out of there the moment I spotted the figure and only brought him back after it vanished. Described it to him, though, just in case."

"What'd he say?"

"He wished that just once we'd cross paths with a metahuman with the power to make flowers blossom or some other innocuous ability."

Cisco shrugged. "Probably end up being carnivorous flowers. With poisonous pollen to boot."

"Yeah." Before they could discuss the subject further, Barry's phone rang. He glanced at the caller ID. "Iris. I haven't had the nerve to speak with her after last night. I know nothing happened to her father, but the mere chance that someone got that close to him has only made her more anxious. I can't blame her, but I also can't carry Joe off to some safe place and lock him up there until Mardon's captured."

"Can't imagine Joe would be too crazy about being shunted off somewhere either." Cisco got up and adjusted three electrodes still attached to Barry. "Hold still now."

"All set," Caitlin called from her console. "Everything ready for real-time comparison."

Cisco leaned down and typed in some instructions, then hit a button.

After several seconds, he frowned, returned to Barry, and adjusted the electrodes again.

"Mind telling me what you're looking for while you poke me with those things?"

"As a metahuman you know you radiate a certain level of energy. Most machines can't read it, but naturally we've got ones that can at S.T.A.R Labs. Your level is far lower than it should be even taking into account all your activity. In fact, there shouldn't be much difference at all."

"But there is?"

"Yeah. The difference is decreasing, but it was definitely noticeable when we first started. Hang on."

Cisco repeated the procedure. After studying the screen a moment more, he ran a hand through his hair. "You're pretty near normal again. How do you feel?"

"Still beat, but not like I need to curl into a fetal position. I just assumed it was the coffee finally kicking in. I've had three cups since I got back here."

"H.R.'s coffee is strong but not that strong." Cisco tapped the screen. "Come here and take a look at a comparison Caitlin and I ran."

Joining them, Barry eyed the data. "I see some numbers that look similar and some other numbers that don't. One of you care to clarify?"

Caitlin pointed at the readings. "This is you during the flooding, the landslides… and after arriving at police headquarters. Do you notice anything?"

"Yeah, those are some of the numbers with similarities to other numbers."

Cisco tapped the three numbers in question. "Those are your rates of depletion. In other words, when you lost the most energy tied to your speed abilities. I can understand the first two, but you lost energy at a comparable rate at headquarters when you didn't even have half the overall activity."

"But there *was* some trouble. When I tried to get to that figure on the roof, the wind picked up incredibly. Someone is obviously tied into all this."

"Yeah, but who is he? There was some fluctuation in other readings I had, but I was able to pinpoint those as belonging to Mardon. I couldn't pin down where he was, but he definitely had some effect on the storm… Of course, we knew that already, but still, it's *verified*."

Barry's phone rang again. A quick glance revealed that it was Iris.

"You can't hide from her forever," H.R. pointed out. "And if you consider it, do you really want to?"

"Of course not." Barry pulled the electrodes off. "We done with the experiments, Dr. Cisco?"

"Evidently. Are you going to call her?"

Barry had already started dialing. "Not yet, but I am going call someone close to her who might be better able to help us work this out." He paused. "Oh, Cisco! Almost forgot!" Barry pulled the toothbrush out. "Here."

Cisco made a face as he caught it. "Great. You couldn't get me something like a comb or a cup?"

"Couldn't find anything. Will it do?"

"It should."

"Terrific." Barry finished dialing, then hit send. "I hope he answers. He may be the only person who can see it both their ways."

"Ah!" H.R. sat up. "You're calling her brother! That could be a very smart move... Or perhaps not."

Ignoring this last comment, Barry listened. Unfortunately, instead of hearing ringing, a busy signal greeted him.

"Busy!" He disconnected. "Of all the times he has to choose this moment to be busy with someone!"

"Not just someone," H.R. interjected. "Maybe she wants to talk to her brother too. That *was* Wally you were calling, wasn't it?"

"Yeah. I was hoping he might be able to convince her that I—"

"We," Cisco corrected. "Joe's our friend too."

"The point is: Joe will be safe. She should understand that. Why won't she?"

"Well, maybe because it *is* her father," H.R. answered. "We all know what you went through to try to bring your mother back, Barry."

"H.R.!" Cisco reprimanded.

"No, I deserved that, Cisco." Barry looked at the phone, then tried one more time. Once again it was busy.

"They must be having a heck of a conversation," Cisco offered.

"Yeah." Barry put his phone away. "Poor Wally."

"No, you listen to *me*, Wally!" Iris West declared over the phone. "You've said nothing to me that either Dad or Barry hasn't said already, but it just won't do!"

"Well, if they can't say anything to calm you, what am I supposed to do?"

In truth, Iris didn't really have an answer for Wally. Both her father and Barry had gone out of their way to avoid having to speak with her on the subject, Barry even physically dodging her.

That last had opened up a sore spot. It was bad enough that she had always had to pretend not to be worried about her father's safety, but now she had to do the same with Barry. Part of her anger at him had actually been the realization that she could lose both of them at once. Iris liked to think she was as strong as anyone, but the thought of such a terrible thing happening even now sent shivers down her spine.

"Hey, sis? Are you all right?"

Iris kept silent as a third horror occurred to her. Wally now had abilities like Barry's. Thus far he had only been involved in a few incidents, but even those had ended up with highly dangerous encounters with metahumans... especially Savitar.

Savitar. Horrific images of the dark speedster filled her head. Savitar had actually tricked Wally into opening a portal into the Speed Force—the essence of all swift metahumans' abilities—but in the end it had also been Wally who had rescued her from Savitar's murderous intentions. She was grateful to her brother for that, but the entire episode now just verified for her yet again how much danger her father was in—how much danger all *three* of the men closest in her life were in. She knew that

Mark Mardon was as obsessed about revenge as Savitar had been and would not stop until someone stopped *him*.

"Sis? Is something wrong? I'm coming right over there!"

A gust of wind sent Iris's hair fluttering. She looked up from her phone. Standing in the middle of the apartment she and Barry had moved into together was her brother. Despite some questionable choices in the past, such as becoming involved in illegal street drag racing, Iris had always thought that he had a rather innocent face. Wally had fuller features than hers and short-cropped hair. He wore a dark casual jacket and jeans and had a lithe build that made him look even more like a speedster than Barry actually did.

And that very speed he had just utilized to rush all the way over from the club he had been at to the apartment—more than two miles away.

"Are you all right?" he asked anxiously. "You look all right, but are you? Is there anyone else here?" He shimmered, then added, "No, all the rooms are empty…"

"I'm fine… I'm fine, Wally. I got to thinking about Savitar…"

"He's gone, Iris! I swear he is!"

"I know… I know… But that emphasized to me what I've been trying to get through to you, Dad, and Barry! Dad has no powers—"

"No powers? Have you ever had an argument with him? He's got this ability to—oh, wait. You've got it too. Never mind."

"Don't make fun of me," Iris warned.

"There it is." He grinned sheepishly. "Listen, Iris. You know him better than I do. Thanks to Mom, I didn't even know he existed until a couple of years ago. Now we get along fine, but he's not going to listen to me any more than he will you or Barry—"

"I know that. I do. I don't expect you to convince him otherwise. What I want from you—"

He put up a warning hand. "I'm also not going to try to carry him off to some safe place! He'd never stay there—"

She nodded. "I know. I want something else from you, I think. I want you to promise me something, that's all."

"What's that?"

"Promise me that whenever you have a chance, you'll keep an eye on Dad."

"Yeah, of course, but—"

"And don't tell him you're doing it. In fact, don't tell any of the others. One of them might blurt it out to him out of respect for his feelings."

He exhaled strongly. "You really *are* trying to put me on the spot, aren't you? You know what he'll do if he finds out?"

"Please, Wally!"

He folded his arms and studied her. "All right, but you've got to cut Barry some slack on this. You know he'll do everything he can. He'd give his life for—"

"I know!" Iris immediately grimaced. "I'm sorry. Just don't… Never mind."

"Listen, I won't cross Dad, but I will keep an eye on him, I promise! He won't even know I'm around. Between Barry and me, we'll keep him safe, okay?"

Iris suddenly lunged forward and hugged her brother. Wally hesitated for a moment, then returned the hug.

"Just be careful."

"Like I said, he won't even know I'm around. I swear!"

Iris started to correct his misconception, but her cell rang. Turning from Wally, she glanced at the caller ID. "It's Caitlin. I wonder what she wants."

"This looks like a good time for me to leave," her brother suggested. "I'll let you know how things go, all right?"

"All—" was as far as Iris got before finding herself standing alone. She took one quick look at the door— seemingly shut the entire time—then answered the phone. "Caitlin?"

"Iris… Hi." Caitlin's voice was quiet, even hard to hear. "I was wondering… I was hoping you'd have lunch with me… if you don't mind this never-ending storm."

Iris looked at the phone's clock. "Sure! Noon?"

"That would be nice."

"Where do you want to meet?" A selfish thought occurred to Iris. "Never mind! How about I just meet you back at the lab and we take it from there?"

"All right. Thank you."

"No prob—"

The call disconnected.

Brow furrowed, Iris peered at the phone. Frowning deeply, she started to call back, then thought better of it. Her attention immediately shifted back to her father and Barry. Wally had assuaged some of her concerns, but there were still others. Only a direct confrontation with Barry would solve them, even if it threatened to put a wedge between them.

Iris sighed. This was not going to be easy, but with Mardon loose, she had to face Barry as soon as possible.

The storm continued unabated. For Cisco and H.R., that was not so much of a problem. They both pretty much lived at the lab. For Barry, while it was certainly a second home, it was not his *principal* home. That was the apartment he and Iris had finally gotten nerve enough to lease together.

Just may end up being very short term, Barry thought with regret. He knew that he had to do something to appease Iris or he risked losing her, which he considered unthinkable.

Thunder chose that moment to shake the building. Barry almost felt as if Mardon were somehow laughing at him. He wondered what the Weather Wizard was plotting and how it involved the indistinct figure on the roof.

Cisco swore.

"What's wrong?" Barry asked in concern.

Cisco held up the toothbrush. "I've been trying to vibe this thing on and off since you gave it to me, but all I keep getting is a vague image of the storm itself! I don't know if it's due to the strange energy fluctuations in the weather or something to do with Mardon himself." He put the toothbrush down. "Maybe later."

"Sorry, Cisco. You tried—"

The lab door opened. Caitlin, still bundled up from the weather, slipped inside. She didn't look very happy: not a terrible surprise considering the journey.

Barry darted over to the coffee, poured her a fresh cup, and stopped in front of her, all before she managed her next step. Unlike most people, Caitlin was undaunted by his action. She looked from him to the cup.

"Thanks. I could really use this."

"When you didn't come in first thing this morning we assumed you were going to stay home."

"I just couldn't. It felt so claustrophobic." She took a sip, then peered beyond him. "This has pretty much become home for all of us, it looks like... Well, except for you. You and Iris."

The building shook harder, the quaking punctuated by bright flashes of lightning. Cisco swore, making both Barry and Caitlin turn to him.

"Well, you don't have to be a genius like me to know this isn't natural," Cisco commented wryly. "I'd have to say the Weather Wizard is up to something right now!"

"Track it, Cisco," Barry ordered. "I'm already heading out."

"Care for an umbrella? It's gotten just a little stormier out there, I think."

"Yeah, good thing I had those swimming lessons as a kid. See if the system's picking up anything and contact me."

"I'll be on it right—"

Barry didn't wait for Cisco to finish. Already fully clad as the Flash, he raced out of S.T.A.R. Labs and back into the maelstrom.

Arms outstretched, the Weather Wizard hovered high over the storm-wracked city. Mark Mardon kept his eyes shut as he summoned the forces inherent in the system and bent them to his control. Never before had he felt so much a part of the elements around him. Never before had he felt as if there was nothing he could not potentially achieve, if only he concentrated enough.

"Yes…" he murmured. "Yes…"

"Do it!" came Clyde's voice. "Let's see what you can do, bro! Let's see it!"

"All right…" Mardon concentrated.

Below him, the clouds no longer rippled, but rather *swirled*. They spun faster and faster.

"Come on, Mark! Come on!"

A gap opened in the center of the swirling clouds. With each breath the Weather Wizard took, the hole increased in size. In less than a minute it had expanded to a size several times that of a football field.

The turbulent clouds thundered ominously.
The Weather Wizard grinned...

Back in S.T.A.R. Labs, Caitlin slipped off her coat. She took another long sip of the coffee, then leaned over Cisco to see what he had recorded.

"It's building up," Cisco informed her. Behind them, H.R. quietly seated himself and watched. "Seems to intensify each time the thunder comes." Yet another roll shook the lab even as Cisco spoke.

Caitlin watched as what her colleague said was verified on the screen—

A sharp pain struck her in the temple. Cisco, his attention on the readings, failed to notice. Caitlin took a deep breath. The pain subsided.

"You're not coming in very clearly!" Cisco said into his mic. "Let me make an adjustment."

Caitlin grabbed another headset.

"I said give me something!" Barry called. "I'm circling the area where the storm's hitting hardest... more or less!"

"Working on it!" Cisco replied. Off mic, he said to Caitlin, "Keep an eye on his readings! If he starts to burn out like he did last time, let me know immediately."

"Be just a second." Caitlin sat down in front of the next screen and called up Barry's vitals. She already saw differences in what they should have read. Cutting off her mic, Caitlin turned to Cisco. "He's already started. It's not as sharp as the last time but still noticeable."

"Keep an eye on him in case there's a radical shift." Into his mic: "He's got to be nearby! Tell me what you see that looks different from any normal storm."

"What doesn't?" the Flash responded. "There's lightning shooting down at unnatural angles, places where hail is dropping out of nowhere, and man-sized whirlwinds wherever I look!"

Caitlin tapped quietly on the desk. When she had Cisco's attention, she cut off her mic and said, "There's been a change in his readings. If they keep up like that, he's going to start wearing out soon. I've never seen anything like it."

"Uh oh."

"What's that? Did you say something?" the Flash called.

Caitlin glared at Cisco and tapped her mic to remind him to cut it off next time. He nodded, then replied to Barry, "There's something happening with—with the storm! Pace yourself! You don't want to burn out!"

"Why aren't you telling him?" H.R., out of mic range, asked.

Caitlin looked at Cisco. After a moment, he cut his mic and muttered, "For now he's well within safe range. If that changes, yeah, we'll warn him immediately. Right now it's an added thought he doesn't need. I've already warned him to pace himself. He couldn't do more, anyway!"

H.R. looked to Caitlin for confirmation. She nodded reluctantly. "It's also very possible we're wrong about it even being anything Mardon is involved with. We need to know more before making Barry too concerned about it."

"Hey, guys!" the Flash shouted. "Remember me? Out here enjoying the weather? Are you getting any new and very weird readings from the storm?"

Cisco focused on his screen again. "Why?"

"Because there's a hole developing in the sky above me."

Caitlin immediately looked at her screen to see what effect this potential new menace might be having on Barry himself, but just before she could focus on his readings, the pain in her temple returned several times stronger. Managing to keep from gasping, Caitlin tried to read the numbers.

"Are you serious?" Cisco was asking the Flash. "A hole?"

"Yeah! All the clouds and lightning are spreading away from it and I'd swear that the sky is darker inside that area…"

Caitlin could hear the Flash saying something more, but the pain in her temple was increasing heavily. Gripping the chair tightly with one hand, she instinctively twisted away from the others.

At that moment a female voice called out. Through her agony Caitlin saw Iris entering the lab.

Without thinking, Caitlin dropped the mic and left

her chair. She forced a smile as she neared Iris. "I just need to step out for a moment and then we can go."

"Are you sure? It got worse than I thought on the way here. We can always use the vending machines—"

"No, there's that sandwich place on the other side of the street. That won't be too bad, will it?"

Iris shrugged. "If you really want to... What's going on? I don't see Barry. I thought—"

Caitlin's temple pounded. She brushed past Iris. "I'll be right back."

She all but darted out the lab. Instead of heading to the restrooms—as Iris no doubt thought—Caitlin went to one of the auxiliary labs seldom used these days. There, with only the dim light of the storm-wracked day to illuminate the room, she leaned against the nearest console, shut her eyes, and tried to calm her nerves.

How long she stood there she neither knew nor cared. All that mattered was stopping the pain... and something else. With the last powerful beat in her temples, she had felt that now-familiar cold sensation within, the same cold that generally accompanied the stirring of her metahuman powers.

A slight crackling sound stirred her from her efforts. She opened her eyes... and gasped.

Frost covered the console and its nearby surroundings. Frost, in a room just above seventy degrees.

"No... No... No..." Caitlin looked at her hands. Pale, cold hands. Killer Frost's hands, appearing of their own accord.

She leaned toward the computer screen and tried to make out her reflection in the frosted glass.

Her skin and hair had already begun to change.

"This isn't right. I have control of this now. I do." Desperately, Caitlin grabbed at the wrist device. Cisco had taught her how to manipulate the controls in case she reached a critical point. Up until now Caitlin had been able to force back her powers, but this time she did as Cisco had explained.

The device vibrated briefly. Caitlin felt the coldness cease spreading... but unfortunately it did not recede.

There was another crash of thunder—

Caitlin gasped again as she felt the chill subside slightly. Encouraged, she concentrated harder on suppressing it. To her relief, it began to fade. In seconds, her hands had returned to normal and the frost had started to fade from the console.

"Caitlin?"

She spun around at the nearness of Iris's voice in the hallway. Smoothing her dress and pushing back hair that had fallen in her face, she hurried out to meet the other woman.

Iris spotted her just as Caitlin shut the lab door behind her. "Caitlin! I got worried. Are you all right?"

"Fine. I'm fine. I was in here earlier and remembered I'd forgotten to put something away."

"H.R. said you barely got here before I did," Iris commented. "Aren't you feeling well? We could've done this another time."

"No. No." Caitlin smiled as best she could. "I really want to spend some time with you. I know things have gotten complicated for you with Barry and we hardly ever have time to see one another because of that."

"What—"

"Hello, ladies!" H.R. came upon them with the suddenness of a ghost. He put a companionable arm around them both. To Iris, he said, "Cisco and I are sorry you didn't catch Barry, but he probably won't be coming in for some time. There's no sign of the Weather Wizard, so he's just going to patrol the city looking for anyone who needs help out in the storm."

"The hole—" Caitlin blurted, finally recalling what had been going on before her incident.

"Is gone. Just like that a minute ago. Barry's checked out the location thoroughly, but no sign of—no sign. Looks like it was nothing."

"Barry's okay?" Iris asked anxiously, mirroring Caitlin's thoughts.

"He's fine!" He turned to Caitlin. "Everything reads normal."

"Oh, good," Caitlin responded.

"Now, you two run off to that lunch Iris said she came for. If Cisco needs anything… Well, he can try to explain it to me. Go!"

Iris took Caitlin's arm. "He's right. We both need a little time to relax. Come on."

Caitlin gave H.R. a last look over Iris's shoulder. He solemnly winked, then made a gesture for her to keep moving. H.R. would clearly not tell what he had seen before and now that the device had been adjusted properly, Caitlin felt certain that this would be the last time she had to fight her powers.

With growing reassurance she walked out with Iris.

Cisco tapped a pen against the work desk as he studied the screen, only stopping both activities when H.R. returned.

"Any more new signs of that hole?" H.R. asked.

"No. No, it vanished as quickly as it appeared and hasn't been back. Barry's searching the riverfront again, but I doubt we'll find anything there either. Can't help feeling the Weather Wizard's been testing something. Exactly what though I don't know." He leaned back. "Are they gone?"

"Yes."

"Those readings from her were really strong, H.R., really strong. If they'd continued much longer, we'd have had a complete transformation. She would've become Killer Frost without even trying."

"That's why I told you about the first time even though I promised not to."

"It wasn't the first time. I just checked. There's been at least half a dozen incidents. Fortunately, nothing strong enough. Still, we've got to do something. The device isn't working right for some reason. I need to get her in here as soon as possible and find out why. I tell you, man, these last readings scare me."

"Does she know you made the device so that it would alert you if she started to change involuntarily?"

"No. I didn't want her to worry that her condition might have turned that bad—"

"So don't tell her yet then." H.R. suggested, grabbing his coffee cup. "Just like you two did with Barry. Try to figure out a solution so that she doesn't go into fear mode. That might make her fully transform… and where would we be then? With Barry, we were talking pretty temporary, minutes maybe… but with Caitlin, she could lose control permanently. She clearly thinks she can handle it; let's not upset that until you can do something about it."

"Yeah." Cisco nodded. "Yeah, that's what I've been thinking too. We need to be able to fix it. The device seems to be helping her again. That'll buy us the time we need to figure out a better solution…" He swiveled his chair to face the screen again. "… and maybe while we're at it help Barry catch the Weather Wizard."

5

Sweat, not rain, dripped from Mardon as he knelt in the center of the room, exhausted. His pulse still pounded and his breathing came in gasps at first.

"It didn't work, Mark… It didn't work… You let me down again."

"No…" the Weather Wizard muttered, his gaze on the floor. "No… it came close. I'm sure of it. We just didn't gather enough energy together. Got to do better next time, that's all. And if that's not enough, figure out how to get even more."

"All right, all right," Clyde's voice came from near his head. "So we go out and do it again right now!"

"No… not now. Too exhausted… and have to think." Mardon ran a hand through his soaked hair. Blinking, he looked up in the direction of his brother's voice, only to see nothing.

"Well, soon, right?" Clyde demanded from the shadows again. As Mardon stared his younger brother coalesced from the darkness. The breeze that accompanied Clyde forced the Weather Wizard to blink a moment. When he finished, it was to see Clyde standing over him.

"Soon, right." Mark started to reach out a hand so that Clyde could help him up, but then remembered what had happened the first time. That made him vaguely recall when he had been lying face down in the storm just after his escape. At the time he thought he had felt hands lift him up, but that was not possible.

He shook his head. So many things were not supposed to be possible. Controlling the weather. Racing at supersonic speeds on foot. Mardon knew some of the other metahumans who had been created that same night and each one of them had had some ability that should have been "impossible"... until it was not.

So why wouldn't conquering death, another "impossible", fall as easily as the others? the Weather Wizard asked himself. In truth, even before his escape, Mark had been mentally fighting with himself over the possibility. That was what had made Clyde's ghostly return all that more significant to him. *Maybe I already felt him trying to come back...*

His legs ached. Mark pushed himself back to a sitting position. "How long have I been out?"

"Yeah, I don't exactly carry a watch these days, bro. Hours. That good enough?"

The Weather Wizard nodded. His stomach growled,

verifying the lengthy span of time. Forcing himself to his feet, he went over to the small cache of supplies he and Clyde had stored in the safe house. It had never been planned that they would stay more than three or four days in any location, so the cache had been meager to start with. After his escape Mardon had eaten a full day's rations in one sitting. That meant that with the meals that had followed he had reduced his supplies to just a few cans and some very dry crackers.

"I need more," Mardon muttered. "I need a lot more."

"Yeah, I'd like to eat, but you see... I can't anymore."

Mardon immediately felt ashamed. Here he was concerned about selfish matters when Clyde couldn't even touch the tiniest morsel.

"Sorry," the Weather Wizard murmured. "Soon as I get you back, I'll make sure you get the biggest steak dinner possible."

"With a baked potato smothered in all the fixings?"

Mardon grinned at the memory. "Yeah, smothered. I'll set it all right again, Clyde. I swear!"

"You keep saying that until you do it." As he spoke, Clyde started to fade into the darkness around Mardon. The wind picked up at the same time. "And make sure you do it..."

No, it definitely did not help to be the fastest man alive when one had no idea where to find one's enemy, the Flash thought as he completed his two hundredth thorough search of Central City. There were, of course, places that he could not legally enter, but the Flash had refused to give in to any temptation that might make him forego those legalities. One way or another, he would find Mardon honestly, even if he had to search the city a thousand times or more.

Barry knew that he was also using the endless search for the Weather Wizard as an excuse not to talk with Iris about the growing gulf between them. It didn't help that Joe had also started pestering him to deal with his daughter. That Joe had not dealt with the situation either was not lost on Barry.

This is ridiculous! All we need to do is talk this out, the three of us! If we could—

He barely evaded the lightning bolt that came crashing down right in front of him. Despite the near miss, the Flash was not overly disturbed; frighteningly, he had become almost accustomed to the storm's unabated assault on him. By this time they were all pretty much certain that the storm was actively trying to either kill or disable the Flash. Yet if the Weather Wizard was responsible, his efforts showed a severe lack of focus.

That had evidently sparked some idea from Cisco, who took readings from each attack and matched them with previous ones. Unfortunately, each time the Flash hoped for progress, Cisco's call concerned more mundane problems.

"Got a new one for you!" he called to Barry. "Power outage on 54th Street!"

"I'm already there." The Flash was, too, having crossed eighteen blocks even as he spoke. He quickly surveyed the vicinity. "Looks like the entire area's out. How long ago?"

"Five minutes! I would've noticed sooner, but with everything else, it fell between the cracks!"

"Not a problem. I didn't pay it much mind either and I'm out here! Are they on it?"

"Yeah, there's a crew close by. Thought you'd want to keep an eye on them in case they have trouble."

"Will do and—hold on!" Out of the corner of his eye, the Flash caught a glimpse of a furtive figure with a tiny flashlight moving through an unlit store. "I think we've already got some looters!"

Cisco said nothing as the Flash raced to the store. As he neared, he noted two more figures. All three wore scarves over their noses and mouths. One held a shotgun while the others continued rummaging through the store.

Barry smiled grimly, welcoming the brief respite. He raced around until he found the door the trio had ripped open to get in.

"Never mind the safe," muttered the man with the shotgun as the Flash entered. "Just hurry up and take what you can carry—"

The Flash paused a few feet in front of him. "Hi!"

The looter swore and fired… or would have if he had still had a shotgun in his hands.

"You did say to take what I could carry," the Flash

remarked with a slight smile as he raised the shotgun for the crook to see. "Not that I really have any need for it."

The Flash raced to the front corner of the store, set down the weapon, and returned before the looter could even realize that anything had happened. Snarling, the disarmed crook swung at Barry.

By then, the Flash had already left him again to inspect the other looters. One carried a handgun stuffed in a pants pocket while the other appeared weaponless. Having taken stock of any potential threat they were to anyone who found them, the Flash removed a box from the looter with the handgun, took the weapon and set it with the shotgun, then moved the motionless figure to exactly where the speedster had just been standing.

The first looter's fist collided with the jaw of the unsuspecting second crook. As Barry had judged, the blow would have been a strong one if it had connected with his own jaw. The second looter tumbled back, the punch rendering him unconscious.

As the first crook gaped at what he had somehow done, the Flash returned to the third, who was just noticing what had happened to the other pair. Barry paused behind him, then tapped the man's shoulder.

The looter instinctively swung the flashlight Barry had seen him using earlier. The Flash seized him in mid-swing, carrying him to the first looter… where the third crook instead succeeded in hitting the first.

The blow did as well as the first Barry had set up.

The first looter dropped like a rock, leaving the Flash alone with the second.

The final looter dropped his flashlight and raised his hands.

"Smart," Barry commented.

Seconds later, he left the looter and his two unconscious partners bound in strong tape found in the repair section of the store. The brief confrontation had revitalized him. He prepared for a new and more thorough search of Central City—

—And a hailstorm spanning more than half the city battered hardest right where he ran.

The hail came down behind the Flash with a ferocity that startled him. "Cisco, are you getting any odd readings on this?"

"At this point I'd be surprised to find one that's *normal*! They're all over the place, but there's some that I'm matching up with what we've got from your previous fights with the Weather Wizard!"

"Doesn't he ever sleep?" Barry asked as he outraced the hail.

"You'd think—hang on! You just may have hit on something!"

"So long as something doesn't hit on me—" Barely had the Flash made the remark than a wall of hail poured down. The velocity with which the hail struck made the padding in the suit of little value. The Flash grunted in pain as he tried to pick up speed and get ahead of the deadly assault.

He finally exited the hail. He knew he dared not slow his pace though. Veering to his right, the Flash raced on until he was far from the danger.

The moment he found a proper overhang, Barry contacted Cisco. "That was too close! It had to be Mardon's doing! He calculated for my speed by putting a danger ahead where he knew I'd run right into it!"

"That may be the case… or it may be even crazier than we think!"

"What's that supposed to mean?"

Cisco cleared his throat in a manner that the Flash noted often presaged some strange piece of information. "We've been assuming a connection between the storm and the Weather Wizard from the beginning even though his condition in Iron Heights should've prevented that, right?"

Barry eyed the foreboding sky, wary of the next threat it might unleash on him. "But we guessed correctly, didn't we? It was him!"

"Yeah, that's the thing though. We shouldn't have been right. The Weather Wizard should have been tightly under control!"

"And he wasn't? How?"

"Haven't figured that out exactly," Cisco replied, "but I did verify that he's definitely influencing this storm."

"Why do you say it like that?"

"You asked me if Mardon ever slept. I know how you meant it, but it made me look over some records from Iron Heights—"

Barry frowned. "Do they know how often you dig into their records?"

"You know me. I am the epitome of subtlety in all things, especially hacking. Anyway, they kept a twenty-four-hour-a-day, seven-days-a-week monitoring of his thoughts. Not sure exactly all the reasons why, but what's important is I finally got a match with what *we've* been recording."

"Cisco, you're still not making any sense."

"Our data matches what Iron Heights recorded after they hooked him up to the latest helmet, the one that's got some background design data from the Wizard Wand. Those particular readings come from whenever Mardon was in REM sleep."

Barry wasn't certain he had heard correctly. "When he was *dreaming*?"

"Exactly! For some reason his subconscious stirred up and began to have an effect on his metahuman abilities. This whole storm *is* due to him and he might not even realize it *himself*!"

"Great. Bad enough we have to fight him, we have to do it in a storm from out of his dreams."

Cisco chuckled. "Yeah, I didn't think you'd care for that. Still, it gives us a better chance of maybe finally triangulating where the Weather Wizard is actually located! I've been trying to do it strictly using the data we have for when he's active. Now with this I can possibly use the storm itself to triangulate using his subconscious—"

"I'll just take your word for that and hope you can accomplish it swiftly. Anything I can do to speed it along?"

"Nope! Just keep running. The storm'll do the r.est!"

The Flash blinked. "Wait. Am I being used as bait so that you can get better readings?"

"Pretty much," Cisco answered, not sounding at all guilty.

Eyeing the storm again, Barry scowled. "All right. Just make sure you find what you need as soon as you can. Maybe Caitlin can—"

"Uh... she had to step away. I told her to go take a break for a bit. She didn't sound well."

"Oh."

"Yeah, just me and H.R. here for the moment. We got your back, Barry. Don't you worry!"

Thunder boomed ominously. "Sounds like it's starting up again, Cisco."

"Better run like you mean it."

"Oh, I will. I will." The Flash inhaled, then, with a last look at the swirling heavens, charged into the chaos.

Thunder rolled and the storm stirred to greater fury again. As the Flash neared some of the taller buildings downtown, lightning struck around him.

"Not getting a second chance," the Flash commented as he evaded the bolts. "Going to have to try harder than that, Mardon—"

One bolt hit the towering office building he was just racing up to. Despite the thickness of the safety glass, dozens of huge panes shattered. Shards flew everywhere.

The Flash circled around, ready to deal with any sizable piece nearing the ground. Due to the storm, there were few pedestrians out, but there were a handful of cars in each direction. He also knew that he had to check inside to see if any harm had come to anyone in the offices—

Then, before the deadly shower of glass could fall very far, a powerful wind swept the fragments up as if they were simply leaves. Barry tried to keep an eye on the glass as it spun around and around, then the spinning stopped, and for one incredible moment the gathered fragments hung suspended in midair.

The Flash shook his head. "Uh oh…"

"What's going on there?" Cisco asked anxiously.

"I think—"

There was an ear-shattering boom. The Flash felt an exhausted tingle run through him.

The jagged pieces of glass shot in every direction.

Joe West would have rather faced a biker gang than his daughter's frustration with him over his decision not to hide, but despite that he had finally agreed to meet with her for dinner. For the most part, the meal had gone well, if in a frosty way. Neither he nor Iris had wanted to be the first to broach the subject of Mark Mardon and so they had turned to any subject that could give them the pretense of a happy meal.

Unfortunately for Joe, the detente didn't last long enough for him to finish what had been a pretty good dessert.

"Dammit, Dad! Were you going to try to avoid telling me? I heard that he was seen near police headquarters!"

Joe swallowed a forkful of cheesecake. "Who?"

"Mardon! The Weather Wizard of course! Please don't play games with me!"

"We have no official confirmation of Mark Mardon near the building. Barry reported seeing someone on the roof, but he couldn't make out who it was."

"Well, who else could it have been?" Iris demanded.

"Have you forgotten just how many metahumans we've had the misfortune of confronting this last year alone? It could've very well been one we haven't met yet."

She leaned back and took a sip of her wine. "I hope that's not supposed to reassure me. Don't think Mardon is the only thing that concerns me about your job since the first metahumans appeared. He just represents the worst possible situation involving them. He personally wants you dead."

"I've had a lot of men want to kill me, sweetheart. You know that."

"But none of them could literally control the weather."

Joe took another bite of cheesecake. "Technically not true. His brother had similar abilities. Just not as focused."

"Thank you. That doesn't make me feel better either."

"I don't know what I can tell you. Here." He pulled

out his cell. "Got you and Barry on speed dial… Heh, I guess Barry literally. I'm not going to let him carry me off to some safe house, but he knows we can reach each other nearly as fast as he can run. Got your brother's number set the same way. Reminds me. Haven't talked to him in a couple of days. He okay?"

"Wally's fine," Iris quickly answered before taking a longer sip of her wine. "Never mind him."

"Listen. I can give you all kinds of reassurances, but I doubt any of them will work. There's also more to this than just me. I know you worry about Barry. I worry about Barry. But just like me, he's going to do what he has to do. If you love him, you've got to accept that."

"Dad—"

"Barry's one of the most intelligent and capable young men I know. I wouldn't have allowed him to court you if he wasn't."

That made Iris truly smile for the first time since they had gotten together here. "'Wouldn't have allowed him'? You wouldn't have had a choice. You've *never* had a choice where Barry and I were concerned."

He chuckled. "How about moving on to another subject? I tried to call you yesterday around lunch, but got your voicemail. I didn't bother to leave a message."

"Oh!" She took a look at her phone. "You did. I was with Caitlin. She called me wanting to do lunch. She sounded as if she needed to tell me something, but we spent most of the meal… Well, a lot like we spent the bulk of this one. She didn't seem well."

"What's wrong with her?"

"I'm not quite sure. I'll be seeing her again soon. Hopefully, she'll be better by then."

"Hope so—"

There was yet another crash of thunder. The restaurant shook and the lights briefly went out.

Joe signaled the waiter. "And there's reality returning. Sounds like the storm is getting more violent again. Let's get you home. In fact, maybe I should give you a ride and tomorrow we can pick your car up."

"Don't be silly. I'll be all right. I can certainly drive the short distance. I made it here, didn't I?"

"I know better than to argue, but I will follow you, just to make sure."

"And I know better than to argue about that. Fine."

Despite the renewed intensifying of the storm, the drive back proved much smoother than either of them had expected. Iris pulled in, then, umbrella in hand, ran to her father's vehicle.

"There's no sense for you to get out. Go home. Call me when you get there. And drive carefully."

"You just get inside! Go!"

She gave him a smile. "Goodnight, Dad!"

Joe sat where he was, watching until Iris disappeared inside the apartment complex. He grinned, happy the gulf between them was shrinking: maybe Barry and Iris could do the same soon.

Lightning lit up the vicinity. The rain became a downpour again.

"Damn," Joe muttered. "I knew it couldn't last."

The lightning flashed again... and in his rearview mirror Joe saw a figure standing behind the car.

He had the car in park and the door open with a swiftness the Flash could have appreciated. In the space of a breath, the seasoned detective stood facing the rear of his vehicle, his gun already drawn.

There was no one there.

Entirely ignoring the rain, Joe surveyed the area. Seeing nothing, he climbed back inside.

In doing so, Joe missed the ominous form descending to the ground with arms spread wide. The Weather Wizard's expression was an open symbol of the hatred he felt for the man in the car. Bolts of lightning played around Mardon, each the result of his burning fury.

He had only just landed again when something made Joe look back one last time.

"Damn!"

Mardon waved his left hand to the side and a fearsome gale struck the detective's vehicle, shoving it hard against the curb. The force threw Joe across the seat.

Without hesitation, the Weather Wizard swung his right hand to the opposing side. Joe's car slid that direction, this time going over the curb and colliding with a lamppost. Electricity crackled as the lamp first buckled, then toppled over onto the vehicle.

Joe attempted to reach the passenger door, but a third gust not only pushed his car free from the live wiring, but sent it tumbling across the street. Joe went tumbling with it, his gun finally slipping free in the process.

The car shook madly. Thunder echoed, all but deafening Joe. It almost felt to the detective as if he were trapped in a storm cloud; not an impossibility, he knew.

Joe managed to remove his phone. Unfortunately, the car shook harder and the device slipped free before he could hit the panic button Cisco had installed on everyone's phone for just such emergencies. The phone dropped near the gas pedal.

Throwing himself after the phone, Joe did his best to partially wedge himself between the wheel and the pedal. He kept one arm thrust downward, hoping that the limited space left would mean the phone would slide to him.

Again, the car slid to the opposing curb, colliding hard. As every bone in his body shook, the detective started to suspect that Mardon was trying to torture him before finally striking the fatal blow.

The phone slid near. Joe grabbed for it.

His elation at retrieving the phone dissipated when he saw that someone was trying to call him and that the someone was none other than Iris. Joe tried to disconnect, but couldn't quite adjust his grip enough to do it.

"Hang up, hang up!" he muttered. Joe prayed that Iris would give up and just go to bed. The last thing Joe wanted was for Iris to decide to leave her apartment and look for her father. Mardon had thus far kept his obsession focused on the detective alone, but it certainly would not mean much to the Weather Wizard to add Iris to his list.

The call attempt finally ceased. Joe continued to pray that Iris would just go to bed. All that mattered now was for him to try again to hit the panic button.

His car spun hard in a circle.

The shift in forces was so abrupt that once more Joe lost his phone. Swearing, he tried to grab it again, only to have it slide under his seat.

"Damn!" Joe forced himself up. As he did, the car swung around to face Mark Mardon. In the almost constant flashes of lightning, Joe could see the Weather Wizard smile darkly at him.

And then he saw something—or rather *someone*—else just behind Mardon's left shoulder. A shadowy figure to whom the rogue appeared to be listening. The Weather Wizard nodded to the figure, then looked again at the trapped detective.

Mardon winked at Joe.

The car began spinning violently, propelled, he suspected, by a powerful whirlwind. Spinning and yet still moving quickly in one dread direction.

Joe caught glimpses of the thick wall that grew closer with every circle. Gritting his teeth, Joe pictured Iris one last time.

The car shattered as it struck the wall hard.

6

The Flash stared at the sinister downpour, well aware of the chaos and carnage it would cause if left unchecked. Barry couldn't anticipate where every dangerous piece would fly, but he could hazard a good guess as to their range. The moment they started flying, he ran.

The cars driving along the streets were his first goals, these were the closest of the targets carrying potential victims. Barry judged which would be out of range, then leapt on top of the first of those that he knew would never make it to safety. Even for someone who could run as fast as he could, the number at risk was daunting.

As the first wave of shattered glass reached the Flash, he went into action. Those pieces small enough for him to grip he plucked out of the air, then carried over to the curb where they would do no harm. Those too large for him to grasp properly he studied with a calculating eye, noting the angle at which they fell and where they would likely land. Once certain of his estimations, the speedster then hit each at just the right spot with his hand, sending the jagged projectiles spinning away.

Four, five, seven, twelve, twenty cars and more. After the thirtieth, the Flash looked around and found, to his relief, that the rest would be safe.

Without hesitation, he headed to the office building from which the shower of glass had originated. Racing through the ruined entrance, he ran up the eighty floors of emergency stairs to the top. There the speedster checked every office, locating those that still had employees and others in them. One by one, he carried each innocent to safety without them even realizing they were moving. Floor after floor the Flash ran, until finally he had the building cleared.

When that was done, he returned to the streets and raced around, locating every person inside and out who stood in the path of the glass spray. Time after time, Barry either plucked deadly shards from the air or battered them aside so they hit the streets or walls without harming anyone. The effort proved a much more complex one than with the cars; the speedster had to check not only the sidewalks, but the fronts of stores and restaurants, alleys, and subway stairs.

As he gathered everyone, the Flash couldn't help wondering what the Weather Wizard was up to this time. Random violence had been more Clyde Mardon's way. Mark generally used it as a means to achieve goals... but what was the goal of this? Barry had expected his adversary to attack him while he was trying to save innocents, but thus far Mardon had attempted nothing. That made no sense whatsoever to the speedster. Considering how possessed the Weather Wizard had been where the Flash and Joe West were concerned, it seemed to—

Barry swore. "Cisco! Do you hear me?"

"I'm with you! What's up?"

"We need to locate Joe! Check anywhere he might be. Now!"

"On it!"

As the Flash ran, he also tried to think where Joe might be at that moment. Joe was not on duty, which meant the possible locations multiplied. Naturally, the first possibilities that came to mind involved Iris and Wally too, but there were so many more. Time, though, was of the essence, even for the—

"Cisco! His phone! He's got to have it on him!"

"Already checked! I tried to ping it, but no luck! The weather's interfering with that too!"

Barry continued running, though he was not quite sure where. Part of him wanted to make certain Iris was also safe, but—

Iris.

She had already been one of the most obvious choices on his list, which made the chance that Joe was with her more than worth checking out.

"Heading to the apartment, Cisco! If he's not there, I'll try Wally!"

"Gotcha! Already checking some of his hangouts! I'll let you know the moment I find anything!"

The Flash sped through Central City, the people and the storm both frozen fixtures as he raced toward the apartment. Still, despite time seemingly stopping for the Flash, he knew that not only did it proceed, but the Weather Wizard had purposely set him up to use valuable seconds while the rogue went after Joe West.

The apartment complex came into sight—

—And so did the fact that Joe's car not only hung high in the air, but was also just about to crash headlong into a very solid wall.

Barry picked up speed. He used momentum to let him run up the wall Joe was about to hit and reach the driver's side door. The Flash tore open the door and pulled him from the car.

He brought the detective over to a spot near the apartment complex entrance, then stopped.

"Damn—" Joe blurted, his arms covering his face in expectation of the collision, then he looked up at Barry, seemingly dazed.

"Barry! How did I end up here? How the hell could even you have been able to—"

Behind them, there was a loud, horrific crash as the detective's car hit the wall hard. Despite being sturdy, the vehicle shattered against the wall. Fragments flew everywhere.

"Go get Iris!" the Flash ordered Joe between gasps for breath. "Go get her and hide! Do not let Mardon see you!"

"Are you all right? What just—"

But the Flash had already turned and headed back to the crash, racing around seeking any innocents in the path of the debris. He moved two people, then went around plucking or battering smaller pieces of the car before they could hit other people.

When everyone was inside, and outside seemed secure, Barry turned to where he expected Mardon to be. Instead, atop a store to the right of where Joe's vehicle had met its untimely end, he once more caught sight of a murky figure.

"Not getting away this time," the Flash swore.

Yet no sooner had he thought that, then a fierce hailstorm struck all around him. Instead of pursuing the figure as he had hoped, Barry found himself having to dodge the savage onslaught.

He recognized his terrible mistake the moment he moved. The hailstorm had left him with but one logical path and he had taken it. Too late the speedster realized he was doing exactly what Mardon wanted.

"Whoa!" A whirlwind that the Weather Wizard had likely conjured up at the same time as the hailstorm stood directly in the Flash's path. Mardon had correctly calculated that with the Flash's attention on the hail, there would be absolutely no chance he would notice something all but invisible before he ran into it.

The whirlwind threw the Flash and several pieces of debris high into the air. As it did, over the din of the full thunderstorm the Weather Wizard's laugh resounded like thunder.

"Run here, run there, run everywhere!" Mardon shouted madly. "Appreciate your help, Flash! I won't be able to do this without you! Only fitting though, I guess, since you're partly at fault in the first place!"

The Flash had no idea what Mardon meant and didn't try to figure it out. Instead, he looked for any solid surface, be it a wall or even—

One of the battered doors left from the remains of Joe's car flew dangerously near the speedster. The Flash had no doubt that the Weather Wizard intended for it to either distract or eventually hit him, but for Barry it was just what he needed.

As it came around, he slammed one foot on it. For anyone else, it would have been an impotent gesture, but for the Flash it was all the surface he required. He pushed himself forward, then got his other foot on and pushed again. The action gave him just enough momentum to reach what was left of a seat flying by, and he kicked off onto an upward trajectory.

He caught a board next, then leaped out. Landing hard on a rooftop, the Flash quickly spun around to look for Mardon.

The Weather Wizard stood at the far end of the street, eyes still on the whirlwind in which he had trapped his adversary. Taking a deep breath, the Flash located the roof's maintenance ladder, then climbed down in less than the blink of an eye.

Unlike with the looters, the speedster knew that he couldn't just take Mardon down, not until the Flash forced him to stop all his storm-related chaos. The Flash darted down to where the rogue still stood watching the whirlwind and reached out.

The Weather Wizard's reaction to the speedster's tight grip on his throat proved somewhat anticlimactic. In fact, Mardon seemed almost to have expected the Flash to strike as he had. The Weather Wizard let out a slight gasp at first, but otherwise simply stared expectantly at his foe. Mark Mardon's eyes were sunken in as if he had not slept in a week. He looked strained, a vein in his neck visibly throbbing. His breathing was rapid and he looked as if he had lost at least fifteen pounds.

"Call it all off, Mardon," the Flash warned as he tried to ignore his foe's physical transformation. "Call it all off or I'll take you on a speedy little trip that'll have you begging to stand still again."

"You're really no good at threats, you know that?" the Weather Wizard rasped. "Just helping to kill people when their backs are turned." He suddenly raised his voice to a shout. "Isn't that right, Clyde?"

"'Clyde'?" Utterly baffled by his adversary's declaration, the Flash automatically turned in the direction Mardon looked. Part of him immediately berated himself for falling victim to such an old ruse. There could hardly be anyone there, especially the late, unlamented Clyde Mardon.

But there *was* someone on top of the nearest roof.

Someone who, as before, the speedster couldn't really make out… yet who, now that a name had been put to him, *did* have a stance and general frame that reminded him of Mark's younger brother.

"Clyde?" the Flash blurted. "Clyde Mardon?"

Another wind tore him from the Weather Wizard and threw him toward the building directly across from the apartment complex. However, just before he would have hit, the wind abruptly pulled him back.

"No, not yet, Clyde! It's not enough yet!" Mardon shouted to the figure, as if having heard something. "But, yeah, we can toss the cop around a bit more!"

As he spun around in the wind, the Flash tried to spot Joe. He could only hope that the detective had done as suggested and taken Iris and fled.

"Now, where do you suppose he might be hiding?" the Weather Wizard asked, this time to no one in particular. "Maybe he scurried into some hole to hide just like any other rat!" Mardon chuckled. "Or maybe he went back to that girl he dropped off over here—"

"Give it up, Mardon!" Joe shouted from somewhere. "Give it up or I'll be forced to fire!"

The wind holding the Flash weakened as the Weather Wizard reacted to the unexpected command. Expression contorting, Mardon searched for where Joe was located. "Come on out, West! Doesn't matter where you hide! The storm—my storm—is everywhere!"

"Don't need to hide," the detective returned. "Just need one shot. Just one."

The Weather Wizard spun to face the spot where it now seemed Joe stood.

"Last chance, Mardon!"

The Weather Wizard started to point. "Yours... not mine, West! Yours—"

Joe fired.

The wind assaulting the Flash vanished... or rather redirected toward the shot. Barry dropped, hitting the street hard despite his padded outfit. He lay there stunned for a moment.

The Weather Wizard stood undaunted by the shot. Barry knew Joe's marksmanship well enough to appreciate that if Mardon had not been hit, it was only due to the intense wind he had shifted toward the detective.

Joe turned the gun toward the roof where the shadowy form still stood. The Flash doubted that Joe meant to shoot, but whatever the reason for his decision, it had a profound effect on the Weather Wizard.

"Clyde! No!" the Weather Wizard shouted, his tone one of fear.

The wind shifted immediately, raising Mardon up into the air and toward the roof while also whipping up loose debris all around the area. Arm protecting his eyes, Joe stepped back. He tried to get a clear shot at the Weather Wizard but apparently couldn't concentrate his aim well enough.

The Flash, meanwhile, finally recovered enough to get to his feet. As the Weather Wizard passed over the roof, the figure faded from the Flash's view. Barry took a deep breath and started after him. Unfortunately, he had only gotten two blocks when he began to slow and stumble. His heart seemed to have trouble beating fast enough and his breathing became a struggle.

A buzzing arose in his ear. The Flash tried to make out what was being said but finally gave up. "Can't understand you, Cisco! Can you repeat it?"

The buzzing increased, then subsided. Barry grimaced. Once again, fighting around the Weather Wizard—with Mardon's unique mastery of the elements including lightning—had ruined the communication device.

He made one more attempt at a search, but could not locate the Weather Wizard's trail. With some reluctance, the Flash returned to Joe West. Standing with him were several policemen who had clearly just arrived on the scene. For Barry, they all faded to the background the moment Iris herself descended from the apartment complex.

Barry hesitated, then headed to Joe.

"Couldn't keep after Mardon," he informed the detective.

"Yeah, understandable." Joe sent the men he had been talking to away. They spread out to cover the scene. "No one can hear us now if you want to talk about anything more personal."

"Speaking of personal, Iris is heading toward us."

Joe didn't turn in her direction. "She won't get far.

I left word that no one is to enter this area without my permission. Not even her."

Indeed, at that moment, one of the uniformed officers stepped in front of Iris. An animated and not entirely friendly conversation ensued, with Iris constantly trying to catch either her father's or Barry's attention.

"Yeah, I don't think that line of defense is going to hold long," the Flash whispered. "This *is* Iris we're talking about."

"Long enough. By the way, thanks for showing up in time to save me from being scattered all over the place. I thought I was keeping a good eye out. More fool me."

"If you hadn't fired when you had, I might've been splattered against a wall too. We're in together, Joe. Mardon wants both of us."

Joe rubbed his chin. "Uh huh, that brings me to what I need to talk with you about right away. Did you hear what Mardon shouted up there? Or maybe actually to *whom* he thought he was talking to?"

The Flash nodded. "I heard it. He was talking to *Clyde*. His dead brother."

"Yeah. The man I shot. You know what's even worse?"

"No."

The detective leaned closer. "Part of the reason I turned the gun so quickly from Mardon to the figure on the roof was because just for a moment... I swear just for a moment... I thought I *did* see Clyde Mardon up there."

7

As Cisco waited for his latest adjustments to hopefully restore communications again, he took a surreptitious glance at where Caitlin usually sat. She had been in a fairly good mood when she had first arrived, but a short time earlier, just after their dinner break, she had suddenly stepped away without a word.

Neither he nor H.R. had gone after her, both hoping, so Cisco suspected, that she would return shortly.

She had not. Now he was regretting that decision as well.

"What do you think?" H.R. asked.

"She should've been back long ago. One of us should have followed her. Just in case."

"I was, uh, actually referring to your attempt to patch up communications, but yes, she should have. Do you want me to go check on her?"

Cisco returned his attention to his efforts. "Still a

minute or two before I have any idea if it'll work. Let's leave her that much longer."

"All right… but what does the device say?"

With the flick of a switch, Cisco brought up the data in question. His brow wrinkled as he digested the information streaming before him. "Well, that's interesting…"

H.R. pulled up a chair and looked at the screen. After a moment of consideration, he admitted, "Yeah… Still means nothing to me. I'll take your word as usual. What do you find so interesting?"

"The time things start to fluctuate is always recorded, as is the duration. According to this it began the same moment things got to their worst between Barry and the Weather Wizard."

"You're saying there's a connection. I don't like the sound of that."

"I don't either. It looks like the energy fluctuations that enable Mardon to control the weather are on a similar wavelength—for lack of a better word at the moment—as Caitlin's. I've triple-checked. There's no denying the data. It's more than that though. I'm sure of it."

H.R. rubbed his chin. "Well, her powers are also kind of weather-related. Could that be it? Could it be as simple as that?"

"Not sure. I'm going to have to research that further. From these readings, it looks like she should be okay now. Let her rest a little. I've still got problems with our communications with Barry. I need to get that taken care of immediately. Fortunately, his readings are showing exhaustion but calm right now, so the fight is over."

"Where'd you say his location is?"

Cisco started reading it off to H.R., only to stop after the street address. "Talk about close to home…"

"Do you think he's talking with Iris right now?"

"From these low readings, I doubt it. Each time they've been near enough to talking things out, Barry's readings shoot up almost as much as when he's been fighting the Weather Wizard."

H.R. shook his head. "Isn't love wonderful?"

"For the last time, officer, that is my father over there. Joe West. My name is Iris West. I just left him a few minutes ago! He is probably even in charge of this situation. You do know who you're taking orders from, correct?"

The hapless police officer whom she had been harassing nodded sympathetically. "Yes, ma'am, and I knew who you were even before you introduced yourself. Seen you with him several times and read your byline in the newspaper more than once. You still can't go to him. I'm really sorry. Those are my orders. No one gets through."

"I don't see why that includes me. You know I often cover the police." She gestured in the direction of her father. "Now see, he can't even make up his mind! Now he's waving me to him!"

The officer glanced over his shoulder to check—and Iris raced past him.

"Ma'am! Please come back here right now! Ma'am!"

With the police officer on her heels, Iris ran toward her father. She knew she might not have been as quick as Barry or Wally, but she had never been slow. Iris managed to keep just enough distance between herself and her unfortunate pursuer until she finally caught up with her father.

Of course in the meantime Barry had simply vanished.

"You and I need to talk," she muttered to Joe. "Right here and right now."

"Yeah? I thought we just did." Still, with reluctance he waved the officer away. "It's fine, Perez. I'll deal with her."

"Yes, sir!" Perez saluted him, then spun on his heel and took off in the direction from which he had come.

"You will?" she asked, not at all pleased. The events of the last few minutes had erased all the good will she and her father had built up over their meal. Aware that no one could hear them, she angrily replied, "Well, I don't want you to *deal* with me. Where's Barry?"

"He was here a moment ago. You know how it is with him."

"Too well. I'll ask again. Where is he?"

Joe spread his hands. "Iris, I really don't know—"

Before he could finish, she caught sight of a figure by the apartment complex. Barry... *just* Barry in civilian garb. Not the Flash. He stood by the steps looking as guilty as she thought he should be.

"Excuse me, Dad." She brushed past her father, who made not even the slightest attempt to stop her.

Hands in his coat pockets, Barry quietly waited. His pitiful expression finally doused most of Iris's anger. Most, not all.

"You've been avoiding me," she started, trying to maintain her frustration with him. "You've been avoiding me for no good reason, Barry! That's not how we treat each other!"

"I'm sorry, Iris. I really am." He briefly looked down. "You're the last person I'd want to avoid. You know that. You know how I feel... How I've always felt."

She softened more, then glanced back at her home. The building had some superficial damage, but fortunately—or unfortunately—the focus of the attack had been on the Flash. "I know all that, of course, Barry, but this is different. Mardon came after my father, Barry. Just like I feared. From what I saw out here, he came pretty close to killing him too, didn't he? *Didn't* he?"

"I got there in time. You saw him. He's fine. He's already taking charge! Joe is just—"

"None of that is the point."

"Listen. I did have a talk with him, I swear it. He will not accept being hidden away. Look at him!" He thrust a hand at the crime scene. "Look at him, Iris."

She knew that she didn't have to look, but she looked nonetheless. Sure enough, her father was directing matters with the usual thoroughness and energy that had garnered him so many accolades in the police department. The men around him moved with the confidence one had when able to trust in the competence of one's commander. Iris had seen that before from the officers serving with her father. Her pride in him battled with her concerns.

"He's only human, Barry," Iris insisted, crossing her arms tight for emphasis.

"And Mardon and I are not." Before she could try to rephrase it, he added, "It's fine. I know what *you* mean, I know that, Iris. Everything changed that night, including how people like Joe need to do their jobs even with metahumans like me, the Weather Wizard, and the rest around."

"I love you, Barry, but you can be so slow for someone so fast. It started out with me worried about Dad, but what you've just said only reminds me of who else I'm concerned for. Very concerned for." She poked a finger in his chest. "You, you idiot. Every time you race out there to fight someone like Zoom, the Mirror Master, Captain Cold, or anyone of those other Cisco-named madmen, I fear I'm going to lose you just after I've found you!"

"Iris…"

"And now to top it all off, I have to worry about my brother as well! Ever since Wally gained his powers, I've had to pray that he won't literally run headlong into danger without at least thinking it through first!"

"I've tried to impress upon Wally all the mistakes I made, so he could learn from them without repeating them. I've also tried to be as careful as I can be, Iris." Barry took her hand. "I'd like to come back each time too."

"I know. Barry, it's just—"

Sirens went off. Barry and Iris turned to the direction from which the sound came. In the distance, they made out speeding fire trucks.

Barry looked even guiltier. "Iris… sorry. I've got to follow after them. I've got to."

"You—" It was too late. As had happened so many times before, she found herself speaking to empty space.

Cold. So cold. So very cold. Caitlin thought.

She suddenly smiled. *How delightful…*

Cisco tapped his mic. "Yo! Can you hear me now?"

There was a crackle, then, "I hear you! Is this going to work from now on?"

"Hope so! What happened with Mardon? The readings were all over the place!"

"You wouldn't believe it. I'll fill you in quickly. I'm heading after some fire trucks!"

"Got it." Cisco listened as Barry quickly explained, then with a nod despite the fact that his friend couldn't see it, added, "That confirms a lot of the data I saw." Cisco leaned forward. "Where are you again?"

"Helping the fire department. I just finished removing potential victims from an electrical fire. Going to try to help put it out."

"Well, listen. How are you feeling? Your vitals are way down."

"Like I could really go to sleep now, even on the street. I'm just glad things seem to be calming down here. I'll move on from here in just a minute."

"Don't worry about anywhere else," Cisco returned. "Right now, everything seems to be being handled by the EMTs and law enforcement. You head back here. We need to check you out."

"Will do. Just have to take care of one more thing…"

Cisco eyed the vitals again. "Do me a favor, take a little time with it. Pace yourself. You really need to get some rest when you get back too."

"You have no idea. See you soon."

Cisco cut the link, then typed in some more data. "H.R.? Hey, H.R.!"

"What?" blurted the older man from his chair. "Sorry. Dozed off."

Inputting one last number, Cisco switched to another screen. "There she is. Caitlin hasn't come back. She's down the hall. According to the device, she must have dropped off to sleep like you. Maybe go and discreetly wake her. I could use her help on this problem with Barry's growing exhaustion. It's looking very odd. I don't like it."

* * *

Steaming cup in hand, H.R. departed the main lab. The silence in the hall made him pause for a moment.

"This place can get much too creepy," he whispered to himself. "We need to channel some music here. Really cheerful music."

He peered down to the doorway of the room where Caitlin was supposed to be, noting that what little of the interior he could see through the glass entrance was dark. Indeed, when H.R. got to the room, it was to see not only that there was no light on inside, but that Caitlin was obviously not within.

"Hmm." H.R. looked at the various entrances around him. None gave any hint that Caitlin was in one of the nearby rooms.

He started to call out, then thought better of it. Keeping the cup balanced, H.R. walked down the hall. As he did, he eyed each doorway for some hint of Caitlin's presence.

H.R. had gone some distance when he felt an odd coolness in the air. Stepping close to an air vent, he reached up.

"Hmm." There was no cold air blowing, but this part of the corridor was noticeably cooler than near the main lab. "Not good."

He considered going back to Cisco, but then remembered what Cisco had said about Caitlin's readings. Shrugging, H.R. continued searching the rooms.

As he reached the far end, he heard a slight sound within. He paused to listen, but it didn't repeat itself. After some consideration, H.R. reached for the handle... only to hesitate when he realized that he could see his own breath.

"Must be the air conditioning. Must be. Sure." Without thinking, he took a sip of the coffee, then tried the door. H.R. was not encouraged by the fact that the handle felt very cold. This did not fit with how Cisco had described matters.

An even chillier wave of air washed over him as he entered. His breath now came out in stronger and stronger puffs of fog. His skin had goosebumps, although not all of them were due to the cold. Despite having heard a sound, H.R. found the room as dark as the rest. He shut the door carefully behind him and moved deeper into the office.

H.R. had taken just a few steps farther when he heard the quiet breathing. At first, the regularity of the breathing made it sound as if whoever was inside were asleep, but then H.R. heard very slight mumbling.

"Caitlin?" He remembered the last time he had found her. "Are you all right? Tell me you're all right!"

The mumbling increased for a moment, then softened to previous levels.

"Cisco and I thought you might like a nice, warm coffee right about now," he commented soothingly. "Wouldn't that be great? Got one right with me. Care for a sip?"

He still received no answer. The mumbling continued its unnerving rhythm.

Listening closely, H.R. located the area where it had to come from. He started to reach for the light switches, but hesitated.

"Caitlin? What say we turn on a little light? Would you like that? I know I would!"

Still no answer. H.R. bit his lip, then turned on those lights farthest from where he believed Caitlin might be.

There was no change in the mumbling. H.R. exhaled, then headed toward the voice.

With every step, the air felt colder, sharper. H.R. nearly lost his footing at one point, belatedly discovering a patch of ice created by water spilled from a small cardboard cup lying nearby.

"Well, maybe you don't want anything to drink after all," he went on, trying to keep his voice level. In his mind, he noted Cisco had clearly either misread Caitlin's vitals or there was a glitch in the device itself.

Either way it really doesn't matter much, does it? You're here, H.R., and that's what truly matters. You're the one who has to decide now what the next step is…

There was a slight movement. H.R. almost turned about, but thought better of it. He slowly came around a table to where he felt certain Caitlin had to be.

"Oh, dear…"

Caitlin sat with her legs crossed and arms clutching her body. She rocked back and forth, her gaze fixated on the empty air ahead. She continued to mumble something H.R. couldn't make out. Frost covered her immediate surroundings, including portions of her.

Even all that didn't bother him as much as two other things. The first was a streak of white in her hair, a streak he could swear was slowly spreading before his very eyes. The second was a less obvious change, unless one knew Caitlin. That was the smile she wore as she rocked and muttered. The smile with an edge to it that sent an emotional chill down his spine to match the physical one he also felt standing so near her.

"Killer Frost," he whispered, "and not by choice, it looks."

Caitlin stirred. She slowly turned her unblinking gaze to him. As she did, her arm shifted and he caught a glimpse of her wrist. Cisco's invention blinked weakly through a layer of ice that appeared to have formed out of thin air.

Caitlin continued to stare at him, and H.R. offered her the best smile he could muster. Her own smile remained fixed.

"Hi... Caitlin. I brought some coffee." He offered the cup. "Why don't you stand up and have some? It'll do you some good, I promise."

She looked at the cup as if not certain what it was. Her brow wrinkled in a clear attempt at thought.

"I made it the way you like it." H.R. could not recall at that moment just exactly how Caitlin liked her coffee or whether he had actually done as he had said.

All that mattered was that the cup seemed to have attracted her attention.

"Hurry. While it's still hot. Take it."

"Coffee," she muttered. "Coffee."

"Yep! You want some?" H.R. steered the cup closer to Caitlin's hand. He placed the still-hot cup in his palm and turned the handle toward her. "Go on."

Caitlin slowly reached for it. As her fingers wrapped around the handle, her expression softened. She looked at the mug as if it were the oddest thing that she had seen in her life.

"I'm cold," she said just before sipping.

Trying to ignore the burning pain in his palm, H.R. nodded. "Yeah, it is a bit nippy. Keep drinking. You'll warm up just nicely. Go ahead!"

She did as he said. At the same time, the streak in her hair began to fade away. H.R. noticed the office also begin to feel warmer. Around him, the frost faded away, the last of it the layer over Cisco's creation.

"That's better," Caitlin said as she neared the bottom of the cup. "Thank you."

"How are you feeling?"

She took another sip. "It's improving rapidly, but that's not exactly what you want to ask me, is it? Go ahead. I'll answer as best I can."

After a moment's hesitation, H.R. leaned against a desk. "This was a bad one, Caitlin. You weren't in control."

"I know. I actually felt it coming on, so I stepped away.

I knew I could handle it better if I could concentrate…
At least, that was my thinking at the time."

"'Handle it'? Caitlin, you should've seen yourself!
This wasn't anything at all like last time—"

Caitlin cradled the cup. "I know. It surged strong
when we were keeping tabs on Barry… I came in here
to do some breathing exercises I'd learned. I'd nearly
finished when you came in."

"To be frank, it didn't look like it."

She held up the wrist wearing the device. "Look. It's
acting perfectly fine. I just need to make one more slight
adjustment." Caitlin frowned. "Does Cisco know?"

"He's been pretty busy," H.R. remarked. "I couldn't
say everything he knows."

"He'd probably have said something to me."
Caitlin worked with the device. "This should do it. I
was too tentative when I adjusted it last time. Cisco
told me what to do, but I only made a slight increase.
I've corrected for that. Since the machine didn't report
anything troublesome to him this time, either, we
clearly don't need to worry him."

H.R. had a sense of déjà vu. He now regretted some
of his last decisions and suggestions where Caitlin was
concerned. "Uh, do you—"

"How's Barry doing?"

"Hmm? He's good. His levels were going down
again, but they flattened off once the fight ended."

Caitlin's face screwed up in thought. "That's
happened more than once! Somehow it's tied into

what the Weather Wizard is doing. Mardon can manipulate all the energies in the weather because of his metahuman abilities. I wonder if he's managed to draw Barry's energies in the process."

"I don't like the sound of that. Is it possible? I mean, it does seem similar to something Cisco was saying."

"He probably saw it in the data. We've only scratched the surface when it comes to understanding what happened then. The diversity of abilities given to those affected. Why some gained greater powers than others. Why more gained no known powers at all. I doubt we'll find out everything in our lifetimes."

She seems as if all that frost stuff never happened, H.R. marveled. *She's back to being… Caitlin.* He wasn't certain how to take that. H.R. knew very well that he was often out of his element when it came to what the others had to deal with. He was not Harrison Wells, scientist. He was Harrison Wells, fraud, who had been given a chance of a reprieve for his past misdeeds by people who had once been friends of his counterparts from other Earths. Despite his often-confident demeanor, H.R. actually felt he did not deserve any true voice in these matters. Caitlin and Cisco certainly knew better what needed to be done when dealing with the idiosyncrasies of the metahuman situation. Besides, he knew that Caitlin remained unaware of Cisco's growing suspicions about her health.

Cisco'll be on top of it, H.R. told himself. *He'll make certain. Everything will be fine.*

Caitlin suddenly looked around. "How long have I been here? I've lost track of time."

H.R. told her. Caitlin didn't even bat an eye.

"I must have dozed off. This storm has kept me awake a lot."

Not knowing what else to say, he replied, "Yeah, I think it's hit all of us."

"We'd better get back to Cisco! I need to tell him some of my ideas."

She rushed past H.R., exiting the room before he could gather his wits. H.R. shook his head, then quickly followed after.

8

Mark Mardon slumped against the wall. He felt as if he had not slept in weeks. That sensation was made worse by the fact that he had not accomplished what he had set out to do. He was close, of that he was certain, but close still meant nothing if he didn't manage to push things to their needed conclusion.

Something his brother was more than willing to point out as well.

"All that splashing! All that noise! What did it all amount to? Nothing, Mark!"

The Weather Wizard managed to nod. As usual, Clyde echoed his own self-recriminations. "I know. I know. We almost had it though, I swear! I could feel it…"

"You could feel it… but I still can't feel anything but regret, bro. I'm still dead and isn't that all that matters?"

"Yeah." Mark's heart had not slowed down since his fight with the Flash. He continued to try to draw enough air into his lungs in the hopes that doing so would help his heart return to normal. "Yeah, that and… and…"

Clyde abruptly hovered over him. "Go ahead. Say it, Mark. Say the other thing that I need done… and that isn't yet."

The Weather Wizard could hardly deny him, especially considering that other failure burned inside almost as much as not having brought his brother back. "I'll get both of them next time. I *will*."

"You will?" Clyde's growing fury matched the older brother's overriding guilt. "You *had* the detective! You *had* Joe West! Maybe the Flash has got all the fancy power and the funny suit, but Detective Joe West is the guy who drilled me, Mark! A damned unpowered cop! Do you know how humiliating that is to *both* of us?"

"Of course I do—"

"Then why the hell didn't you at least kill *him*? You had him and you toyed with him!"

Struggling back to his feet, Mark tried to defend himself. "You know why I delayed. I had to get the Flash running himself ragged! Remember what we found? When he and I—hell, maybe all those like us— are at our most active, that's when whatever energies it is making us like this are most volatile—"

Clyde grinned coldly. "Listen to you. Always the one better with words. Words. I needed action and I get words."

"Stop that!" Without thinking, the Weather Wizard thrust a hand toward his brother. Lightning played from it, striking out at Clyde.

The bolts shot through him.

"*No!*" Mark shouted, horrified at the forces he had just unleashed on the only person that mattered to him. "No! Clyde!"

His brother's body scattered as if made of dust. A harsh wind rushed from the vacated spot and at the Weather Wizard. Mark shielded his face as he tried to come to grips with his horrendous error.

"Don't go, Clyde! Don't go!" Mark stretched a grasping hand toward the spot. "I'm sorry… I'm sorry… I didn't mean to do it…"

The wind swirled around him, then gathered at his brother's last location.

"That's it, Clyde… You'll be all right…"

As he begged, a human shape formed in the wind. Its movements mimicked those of the Weather Wizard perfectly. An anxious Mark watched as the body and limbs coalesced, finally coming into definition.

Clyde's face formed. Clyde's angry, judgmental face.

"Did that make you happy, Mark? Maybe you like me better dead. We were always competitive, you and I. Maybe you want to be the one and *only* Weather Wizard!"

"No!" Mark insisted, vehemently shaking his head. "No! I wouldn't go through all this if I did—"

"All what? You should be ruler of this city, but instead you're still holed up in a leftover dump we used when we were hiding from the cops! You're gonna have to move from here too! You know the Flash has friends, brainy friends. They've got to have been trying to get a fix on you since Iron Heights!"

The Flash's brainy friends...

"The wand!" The wand would have solved a lot of his troubles. The wand might have been enough to help him finally cross that threshold needed to bring Clyde back to life.

But the wand was beyond him, hidden who knew where.

"Yeah, the bloody wand. A shame they didn't make two, one for each of us once you get me back."

"Would like one right now just to get the job done," the Weather Wizard muttered. His eyes widened. Suspicions he had had about another device returned.

"You're thinking about your escape, aren't you? You've been wondering all the while how you finally got out."

Mark suddenly felt as if he had swallowed a desert. He stumbled past a couple of pieces of dusty furniture to the cache. Unfortunately, there were no bottles of water left.

"Are you that slow, bro? You're the lord of the storm! Conjuring a little water for yourself is simple!"

"Don't want them to locate me..."

"Then we leave for the other safe house. This dump was getting to me anyway." Clyde cupped his hands in encouragement. "Go ahead! A few raindrops."

Rubbing his forehead, which had begun to pound around the same moment he had cast the lightning at his sibling, Mark focused.

A peculiar haze formed a couple of feet over his upturned palms. Gritting his teeth, the rogue kept up his effort.

Droplets of water begin dripping into his cupped hands. Mark waited until he had enough, then brought it to his mouth before it could slip through to the floor. In the meantime, the haze faded away.

After swallowing every bit he could, the Weather Wizard rubbed his face with his wet hands. The cool moisture brought a measure of calm back to him, which in return enabled him to concentrate better on the theories he had about his escape.

"The wand. All the while I had that last piece of electronic garbage on my head, keeping me helpless, there was a familiar feeling. Something that reminded me of the way I felt when the wand was used."

"Go on... Go on," Clyde whispered abruptly by his ear.

"Whatever they used," the Weather Wizard muttered, "had to use some of the same technology. At first, it did what they wanted, but somewhere along the way, just like with the wand, it started to focus my power, not nullify it after all." He ran his fingers through his hair. "Wonder how?"

Clyde now hovered by his other ear. "What does it matter how it worked? Maybe you could see if there's some way you can make use of it to help me! Maybe it's just what you need."

"That means heading back to Iron Heights."

"So? You afraid of a few guards?"

Mark growled at him. "Nothing about Iron Heights scares me. *Nothing* scares me, Clyde. You know that."

"Yeah, nothing scares me either, except you failing me."

Gritting his teeth, Mark summoned a wind to carry him aloft. It brought him through the skylight he had shattered the first night arriving here. He soared up into the storm, the rain bending around him as he moved.

The storm's fury revived as the Weather Wizard flew over Central City. He noticed none of it, attention fixated on the ever-nearing shape of the penitentiary.

Lights flooded Iron Heights, far more than the Weather Wizard recalled. The reason was a simple one and a credit, as he saw it, to his tremendous abilities. After only a few days since he had escaped the place, the authorities had been forced to take what immediate temporary measures they could to maintain security.

A constant stream of searchlights poured over the damaged wing. Mark paused just out of sight, then stretched one hand toward where his old cell had been.

An onslaught of wind, rain, and hail struck the area. The Weather Wizard considered lightning as well, but decided that might destroy just what he had come to investigate.

Frantic shouts only audible between bouts of thunder made him smile. Mark would have done a lot worse to his former jailers if not for his need to take care. As they ran from the storm, the Weather Wizard descended into the chaos.

"Look at 'em go!" Clyde roared next to him as Mardon alighted. "Pity you couldn't take out a few permanently."

"There will be another time." Mark was not at all disturbed by his brother's abrupt appearance. To his mind, as a ghost, Clyde could be anywhere at any time.

"You think you'll find anything?"

"That's why I'm here." The rogue strode calmly through the ruins of the wing, once more the fearsome elements of the storm avoiding him.

Clyde stood in front of him. "You know he may very well show up."

"He's going to have enough trouble on his hands." Mark paused to look up at the turbulent skies. "I'm getting stronger by the day, Clyde! I can handle more and more of it! My power extends throughout the storm. I can create havoc on the other side of the city while I handle matters here."

Clyde only grinned, not seeming to see the obvious circles under his brother's eyes or the straining vein in the Weather Wizard's neck. "Yeah... not enough, though. Remember that. Not enough."

"It will be. Soon."

He located his cell, now mostly a pile of concrete, brick, and steel. The authorities had not yet had the opportunity to clear it away, in great part thanks to the incessant storm.

"Lot of heavy trash here," Clyde remarked.

"Pebbles and sticks." The Weather Wizard inhaled, then concentrated.

In the center of the rubble, a small whirlwind formed. As Mark stared at it, the whirlwind began to swell. Small bits of refuse became swept up into it.

Glaring, the Weather Wizard increased his efforts.

The whirlwind became a small tornado. Larger pieces of brick and concrete stirred from the ruins, then slowly rose up before his eyes.

"Come on, bro! Come on!"

Egged on by Clyde—a comfortably familiar sensation from the past—Mark Mardon threw his full strength into the tornado.

The tornado exploded into a giant and yet its horrendous winds did not extend beyond the area the Weather Wizard desired.

"That's it, Mark! A good five on the scale, eh?"

"I've just upped the scale. This'll be a six." Mark eyed a particular spot in the rubble. The tornado shifted minutely. As it did, it began ripping up huge chunks of concrete as if they were styrofoam.

"Ha! Now we're talking big!"

It's the storm, Clyde," the Weather Wizard rasped. "The original one. It's feeding me just like I'm feeding it. I'm getting better at holding all that power. Do you see it?"

"Yeah, you look just like a god!"

Sweat succeeded where rain had not in drenching the Weather Wizard. He noticed none of it, caught up in the astonishing sight of massive pieces of wall and ceiling rising into the tornado at *his* command. Within seconds, nearly all the area of the cell had been cleared.

As tons of material swirled over his head, the Weather Wizard stepped into the clearing and began searching.

"This storm is getting crazier… if that's even possible," Cisco rumbled. "I'm getting readings on both sides of the city that could be Mardon."

"How's that possible?" asked Barry, cowl shoved off.

"It's like the energies involved in Mardon's abilities are becoming totally intertwined with the natural ones of the storm. Remember, this storm existed before he gave any indication of being able to escape."

"We still haven't come up with an explanation for that, have we? They had him pretty secure, didn't they?"

Cisco nodded. As Barry watched, he called up another program. "Get a load of this. All perfectly well until then—"

A warning signal erupted from the computer.

"What is it?" Barry asked, cowl already on. "Mardon?"

Cisco's fingers danced on the keyboard. "Must be! Alarms going off all over that area! You see the address—" When Barry didn't answer, Cisco looked up… and found himself talking to no one. "Yep! Guess you did."

Turning back to the console, Cisco grabbed his headset.

* * *

Barry sped through the storm, every nerve taut as he waited for it to start striking at him. He had the advantage of swiftness, but the storm had the better advantage of being *everywhere*. If Mardon thought the Flash was heading toward him, the Weather Wizard would unleash everything. Not for the first time he reminded himself that running fast didn't help when there was nowhere to run.

The main part of the interstate lay ahead. The Flash didn't have to have Cisco's readings to sense the incredible forces suddenly building up over the gargantuan cloverleaf. Nothing had as yet happened and that worried him most of all. The immediate implication in the Flash's mind was that Mardon was waiting for *him*.

"All right," murmured Barry. "I'm here. What've you got?"

Cars moved along the interstate at a fair clip. The Flash noted the rain had slowed to a drizzle.

"Cisco, you copy?"

"Go ahead!"

"How's the storm acting over the rest of the city right now?"

"Pretty much miserable! Trying to get police and fire reports, but the electrical part of the storm is wreaking havoc. If I hadn't upgraded our system in response to the problems we'd had earlier, we wouldn't be speaking right now!"

"I stopped a mile from the address you had online. Are the readings still crazy?"

"Yes... and no. How's it look there?"

"Hardly a drop coming down. In fact, it's so calm, traffic is picking up speed. The rest of Central City would want to be so lucky... I think."

"What're you thinking?"

Barry didn't answer, the dread truth having suddenly occurred to him. He knew he was right about Mardon waiting for him and didn't even need the first lightning bolt to tell him that it might already be too late to stop what the Weather Wizard planned.

The respite the cloverleaf had experienced ceased instantly. Walls of rain came crashing down on the interstate. Lightning strikes hit strategic spots throughout the vast concrete structure. Several cars lost control as conditions dropped to catastrophic in the blink of an eye. They, in turn, veered toward other vehicles or the safety walls designed to prevent them from driving off the cloverleaf and into the air.

The Flash raced along the structure, quickly noting which cars were in the most immediate danger. He plucked out the two passengers of the first vehicle, carried them from the interstate to a place of safety, then returned to turn the wheel so that the empty car ended up on the side of the highway. Even before that one could move, the Flash rushed to the second car and did the same.

Lightning struck the cloverleaf, more lightning than Barry had witnessed thus far in the monstrous storm. It had actually struck at the very moment the speedster had reached the interstate, but only now did he comprehend what it presaged.

"Oh boy…" He picked up his pace, moving to the next auto and the next, clearing out the occupants and directing the emptied vehicles as quickly as he could.

The necessity of rescuing people meant that minuscule moments of time still passed. That, in turn, gave the lightning the chance to affect the cloverleaf.

Battered by the barrage, several portions of the cloverleaf cracked, then collapsed. Huge gaps opened up, cutting off some parts of the interstate from others and trapping vehicles that the Flash had thought momentarily safer.

He raced to the cars now teetering at the edge of the shattered cloverleaf. Momentum enabled him to span the gap between the two portions of the interstate. Once on the other side, he pulled out the back passenger of the nearest vehicle, then quickly searched for the best path to safety.

Unfortunately, that meant having to cross another crumbling section. Inhaling, the Flash jumped onto one of the safety barriers on the shoulder and used that to give him the few necessary extra feet to reach the other side. Then, midway to the next, Barry stumbled. It was only a slight misstep, but it was followed by another. The same exhaustion he had felt during the previous rescue missions began to plague the Flash more and more as he pressed on.

"Cisco! I'm starting to flag!"

"We just saw! It gets worse!"

Barry made a face. "How?"

"Police reports are all over it! Mardon's back at Iron Heights wreaking havoc!"

The speedster eyed the interstate. "I can't get there yet! I can still move fast, but I need every ounce of strength right now for the rest of his victims here!"

"Yeah," Cisco replied. "Probably just like he planned."

"What's he up to, Cisco? We need to find out! It's like he's trying to draw tremendous amounts of power together—hold on!"

Picking up his pace again, the Flash raced up the side of one of the great columns in the cloverleaf and onto another part of the interstate. As he neared, he kept an eye on the overpass above. There, the stress created by the rest of the destruction had caused those columns to fracture. Several chunks of concrete rained down on the three trapped cars toward which Barry raced.

Despite his increasing weariness, he pushed harder, reaching the first vehicle while the falling concrete was still high above. The Flash seized the two small gaping children in back, carried them down to safety, then went back up for the mother and father before the concrete had dropped more than a foot. He emptied the next auto in nearly the same brief moment of time, but it was enough to allow the heavy chunks to drop more than halfway to where the Flash worked.

He stumbled again, lost his footing and fell to his knees. As he landed, he looked up desperately.

The massive piece of concrete was plummeting toward the last car.

"I can feel him through the storm," the Weather Wizard remarked as he continued his search. "I can sense every movement. He's faltering."

"Just so long as we get what we need from him before something happens to him, okay?"

"I know what I'm doing now," Mark snapped back, jutting an index finger to the swirling fragments he had cleared from the vicinity. "Just be quiet while I—there we go!"

The Weather Wizard shoved aside some smaller bits of concrete to uncover an electrical connection. Near it lay some fragments of the arrangement linked to the helmet Mark had recently been forced to wear. Even from where he stood, he could sense the residual energies.

Going down on one knee, the Weather Wizard picked up a part. To his disappointment, there was no charge.

He concentrated. Holding out one hand, he produced a tiny cloud.

A miniature bolt struck the link from the broken arrangement. The Weather Wizard eyed the rest of the damaged system. A brief hint of power coursed through the setup, then faded.

"Quit your games," Clyde urged him from behind.

"No games. Just checking to see if there's enough of the system intact—"

"I wouldn't worry about anything except how you're gonna decorate your cell walls over the next few decades!"

"Flash?" Clyde blurted.

"Flash?" The Weather Wizard repeated.

"Gained a stutter, Mardon?" said a figure at the edge of what had once been the rogue's cell. "No, I'm not him, but I do pretty good myself!"

Mardon straightened to see a young, athletic African-American figure in a gold-and-red outfit akin to the Flash's. The figure gave him a confident smile.

"The Kid Flash," The Weather Wizard mocked.

"Just 'Kid Flash' will do! Care to make it easy on yourself and just surrender?"

"To an understudy? If the Flash can't stop me now, how will you?"

No sooner had he finished the question than Kid Flash stood just inches from him. The speedster continued to smile. "I'm pretty fast! Sometimes even faster than him!" He eyed the Weather Wizard. "Maybe prison might be good for you. You take a peek in the mirror lately? You don't look very well—"

"Stop playing with children, Mark."

Kid Flash's smile faded. "What was that you said, Mardon? Who're you talking to?"

Mark Mardon gave Kid Flash a nasty smile. "I said, did you hear that *thunder*?"

An earth-shaking boom erupted from the Weather Wizard, Mardon having been forming the conditions even as Kid Flash had been speaking.

The gold-and-red speedster flew back from the force and crashed hard into a large pile of rubble. Kid Flash let out a yelp as he bounced over a piece of concrete before landing atop the pile.

"Should've stayed on the bench until you were seasoned a little better," the Weather Wizard remarked.

Wally rose… and ran at him.

He collided with several large pieces of concrete and brick Mardon had already let fall before Kid Flash had even stood up. Stunned, the speedster stumbled back.

"Think ahead, that's the key to dealing with you swift guys. Got the Flash feeding me through the storm running around saving innocents! Don't know why I never figured out that part before. All that surge in energy, just like in a storm. Of course, didn't start until they hooked me up to that last device! Idiots! They not only gave me the way out of here, but they made me stronger!"

He spoke to emptiness, Kid Flash having already moved.

Hail surrounded the Weather Wizard like a wall of bullets. Mardon laughed as he heard his adversary cry out.

Head bleeding, Kid Flash pulled away from Mardon.

"Fast on the feet, slow in the head, eh, Clyde?"

"Put him out of his misery, Mark," his brother said.

"Yeah, he's not got enough to help us."

Kid Flash raced at him again, only to slip on an icy patch where once there had been puddles.

"You still haven't learned. Too bad for you."

Before the speedster could regain his balance, the vast tornado the Weather Wizard had first summoned dragged him into the sky. As Kid Flash went soaring away, Mardon turned from the ruined cell.

"That's it. We're done here."

"Yeah? What about their toy?"

The Weather Wizard gestured at the departing tornado. "Learned all I need. They made one big mistake. They had it locked into my head for weeks. *They* made me better. I don't need it or the wand now." He took one last look at the huge whirlwind. "They made me into a real god, Clyde. A *real* one."

9

Despite the pain wracking him, the Flash shoved himself up and headed to the last car. Inside, he made out five startled-looking elderly women.

Racing to the back door, he unhooked the first and carried her away. Despite having to fight the increasing exhaustion as well as the pain, Barry pushed as hard as he could. He set the first woman down and hurried back.

The concrete had dropped conspicuously closer by the time he returned. The Flash gingerly took out the second woman and rushed to safety.

The third went as easily as the first two, but in that time the huge chunk of concrete had nearly plummeted to the car's roof. Barry forced himself to increase his pace even though his body screamed for him to rest.

He got the front passenger out and brought her to the others, but as he hurried to grab the driver, his body rebelled against him.

"No you don't..." the Flash gasped. Ahead, he looked in horror as the concrete moved slowly but effortlessly into the metal roof.

Fighting every step of the way, the speedster made it to the driver's side just as the woman appeared to realize what was happening above her. One of her hands had instinctively reached for the seatbelt, complicating Barry's efforts. As he peeled her fingers away and undid the safety belt, the concrete pressed the roof down to the woman's head.

Grabbing her by the shoulders, the Flash pulled her out. The roof caved in to the steering wheel. The slight relative movement of the car compared to the speedster nearly tripped the Flash, but he managed to get both himself and her away just as the cement finished crushing the auto.

Leaving the smashed vehicle behind, Barry carried the last occupant to the rest. As he set her with her companions—and near an emergency vehicle already handling victims—his legs buckled.

"No... not yet..." Straightening, the Flash sped back to the crumbling cloverleaf. He leaped across the jagged, widening gaps and continued ferrying innocents to safety.

He dropped off the last one, then immediately dropped to his knees before several of the startled folk. A few moved to help him, but through gasps for air, the Flash waved them off and said, "I'll be fine. Keep moving."

Cisco's voice broke through in his ear. "Sorry to ask this of you, buddy, but can you still run?"

"I'd rather lie down and sleep for a thousand years, but what is it?"

"Wally went after Mardon at Iron Heights... and got sucked up into a tornado! Right now he's doing a Dorothy Gale high above the area!"

Barry started running.

He came up on the penitentiary in time to see the tornado moving off from the facility.

"Cisco! Can you locate him in all that? Is he even still alive?"

"His readings are all over the place, but he's alive! In the upper part!"

"Of course." The Flash eyed the tornado's immediate surroundings, then ran toward the monstrous whirlwind. Seeing the tons of material being tossed around so effortlessly, he knew that the potential danger in the cloverleaf paled in comparison.

"Looks like I need to pick up more speed," he murmured, already feeling the wear and tear on his body as he accelerated. "A lot more."

As his velocity increased, the tornado seemed to slow its spinning. Try as he might, though, the Flash couldn't accelerate enough to see the whirlwind as if it had completely frozen in place.

"Not good." He eyed the ruined areas near the tornado's base, picked the highest spot, and ran to it. Even as slowly as it moved in comparison to him, the tornado still radiated immense power. Barry knew that if he hesitated even for a moment, he would be swept up just like Wally.

He scanned the tornado, studying the refuse swirling around in it. Then, reaching a roofless building just below, the Flash raced to the top and threw himself into the maelstrom.

Just as he hoped, he landed atop a metal door clearly ripped from Iron Heights. Barry wasted no time, running to the other end and jumping to a block of stone a few feet up. His footing continually proved unstable, barely giving him time to recover.

On the far side of the tornado, he caught movement heading against the spin. Wally, looking as exhausted and in pain as he felt, doing the same as Barry, but clearly with more difficulty.

As the Flash neared, Wally noticed him. He tried to get to his friend, but the rubble didn't give either a perfect path. Barry knew how overdone he felt and he knew that Wally, not as experienced as him, was in some ways worse off. He pushed on—

Suddenly, he felt the broken board on which he next stepped sink. The Flash could think of only one reason why; the tornado had ceased to exist. Mardon had left Wally where he was as a trap for his true enemy.

Wally began to descend. It was still a very slow movement, but a definite one. Barry knew he had only a second or two before they plummeted to the ground.

Despite the risks, the speedster leapt to one

questionable surface after another. Even so, he started to sink farther than Wally. Grunting, the Flash accelerated his efforts, finally reaching his friend.

"This—wasn't—supposed to work out like this!" Wally shouted.

"Hold tight!"

With Barry guiding them, the pair moved from piece of rubble to piece of rubble, not daring to slow their pace and risk becoming part of the tornado's collapse. Even so, the necessity of keeping together forced them to make a circuitous route toward the ground.

Unfortunately, the Flash saw that their path would end several floors shy of a landing. That left only one choice.

"When we get to that last piece of wooden fence there, we stop! It's the only thing large enough to support both of us!"

"Are you crazy? We need to keep moving!"

"Just follow my lead!"

They came to the end… and stopped as Barry had ordered.

They and the wooden fence plunged.

"Now!" the Flash roared.

Just before the fence would have struck, the pair jumped. Normal reflexes would have left both men dead, but the Speed Force enabled them to do what should have been impossible. The pair landed while the fence and the rest of the falling debris stood frozen in comparison.

Wally and Barry kept moving until they were far from any threat, then dropped on all fours in exhaustion under a store awning.

Behind them, the rumble of thunder was briefly drowned out by the crash of several of the larger bits of rubble hitting the ground.

"I cannot—believe—we did that!" Wally rasped.

"It worked…" Barry whispered in awe. "It worked…"

"Wait! You weren't sure it would?"

"Not… entirely."

Wally shook his head. "Talk about learning on the job."

"You should have never gone after Mardon on your own. Why did you do that?"

Wally made a face. "That's my father he wants to kill. After what happened the last time between you and the Weather Wizard right by Iris and him, I had to do something! Bad enough I let her down after I promised—"

Barry stared at him. "Wait! What did you promise?"

"To keep an eye on Dad when you couldn't."

"Well, no more of that. Not, at least, without the rest of us involved."

"I'm not going to argue. Listen, though, you know Iris wasn't just worried about Dad; she was concerned about you too."

The Flash nodded. "Starting to figure that out. She knows there's nothing I can do. If I stop being the Flash, where does that leave Central City?"

"Hey, maybe you're looking right at him!"

"I doubt that will make Iris any more happy." With some effort, Barry rose. "The only thing we *can* really do is grab Mardon and make certain he never escapes again."

"Suits me, if it can be done—"

"Hey, guys!" Cisco called over the coms. "Didn't dare to say anything while you had to escape that tornado. Mardon's gone, of course, but why did he stay as long as he did?"

"He was looking for something in the ruins," Wally offered. "Something electrical."

"'Something electrical'," Barry repeated. "What would there be that he'd want in that regard? Cisco?"

"I think I've got an idea and it isn't a pleasant one, dude," Cisco returned. "First, though, you two need to come back to the lab. You're both burned out pretty bad. We need to check your vitals."

"We're on our way," Barry promised.

"Copy that."

As Cisco's voice faded away, Wally's expression soured.

"What's that face about?" the Flash asked.

"Just thinking of something else that happened when I confronted Mardon. Man's crazy as hell! When I spotted him, I paused out of sight for a moment to get a better read on him. He kept talking to himself, or at least I didn't see anybody."

"Talking to himself? What do you mean?"

"Well, I thought there was someone else, but when I

looked again, there was no one. Thing is, he acted like he was talking to his brother, Clyde!"

"Clyde..." Barry nodded. "Yeah, I heard him mention Clyde too."

"The man *is* dead, isn't he? Clyde, I mean?"

"Your father made sure. Still, I thought I saw someone going after Joe and the Weather Wizard called his brother's name. Trouble is, I never got a good look at who it was."

Wally rubbed his head, then winced. Only then did Barry see the vicious bruise. "We've got to get you back to the lab. How is that?"

"Throbbing in time. Wouldn't be a bad beat if it wasn't my head."

"Come on!" Linking his arm with Wally's, the Flash led him back to S.T.A.R. Labs. The storm hit at them hard, but not in any noticeable way that made it seem that Mardon was influencing it.

Barry breathed a sigh of relief once he had Wally in the lab. H.R. joined him in assisting Wally to a place where he could lie down. As they did, Caitlin came in the room.

"My God!" She dashed over to investigate his injury.

As Barry stepped back to let Caitlin deal with the situation, Cisco casually pointed at the monitor. "Interesting readings. Wanna see them?"

"Will I understand them?"

"Heck, I still don't know if I do."

"Hold on just a moment more," Caitlin said to Wally. "There, that should be good for now."

"Thanks, Caitlin." Barry joined Cisco, Caitlin following. "Tell me what I'm looking at."

"This is you," his friend commented, tapping on one set of lines. "See how they dip at this point and keep dropping until here, where they level out?"

"Is that now, that last spot? That's awfully low, isn't it?"

"Too low," Caitlin interjected. "You don't want to drop like that so often."

"Yeah, she's right. For the moment, though, if you get some rest and some vitamin shots, that'll help you physically. Speedwise, you definitely need to rest, Barry."

"You have no idea how much I look forward to that. How can Mardon be up to doing all this?"

Cisco looked sheepish. "Honestly, I'll have to get back to you on that. Look at these other readings now."

"They look more consistent than mine."

"They belong to Wally. You can see that there's some decrease here and some acceleration here, but those are due to normal criteria."

Barry grunted. "So why is Wally lucky… if you can say that?"

"Well, yours shift each time the Weather Wizard is involved, right?" When Barry had nodded, Cisco continued, "And we see that Wally's don't, even when he faced Mardon directly. The only thing I get out of that is that whatever he's doing to you he isn't bothering to do to Wally."

"Why? Because of his brother's death?"

"He is kind of fixated on that, Barry. Still, it's got to have some more purpose than just to weaken you, I think."

"But what?"

"Haven't figured that out yet. I did find something else interesting, though." Cisco typed up a new screen. "Been trying to filter through all the bizarreness of the storm and its link to Mardon. You know those moments when you thought you saw someone with him? Look at this."

"Is that Mardon's reading?"

"I don't know *whose* it is, but it floats along with his like they're tied together at the hip. He has a reaction; it has a reaction... or maybe the other way around. Sometimes it's hard to tell."

"So, I *did* see someone. Another metahuman."

Cisco looked uncomfortable. "I don't know how to answer that one. Metahumans have certain types of readings. There's a trace of something like it, but... it's almost just in the background."

"English, Cisco?"

"If I could describe it in more theatrical terms, it's almost like the *ghost* of a metahuman reading."

Barry's eyebrow arched. "'*Ghost*'."

"Sorry. Can't do better right now."

A thought unrelated to their conversation suddenly occurred to Barry. He looked at the clock on Cisco's screen. "Keep trying. I need to make a phone call."

"Sure."

Barry moved to a quiet corner, then pulled out his phone and called.

"I suspect you've had an interesting night," Joe commented at the other end.

"Very much. Listen, I think I'd better stick with you when you leave headquarters. We can—"

"Now hold on!" Joe growled. "I thought at least you and I still had things settled! I'm back to square one with Iris after that trouble by the apartment! Do you know she tracked me down again and told me I should take a leave of absence until this blows over?"

"It wouldn't be a bad idea—"

"Now don't you start! In case you haven't noticed, Barry, I'm a detective in the Central City police department! I chase crooks for a living! If I go into hiding for Mardon, what good am I at all? Is Iris going to ask me to take leave the next time I cross paths with some new metahuman or maybe even just some mobster with strong underworld ties? Where does it end?"

Barry hesitated. "Listen, Joe. I know Iris is having a hard time with this. She's not too happy about my activities, either—"

"Maybe it'd be better if you took a leave of absence, hmm?"

"Joe. Listen. Never mind what I said. There's something else. Wally—"

Joe's voice rose. "Wally? What about Wally? Oh my God, did he go out hunting for Mardon? That's it, isn't it! What happened! Is he—"

"Joe! He's all right." Barry nervously rubbed his chin. "Well, he got a bad bash on the head from a piece of concrete, but it's not too serious. He'll probably have a headache for a while."

"That's it! I was never happy when he gained those powers! This is the last straw! I'm going to make certain that he puts an end to this!"

Barry waited for him to finish, then asked, "And how well do you think that'll work, Joe? You may not have had a chance to raise him, but Wally's certainly got your stubbornness. I wasn't happy either that he went after Mardon, but the best thing we can do is see that he's properly trained. Like it or not, being a speedster is part of Wally now."

The detective let out another growl, this one tinged with frustration. "Yeah."

"As for you—"

"As for *me*," Joe interrupted. "You really don't have to concern yourself at the moment. Thanks to that last stunt Mardon pulled near the apartment, the chief's decided I am a liability on the street and for now I have been reassigned to the basement level. Let me repeat that for you! I have been reassigned to the basement level! So, for the time I'm on duty every day, you've now got nothing to worry about!"

"Joe—"

"I've got to run, Barry. Bye."

"Joe?" Barry waited for a few seconds, but there was no reply. Joe had hung up.

"Barry? Are you all right?"

He turned to Caitlin. "Sure. You look bothered. Something with Wally?"

"No. He'll be fine, though I hope we can convince him not to do anything like that again. The strike wasn't a deep one, but another might have cracked his skull."

"Yeah, he and I have to have another talk about what it means to be a speedster. I don't think he realizes that there are some limits."

She smiled slightly. "Well, if this didn't teach him a little bit about that, you've got your work cut out for you."

"I probably do." He noticed she had a coat on. "You're leaving?"

"I'm meeting Iris again. Barry, you two really need to talk. She's all wound up about her father, Wally, and especially you."

"We talked. After the Weather Wizard tried to kill Joe outside the apartment. Unfortunately, that didn't make it conducive for a productive conversation."

Caitlin gave him a reproving look. "She mentioned that over the phone. You're right. I wouldn't exactly call that a successful conversation. When she and I met yesterday, all she could speak to me about was her need to talk it all out. I'd say from my phone call with her earlier today that she still feels that way."

"It's a little complicated right now with Mardon tearing up the city, Caitlin—"

"I know. *She* knows. But when is a good time with you, Barry? There's always some threat."

"Yeah."

"Just do it, Barry. It's best for both of you." Caitlin squeezed his arm and gave him a parting smile. Barry nodded, then headed to Wally, who was sitting up.

"You were talking to my old man, weren't you?" Wally asked.

"It won't surprise you to know that he wasn't too thrilled about what went down at Iron Heights."

Wally shook his head. "*He* wasn't thrilled? Me, now I know how it feels inside a clothes dryer!" He tried to rise. "Still, that reminds me, I've got to get going."

Once on his feet, though, he wobbled.

"Easy there," H.R. said, giving Wally a hand. "You need to rest a little longer. Maybe a lot longer even."

"No. I've got to go—"

Barry realized why. "You're still trying to keep an eye on your father, aren't you?"

"I promised Iris… and myself."

"Well, Joe wasn't too happy, but he's been assigned to desk duty in the basement of police headquarters."

Wally grinned. "You're not putting me on, are you?"

"No."

"He'll be frustrated all right… but thanks. He should be safe there until my head stops beating."

H.R. looked at Barry. "Might I suggest you take the same advice?"

Barry realized his comment was not without merit.

"Yeah. I suppose so."

From his chair, Cisco called, "It's all quiet out there... so to speak. No Mardon. Just the storm. I've got the emergency channels all tuned in, so if anything comes up, we'll know pretty early." He swiveled the seat to face Barry and Wally. "Caitlin suggested you both not leave until you're rested and I concur. You need some serious downtime if you want to face Mardon and not get tossed around like Dorothy and Toto!"

Nodding, Barry said to Wally, "They're right. Your father's safe for now. Let's leave him be and make certain that we're ready for whatever the Weather Wizard throws at us next."

"The Weather Wizard," Wally repeated, briefly wincing as he touched his bandaged wound, "and whoever the heck that is shadowing him..."

Joe tapped his fingers on the desk, thinking. He stared at the windowless walls surrounding him. Making a face, the detective picked up his phone again and dialed.

The line rang. And rang. And rang.

Joe checked his watch. "Where are you, Iris?"

The phone continued to ring. Finally, the voicemail came on.

"This is Iris West. Not available at the moment, but if you leave a message—"

He hung up. Setting the phone back down, Joe eyed the walls again... and sighed.

* * *

Iris thanked the restaurant hostess and sat down across from Caitlin, who was nursing a coffee. "Hi! Long time no see! Must be years!"

Caitlin smiled at the light joke. "Yep, all the way back to yesterday."

Iris set her purse on the chair to her side. "Seriously, I'm not at all sorry to do this again so soon. Between my father and Barry especially, it's been hard to concentrate on work or anything else. Do you know Barry's slept at the lab for the past few days?"

Caitlin sipped her coffee. "Well, he has been kept busy with the storm and the Weather Wizard."

"I know, I know, and I guess that makes some sense, but we'd hardly seen or talked with one another the two or three weeks before that as well."

Caitlin set down her drink. "I hadn't realized that."

"We kept it between us. It's all about the same thing, though. It's just what I'm arguing with Dad about, too."

"The risk. I know. Things have changed so much since that night. I thought you said you were working things out with your father, at least. You were going to meet with him to discuss it."

"I thought I had… until Dad nearly got killed right on my doorstep. Now, I don't know what to think." A waitress brought her a coffee. "Oh. Thank you."

"I made an assumption on a lovely day like this that you'd want it," Caitlin explained, grinning. To the waitress, she asked, "May I have another, please?"

"Yes, ma'am."

"Thanks for ordering it, Caitlin. I know it's not that cold out, but the rain makes everything feel damp and uncomfortable."

"You're welcome."

Iris took a sip. "Have you heard from Julian?"

"He'll be back in a couple of days. One thing lucky; he just missed all this crazy weather."

"Not to mention all the trouble with Snapshot."

Caitlin frowned. "He was sorry about that happening. He wants to prove he'll be a good part of the team."

"He will. You recommended him, after all."

The waitress brought Caitlin's new coffee. "Thank you." Cradling the steaming cup, Caitlin said to Iris, "I know. I'd rather it just snowed then or something."

"Be careful! With the Weather Wizard, we may get that yet! We've certainly had enough hail."

"My car has more than a dozen dings in it. I thought of taking it in, but I didn't see the point until Mardon was captured."

Iris tapped the table. "If he ever is! Why is he so powerful? This is worse than last time!"

Caitlin pressed her palms against the hot cup. "Cisco and I are still looking into it—" She winced. "—n-nothing definitive right now."

"Are you all right?"

"Just a headache. I blame that on the weather too."

"I can understand—careful! You'll burn your hands!"

Glancing down, Caitlin saw her hands. "It's all right. The coffee's not that hot."

"Really?" Iris touched her own cup. "Mine's still like lava! I thought with the steam rising from yours that it had to be at least as bad."

"No. Not really." Caitlin winced a second time. She immediately took a strong swallow of coffee.

Iris blanched. "Are you sure that's cooled down enough?"

"It's *fine!*" Caitlin abruptly snapped.

Both Iris and the handful of customers seated near them looked at Caitlin in surprise.

"I'm sorry!" Iris responded. "I was only concerned—"

"No." Caitlin shook her head. "No, I need to apologize. I don't know what came over me. It's been crazy at the lab, I guess." She reached across the table and set her hand atop Iris's. "I'm so sorry…"

Iris opened her mouth, then shut it. She glanced at their touching hands.

"Iris?"

"Your hand is *cold*. I mean, like really cold. Caitlin, are you—"

Caitlin quickly withdrew it. With her other hand, she raised her coffee to drink.

Her lips touched ice.

She set down the cup, grabbed her purse, and jumped to her feet.

"Caitlin? What's wrong?"

"I just remembered something urgent. I-I apologize! We'll talk tomorrow!"

"Caitlin?"

The other woman didn't answer, instead rushing out. Iris instinctively got up to pursue her, only pausing to leave some money on the table.

"Caitlin!" She hurried after her, exiting the restaurant only moments later. By then, though, Caitlin had vanished. Iris looked in both directions… but saw no sign of the other woman.

Back in the restaurant, the waitress returned to the table. She picked up the check and the money, then paused when Caitlin's coffee caught her eye.

Picking up the cup, her eyes widened in disbelief as she tipped over the cup and the contents stayed inside. She used a finger to touch the coffee… and found it frozen solid.

1 0

The storm continued its relentless onslaught of Central City, yet there was a noticeable shift, a lessening from the days before. Most of the city's inhabitants saw this as some relief, but to the Flash it only meant more frustration. The Weather Wizard appeared to be lying low and the possible reasons for it greatly disturbed him. Mardon had something new in mind, something the speedster was certain that he would not like in the least.

Despite a lack of any trace of his adversary, the Flash redoubled his efforts in his search, trying constantly to locate places that he had failed to search previously. None proved to be the rogue's hiding place.

And even though Barry suffered no more sudden depletion of energy, by the end of a very long day he was ready once more to keel over.

"Any-anything?" the Flash asked.

"Nothing," Cisco replied with a yawn. He stretched.

"God! Somebody get the jaws of life! I think I'm fused to the chair!"

Barry slumped against the edge of a table. He took a bottle of water H.R. offered him. "Thanks. When's the last time you went home, Cisco?"

"Feels like years. No sense going home any more than necessary. Not, at least, until the Weather Wizard is finally captured."

"Listen, I appreciate the dedicated help, but you don't need to do this. Maybe Caitlin could fill in for a while. She knows most of what you do—"

"She's not in today."

Barry looked up. "What's the matter with her?"

"Just a little under the weather," H.R. offered.

Both Barry and Cisco gave him a look.

"Sorry. Didn't mean it like that."

"She's just worn out, Barry," Cisco interjected. "I'll call her later on to see how she's doing."

"Okay." Barry opened the bottle and downed the contents without pause. "I think I could use a sandwich."

"I'll get—" H.R. started to offer, but Barry had already headed to the refrigerator they had installed due in great part to most of them living a good chunk of their days and nights in S.T.A.R. Labs.

Barry removed what he needed and shut the door before the light inside could even come on. On a clean table next to the refrigerator, he'd set out the bread, condiments, meats, cheeses, and salad pieces he needed.

"—you one right away," H.R. finished.

"Thanks," replied Barry, shutting the refrigerator after returning the leftover ingredients. On the table sat half a dozen thick sandwiches. "I took care of it."

Not bothering to wait for any further response, Barry seized the first sandwich. As the others watched in horrified fascination, the Flash devoured it in several rapid-fire bites that took all of three or four seconds. Without pause, he plucked up the second and did the same, repeating the process until all six sandwiches had been consumed.

"You know," H.R. went on, "my mother said you should never gobble your food down. Not healthy."

"Don't worry. I paced myself."

"Yeah?"

Barry patted his stomach. "That should tide me over for a couple hours."

H.R. looked a little dubious. "You ever consider joining a hot-dog eating contest?"

"Seriously, Barry," Cisco added. "You put away a lot of calories because of your abilities, but you've nearly doubled your daily amount since Mardon became a problem."

"I'd say he's more than doubled it," H.R. piped in.

"I can't help it. Once I slow down, I start feeling the hunger."

"We've got to put a stop to whatever the Weather Wizard's doing before you burn out completely."

Barry joined him by the monitor. "You tell me where to find him, Cisco. I've searched everywhere I can, but that still leaves countless places I can't get to. We need to track him. Unlike most metahumans, when Mardon uses his abilities, it shows up pretty good. So why can't we get a bead on him? If anything, he should be more obvious than ever."

"All the energy feeding into the storm is still making it impossible to get enough data to pinpoint him. I'm getting very close, though, I think."

"We need to find him before he can unleash whatever it is he wants to do." Barry pulled up his cowl. "Maybe I'd better get out there right now. I might find us a clue, or at least draw him out—"

Cisco frowned. "Barry, before you do, I need to carry out a couple of brief tests. Do me a favor and lie down for them. I'll be right there to hook you up."

"Short?"

"Promise."

"All right." Barry disappeared, seemingly materializing from nothing a moment later by the research table. Keeping his cowl pushed back, he climbed on top of the table and settled down to wait.

Cisco returned to the keyboard. "I will be just a moment longer."

"Sure," Barry answered, yawning.

"Need to input some numbers."

"Numbers. Got it."

"Argh," muttered Cisco. "Have to retype some of this. I must've missed a decimal point before. Hang on there, Barry. I promise I'll be done here before you know it."

There was no response from the table.

"He's asleep," offered H.R., "which I'm sure was your hope."

Cisco leaned back. "Uh huh. He's burning out faster than ever. It has to be in part due to the fact that they're both metahumans, but there's more, I think. The Speed Force must be linked to the natural elements in some way though, to make him so susceptible."

H.R. straightened. "What was that?"

"Here, look on the big monitor." Cisco typed in a couple of instructions and one of the wall monitors flicked from showing weather reports to a series of ever-shifting graphs.

The older man chuckled. "So, how many times must I tell you showing me these things doesn't help. I'm not Harrison Welles... I mean not *that* one."

"Here, I'll explain. You see these six lines?"

"Uh huh."

Cisco adjusted the screen to cut down to six graphs. "I had these six chosen at random from some of our encounters with metahumans. I've not bothered listing them by name because that's not important. What is important is that if you study them long enough, they have similar points here and there: traits of all metahumans."

H.R. nodded slowly. "Okay. I got that. All metahumans share certain energy traits."

"Right, but in some cases, like with Barry and the Weather Wizard, there are more points of similarity.

Depending on what those points are, those abilities then share a common core."

"And this can be affected by another metahuman?"

"I wouldn't have thought so," Cisco replied, changing the image to two new graphs. "It should be beyond the ability of any one metahuman, but, yes, somehow it has in the case of Barry and Mardon."

"How?"

"Look. Let me try this again from the beginning. From everything we've studied, it's a fact that not everyone out when the original burst happened became a metahuman. We've found plenty of people who remained unchanged."

"Okay, I got that."

"That could mean that everyone who *was* affected had some trait in common. A gene or something else. Maybe someday we'll figure out what, but what's more important is that Mardon's powers not only now effect the elements of the storm to a degree they never could before, but I think that because they involve meta energies, they now affect other metahumans as well. Maybe make someone else's powers more unstable or even, with an assist, draw those meta energies to the Weather Wizard, making him kind of like a parasite."

H.R. whistled. "What could do that?"

Cisco rubbed his jaw. "That's the thing. It'd need quite a boost from something pretty much attuned to Mardon. Like the wand."

"But he doesn't have that."

"No. I'm beginning to think I know how it all started: just not how it's going to finish."

H.R. cocked his head. "And there you go losing me again. Well, it was nice while it lasted."

"Don't feel too bad. I'm not much farther ahead. I'm going over the Iron Heights info again." Cisco glanced at where Barry slept soundly. "Maybe I'll have some answers by the time he wakes up." He looked at the data on the large monitor and sighed heavily. "Maybe."

"So, why don't we just get the wand again?"

Cisco shook his head as he called up another set of numbers. "The device the prison implanted in the Weather Wizard's head is on the same wavelength. If we try to use the wand, it's more likely that he might usurp its abilities."

"So, we don't do that. Definitely not."

A warning beep emanated from Cisco's computer. He took another look at Barry, saw that the noise had not even disturbed him, then quickly turned back and summoned up the reason for the warning. Data flowed madly across his screen.

"What is it? Mardon?"

"I don't know. Better go wake him up after all."

H.R. quickly went to obey. He tapped Barry on the shoulder, but when that failed to rouse the speedster he shook him, calling his name.

"Don't play around. This is really odd stuff that's going on here. If I can get a fix on it, maybe Barry can catch the Weather Wizard before it leads to any trouble."

"I'm not playing around. He's really deep asleep—and I do mean asleep."

"Great." Cisco started to get up to help, then found himself drawn back to the console by a new rash of readings. "These make no sense. Just what the heck is happening?" Typing in a few numbers based on what he saw, Cisco sat down and stared. What he read made his eyes narrow. "Just what *are* you doing, Mardon?"

"Wake up, my lord," Clyde's sarcastic voice had whispered in his ear. "Can't sleep your life away…"

It had taken the Weather Wizard all his strength to do as his brother said. Even though in some ways he felt more powerful than ever, it seemed to be more and more of a struggle to get started.

"More importantly, can't go sleeping *my* life away again, bro," Clyde added in a far more bitter tone. "Not ever again."

That had snapped the Weather Wizard in to action at last. Even though his situation in the hospital after the crash had not been his doing, the notion that he had been unconscious—asleep, as he guiltily thought it—when Clyde had been murdered.

He had woken up to a powerful thirst and hunger. Despite the ease with which the incursion into Iron Heights had gone and the easier time dealing with the Flash's would-be protégé, the Weather Wizard had been left much weaker than he had imagined. Not trusting the old safe house, Mark Mardon had found another location he hoped the Flash would not yet have thought to investigate. Clyde had insisted that his brother seize some skyscraper and declare his glory, but the Weather Wizard had not wanted to be bothered with ruling Central City until he lived up to his promise to Clyde.

It had taken only seconds to sweep down to a food store on his path, blast the windows open with a gale-force wind, and use that same gust to lift up enough food and drink to supply him for several days. For his new safe house, he had chosen a warehouse he and his brother had been familiar with through their contacts in the underworld. It would serve long enough to see his brother resurrected and the Flash and Detective West dead.

By the time he had satiated himself, the pile of refuse and empty bottles lay stacked high. The Weather Wizard paid no attention to the fact that although he had just devoured enough calories for two days, he somehow looked leaner and even more strained.

"Quite a feast," Clyde had said. "Do you know how much I yearn to taste food again, bro? How sweet even water would taste?"

"It won't be long. I'm ready to start."

"You think it'll be enough this time? You think you've got it under control? You've failed me before—"

"I know!" shouted the Weather Wizard. "I know!"

Clyde hovered there, silent. The older brother's rush of anger faded, overcome by even more guilt.

"I'm sorry, Clyde! So very, very sorry…"

His brother merely stared.

"I really think we've got a better chance this time, Clyde! It's gone just as I planned. I'm holding together the entire storm now in addition to gathering in all that energy. I was right. The Flash is part of the key. Even he fed me power!"

"Do it," Clyde murmured. "Let's see what you got, bro. Show me. Show me…"

"Yeah… show you." Mark took a deep breath, then spread his hands. The room crackled with gathering energy. Small flashes of lightning erupted around the Weather Wizard. A wind rising out of nowhere brushed the older brother's hair back.

Clyde stood directly in front of the Weather Wizard, his expression one of monstrous anticipation. The Weather Wizard matched that expression as he began to release the pent-up energies and mold them as he desired.

"Don't move," Mark ordered Clyde. His brother did not answer, already standing as still as a statue. Indeed, Clyde didn't even blink. His eyes just continued to stare into the Weather Wizard's: to the elder sibling it seemed as though the specter silently demanded that Mark not fail him yet again.

The Weather Wizard slowly started drawing his open palms together. Caught up in his efforts, he failed to notice not only the tremor in his hands, but how much stronger it became as he progressed. In the empty spaces to each side of Clyde, Mark created twin whirlwinds. Miniature storms within each crackled with lightning and raged with thunder. Each was a manifestation of the energies the Weather Wizard had gathered within him. Mark grinned as the storms trebled in intensity yet remained sealed inside the whirlwinds. But still he knew it was not enough. Teeth bared, the Weather Wizard forced more and yet more from himself. The whirlwinds shook and twisted out of shape, the storms growing so violent that they could barely be contained.

Mark Mardon could not fathom anyone ever having wielded such might. He *was* a god.

Throughout all the fury flanking him, the figure of Clyde never moved so much as an inch. The Weather Wizard smiled once more at his younger brother, then brought the two whirlwinds together.

They merged just as they engulfed Clyde, who made no sound as he disappeared into the storms.

Mark now raised one hand palm up. The misshapen whirlwind created from the other two swelled, growing several times its original size until it nearly touched the high ceiling.

The two storms became one. The new storm raged and raged, lightning striking over and over and over within the tornado the Weather Wizard had now formed.

Once more bathed in sweat and with pulse pounding, the Weather Wizard stirred the restrained tornado, increasing its spin. Head pounding, he surveyed his work one last time... then unleashed the storm's full energies where his brother stood.

Outside, the main storm abruptly unleashed a new barrage of lightning and thunder. The temperature dropped several degrees, rose again, then dropped even more. Winds whipped up that blew in every direction.

Body quivering from effort, the Weather Wizard fought the energies' natural tendency to disperse. Each time part of it tried, he turned it into itself with the results being that any discharge spilled into where Clyde stood.

At last, he had everything where it needed to be. Growing well aware that he couldn't hold it all together much longer, Mark forced it all to converge at one point in the center.

The explosion that followed ripped through the room. A devastating force threw the Weather Wizard several yards back. Winds immediately formed around him, but they failed to grow strong enough to protect him fully before he hit the floor.

Stunned, Mark fought with blurry eyes to see what had happened to his brother. At first, all he could see was blinding light. Then, as the energies continued to shoot off in every direction, the Weather Wizard made out a faint, manlike figure in their midst.

"Clyde?" His voice cracked and ended in a prolonged cough.

The figure moved toward him, his movements strange, almost as if he rolled...

"Clyde?" Mardon asked again, this time managing to suppress the cough.

The form solidified. Mark's brother grinned. But barely had Clyde become recognizable than the Weather Wizard's sibling disintegrated into a small dust devil. The tiny whirlwind dipped left, then right.

"No! Clyde! No!" The Weather Wizard tried to push himself to his feet, but failed. All he could do was watch helplessly.

To his tremendous relief, though, the whirlwind again coalesced into Clyde. The younger brother stepped forward.

And at that moment, the Weather Wizard saw that Clyde was now translucent.

"No..." Mark slumped back. "Damn it... No..." He put his hands over his face. "No... No... No..."

"Failed me again, Mark," came Clyde's bitter voice. "How many times is it going to be, bro? Anyone would think you really don't want to help me! Is that it? You *do* want to help me, don't you? No matter *what*?"

"It should've been enough. It should've..." the Weather Wizard defended. "It should've been." He shut his eyes and tried to focus. "Thought it through... thought I did anyway."

"You've let me down again, Mark. We were supposed to be there for each other, just like I was always there for you. I would never have failed *you*..."

"Shut up, damn you!" Extremely drained, Mark rolled onto his side. He could just barely see his brother now, but the ghostly image of a moment earlier still burned into his thoughts. "I'll get it right…"

His exhaustion overtook him. The Weather Wizard lay still.

Clyde stood frozen, then slowly lost all definition. The last vestiges faded into a mass of swirling wind that hovered for a time… and then faded away.

Caitlin had had no strength to go to work. She had ended up sleeping twice as long as usual and had only been able to get up to feed herself. Her relative helplessness infuriated her, but she had been unable to fight it. Ironically, the storm had become such a constant that as turbulent as it had grown Caitlin barely noticed it anymore.

But then there had come that one rumble of thunder, that one flash of lightning—and suddenly Caitlin had had a sense of claustrophobia that had shaken her so suddenly that she had dropped the plate she had been holding and not even worried about cleaning it up.

She had rushed to the living room, the emptiest spot in the apartment. For a breath or two, that had helped, but then the sensation had returned twice as strong. Caitlin had tried deep breathing to no avail. Her heart had begun pounding, and suddenly she felt as if she had been locked in a sauna. In desperation, Caitlin had gone to the refrigerator. Opening the freezer door, she had inhaled the wonderful cold air.

She had not noticed it: the odd, violent change in the storm that had come to a sudden conclusion. Yet, by then, what it had stirred in her had no longer needed outside stimulation. Now Caitlin pressed against the open freezer, not caring what it did to the contents. More and more she savored the cold, wanted to be a part of it. Frustrated, Caitlin stepped back and looked around for anything that might help. She spied the thermostat and rushed to it. Without hesitation, she threw the air conditioning to full blast at the lowest setting she could. Chilly air immediately filled the apartment.

Sighing happily, Caitlin opened her arms to embrace the cold. She spun once… then stopped when she found herself facing a mirror hanging on the wall.

A long streak of her hair had turned as white as snow… or frost.

Gaping, Caitlin hesitantly touched it. As she did, her skin took on a pale cast. Her eyes widened. Caitlin ran a finger over her cheek.

A light flashed on Cisco's device.

"Oh my God!" Caitlin stumbled back. A puff of mist escaped her mouth. Steeling herself, she growled, "No… I'm in control… I'm in control! No…"

Yes… a part of her mind insisted. *Be free at last…*

"No!" She quickly reached to adjust Cisco's machine, but as her fingers touched it, a layer of frost swiftly spread from the tips over the surface. Caitlin tried to wipe it off, but only strengthened the frost. As the layer thickened, she felt the abilities of the device lessen.

"Cisco… He'll be able to help." She rushed to her purse and grabbed her cell phone. Dropping the frost-laden bag, she started to dial.

A fresh layer of frost quickly enshrouded the phone. Caitlin tapped the touchscreen hard, but the frost had already grown too thick.

She brought the phone up to her mouth. "Phone!"

The screen slowly changed, revealing Caitlin's phone and email list. Heartened, she quickly added, "Call—"

The list faded away. The screen went black.

Caitlin dropped the phone. She started for the air conditioning, but only made it a few steps before falling to one knee.

Sit… Rest… Let it happen…

"I will *not*," Caitlin managed. "I control my powers now. Me!"

Forcing herself to her feet, she struggled to the thermostat.

"Heat. Heat." As quickly as she could, Caitlin adjusted the controls. She put the heat on as high as it would go, then wrapped her arms tightly around herself. "Come on! Warm up!"

The system clicked on. Impatient, Caitlin went to the nearest vent and waited for the warm air to engulf her.

The cold gave way… for a moment. Just as Caitlin had started to believe her plan would work, the apartment got noticeably chillier. Worse, she realized that she was the source of that new cold.

"No! I will not give in! I will not!" Gathering her strength, Caitlin tried to will the cold away. She would not permit her powers to overcome her. She was in control.

The cold eased… and then once more returned with a vengeance.

"No!" Caitlin insisted to herself. "No!"

The cold receded. The cold advanced. Receded. Advanced. Receded—

It was too much. Caitlin's thoughts spun. She attempted to go the couch, but dropped to one knee halfway there.

"No…" Caitlin fell face first to the floor.

She lost consciousness.

Frost extended from her fingertips and spread along her arms, her torso, and quickly to her legs and feet. In seconds, a layer covered her entire body. A few seconds more, and it had thickened enough to obscure her from view.

And all the while, the apartment kept getting colder and colder.

1 1

"As peaceful as he looks, we should really wake him," H.R. said.

"In a minute," Cisco answered for the tenth, eleventh or maybe twelfth time. He still hoped to make sense of the new readings he had just gotten. They had to be the results of the Weather Wizard's unknown plans. "We may have a location on Mardon."

"You mean that awful ruckus we just went through? I mean, clearly it was him, but how was this incident different?"

"Mardon just funneled a lot of work into something, so much so that the storm couldn't mask it very well! I think—"

A signal went off. Cisco immediately summoned up a new page.

"Caitlin!" he breathed.

H.R. instantly straightened. "What is it?"

"Let me double-check." Cisco's fingers moved

furiously on the keyboard. His expression tightened. "Caitlin's not doing well."

At that moment, a yawn escaped Barry. Cisco and H.R. looked at the speedster, now sitting up, then at one another.

"What should we tell him?" H.R. asked.

In answer, Cisco switched back to the readings he had been studying before. "What he wants to know."

Barry stiffly pushed himself up on his elbows. "I guess I was more exhausted than I thought. Did you get the readings you want—" He caught sight of a clock. "I've been asleep *that* long?" Barry's expression tightened. "Cisco… you shouldn't have done that. I need to be out there."

"It was necessary, man, but enough of that right now. I think I may have located Mardon."

Barry suddenly stood next to him. "Where?"

"One second more… Yeah, I think that's it." He typed. "There. An exact address. Oh, that's clever. 5515 Whispering Wind Avenue. Not too obvious a choice, is it?"

"5515 Whispering Wind Avenue. Got it," Barry's voice said, the speedster himself already gone. It was an effect both Cisco and H.R. had experienced several times before and yet still one that made both men start for a moment.

"We may not have much time left," Cisco commented grimly. Switching back to Caitlin's readings, he jumped up. "Get the car ready. I've got a couple of things here to grab!"

"We're heading to Caitlin's?"

"Yep."

"What about Barry?"

"Been putting together a new portable setup, though I wasn't planning it for this. I'll be able to keep in touch with him and give him all the backup he needs. Sometimes I am so brilliant I impress even myself!"

H.R. nodded. "All that means I have to get us there. Have you considered that?"

"Considered what?" asked a feminine voice from the entrance.

"Iris!" Cisco blurted. "What're you doing here?"

"I haven't been able to locate Barry anywhere else," she replied as she neared them, "so I figured that he had to return here eventually. Certainly before he bothers to come back to me."

"You just missed him," H.R. offered.

Cisco nodded. "Yeah, he needed to rest up here before he could go out again. He's been asleep for hours." He gestured at the screen. "I just finally tracked the Weather Wizard to a specific location. Barry should be there already. I was just waiting for him to contact me—"

"Then why do you look like you're about to leave? Is there something wrong with Barry that you're not telling me? I came to finally hash things out between us, but if he's in trouble..."

Iris pushed past Cisco to peer at the screen. Cisco looked at H.R., a sudden expression of concern on his face.

"This says it's for Caitlin, not Barry. Why are you looking at this? Is there something wrong with—oh dear God! Cisco, is this all accurate? Am I reading it correctly? How long has it been going on?"

"Listen, Iris—" Cisco began.

She whirled on him. "It makes sense now. Her cold hand. Her demeanor. You think she's falling victim to her powers! Tell me, Cisco!"

"We were just on our way to check on her," H.R. commented.

"H.R.!" Cisco growled.

Iris looked thoughtful. "What about Barry? I know you wouldn't leave him alone, especially with Mardon!"

"I've got this portable equipment. The earpiece is already in, so if he wanted to say anything, I'd already know. I would never risk his life, Iris!"

She looked somewhat mollified. "Does he know about Caitlin?"

"I didn't think he needed to have that extra burden right now."

She gave him a reproving look, but then nodded. "And you'll be able to keep in contact with him at *all* times?"

Cisco crossed his heart. "I'd never risk Barry, Iris. How could you even think that?"

"Then we'd better get over and see what's happened to Caitlin."

Much relieved, Cisco grabbed the last of his gear. "Mind driving? It's you or H.R."

Iris nodded. "I'll drive."

"Thank you," murmured H.R. "Really. Thank you."

A voice suddenly echoed in Cisco's ear. "I've circled the area to make certain that there were no traps!"

"Hang on," Cisco told the others. Adjusting a portable mic, he replied, "Say that again, Barry?"

"I said I've circled the area—about a hundred times—to make sure that there are no traps. Going in now to search for him."

"Listen, Barry—" Cisco stopped as a powerful surge of static cut him off, not to mention nearly deafened him. "Barry?"

"What is it?" asked Iris worriedly.

Cisco covered the mic. "The damn thing's cutting out. I thought I'd compensated for how Mardon's altered the storm." He set down the portable set. "I can't leave."

"But what about Caitlin?" H.R. interrupted.

Iris watched as Cisco quickly returned to the main console, then made a decision. "H.R., you and I will go check on her. Cisco, did you hear? H.R. and I—"

Cisco nodded, then signaled for silence. Now at the console, he muttered into another mic. "Go ahead, Barry. Try again."

With a hesitant sigh, Iris waved for H.R. to follow her. H.R. eyed Cisco for a moment, then trailed behind.

* * *

The Flash circled the address yet again, keeping just far enough away to hopefully evade any detection by the Weather Wizard. To Cisco, he said, "That's it. I've definitely cleared the vicinity of any traps and such. I'm going inside now. Yes, that's what I said. Any noticeable shift in the storm?"

"Negative! Listen, let me call in Wally on this. He could be very—"

"No! He almost got killed last time! Mardon is too savvy for him. I'll handle this."

"All right… Just be careful! Mardon may just be sitting in there, waiting to strike as you enter."

Barry chuckled. "You're starting to sound just like Iris. You know I'll be careful."

With that, the Flash veered toward the address. He picked up speed as he neared the structure, well aware that he had to catch his adversary completely by surprise. The Weather Wizard had already proven that he knew just how to compensate for Barry's speed. So long as Mardon believed that he was safely hidden, the Flash had a chance to catch him without danger to anyone in the vicinity, let alone the speedster himself.

He zipped toward the side of the building, then reached for the first door handle. The speedster pulled open the door, and immediately raced to the second entrance where he did the same. He then raced to the third and opened that too.

To the normal eye, all three doors opened simultaneously. The Flash peered inside each doorway, checking for any visible traps. To his surprise, there were none. The Flash retreated for a moment and contacted Cisco. "Just tried three entrances and nothing happened. From what I saw looking in, it's likely he's not in there anymore."

"Hard to tell from the readings," Cisco returned. "And I've still not been able to get a vibe off of the toothbrush. It's all the storm again, but there's no hint of him anywhere else in the city at the moment. Your call on going inside."

"Oh, I'm going inside. We can't afford not to look... which hopefully isn't what the Weather Wizard was thinking too."

No sooner had Barry said it than he returned once more to all three entrances. Again, he saw no hint of a trap. With no other choice, Barry randomly chose the third door.

He entered a vast room that looked as if it had been through a terrible war. Although the building itself had shown no visible signs of damage on the outside, the walls, ceiling, and floor were all marked by burns and cracks and areas tattered by other unidentifiable forces.

"Cisco, now that I'm inside, can you get any readings of this place through the suit?"

"Hang on." After a pause, Cisco answered, "Yeah, getting readings all right. Don't know what Mardon was doing here, but he poured a lot of that energy I picked up right in this place. Funny, though..."

The Flash peered at the burned walls, the scorched floor. "What could possibly be funny? This place looks like a wreck."

"It shouldn't even be *standing*. That's what's funny… strange. Amazing, actually. He kept it all focused in here on something."

"But what?"

"No idea. Whatever it is, though, it has to be the reason for everything odd he's done since he escaped."

"Yeah." The Flash rubbed his chin. There were traces of food wrappers and even ruined food. Mardon had not worried about any of the niceties of civilization while here. Barry had seen the lairs of animals that had been kept much neater. "It looks like once he finished what he was doing here, he left. Maybe not right away, but soon after."

"So we've lost him again. Figures."

"Looks like it. Give me a moment, though. I'm going to see if there's any clue to where he is or what he might be planning next."

The moment he finished talking, the Flash raced around every corner of the interior, studying the walls, searching the floor, turning over and checking every bit of trash. The speedster even ran up the walls so that he could better inspect the damage done to the ceiling. When he was done, he returned to his original location.

"Sure. Go ahead," Cisco was still answering.

"Done. Not too much out of the ordinary. Did find one thing of interest though." The Flash held up one of a small bundle of papers and inspected it again. "A picture of Clyde Mardon from the newspaper. Actually, four of them. It's like he gathered clippings somewhere along the way."

"A little obsessive, but certainly understandable except for the fact that someone's actually *reading* a newspaper these days instead of just calling it up online. Anyway, like I said, the obsession makes sense. He and his brother did everything together and we already know how bad it hit Mardon when he found out Clyde was dead."

"Yeah, but here's another thing," Barry went on, now peeking at a fragment of paper in his other hand. "Actually found a fifth one… or what's left of it. Lying with a few other pieces of refuse right where it looks like Mardon unleashed all this energy. I think the only thing that helped keep this image from being vaporized was the fact that it also got soaked as heck. I could barely make it out, either way, but it's definitely another image of Clyde Mardon."

"Now that is really odd. Wonder what it means?"

"One last thing. A lot of this is very fresh. I doubt we missed him by very much. You able to track anything yet?"

"No activity at all that we haven't attributed to the storm," Cisco answered. "It's almost like he faded away."

The Flash eyed one of the clippings. "Faded away. You know that figure I saw on the roof? The one that Joe also saw?"

"What about it? We figured it was some metahuman we haven't crossed paths with yet. That makes the most sense. Maybe even one who's convinced the Weather Wizard that he *is* Clyde Mardon."

"Maybe. But I keep thinking how Mardon acted and how certain he was just who he was shouting to. He had no doubts that it was Clyde. I'm not sure he'd be fooled by a fraud, although I could be wrong."

Cisco was silent for a moment. Then, "What're you getting at, Barry? If it's not another metahuman in disguise, then what is it?"

The Flash held one of the clippings as far away as he could, imagining the figure in it to be even farther away and in a darker location. "I don't know. Do you believe in ghosts?"

Another day in the tombs, Joe thought as he looked at the old clock on the painted cinderblock wall. *Tombs, all right. I wonder just who the hell even designed this place?*

The detective glanced at the other windowless walls. The basement was generally used for data and record storage. Most of the officers around Joe were either very near retirement or permanently injured. Joe respected all of them highly, but still chafed at not being out on the streets. He had spent years helping keep Central City safe from all kinds of hoods. That was where he belonged, not down here.

But his superiors had deemed otherwise.

Sighing, he finished the paperwork in front of him, stamped it, then set it aside for later filing. As he reached for the next batch, Joe paused to look at his phone. He and Iris had hardly talked since the Weather Wizard's last attack on him and that bothered Joe a lot.

Might as well do it, he thought with some trepidation. Picking up the phone, he called up Iris on the speed dial. Joe listened as the phone rang and rang and rang. However, when the voicemail came on, he didn't bother with a message. Instead, he dialed Wally... only to receive the same result.

Making a face, Joe set the phone down. He glanced up at the clock again—which hardly seemed to have budged in the meantime—and not for the first time calculated to the very second how much time he had left on his shift.

Wally West looked at the clock on his phone and did a calculation of just how long his father had left on his shift. That done, he sighed in exasperation and settled down again.

Wally watched police headquarters from a dark corner far across the street where an awning protected him from the storm. While he could have been on the other side of Central City and still reached headquarters in less than a single breath, after his debacle with the Weather Wizard, Wally had wanted to take no chances... especially with his father. By keeping an actual eye on where Joe was, Wally felt certain that nothing could go wrong.

His phone vibrated again. Wally glanced at it, this time answering. "Hi."

"Where are you?" Iris asked.

"Watching Dad like I promised. I had free time, so I thought I'd stick close by police headquarters. It doesn't help to be fast if I don't hear about what's happening until it's too late. I'm not going to let something happen because of that."

Her tone when she responded was full of both relief and concern. "I don't know how to thank you for doing that, Wally... but just be careful yourself, all right? Don't take Mardon on if he shows up. Just grab Dad and go."

"I'll do that. I promise." *But once he's safe, I'll deal with Mardon right, you'll see, Iris.* He took a quick look at police headquarters. "He won't be on duty much longer. I'll follow him home and once I know he's sticking there, I'll check in at regular intervals... without him knowing, natch."

"That sounds reasonable. Remember what I said, though. I want you to be careful too. Please."

"Don't you worry." He frowned as he heard background noises from her side. "Where are you? Are you in a car in this weather?"

There was a long pause. "Caitlin wasn't feeling well, so I thought I'd check in on her."

"Not too serious, I hope."

"No. Wally, I'm in traffic. I'll talk to you later."

"Sounds good. Like I said, don't you worry. Drive careful. I worry about you too, sis."

"I'll be fine. Bye."

Wally let her disconnect, then resumed watching headquarters. "Just let him come," he whispered to the air. "Once Dad's safe, Mister Wizard's all mine." Then, glancing at his phone, he added, "Sorry, Iris. You just wouldn't understand. I've got to take care of it. Guess I'm just more like Dad in that way than even I figured."

"Sorry about that," Iris said to H.R. as she turned onto the next street. "I suddenly felt like I just had to call him. I had to know he was all right."

H.R. raised both hands slightly. "You won't get any argument out of me. I think it's good to have family. Never really had much of one myself on my Earth."

"Thank you for understanding. Here we are, thank goodness." She pulled into a parking place at Caitlin's apartment complex. "Let's hope it's not bad."

"Let's," H.R. replied in a dubious tone.

They dashed from the car to the entrance. H.R. stepped back and leaned against the other side of the doorway as Iris tried the buzzer. After four futile attempts, she looked to him for a suggestion.

His gaze flickered to the sealed glass door keeping them from Caitlin. Something inside caught his eye. "Try one more time."

Frowning, Iris turned back to the buzzer. As she pressed it, another occupant opened the door and stepped through.

"Oh. Pardon me!" H.R. exclaimed, jumping out of the man's way in what Iris thought a somewhat exaggerated manner.

The man nodded briskly and moved on to face the storm.

"She still isn't answering," Iris muttered.

"Not a problem anymore." H.R. indicated the door, which was now slightly ajar.

Iris looked down to see his foot in the doorway.

"Saw him coming. Hoped it might work with you and the weather as distractions."

Patting him on the shoulder, Iris rushed into the building. With H.R. at her heels, she headed up to Caitlin's apartment.

"Everything seems pretty calm," Iris muttered as they moved unhindered through the building. "Maybe she actually is just a little sick."

"Maybe."

They reached Caitlin's floor. As they stepped into the main corridor, both instinctively came to a halt.

"Is it noticeably colder here than downstairs?" H.R. asked.

"Could be just the way the air conditioning for the common areas is set." Still, Iris's expression indicated to him that even she did not believe what she said.

Moving more cautiously, they came to Caitlin's door.

"It's even colder here," Iris murmured. With the utmost care, she reached for the handle.

"Hang on a moment!" blurted H.R. As Iris pulled back, he covered one hand with part of his shirt and took hold of the handle. Gritting his teeth, he said, "Oh boy, that's cold! We're in luck, though. It's unlocked. Here we go."

He pushed open the door enough for both of them to enter. A wave of Arctic cold pressed against them, but they stepped inside nonetheless. H.R. immediately shut the door behind him.

"Oh my God," Iris blurted.

"Yep," echoed H.R. warily.

The entire scene before them was bathed in glittering frost. Couch, table, walls, fixtures… everything.

H.R. shook his head in horror. "It's almost pretty…"

Iris looked behind him. "That's funny… Oh."

"What is it?"

"I felt a faint warmth. Look at the thermostat. It's practically set to broiling, but you have to stand right in front of it to even feel anything."

"That's not good, but at least there's a little hope." He folded his arms over his chest in a vain attempt to keep some body heat. "Clearly, Caitlin tried to fight it."

"'Tried' being the operative word. This doesn't look very much like success. We need to find her quick—" Iris gasped.

H.R. followed her gaze to a spot just off the center of the room and partially obscured by a couch. "What is that? All ice?"

"More likely Caitlin. Help me!"

They rushed to the low mound. Iris bent down to study it, carefully rubbing one hand over the top.

She pulled back in horror. H.R. grabbed her by the shoulders in support as both looked wide-eyed at what she had uncovered.

Caitlin lay on her back, seemingly staring at the ceiling. Her skin was frost white, her lips almost blue. Most of her hair had turned the color of snow.

They both knew that look. They both knew the name that went with it.

"This is bad," H.R. finally managed. "So bad."

Iris carefully put her hand back on the mound. When nothing happened, she pressed slightly on it. To the surprise of both, the area beneath her hand crumbled.

"It's like a shell... of frost..." H.R. offered.

"Or more like a cocoon. Look at her. She's slowly changing. We've got to wake her before it can't be reversed." Unspoken by her was the possibility that it was already too late.

"Is that wise? What if she doesn't... respond well?"

"We have to take that chance," Iris insisted. "We can't leave her like this."

H.R. looked anxiously at Caitlin, then nodded. "Cisco. His device. On her wrist. Maybe we can get to it."

They battered at the frost over her arm. Iris carefully

raised Caitlin's arm up so that they could view the mechanism.

Another, thicker layer covered Cisco's creation... and only Cisco's creation.

"Now that looks like a lot more than just a little fragile frost," H.R. pointed out.

Iris gingerly touched the surface, then recoiled. "I've never felt anything so cold!"

"But why is this so much harder than the rest of this mound?"

Gazing at Caitlin, Iris finally answered, "It's almost as if her powers are focused on the device... intentionally."

"Caitlin wouldn't do that—"

"I didn't say she did. I said her powers."

He gave her a blank look. "How does that happen?"

Iris looked around for something to use to warm up the device to melt its frosty covering. "Never mind that now. She has one of those portable candle lighters in the far right top drawer in the kitchen. Go get it while I call Cisco!"

As H.R. obeyed, Iris dialed.

"What's up, Iris?" Cisco's tone hinted of grave concern. "How is she? I've been getting more and more questionable readings for the past few minutes."

"Not good. We're trying to melt a thick layer of frost around the machine you gave her—"

"What? That shouldn't happen!"

H.R. returned with the long-stemmed lighter. "Got it."

"Hold the trigger there and squeeze," she instructed. "Should get a little gas flame."

"And gently heat the surface. Right." He went to work.

To Cisco, Iris asked, "Do you think we can reprogram it once we get through?"

"Temporarily at best. Let me know as soon as we can do anything."

"Starting to get through," H.R. informed her. "Shouldn't be much more than—"

The half-melted covering refroze.

"Uh oh." H.R. held the flame closer. Unfortunately, as both watched, now only a slight hint of unfreezing occurred before freezing happened again.

"What is it?" Cisco called. "If she's gone full Frost, you guys maybe better get out of there."

"It's the coating on your device! It's refreezing as fast as it melts!" Iris blurted into the phone.

"Uh… Iris…"

She looked at H.R., who stared at Caitlin with wide eyes. Iris immediately followed his gaze to the other woman.

Caitlin stared back.

Mark Mardon stirred. As he did, a wind blew in his face. He blinked, trying to clear his eyes. Through his blurred vision, the Weather Wizard made out an indistinct figure.

"Clyde?"

He blinked several times. The figure finally coalesced into his brother.

"About time you woke," the younger sibling responded. "You sleep like the dead." He chuckled at his joke.

"Where the hell are we?" This was not the building where he had tried yet again unsuccessfully to bring his brother back.

"You don't remember? I brought you here, just like on that first night after Iron Heights."

Try as he might, the Weather Wizard could summon no memory of the journey. "But you can't touch anything."

Clyde scowled. "Go ahead and be ungrateful! I'm the one who should be ungrateful after that last try!"

Mark jumped up. "Easy, Clyde! I didn't mean anything by it! It's all appreciated, especially after what happened... or didn't."

The younger brother beamed. "Good. How're you feeling now?"

Stretching his arms, the Weather Wizard grinned wide. "Feeling pretty good. Feeling pretty clear in the head too."

"Yeah?"

"Yeah... Clear enough to know how best to handle the Flash. How best to set him up for how we need him."

"Oh? And how's that?"

Mark grinned. "We're going to play an old favorite just for him."

1 2

Wally raced back to his observation point, having only been gone exactly one second. He had returned home, changed clothes, eaten some food, and returned in that time. Confident that he had missed nothing, Wally now debated one last step.

Exhaling, he dialed his phone.

"Central City Police Department. Detective Joe West speaking."

"Hey. It's Wally."

"Wally? Something wrong with you? Iris?"

The tremendous concern made Wally smile. "No, Dad. Nothing wrong with us."

"Well, so to what do I owe this honor? Not that I'm complaining."

"Are you still getting off in an hour?"

"You know it. One long, long hour."

Wally laughed, then sobered when he recalled why he had contacted his father. "I'll be there to pick you up."

"Oh, not you too," Joe moaned. "I thought you were on my side."

"I am… and on hers too. This is about all of us."

His father's tone shifted. "All of us? Listen, Wally, I don't want you ever facing Mardon again! You got that?"

Shaking his head, Wally interrupted, "I'm going to meet you when you leave. Talk to you then."

He hung up before Joe could say anything else.

Iris stared into Caitlin's open eyes… and after a moment realized that they didn't actually stare back.

"We've still got a chance," she murmured to H.R.

"Not at the rate this is going. Is there anything else we can use?"

Iris wracked her brain, but could think of nothing more focused. "No, we've got—"

Caitlin's eyes blinked once. Iris watched, but when Caitlin didn't blink again, she went on, "—to try to—"

Again, Caitlin blinked.

"What is it?" H.R. asked anxiously.

"She seems to be responding to my voice—there! Look! She blinked once." Iris leaned over the other woman. "Caitlin! It's me. It's Iris."

Another blink.

"That's right, Caitlin! Listen to my voice. Focus on it. We're here for you. H.R. is with me."

"Hello," he greeted weakly.

"Come on, Caitlin! Follow my voice back!"

"I saw that time! Two blinks!"

Iris nodded. "I saw them too. Caitlin, you can do it. You can do it—"

"God!" H.R. blurted. "Did it just get *colder*?"

"Her skin's almost utterly white!" Iris cupped Caitlin's face. In a stronger, more determined voice, she called, "Caitlin... Caitlin..."

The eyes shut. At first, Iris feared the worst, but then she noticed a warmth beginning to spread.

"That's right, Caitlin! You can do it! You can do it!"

"Is that a slight flush in her cheeks?" H.R. asked.

Iris looked. To her relief, she did notice a slight hint of color in Caitlin's face. "You're doing it, Caitlin! You're doing it!"

"The hair's changing back too," H.R. added. "See?"

"Come on, Caitlin!" Iris called. "You're almost home."

"I-Iris?"

The eyes opened slightly. Iris kept her gaze on Caitlin's.

"Iris... So cold..."

"I know."

"Tried to make more heat. Didn't work."

"We saw that. You did what you could. Keep fighting. You're almost back to us!"

Caitlin moaned. Iris at first took the reaction for a lapse, but then saw that the color in the other woman's cheeks had improved several times over.

"You can do it!" she repeated. "You can!"

"I can actually feel some heat from the vents," H.R. muttered.

"Now's our chance. Try to work on the device."

He did as she bade, gently running the lighter over the frozen mechanism.

"It's melting better again," he reported to her.

She slid the phone to him. "As soon as it's free, talk with Cisco."

"Got it."

"Come on, Caitlin," Iris encouraged. "Come on."

"There!" H.R. set aside the tool and grabbed the phone. "Okay, Cisco! Please make this easy!"

Iris paid them no mind. She knew that she had to keep speaking to Caitlin. Any hesitation might reverse all that they had managed thus far.

"Iris…" Caitlin muttered. "I'm cold."

"I know, honey. The heat is on. You'll be much better shortly. Just stay with me. You hear?"

"I'm… trying. I want to go to sleep… but I know I better not…"

"No, that's right," Iris responded with more confidence. "Just stick with me."

Caitlin said something else, but it was too muffled for Iris to understand. Fearing that her friend was slipping, Iris gently rubbed Caitlin's cheek.

She was rewarded with a smile. Caitlin's eyes opened wider this time.

"It's fighting me, Iris…"

"I know. You're strong. We're here. H.R., how are you doing?"

"That's it?" he asked of the phone. "I hope it works fast!"

Setting aside the phone, H.R. reached for the wrist device. He cautiously brought Caitlin's arm around so that he could reach Cisco's creation. With Iris's phone in the crook of his neck, he went to work.

Iris continued keeping Caitlin's focus on her. Every time Caitlin's gaze started to drift, Iris doubled her efforts to keep the other woman occupied.

"You're doing great, Caitlin," she said. "Just a little bit longer and things will be back to normal."

"It feels… warmer."

"Good. Are you hungry?"

A pause. "Yes."

"Well, after we're done here, we'll get something to eat. Sounds good?"

"Yes."

Iris looked at H.R., who was still fiddling with the mechanism. He caught her glance and gave a nod. To Caitlin, Iris added, "That Japanese place we talked about a couple of weeks ago sounds like a good choice. How about we go there?"

Another pause. "Yes."

The continual short answers bothered Iris. "Any idea what you'd like?"

Caitlin frowned. "No."

"How about—" Iris stopped. A strong wave of

cold air swept over her. She immediately turned her attention back to H.R. and his efforts.

He shook his head in clear puzzlement, indicating with one hand that he was doing what he was told.

Iris fixed on Caitlin. "What about—"

Caitlin's skin had grown pale again.

"No." Iris rubbed the other woman's cheek. "Caitlin. Look at me."

"Iris? Is it… cold again?"

"Just for a moment. You just focus on me, all right?"

"Yes." Caitlin's brow wrinkled. "Yes."

The cold air faded. Warmth slowly poured over the trio. Iris smiled at Caitlin, who smiled back. Caitlin's skin returned to normal.

"Got it!" H.R. proclaimed loudly. After a stern look from Iris, he added in a much quieter voice, "Sorry!"

The room got much warmer. Frost began fading— though not yet melting—everywhere. Caitlin reverted to her normal self. She suddenly took a deep breath.

"Praise be!" H.R. exclaimed.

"Iris…" Caitlin hugged her tight.

"Easy, easy…" Iris held her just as close. She felt Caitlin slowly calm.

H.R. lowered the phone. "Cisco says we should bring her back to the lab."

"We will. Soon."

"No," interjected Caitlin more strongly. "Let's go now."

"Are you sure you're up to it?" questioned Iris.

Caitlin exhaled. "No. But I have to be. Let's go right now."

Iris stared into her eyes. What she saw made her nod. "All right. Now. H.R., give us a hand."

"Right. Right."

The two of them helped Caitlin to her feet. As they did, Iris felt the warm air from the heater. Keeping one hand on her friend, she reached for the thermostat.

"No!"

Caitlin's exclamation startled her. One hand still stretched to the thermostat, Iris eyed her.

"Please," Caitlin said more evenly. "Leave it. I'd like it to be... warmer... when I return."

Iris and H.R. shared glances. Iris lowered her hand.

"All right," she answered. "We'll leave it just like you want. Shall we go now?"

"Yes."

Nodding, Iris took hold of her and led the three of them from the apartment as quickly as she could.

Barry returned to the lab to find Cisco alone. "Where are the others?"

"They'll be back shortly," Cisco replied, setting down his phone. "Got those clippings?"

"Yeah, here they are." Barry handed them to him.

Cisco studied the images of Clyde Mardon, then the other side of each. "All the same newspaper. See: they all have the same story on the other side. He must've gathered them the same day."

"Well, we know Clyde's death really stuck with him. If anything, he's gotten worse about it."

As Barry talked, Cisco typed. A minute later, Cisco nodded. "Wasn't too hard to track down. All from the *Central Gazette*: that smaller paper that covers the area beyond Iron Heights, including the very same hospital where Mark Mardon was comatose. When he woke, he must've grabbed every copy he could still find. Almost sad."

"What about the one I found separate from the others? It didn't look like it just fell there. In fact, considering how the area around it was so damaged, it was in remarkable shape."

"Don't know. I—" Cisco studied the Flash. "Barry, buddy, you look all out."

Barry rubbed the back of his neck. "I feel all out. I think I need to get something to eat."

"Yeah?"

"I've *got* to get something to eat."

Cisco started to reply, but Barry had already moved to the refrigerator and removed half the contents. Before his friend could blink, the Flash had made himself several sandwiches, three salads, and a number of other snacks.

"Seriously, dude. The sandwiches again. We're going to have to up the food budget if this keeps up!"

Barry didn't bother answering. He bit into the first

sandwich. The second. The third. The rest... all while alternating with the salads, the snacks, and then water to help down the food.

Cisco groaned. "I think I may never eat again. You devoured *everything*. It's like you're a living Pac-Man, only a lot messier."

"Had to. Cisco, I barely feel full."

Cisco checked on the computer. "You're burning things up at an accelerated pace from yesterday. If this is due to the Weather Wizard, I don't see how he can do all this without burning out himself."

Barry started to yawn, then stopped himself. "No. If I take another nap, I'm liable not to wake up for a few days."

"You won't be able to fight it forever. It's only getting worse."

"I'll do it for as long as I can." Stretching, Barry added, "In fact, I'd better get out there now. Mardon's got to make a move again soon." He paused. "As a matter of fact, I'm going to check on Joe first."

"Suit yourself, but I'm going to keep a good eye on your readings. Even if you think you can handle everything, there's a limit. You ought to know that by now."

Barry didn't answer, having already raced away.

Cisco grunted, then picked up the phone again. "Iris. How's it going?"

"We're on the way. She's all right now, but she insisted we return right away."

"She's right. Honestly, Iris, I would've gone ahead

and opened a breach to you guys except with this weird storm my own powers aren't functioning at a hundred percent. Or even half that. By the way, Barry was here, Iris. He's gone now, though. Said the first thing he's doing is checking on Joe."

"All right."

He cocked his head: it was not the kind of answer he had expected. "Anyway, glad Caitlin's with you. I need to check out that worthless piece of machinery."

"We should be there any moment. I've got to go. The storm's cutting visibility."

"Roger that. See you."

Barely had he disconnected from Iris than Barry contacted him.

"Cisco, any idea when Joe's off duty?"

"Hang on." Cisco typed. "He's due off in about an hour."

"Did you just hack the police department?"

"'Just'? Dude, we've had an in for months—" A signal on the monitor went off. "Wait a moment! We've got something coming!"

"Mardon?"

Cisco switched the view on the monitor. "Don't know. All I've got so far is a growing reading near the ocean."

The Flash's silence after that did not surprise him. "The ocean. Are you sure?"

"Certain."

Again the Flash said nothing at first. Then, "I'd better check it out immediately."

Barry cut contact. Cisco stared at the readings. Even as new as they were, the resemblance to the readings from the previous time the Weather Wizard had struck the coast were impossible to miss.

"Great," Cisco muttered. "Just great. Another tidal wave."

The Flash veered from police headquarters to the coast. He had the utmost faith in Cisco's reading of the new data, which meant that perhaps the Weather Wizard had finally started unleashing his ultimate plan. The fact it was taking place on the coast meant only one thing to the speedster: Mardon was trying to finish what he had started last time.

The destruction of Central City by a massive tidal wave.

I stopped it before and I'll stop it again, Mardon, the Flash swore. He had no doubt that the Weather Wizard intended to magnify this new tidal wave's strength, but to the Flash that just meant that he would have to double his own efforts.

Savage waves struck the shore as he neared. Barry could feel the electricity in the air. He knew the wave was sure to rise far higher than the previous one.

"Cisco! It's just forming! I'm going to see if I can nip it in the bud! Keep me posted on any abrupt changes!"

"You got it! I estimate you've got maybe two minutes before it threatens the shore!"

"Two minutes is more than enough time for me, remember?" Yet despite his bravado, the Flash approached the surging water with caution. Mardon had proven himself smart enough to arrange his traps ahead of time so that the Flash would race right into them.

Barry began running a zigzag pattern, all the while watching for any hint of some trick by his adversary. Still, he knew that the tidal wave did limit him in some ways. Sooner rather than later, the Flash would have to step where the Weather Wizard expected him.

A feeling of déjà vu overcame the speedster as he watched the wall of water build. However, the last time this had happened, the Weather Wizard had had a clear and simple purpose in mind and the Flash had acted aware of that purpose. This time, though, Barry distrusted what his eyes saw; Mardon likely intended more than merely repeating the past. True, the Flash had no choice but to stop the wave as he had previously, but he doubted it was going to be as easy— so to speak—as the last time.

Let's see if this puts your plans off, he thought as he suddenly ran onto the water. Skimming the surface fast enough to avoid sinking, the speedster quickly rushed along the length of the stirring wave, both measuring its potential and seeking any hint of the traps he felt certain had to be there. However, even after repeating the step, the Flash discovered nothing new. Not only did there appear to be no tricks, but the tidal wave looked little stronger than the previous one.

Even more curious, where was the Weather Wizard himself? Barry had hoped to catch his foe in the act, but there was no sign of the rogue anywhere. The Flash knew that Mardon had far more control over his abilities than during their previous encounter, but it still amazed and bothered him that all this could be happening without the Weather Wizard being close by.

Circling back around, the Flash began racing back and forth, building up speed. A wind arose from his efforts, one that intensified as he accelerated. Barry ran faster and faster, ignoring any touch of exhaustion or pain.

The wind grew into a gale, then to hurricane strength. It buffeted the growing tidal wave as no other force could. Ocean water became swept up in the wind, adding to the destructive force of the Flash's creation.

Out of the corner of his eye, he noticed several bystanders who had been so caught up in getting through the storm that they had failed to notice the rising threat from the ocean. Barry debated for a moment, then sped away from his creation to the nearest. One by one, the speedster carried the bystanders to safety far from the ocean.

He was back before his creation could falter in the slightest. The Flash picked up his pace, building up his counter to the tidal wave as swiftly as possible. Faster and faster he ran—

A fog arose. A fog that blossomed directly where the Flash had to run. The speedster plunged into an empty world.

The outline of something massive formed in the fog. Barry adjusted his path—

And suddenly lost his footing on something. He attempted to compensate, but here his speed worked against him. He stumbled, then fell.

Momentum threw him forward. He twisted as best he could, managing to tumble out of the path of whatever lurked in the fog.

But in doing so, the Flash ended up back on land. The uneven surfaces further exasperated his situation. Barry spun in a circle, then crashed against a solid surface with such force that it left him stunned for several seconds. As his head cleared, he heard Cisco shouting in his ear, "—out now, Barry! Hurry! Get out now!"

The Flash rolled over to see a wall of water descending on him. While much reduced in size and strength, the tidal wave still stood several yards high. The Flash attempted to rise, only to have a bout of vertigo send him sprawling again. He looked up as the tidal wave came crashing down—

As the Flash had raced to the ocean, a startled Wally stared as his father left the police headquarters. Joe West had his collar held tight around him and his head covered by a hat as he pushed through the storm to where his car waited.

"You just had to sneak out," Wally muttered.

Shaking his head, he eyed his father for a moment more. "I'm trying to keep you *safe*, Dad."

With a sigh of resignation, he hopped over to his father. Joe recoiled in surprise as Wally appeared in front of the elder West's vehicle.

"God!" Joe exclaimed. "Do you know what a shock you just gave me?"

"It's only fair after you tried to sneak out."

"The chief said I should take off early. I was all for staying and backing everyone during this storm, but apparently I'm a liability now!"

Wally grunted. "And you couldn't call me about this change in plans? Dad, you know why I'm here. You know how dangerous it is for you right now!"

"Listen!" Joe poked him in the chest. "You are my son! I'm supposed to keep an eye on you and your sister, not the other way around. I have never run from a fight and I will not now! I would rather you stay clear!"

"I know how you feel, but this is different! Besides all I want to do is see you home safely. I promised Iris, but I also promised myself."

Lightning flashed. Joe looked up. "Okay, you're here. Fine. Let's get going and—look out!"

Lightning struck where Wally stood—except that neither Wally nor Joe were anywhere near anymore.

Wally set his father by the police headquarters. "Get inside! I'll deal with him!"

"No! Get away!" Joe drew his revolver. "It's too dangerous!"

"You ought to listen to the cop!" the Weather Wizard mocked from above them. "All that concern! Might as well be your father, Flash Junior!"

"The name is Kid Flash!" Wally shouted, racing through the parking lot in order to gain enough momentum to leap up at the hovering figure.

"The name is the *late* Kid Flash, you mean!"

A tremendous wind stopped Wally in his tracks, then shoved him back. He compensated, using the wind to give him an extra boost to the top of a car. From there, Wally jumped to another vehicle, this time a tall truck.

A bolt of lightning hit right in front of the truck. By then, Wally had jumped to his next choice.

Joe fired. The wind gusted, blowing his bullet far from his target.

"Last shot taken, West," Mardon called. He gestured at the detective.

A hailstorm assailed Joe. Covering his head, he tried to retreat into the building.

"Not going to escape this time, West!"

A stunning rush of rain bombarded the doorway, forcing Joe back out into the open. He wasted no time, firing again.

Once more, the Weather Wizard seized control of the bullet. He let it spin around in the wind as he looked again at Wally.

"The Flash wouldn't be caught dead using that stunt against me. You, you'll just be caught dead because of it."

Wally jumped.

The same wind that had seized Joe's bullet trapped Wally in midair.

Mardon descended a few feet. "You quicker than a fast bullet? Let's see how you do against one aimed right at your head."

The wind spun both Wally and the bullet around and around, tossing Kid Flash around like a tiny toy. He flailed, unable to get sufficient traction.

"Round and round we go," the Weather Wizard jested. "Where we stop, you don't want to know!"

Joe fired again. Perhaps distracted by his other victim, Mardon didn't immediately realize the threat. The bullet soared toward its target—

Joe West was a crack shot. It had been no fluke that he had managed to bring down Clyde Mardon so efficiently. Given normal conditions, there would have been no doubt as to his aim. Unfortunately, the powerful wind surrounding the Weather Wizard was more than sufficient to disrupt the bullet's path.

"Aargh!" The Weather Wizard clutched his shoulder. The bullet had not gone in, but had left a distinct crimson graze.

Mardon's eyes widened. The manic look in them startled Joe, but not enough to keep him from trying to fire again.

"Aaargh!" The Weather Wizard gestured in Wally's direction. The spinning ceased. Instead, Wally went flying into the nearest car.

"No!" shouted Joe. He fired.

The hovering figure easily deflected the shot this time. Clenching his fist, the Weather Wizard gestured at Joe. A gale-force wind slammed the detective against the doors to the police headquarters, cracking them and knocking Joe out.

Paying no heed to Wally's still form, the Weather Wizard descended further. Hovering over Joe, Mardon raised a new wind that pulled the unconscious detective's body up into the air.

"Now that's more like it," Clyde, suddenly floating next to his brother, said with satisfaction. "Nice!"

"I'll kill him now. We'll finally be rid of him. He'll finally pay for you, Clyde." As Mardon spoke, his voice took on a strained quality. His body dripped, but with sweat, not rain.

"No. Not yet," the ghostly figure whispered. "We need him to draw the Flash right where we want him. He ought to be just about tenderized by that tidal wave."

"You sure it didn't destroy him?" the Weather Wizard asked dubiously. "That trap you suggested was a tricky one. He could be under tons of water."

"The Flash? Nah. He's ours, Mark. He can't die until we decide he should. You need him to bring me back. Then he can die a thousand different ways."

"'A thousand different ways.'" Mark smiled, his lips curled much farther back than normal, giving him even more of a cadaverous countenance. "Yeah. I know what to do. I know how to bring you back. This time I'll succeed."

"Yeah, this time you'll succeed. That's right, Mark. Let's go."

"Let's go," the Weather Wizard repeated.

He shot up into the air, Joe's dangling body following. The Weather Wizard vanished into the clouds with his prey.

Below, Clyde Mardon stilled. His expression grew slack.

A moment later, he dissipated.

Moaning, Wally tried to move. More than ever, he was grateful for the special padding Cisco had made certain the suits had. His bones still vibrated and his head felt as if it were about to explode, but he would live.

Live with his shame, that is. Not only had he twice lost badly to the Weather Wizard, but he'd failed to protect his father. That after swearing to Iris, his father, and himself that nothing bad would happen.

"Cis-Cisco," he managed.

"Wally? Where are you? Hang on! Let me get your readings—geez! Are you with your father?"

"No." Wally had to wait a moment to catch his breath. "Cisco. Mardon has—him."

"'Him'? Your father? When?"

"Just… just a couple of minutes… ago! I think… I think they're headed east. Tell Barry."

"I'm on it. I'll also get someone over to you—"

"Never mind me…" Wally's mind began to clear.

"One more thing. I saw someone with Mardon. Right at the end. Floating up there just like him. Couldn't really make him out. Always… Always like he was out of focus."

"Yeah, Barry and I figure some new metahuman pretending to be Clyde Mardon."

"Yeah?" Wally groaned as he tried to move. "A-a real strange one, then. I saw him vanish, Cisco. Poof. Just like that. Just like a—like a—"

Cisco didn't wait. "Like a ghost?"

Grimacing in pain, Wally nodded. "Yep. Just like a ghost."

Although somewhat dazed, the Flash nevertheless pushed himself to his feet and ran. Compared to his abilities at their peak, he ran so very slowly. Yet, compared to the tidal wave, he still moved in the blink of an eye.

The only question for the speedster was whether that was fast enough for what needed to be done. Peering at the growing wave as he rushed, Barry could not really trust that it was.

The fog that the Weather Wizard had set up had already begun to dissipate. It had not been designed as a danger itself, only as a distraction at a critical moment. The Flash could have easily broken his leg or worse. At the very least, he could have been left helpless long enough to become a victim of the tidal wave. Mardon had planned cunningly. Fortunately, circumstance and luck had been with the speedster thus far.

Once the Flash himself was out of range, he came around again to better judge the oncoming catastrophe.

The Flash knew that somehow he had to return to his efforts. Whether or not the main purpose of this second wave had simply been to trap the speedster, the Weather Wizard would at the very least leave much of Central City in ruins with who knew how many casualties. Barry couldn't risk that happening.

Taking a deep breath, he picked up speed once more. He raced back and forth several yards ahead of the diminished tidal wave, pushing himself faster than before despite his battered body and rapidly depleting energy. The Flash realized that he probably had enough strength for only one attempt. Anything beyond that and he would likely falter before he could finish.

His body screamed from abuse as he accelerated again. To his relief, however, a second gale-force wind finally rose from his efforts. The Flash adjusted his path to ensure that the wind focused on a direction setting it against the tidal wave. Faster and faster he ran, building it up to the mighty level of the previous and then pushing it harder yet.

"Not this time either, Mardon!" Barry muttered. "This tidal wave's going to be just as much a washout as the last!"

The wave neared. The Flash's wall of wind met it hard. The speedster gritted his teeth and belatedly shielded his ears.

Water sprayed everywhere... but not as one massive wave. Instead, much of the water tumbled back down into the ocean. That which managed to pass the Flash's barrier only created a briefly rougher rainstorm. There would be some light damage, but hardly anything in comparison to what could have been.

Still Barry didn't rest as the two forces met. He continued to strengthen his wall. As weary as he was, as violently as his leg muscles shrieked, the speedster pressed on for as long as there was even a remnant of the original tidal wave left. The Flash easily lost track of just how many times he raced to one end and back. All that truly mattered was that it had to be enough.

Faster and faster and faster he ran, though throughout it Barry couldn't help feeling he could not run fast enough. The wave might have been reduced in size by his previous efforts, but it was much nearer the city now, giving him no margin of error.

The Flash ran until he had nothing left to give, and stumbled to a halt, leaning against the nearest wall, to watch and see whether or not he had done enough after all.

The initial collision had somehow dwarfed the earlier one despite the marked difference in height. A heavy but very brief downpour washed over the shore and the first two blocks. The Flash remained just out of reach of it, waiting to see if there would be any more threat.

The sea churned, then settled back. Barry eyed the coastline, but saw no more trace of the threat. The protections already put in place after Mardon's first attack on Central City would continue to work unless the Weather Wizard attempted something else.

Only then did he realize that Cisco was yelling in his ear. "He's got him, Barry! Do you hear me? Wally tried to do something but Mardon got Joe!"

A chill ran through the Flash. The true reason for the second tidal wave now became horribly evident. Barry shook as he thought of how well the Weather Wizard had played him. Now the worst had happened. "Joe's... *dead*?"

"No! Sorry for that, man! Kidnapped! Wally saw the Weather Wizard use a gust of wind to carry Joe off. Joe was just unconscious. Wally tried to stop him, but couldn't! He's still out there now, searching."

"Where'd it happen?"

"Police head—"

The Flash ran.

"—quarters!" Cisco finished as the speedster paused in front of the selfsame building.

The evidence of the struggle was very clear all over the area. The damage spoke of the intense effort Wally had put in while attempting to save his father. Barry saw that the battle couldn't have happened very long ago: police had just started to take over the scene.

Running so swiftly that everyone around him appeared to freeze, the Flash cased the entire scene from top to bottom and quickly made a judgment as to everything that had happened. He especially noted the damage to the door and to several of the cars in the parking lot, seeing the ferocity with which Mardon had dealt with both Wally and Joe. The vision left the speedster shivering from frustration at the thought that he had not been there to help prevent Joe's kidnapping.

Stop it! he ordered himself. *This isn't going to help Joe! Keep your calm and analyze everything for some clue.*

Moving beyond the police facility, the Flash surveyed the neighborhood. Calculating where the Weather Wizard had to have been when he struck the pair, Barry then tried to follow back the rogue's trail as best he could.

Only when he was far out of sight of the police and under the protection of an overhang did he pause to evaluate his progress. A part of him knew that he should have joined those inspecting the scene. It was not that he didn't work well with the department, but right now Barry felt that if he became embroiled in the official investigation he would be slowed down too much. Mardon had no reason to keep Joe alive for very long.

"He's nowhere to be found!" a voice cried out from behind him. "I tried but I couldn't keep him safe!"

Wally's harried expression as he suddenly joined the Flash matched the other speedster's concerns and then some. Wally had only recently connected with his father. Now the fear of losing his parent again hung heavy.

Putting a comforting hand on his companion's shoulder, Barry replied, "I can imagine what you're going through. Not exactly, but certainly near enough. Joe means a lot to me, you know that. He's always been there for me. So just try to calm down. We'll save him. I promise." After Wally quieted, Barry went on, "I know what Cisco told me. Now you tell me what happened, so we make sure we don't miss a clue."

Wally quickly did, filling in some holes in what Barry knew. What interested the Flash most was the last bit.

"You saw this figure too? The one he called his brother?"

"I mean, I couldn't say it was this Clyde, since I never really paid attention to who he was, but there was someone up there. Never really in focus, and then he up and went poof just like you see ghosts do in the movies! At the time I didn't have much of a chance to let it sink in, but now…"

"Cisco thinks it's a new metahuman using the Weather Wizard's grief, but I'm beginning to question that possibility. I don't know who or what it is, but somehow it's key to a lot of what Mardon's doing, including kidnapping Joe now."

Wally shook his head. "That part doesn't make any sense to me. Why kidnap him? Before, the Weather Wizard tried to kill him in front of the apartment complex."

The Flash scowled. "Did he really, though? I've thought about it. Maybe a part of Mardon wanted to kill Joe then, but I think he really expected that I'd be there just in time. The Weather Wizard knows me better than most of those we face. He might have assumed, rightly or wrongly, that I'd always arrive in the nick of time and used that."

"Man, he sounds loco."

"I'm certainly not arguing that, but it makes him no less clever. Take this kidnapping. I think Joe's still got some time, not that we're going to slow our search in the least. No, I'm pretty sure at this point that the Weather Wizard's building up to something involving me and right now he's using Joe for bait."

Wally looked at him as if he now thought Barry insane as well. "What could that be?"

"I wish I knew." The Flash looked up into the stormy sky. "It's something more than just wanting revenge on me too, although he really wants that badly. Never mind that. When's the last you saw them. Exactly which direction?"

Peering around, Wally pointed. "There. They disappeared into the clouds that way. I couldn't follow after that. I didn't know where to go. He could've flown right over me and I wouldn't have been able to see him."

"Yeah. That's been a problem with him. Most of the others we've faced can't fly, and worse, don't always bring cloud cover with them." Barry grimaced. "Still, we may not be at a total loss. Cisco, are you there?"

"Right here," Cisco announced in his earpiece. "I heard what you were saying. Ahead of you. Been trying something different. On the assumption that the Weather Wizard is of course the cause of things like the tidal wave, I'm using that to measure his control over more than one incident at a time. If we can see what stresses it takes, depending on distance and intensity, then we might be able to locate him no matter where he moves."

The two speedsters looked uncertain. "That sounds like an awful lot of calculating, Cisco," the Flash commented. "Is that possible?"

"Well, it'll take some doing, but I think I should have everything in place not too long from now."

"All right. I guess the best thing to do then is for Wally and me to divide Central City in two and double our search efforts until then. Just hurry, Cisco. We need this."

"I understand, man. Don't you two worry. We'll find him."

Barry looked at Wally. "You see anything, you let us know. Don't go charging in alone. The Weather Wizard's more powerful than ever. You don't want to take any chances. That won't help Joe."

"Don't you worry. I know what I've got to do. Think Cisco can really locate him with some program?"

"We need every shot we can get, that's what I know." The Flash eyed the incessant rain. "You ready?"

"Yeah. Let's do this."

Cisco glanced at his phone. Iris had briefly called one last time from Caitlin's apartment to tell him that they were on their way. The storm had clearly slowed them, which actually benefited him at the moment.

He went to work, but not on the program that he had just discussed with Barry. Instead, Cisco delved back into the circumstances of the Weather Wizard's escape from Iron Heights. Something about it still nagged him. He had his suspicions but needed to verify them.

The knowledge would benefit him in more ways than just satisfying his curiosity. Whatever had happened that night had somehow augmented Mardon's already substantial abilities. That had not been a simple thing to do. To Cisco, that meant that whatever had managed it should be fairly easy to find.

"So, where is it then?" he muttered at the data. "Where is the key? Come on, Cisco! You're a genius, or so you keep saying! Where?"

He skimmed through page after page of the design for the Weather Wizard's cell, including especially all the schematics surrounding the extensive wiring.

And there, deep into that section, he thought he spotted the answer. If so, it had actually been staring him in the eye since almost the beginning. Cisco had seen to it that the information concerning the wand had reached the designers. It had been necessary to do that in order to make certain that Iron Heights could hold the Weather Wizard, since their previous designs had failed to come up with a method to keep his extensive powers at bay.

And so they had done with Cisco's secret contribution just as he had expected. But then someone had decided to try to be too clever. Cisco had purposely left out elements of the wand's design that had in the end actually enabled the Weather Wizard to use it to enhance his powers. Cisco had thought nothing more about it at the time. Now he saw that he had clearly underestimated the designers' own tech savvy.

Someone had followed the same logical path he originally had in expanding on his data. Studying the cell's electronic design, he could understand why. In order for Iron Heights to work where metahumans were concerned, the designers had had to try to take several things into consideration. They had not only needed to create a chamber with four walls, a roof, a tiny window, and a strong door. No, they had had to think about the intricacies of each metahuman's unique abilities and how best to keep them in check.

And so they had, in the system designed to make the Weather Wizard helpless, virtually recreated the concept of the wand. Then they had in their further wisdom created a helmet in order to fine-tune the effects to his brain.

"And it did just that," muttered Cisco as he leaned back to stare at the results. An expression of disbelief spread over his face. "The wand... Oh boy..."

"What's that?"

Cisco turned to find H.R. at the door. "Where's Caitlin and Iris?"

"On their way. I went ahead to see if you needed anything set up."

"How is she?"

"Tired, but normal. What should we do?"

Rising, Cisco went to where Barry had slept. "Give me a moment here. We don't need all these electrodes."

"No?"

"The machine is constantly taking readings. I can access everything I need on the computer or my phone."

H.R. did not look convinced. "We are talking about the machine that failed her more than once, right?"

"That was due to a programming error on my part," Cisco responded. "Even knowing Caitlin as I do, I underestimated her natural strength."

"Not by a little."

At that moment, Iris and Caitlin entered. Caitlin held tight to the other woman as if fearing a fall.

"Right here," Cisco ordered, gesturing to the table. "Hop up, Caitlin."

"What are you going to do?"

"Nothing at the moment. I just want you to be able to relax. Sorry, but I've known for a while that you were having some problems, but I noted you made a few adjustments and seemed to be over them."

She nodded. "It worked for a little while, but of late it's grown so much worse. I don't understand why, though. For the longest time, I had perfect control thanks to what you built."

H.R. offered her a hand. Caitlin climbed up, then settled in place.

Cisco moved to her side and began investigating the device. "Been through some heck of late, but still functioning. Let me run some short internal diagnostics. There are some things the machine doesn't transmit."

"Cisco... I nearly turned."

"But you didn't. Besides, you've got me, H.R., Iris, Barry, and more to watch over you. With a team of friends like us, you've got nothing to worry about." He started pressing buttons. A new screen popped up on the wrist device.

Caitlin's eyes widened. "I've never seen that before."

"You wouldn't need to. This is for repair purposes for the most part. I check it every time we make an update."

"Is Barry still searching?" Iris asked suddenly.

Cisco nodded. "Yeah."

Iris couldn't see his face directly, but Caitlin could. She clearly saw a look in his eyes. Cisco shook his head ever so slightly, in response to which she bit her lip.

"Caitlin, you're in better hands here," Iris went on. "Do you mind if I go make a phone call?"

"Wally's out too," Cisco quickly added, "but Barry made him promise that he wouldn't do anything on his own."

"I don't like that, but I suppose he'll listen. I'll just call Dad then."

"Uh… Yeah, okay." Cisco kept his grimace hidden from Iris. "Actually, could you help me with something here?"

Iris toyed with her phone, then nodded reluctantly. "All right." She put the phone away. "What is it?"

"Keep an eye on Caitlin's face as I check things. Maybe hold her hand too, just for good measure."

When Iris wasn't looking, he winked at Caitlin. She nodded slightly.

"That's it?"

Cisco shrugged. "I'd appreciate it."

"No, it's fine, I don't want anything else to happen to her."

Caitlin smiled at her. "Thank you, Iris. I'm really, really sorry."

As Iris came around the other side, she patted Caitlin on the arm. "Don't apologize for anything! We're friends. How could I refuse?"

"H.R., can you go to the console and read me whatever numbers come up?" Cisco asked.

"That I think I can do."

"Cisco—" Caitlin began.

"You just relax," he quickly interrupted. "Let me see what these readings say."

"The numbers are changing on the screen," H.R. called. "Do you want them?"

"Sure. Go ahead."

H.R. read them off. Cisco grunted, then made some adjustments. He grunted again at what he saw on the small screen from the device, then said, "How about now? Any change in them?"

"No change," H.R. responded.

"No change?" Cisco studied his own numbers, at the moment forgetting that he was keeping everyone around him in the dark about something. He looked up at Caitlin. "Your powers are akin to the Weather

Wizard's in some ways, you know that?"

"You're saying that I'm being affected by what he's been doing?"

"Seems so. Apparently it makes you particularly sensitive to how he's manipulating his own meta abilities. The more he twists the energies to suit his desire, the more it affects you."

"That's not a pleasant thing to find out." Caitlin's expression screwed up in confusion. "But it never happened before. We faced both Mark and his brother and I never felt anything."

"That's because he hadn't been hooked up to that system at Iron Heights then. We provided some of the data, then someone else went and made the same mistake as I did with the wand. Instead of keeping him at bay, they helped him build up his power. I think it might be temporary now that he's not attached to the machine at the Heights, but that might be a moot point if it stretches on long enough."

Iris straightened. "The wand! Why haven't we used that yet? That's how we stopped him last time!"

"Yeah," H.R. interjected. "Why haven't we... Not that I'd know about it since I'm not the same me from then."

"I'd forgotten the wand," Caitlin added. "How could I? Cisco, why don't we—"

Cisco shook his head. "We don't dare use the wand. Right now, with how they wired him in Iron Heights, the wand is more likely to magnify his abilities further,

not control them." Cisco rubbed his chin. "Magnify...
That's what... No..."

The others waited, but Cisco just kept staring off in
thought.

"So what *can* be done?" Iris finally asked.

"I think I can do something, but I need to check
one more item." He made a few adjustments. "H.R.,
what do you see now? There should be two lines of
numbers. Which one is lower and by how much?"

"Second line is lower. Is this time that I'm reading?"

"Yes. So nearly ten minutes before the top started,"
Cisco said.

"Six seconds less. That's it."

Cisco made a few more adjustments. "Okay, I see
what I've got here. How are the readings now?"

"Different, I guess? What do you need?"

"Same gap between them?"

H.R. hesitated, then, "Pretty much the same. Seven
seconds less than ten."

"Before?"

"Before."

Cisco tapped a button on the device. The screen
faded away.

"What is it?" Caitlin asked, the worry clear on her
face. Cisco felt bad for her. She had assumed the device
would keep her safe and it had failed her. In his eyes,
that meant that *he* had failed her.

He stepped back. "We've already confirmed that your
powers are especially influenced by their similarities

to the Weather Wizard's and we know why. Wasn't expecting this though. I'm pretty sure if I double-check other times, it'll all be about the same."

"Please make sense quickly," Iris pleaded. "Can't you see how anxious she's becoming?"

"Sorry, Caitlin. Look, with the storm as it is, it's hard for me even with the computer to catch exactly when the Weather Wizard starts using his powers in any significant manner. Been getting close, but not close enough. Those later sets of times I had H.R. look at, those were the ones the system recorded when it first registered Mardon's use of his powers. The others are when you first seemed to be influenced by his work."

H.R. snapped his fingers. "So wouldn't that help you maybe catch him this time if you had those earlier numbers?"

"You got it. Caitlin, with early detection possible through your reactions, I'd definitely be able to pinpoint him not only before he started anything significant, but also before he runs away!"

Although he and H.R. grew upbeat with this news, Caitlin and Iris didn't look as pleased.

"Can you use the old readings in any way to find him now?" Iris asked warily.

"No. It'd have to be exactly when it was happening."

Iris gasped. "Oh no... No, Cisco. You can't let her do that! Do you remember how near she came to changing completely? You corrected the device, didn't you?"

"Temporarily. I have to do a few more things to make it permanent."

"Well, do it now! Caitlin can't risk another incident like that!"

Cisco spread his hands. "Iris—"

"No!" Caitlin broke in." She patted the hand Iris had placed on her other one. "Iris... I'm so very grateful for all your concern, but I need to do this. I can't let anything happen if it's the best chance to..." She trailed off, but her eyes shifted to Cisco.

Iris didn't miss the look. "What is that? What's going on that *I* should know about? Oh dear God!"

She grabbed for her phone, pulling it up before Cisco could bring himself to say anything.

"Wait!" He ran a hand through his hair. "Iris... the Weather Wizard has Joe. It just happened a short time ago."

"What? After everyone promised me he'd be safe? Where's Barry? And Wally? Are they all right?"

"Wally got knocked around again, but he's okay. He and Barry are out there right now, crisscrossing the city over and over." To Caitlin, he said, "Listen. Between the two of them, they'll scour things like no one else can! We probably won't even need to do what we just discussed—"

Frowning, Caitlin interjected, "I can't take that chance. Not and risk Joe. If I can help you pinpoint the Weather Wizard, I'm willing to take the risk."

"No, Caitlin. I can't let you. Not even for my father."

Caitlin ignored her. "Cisco, is there any way to prevent it from affecting me very much?"

"I've got the device attuned as much as I can without putting together a proper update. We don't want to do that right now, though. Without it on, if Mardon starts to do anything, you might not be able to keep from giving in to your powers."

"So, how likely is this to protect me then?"

Cisco looked guilty. "To be honest, to make sure we get what we need, I'd probably have to return it to nearly what it was when you got struck down in your apartment."

She sighed. "I'm not going to think about it anymore. All right, Cisco. Do it. Put it back the way it was… but get something strong to knock me out if I start changing, whether it's due to Mardon or not. Make it as strong as possible. I don't want you to take any chances."

"I can do that, but it's going to take a very powerful sedative. That in itself could be risky. You know how strong you are. You're like Elsa on steroids."

"Do it. There can't be any chance of danger. You can't afford an uncontrolled Killer Frost as well as the Weather Wizard. Central City certainly can't. If anything should happen—anything at all—you need to put a stop to me before I become a threat." Caitlin swallowed. "Even if it ends up meaning something permanent."

1 4

Slowly, so very slowly, Joe began to emerge from the darkness in fear. As he did, two things took his attention. The first was the throbbing pain coursing through him from head to toe. There seemed like no part of his body that did not hurt. It nearly sent Joe back into the dubious comfort of the deep darkness, but a part of him knew that giving in was not a wise choice. After all, there was a very good chance he might not wake up.

The second thing was the voices. Although he could not yet make sense of their words, he could hear and even feel the intense anger and bitterness in them. There was an odd orderliness to them that for some reason, even then, the detective could not get past.

Finally, consciousness returned enough to enable him to try to open his eyes. As he struggled to do so, fragments of memory returned. He saw police headquarters under attack again, and his son tossed about like a rag doll. The image of the man responsible burned into Joe's mind. Mark Mardon. The Weather Wizard.

And that enabled him to recognize one voice. Mardon's. That recognition stirred Joe to stronger effort. He finally managed to get his eyes open, if only as slits.

At first, only more darkness greeted his gaze. Joe blinked and blinked, gradually regaining his vision. Through tearing eyes, he at last beheld a single shape standing several yards ahead of him. The Weather Wizard. Joe instinctively went for his gun, only to find his arms pinned against him. It slowly dawned on him that not only were his arms bound, but so were his legs. Despite the tightness of those bonds, the detective squirmed around, trying to find some weakness he could possibly exploit.

Unfortunately, his movements, however slight, caught the attention of others.

"He's awake. Finally."

Still groggy, Joe couldn't tell who had spoken. He only finally assumed it to be the Weather Wizard because of the fact that only a breath later Mardon loomed over him. The metahuman forced Joe's chin up.

"Not quite with us yet. Almost. Here, let me give you a little jolt to wake you."

Joe screamed as electricity coursed through him. He felt as if his entire body were burning from the inside out. The detective didn't want to give the Weather Wizard the pleasure of seeing him surrender to the pain, but could not hold back.

The horrifying shock ended abruptly. The agony it caused remained for some time after, albeit to a lesser degree.

"That enough, detective?" asked Mardon as thunder boomed. "Or do you need a little more to wake up properly?"

Joe refused to answer, even if it meant more torture. He clenched his teeth, expecting the worst.

"The big brave lawman," the second voice, now also nearer, scoffed. "Especially brave when he has a gun on an unsuspecting target!"

There was something about the second voice that drew Joe's attention. It was not just that it had similarities to the first, but that the tone and timbre reminded him of someone in particular.

"Easy, Clyde. He's all ours now. He'll get the justice he never let you have. You'll see."

Clyde… Clyde Mardon… the detective managed to think through his pain. *Clyde Mardon… Only he's dead…*

"Him and the Flash. They've both got to pay for what they did to me… but only after you use the Flash to bring me back."

This made no sense to Joe, but then, the fact that Clyde Mardon was even talking made no sense to him. Joe blinked, trying to better see the other figure.

The Weather Wizard solidified in front of the detective. Some of the details of their darkened surroundings did as well. Joe identified the interior as part of a half-completed industrial building. That rang a bell with the law officer. There was a lot of industrial construction going on around the edge of Central City. The knowledge didn't do him any good at the moment, but Joe filed it away nevertheless.

As his eyes adjusted to the dimness, he finally made out the second figure standing far away from both the Weather Wizard and Joe. Joe strained in an effort to see detail, but failed.

"Detective Joe West, Central City Police Department," Mark Mardon growled. "Executioner…"

"Your… Your brother had every chance to surrender," Joe managed. "He chose death."

"The hell he did!" responded one of the voices.

Electricity burned its way through Joe again. He screamed, and when it ceased he fought for breath.

"I think you're *trying* to make me kill you quickly," the Weather Wizard rasped. "Well, it's not going to work." He leaned close to his prisoner. "I'm a lot better with my powers since Iron Heights, West! I can summon storms as I like. See?"

Mark extended a darkened hand palm up to Joe. As he did, energy suddenly crackled over the palm. Mist gathered to create a tiny, but dark cloud. The dark cloud crackled some more, causing several tiny bolts of lightning to play out over his palm.

"You see that?" Mark asked almost gleefully. "I *am* a storm god! Lord of the heavens!"

Joe saw Mark's display… and so much more. For the first time, he beheld the Weather Wizard up close and well illuminated. What he saw shook even a man who had worked in law enforcement on the streets for years.

Mark Mardon was drenched in sweat. He looked emaciated, almost as if he hadn't eaten in more than a week. His skin had a red rawness to it that made it look as if someone had flayed the Weather Wizard alive.

The eyes had an extremely manic quality to them and constantly darted back and forth as if seeking something. Joe noted that the whites were filled with jagged veins.

"Dear God," he muttered without thinking.

"So glad you agree," the Weather Wizard replied, grinning wider. He backed up, in the process dismissing the violent elements in play over his palm. "Pretty soon, everyone will see the truth of that!"

"You'd be better off putting an end to this by surrendering, Mardon," Joe blurted. "Can't you see what you're doing to yourself? Whatever you plan, it's eating you alive! Just look at yourself!"

To his surprise, the Weather Wizard hesitated. "What're you talking about, West?"

"I mean that you look like you're literally burning out! You need help, man! Let me bring you in and we can get—"

The moment of hesitation passed. Anger again filled the rogue's twisted face. "You got a lot of guts, detective, I'll give you that! Most in your position wouldn't have the brass to suggest I should give up everything and go back with you so that they can fit me with a new damned helmet!"

"Mardon—"

The escaped convict tapped his head. "Do you know what it was like having that thing playing with my thoughts twenty-four hours a day every day? Do you know what they considered 'healthy rehabilitation techniques', West? Scrambling my thoughts every few seconds so that I couldn't focus enough to use my powers!"

The news startled Joe. He understood that for a time Cisco and the others had had to take extreme measures to keep some metahumans under control and that Iron Heights had gone on further in their own way. Still, Joe couldn't blame the prison for what it had done. Mark Mardon, his brother, and other law-breaking metahumans presented a danger to people like nothing anyone had ever experienced before.

"But they finally screwed up. They made me stronger instead. You probably saw my handiwork at Iron Heights. I paid them back well, didn't I?"

"All right," Joe conceded. "Listen. I'll speak for you. We'll make certain they don't do anything like that again—"

The Weather Wizard laughed loudly, not a pleasant sound to the detective. Mardon abruptly spun to face the half-seen figure. "You actually hear that, Clyde? Isn't that altruistic of the good detective? What do you say? Should I accept?"

"What a crock!" came an answer.

Joe frowned. Although the figure had moved one

hand dismissively at the time, the voice had come from somewhere else. He shook his head in the hopes of clearing away the last cobwebs. So far, it was obvious the others had no idea where he was. Barry or Wally would have already been here to rescue him. For now, Joe had to do what he could to free himself. That meant that, in the meantime, he had to try to keep the Weather Wizard from proceeding with anything affecting him. Not an easy task considering the delicate balance Mardon apparently dealt with at the moment.

With few other options available to him, Joe tried to continue the conversation. "Just hear me out, Mardon. Obviously I'm not altruistic. I also know you hate me for what I had to do. I never wanted to shoot your brother—"

Snarling, the Weather Wizard gestured at Joe. The detective felt a strong wind wrap around him. Without warning, he was hefted high into the air.

A breath later, Mardon joined him. The Weather Wizard fixed his unblinking stare on the law officer. "Yes, let's talk about my brother, but let's do it in a more appropriate spot!"

They soared through an unfinished gap in the ceiling and into the storm. Immediately, Joe was buffeted by heavy rain, strong winds, and even hail. He could do nothing save try to turn his head away from the direction from which most of the elements came at him. Even then, he was battered hard.

His few glimpses of the Weather Wizard were enough to verify that Mardon didn't suffer from the rain and wind as the detective did. Joe suspected that meant that his captor could have protected him as well, but had just not bothered. The Weather Wizard needed him alive, but apparently just barely.

In the clouds, he finally lost all sense of direction. He only knew that they flew for perhaps five or six minutes before descending.

Joe recalled that Cisco had been working on trying to use the Weather Wizard's abilities as a means to track him. Unfortunately, from what the detective had seen, with the storm acting as interference, Cisco would need a far stronger display of Mardon's powers than this to be able to pinpoint where they currently were.

You have to keep assuming that it's all up to you, Joe. That saved you more than once when you were a beat cop. Mardon's just another hood, no matter how strong he is. You've outwitted better than him.

The Weather Wizard began to descend. Joe didn't thank any power until they were once more safely on the ground. He had not been entirely certain that Mardon would lower him slowly; the Weather Wizard might have decided that he wanted his prisoner alive, but in just what condition was another question.

The rain abruptly cut away from the bedraggled law officer. Joe thanked no one for the meager gift; he was soaked to the bone from the flight.

"Oh, I am so sorry," Mardon mocked as he alighted next to Joe. "Did I forget to shield you from the elements? Here, let me dry you off!"

The wind surrounding Joe spun hard, picking the detective up a few feet and whirling him about. Joe tried his best not to throw up as he went around and around and around. His captor laughed throughout the awful spinning.

Without warning, the wind halted. Joe dropped unceremoniously to the ground. The detective grunted in new pain as he hit hard.

"There," the Weather Wizard remarked with relish. "Now you're dry. So much better!"

Vertigo assailed Joe. He shut his eyes and concentrated, trying to regain his focus.

"Forgive me. I'll keep you fairly dry from here on, Detective West."

"Th-thanks. For nothing."

"My pleasure. Now, why don't you take a gander around us, just for old times' sake."

Not at all certain just what Mardon meant by this, Joe attempted to do as suggested. They were clearly outside the city limits. He made out the silhouettes of distant buildings and tried to match them with places near Central City.

Then he saw the ruined farmhouse just behind them. To anyone unfamiliar with its history, it appeared as if some terrible explosion had ripped it apart from the inside. Fragments still lay scattered in the muddy soil, there being few people out here inclined to even step near what many considered almost cursed land. Three battered walls gave about half the roof just barely enough hold to stay on, although Joe estimated that the balance could not maintain itself for much longer.

Oh dear God. He's brought me back to where it all began. There's no dealing with him after all if this is his state of mind.

"Feels good being in the old neighborhood, so to speak, doesn't it? Makes you want to reminisce, hmm?"

Joe knew that the Weather Wizard meant just the opposite. In retrospect, it didn't come as any real surprise to the detective to end up here, especially having already experienced Mardon's obsession with all things concerning his brother.

This was, after all, where Clyde Mardon had died.

Joe could make out the location from which he had fired and further on the spot where the Weather Wizard's younger brother had last stood. Joe remembered vividly Clyde unleashing the tornado. The detective could also well recall how, immediately after the Flash had succeeded in dealing with Clyde's creation, the furious younger Mardon had drawn a gun to deal with the disoriented speedster.

Joe had had no choice but to shoot.

"Yeah, I can see it brings back all the good old memories!" The Weather Wizard turned away from the detective. "How about you, Clyde?"

Following Mardon's gaze, Joe discovered that the shadowy figure was again with them. Joe couldn't remember having seen him during their flight, which meant that the Weather Wizard's supposed brother had to have followed by some special means of his own. Again, that made Joe suspect some new metahuman. A clever one if he had managed to convince the Weather Wizard of just who he was for so very long.

"To hell with memories," came that other voice. "I'm the only thing I want brought back now!"

The declaration startled Joe in two ways. The first was what the words insinuated, that this figure claiming to be Clyde Mardon also claimed to be wanting to return from the *dead*. That in itself would have been enough to shake anyone, but added to that was the oddness in that voice. Once more, Joe felt as if it didn't come from the same direction as the figure. *But why?* he wondered. *What's going on with that?*

"It'll be soon," Mardon promised his murky companion. "Got the Flash all primed up. He'll push himself more than ever. That'll be enough with all I'm holding together, Clyde! We'll get you back this time!"

"I hope so. I hope so." The figure pointed at Joe. "And then we get rid of that one too. Maybe after we first get rid of that daughter of his we found. Let him die knowing what it's like to lose someone."

For the first time, Joe lost control. "Don't you touch her!"

The Weather Wizard turned and glared at him. "You don't get to demand anything, West, especially that! You owe a life beyond your own if we say so!"

"No! My life for Clyde's, if anything. She's been no part of this!"

Mardon's expression turned feverish. "Maybe you didn't hear me! You don't get to demand anything! You took Clyde and you and yours will all pay if that's what gets him back! Isn't that right, Clyde?"

"You tell him, Mark. You tell him."

The Weather Wizard cocked his head. "Awful quiet now! Maybe you finally got the message!"

Joe couldn't answer, but not because of the Weather Wizard's implied threat against Iris. Instead, Joe was too busy trying to digest a new and monstrous revelation. Now he had some answers, but also more questions... not to mention more fear not just for himself, but for Iris and the rest.

"Yeah, quiet as a mouse now, Mark," Clyde agreed... Only it wasn't Clyde speaking. The voice sounded a lot like the voice the detective remembered from the younger brother, but it wasn't coming from any ghost of the dead metahuman nor even the shadowy figure.

It was coming from the Weather Wizard himself.

Cisco glanced over at Caitlin, who lay calmly on the table. Her eyes were closed for the most part, although every now and then she would open them slightly. However, each time she did, they opened less and less.

He looked at the small cup next to her, the cup in which a tiny amount of something to relax her had been added. Cisco got up and took the cup. Caitlin briefly looked at him, then shut her eyes again.

Iris, seated next to her, stared warily at him. "How strong is what you gave her?"

"Just enough to help her rest a little. According to my calculations, for what we're planning she can be asleep. This way, if anything changes in her, she won't be able to consciously attack us."

Iris didn't look pleased. "Just what are you thinking will happen?"

"I've run every possible scenario. Hopefully, one of the ones where we come out pretty much unscathed."

"'Hopefully'?"

Cisco shrugged. "I—"

The alarm went off. The two stared at his console. H.R., munching on a sandwich from what supplies Barry had left, jumped to his feet.

Cisco hurried back to his station. However, as he reached it, the signal died.

"What is it?" Iris asked.

"Let me see." He typed. "Not him, at least not directly. That's odd. The nature of the storm is changing again. Why would the Weather Wizard—never mind. I'm making some adjustments so there's no mistaking again. How's she doing?"

"Resting." Iris looked at the monitor near Caitlin. "It says here that her blood pressure and heartbeat are normal."

"Good. Then all we need is for Mardon to act." He studied Iris. "Sorry. I know this is especially hard on you. I wish it were otherwise, believe me."

She bit her lip. "I have faith in Barry and you guys. I have faith in my father too."

At that moment Caitlin twitched. The readings on the monitor momentarily jumped, then settled slightly higher than they had been.

"Cisco, does that mean something?"

He looked at the console. "Not getting anything here, but that's the point of this." Cisco added some information. "Making a sweep of all readings from here on. If the Weather Wizard's doing something, we should be able to pick up a slight but ever-increasing level to it. That should help—"

"Cisco!" Iris leaped up as Caitlin's readings began to fluctuate more.

"Let me check over here." He went to his console and looked at the latest readings. Excitement tinged his voice. "That's new! Right at the same moment. Let me cross-check it."

H.R. joined Iris. "When does this go from helpful to dangerous?"

"We're good right now. Hang on. I think I've just about got it."

He typed in a few more numbers. All the while, Iris and H.R. kept watch on Caitlin.

"There! I think that should be it!" Cisco straightened. "Cisco to Barry."

A moment passed, then Barry's voice came online. "I was going to contact you! I'm coming up dry, no pun intended! Wally hasn't spotted anything either."

"Yeah, well, take a listen to this address!"

There was a very slight pause as Barry digested the information Cisco gave him next. Then, "How recent is this?"

"A minute. No more! It's—"

"I'm already there."

On one of the main monitors, the signal marking the Flash zipped across and then down. Cisco shook his head in disbelief. As quickly as the dot shifted, it couldn't actually keep up with the Flash's true speed. Whatever Cisco viewed lagged behind badly.

And so, when the light had made it nearly halfway to the address in question, he knew that meant that Barry had already almost reached his destination.

From another direction, the dot representing Wally shifted only slightly slower than Barry's. Despite both Barry's and Cisco's preference, it was clear that Wally intended to be there for any confrontation.

"Is that my brother?" Iris called.

"Don't worry. He knows enough to follow Barry's lead this time."

"And does Barry know enough now to lead someone in there?"

Cisco kept his expression neutral. "They'll be fine. I promise. Wally will be very careful from here on. You'll see."

"I've heard too many questionable promises— Cisco! Caitlin's readings are changing!"

"How high?"

She paused. "Not high at all. Down, for the most part!"

"Down?" Despite their immediate situation, Cisco had to take the chance of looking at Caitlin's readings. What he saw disturbed him. "That's not possible. Let me make sure the machine is reading things right—"

An intense wave of cold air draped over him. At the same time he heard a surprised grunt from H.R. and a gasp from Iris.

A chill ran down Cisco's spine.

Though Caitlin still slept, her skin had turned frost white in barely a single heartbeat.

1 5

He's completely insane! Joe realized.

The figure that was supposed to be Clyde Mardon remained out of proper view. Joe no longer knew what to make of him or it or whatever it was that lurked out there. All he could say for certain was that it had a human shape.

The Weather Wizard continued to grin, an expression that more and more reminded Joe of a death's head. Mardon looked like a man possessed... and perhaps he was, Joe thought.

"Take a look at it, West!" the Weather Wizard roared. "Feel the storm? Every facet of it is me now! The fools thought that they were binding my powers, but instead they made me a god!"

Joe winced as lightning wracked their vicinity and thunder nearly deafened him. He also noticed the Weather Wizard flinch slightly as the lightning and thunder played out, although from the intense expression on Mardon's face, the metahuman was unaware of his own reaction to his precious storm.

Filing away that disturbing knowledge, he responded. "I can see you need help badly, Mardon. Whatever you're doing, it's tearing you apart! Can't you see that?"

The rogue's expression shifted. His eyes narrowed. "He's trying to keep you from bringing me back, Mark!" the Weather Wizard snarled in the other voice. Simultaneously, the figure behind him moved as if accenting the words. "We shouldn't take a chance. We should kill him!"

"Not yet," Mardon countered, face and voice shifting back to his own. "We need him for the Flash, remember? We need the Flash so we can build up the storm enough to resurrect you!"

Joe stared. Mardon actually believed that he had the power to bring back his dead brother. While it was clear that Mardon was extremely strong—perhaps the strongest metahuman Joe and the rest had thus far encountered—such a feat was certainly beyond him. Still, what concerned the detective most was what would happen to Central City when the Weather Wizard did truly unleash everything. Joe could see a catastrophe far worse than even the tidal wave. And caught up in that catastrophe would be his daughter, son, and everyone else he cared for.

He tried to work his bonds loose. From what he could judge, the Weather Wizard had bound him by hand. Joe trusted from past experience that anyone in such a hurry or so obsessed might very well make a mistake. Now, at last, Joe sensed a weakening. With his captive so helpless and his belief in his power so utterly complete, Mardon hadn't even bothered to check the detective for any other weapons. The slight bulkiness Joe felt by his back at the waist meant that the second gun he had decided to carry a few days ago was still with him. Mardon, with his criminal background, should have thought about a gun being hidden there. It was a piece of luck the detective was glad to have.

"Yeah," Mardon answered as Clyde. "Yeah, that's what I've been telling you all this time, but seeing him has me burning. He shot me like a dog, Mark! Let's get this done so I can make him pay!"

"We will," the Weather Wizard answered as himself. "We just need the Flash here at just the right point. No sooner, no later."

"No sooner, no later," the Clyde personality repeated.

Joe felt one hand finally gain some movement. He began twisting both wrists as much as he could without alerting his captor to his actions. *Just a little more.*

"It's coming soon enough," declared the Weather Wizard as himself. "Soon enough to get the ball rolling... or maybe I should say the storm roiling..."

To put a flourish on his words, Mardon raised his hands and summoned thunder. Now Joe wished that his hands were free just so that he could cover his ears. He felt as if his head were about to explode from the horrific din. In his struggles to block out the continuous barrage of sound, one hand finally slipped free.

The Weather Wizard noticed none of that. Instead, hands still raised, he slowly turned in a circle, then cried out, "I know he's out there! I know he's nearby! Looking to rush in and grab me... Come on, Flash! Everything's falling into place! All we need now is for you to make your move—"

Joe grabbed for the hidden gun and brought it out with one smooth motion. The other figure did nothing to stop him. His sense of justice and duty made the detective hesitate. Joe had never shot a suspect without giving him some sort of chance to surrender. It was not just what he had been taught, but what he felt.

"Damn..." He aimed carefully, calculating where the Weather Wizard's chest would be when the rogue spun around. "Mark Mardon! Keep your hands high in the air and surrender or I fire!"

To his bewilderment, the Weather Wizard not only did not obey, but didn't even turn.

"Go ahead, West!" the rogue called while still facing the other way. "You've got a nice clean shot at my back! Just like you love to take! Go ahead and fire!"

"You know that's not how it's done and that's not how I do it, Mardon! I had no choice!"

The figure slowly extended a dark hand toward the detective. "Not exactly how I remember it, West!" the Weather Wizard said in his "Clyde" voice. "And I got the bullet hole in me to prove it!"

"I don't even know what you are, but you're not Clyde Mardon!"

"What's the matter, detective?" the second voice mocked. "Don't believe in ghosts?"

"Don't know if I believe in ghosts or not, but I certainly don't believe in you!"

"So, go ahead and put another bullet in me then! Go on! You know you want to!"

Joe shook his head, in part in disbelief at the conversation he was having with the two parts of the Weather Wizard's personality and the murky figure. A part of him considered firing a close shot at the shape just to see what would happen, but he needed to save his likely one and only shot for the true threat.

"Gaining some morals, West?" asked the Weather Wizard in his normal voice. He had still made no move to face his foe. "Or just assuming the Flash will pull your bacon out of the fire? Isn't that how you always work?"

While the rest of what Mardon said was utter trash, Joe did wonder where Barry was. He knew that the Flash would not just rush in, but would try to choose the best moment and the best attack. Still, the Weather Wizard could not be allowed to continue unchecked any longer.

"Last chance, Mardon! Surrender now!"

"You'll have to be a little more specific!" the second voice countered. "Which Mardon?"

"There's only you and me here, Mark! Give up this game! I'm sorry your brother's dead, but he left me no choice!"

With slow deliberation, the Weather Wizard, his arms still raised high, finally turned. Joe wanted to fire, but Mardon had not yet given him cause.

The thunder boomed louder, shaking the very ground. In fact, Joe realized that each successive rumble was stronger, harder.

"My brother," Mardon said very calmly, "was lost to me thanks to you and the Flash, but he's returned to me. Now, one last step and I'll have him back completely." His expression contorted and in the other voice he repeated, "Completely. You said it, brother."

Joe kept a bead on his target. Thinking quickly, he responded, "Yeah? If that's your brother, then why is he always standing in the distance, like he doesn't want me to see what he really looks like? How about that? He's the one I owe, if anybody! How about he and I come face to face so I can see for myself!"

"Fine by me!" the "Clyde" voice countered.

"No!" the Weather Wizard shouted. Then, regaining his mask of calmness, he continued, "No, detective. You don't get that honor. Maybe when you're dead, you can come back and give your own thoughts on everything." Mardon's eyes narrowed. "Knew you had that thing on you all the time, by the way. Just thought I'd leave it there so you'd maybe have a false sense of security and believe that if you cooperated, you could pull a stunt like this."

"Keep your hands where I can see them and your mouth shut!" Joe ordered yet again. "If you so much as blink wrong, I'll be forced to shoot! I mean it, Mardon! I don't want to do that!"

"Enough blood on your hands finally? Too late, West."

Mardon's right hand started to move.

This time, the detective took no chances. He fired every round. Joe prayed that if he emptied his pistol, one or more of the bullets would do their work. It was his only chance.

The bullets soared toward different points on their target. Joe had spread out his shots to potentially take out the Weather Wizard in a number of ways.

Mardon's eyes narrowed. The ever-present wind surrounding him turned into a hurricane-force gale.

Come on! Come on! Joe urged his shots. *One of you has to make it!"*

A brief yet complete stillness fell over the area.

Mark Mardon smiled. In that stillness, Joe heard first one tiny thud on the ground, then another, and another and so on until there was one for every shot that the detective had fired.

The Weather Wizard chuckled. "Now that's over, why don't you just behave and perhaps I'll let your daughter live, hmm?"

If Joe thought that he was expected to answer, that notion was erased as the wind shifted to toss him into the air. Joe lost his grip on the gun and watched it fly far out of reach. A moment later, he crashed into one of the remaining walls of the ruined farmhouse. The collision left him senseless for a moment.

The gusts ceased. Joe braced himself as best he could as he dropped the short distance to the ground. No sooner had he landed than the wind erupted again. It pressed him against the wall and would not let up. The pressure was so intense it was all Joe could do just to breathe.

"You'll stay put now," the Weather Wizard said in Clyde's voice. "Enjoy! You're gonna have a fine seat for everything… including my grand and glorious return to life!"

The Flash closed in on the address. Although he had every confidence in the information Cisco had passed on to him, he doubted that it would be that easy to take the Weather Wizard by surprise. The speedster watched every part of the storm around him, certain that something held another of the rogue's tricks.

He could have kicked himself when he had heard the address. Before this, the Flash had assumed that the Weather Wizard would never go to it. After all, what was left to look at? Just memories for the most part. Terrible memories.

After all, it was where the Weather Wizard's brother had died.

Clyde Mardon's death remained burned vividly in the Flash's memory. Indeed, most of the deaths he and the others had been forced to confront in stopping some of the threats to Central City remained strong in his thoughts. Barry regretted every loss, even if most of those involved—such as the younger Mardon—had clearly brought it on themselves.

But more important than any such regret was that Mardon threatened those closest to the Flash. If Barry had to sacrifice both the Weather Wizard's and his own life to prevent anything from happening to the others, then so be it.

The Flash veered slightly to the side and started running in a huge circle encompassing the location where Clyde Mardon had died, along with the neighboring farms. He picked up speed, with each circle tightening the area in question.

The rain grew more relentless as he neared. The Flash kept an eye out for lightning strikes and hail, two of the Weather Wizard's favored short-range assaults.

"Cisco, what's your reading on the storm near me?"

"Two things! One, it's stronger the closer you get to the address—"

"Uh huh. Can definitely vouch for that!"

"Yeah, but it's the second thing that gets me! I've got the entire history of the storm on one side of my screen, but what I didn't pay attention to before was that the original core of the storm didn't begin over Iron Heights, but instead right over where you're heading!"

"Wait? Over Clyde Mardon's scene of death?"

"Yep."

The Flash grimaced. "Well, that can't be good. Keep me informed of any further changes."

"Will do!"

Barry cut the circle tighter. The storm intensified as he did so. Curiously, the focus of this area's madness appeared to be not the Flash, but where he was heading. The Weather Wizard had begun something, perhaps even whatever it was that he ultimately desired.

But we still don't know what it is… The Flash doubted Mardon simply intended the ultimate destruction of Central City, although if it came about, the rogue probably would not mourn.

Tighter and tighter the circle became. In a single breath, the speedster had reduced the area by more than half. The rain proved the strongest of his obstacles, coming down so hard that the Flash could not evade it entirely. Much to his frustration, he also had to slow slightly to avoid some of the less even surfaces around him. It did not escape him that the Weather Wizard could use the soaked farmland to create traps designed to at least slow him down.

The street in front of him was now a river. Suspicious of what might lie beneath it, the Flash jumped isntead onto the country road. He couldn't take it all the way to his destination, but for the moment, it would be useful—

Lightning struck well ahead of him—which meant right in front of him by the time it hit. Prepared, the Flash slowed enough to slip over to the other side of the road and away from the barrage.

The road crumbled beneath him, collapsing into a massive sinkhole apparently barely covered by a thin layer at the surface.

Too late he realized that Mardon had set a different trap, using the rain's ability to seep into every crack in order to undermine this section of land. Now, the asphalt chunks were spilling into the water-filled gap with him. All he could do now was flounder and sink as what was left of the road threatened to crush him beneath it or at the very least drag him deep into the murky water.

The moment he had finished answering the Flash, Cisco had left his station again. With Iris and H.R. still flanking Caitlin, Cisco leaned down to investigate what was going on with Caitlin's condition.

"Is this what happened to her before?" he asked them.

"This?" Iris gestured at the other woman. "Not exactly, but certainly the same direction. Can you do anything?"

"For anyone else I'd have relied on Caitlin for what to do. I figured something to help her relax and sleep would be safe." He reached for the wrist device. "Hang on."

Typing in a few instructions, Cisco returned to his station and changed over things on the monitor without paying attention to what was already on it. As soon as Caitlin's vitals came up, Cisco scanned them for any anomalies. "Looks like maybe I should've given her something stronger. She's asleep, but just barely."

"So what does that mean?" H.R. asked.

"It means that whatever part of her subconscious is tied to her powers has been growing on that level for some time now. That explains what I thought was a mistake in the programming. It wasn't a mistake— not exactly. I programmed it for Caitlin. I should've programmed it with her subconscious in mind instead. I should be able to take care of that pretty quickly."

Iris stared at Caitlin's pale face. "Is there anything we can do?"

"Just tell me if there are any changes, good or bad. Keep an eye out. I'm not going to trust that they'll show up at all on my screen."

"All right," she replied hesitantly. "What about Barry, though?"

Cisco adjusted his headset. "I was just going to check. Hey, Barry!"

Silence filled the lab. Iris and H.R. looked at one another, then at Cisco.

"Hey, Barry!" he repeated.

"What is it?" Iris asked worriedly.

"Let me turn it up and check." He adjusted the settings, then listened. Several tense seconds ticked by. "Static." Cisco said. "Just like the other times. I was hoping it wouldn't happen again, but, of course, it has."

"So we have no contact with him? You can't be serious! First Caitlin and now Barry?"

Cisco shrugged an apology. "It's been happening on and off since Mardon's escape. With all his control over lightning and such, it's not surprising. Should take just a—"

"Uh, Cisco—" H.R. interrupted.

"What is it?" Cisco waited, but after several seconds of silence, called back, "H.R.?"

Still no reply.

Cisco finally looked over his shoulder… and gaped. "Iris! H.R.!"

He had hardly looked away—a minute at most— yet now frost coated everything around Caitlin. The table, the attached equipment, the surrounding floor… all of it glistened with a fine coat of frost.

But that was not what put such an expression of fear and dismay on Cisco's face. What did was what had happened to both Iris and H.R. The pair stood utterly motionless next to Caitlin, their gazes still on Cisco… and their bodies covered in frost.

1 6

"No…" Caught up by the horrific spectacle, Cisco almost inadvertently touched H.R. on the shoulder, only thinking about what might happen if he did at the last moment. He did not want to become part of the monstrous tableau. Nor, though, could he leave his friends in such a condition. It was possible that they were experiencing a cryogenic situation—something the group had come across in the past—but just as possible was the danger that they were quickly freezing to death. Either way, Cisco had to work fast.

He eyed the device. Coming around, Cisco reached for it… only to hesitate again. The layer of frost covering it looked brittle enough to break, but again Cisco wondered whether or not he would simply trap himself.

"Remote!" he blurted, slapping his forehead. "Do it by remote, you genius."

He quickly set up things on the screen, then considered. Nodding, Cisco went back to the device to see what, if any, changes had occurred in the system. After verifying everything with the data on the screen, Cisco realized that his best bet was to keep going back and forth between his station and the device, thus enabling him to continually verify that the data and programming he fed into the latter were actually being accepted. He had already come to realize that not all the data he was sending was actually reaching the device. Cisco knew that would mean he would have to be ready to modify the programs in progress at a moment's notice.

As he returned to his station again, he tried one last time to contact the Flash. "Barry! Dude! Can you hear me? Barry! Can you hear me?"

He received no response in return. Cisco adjusted the system, but only received more static.

"I'll take care of you right after, buddy," he muttered. "I promise!" He knew that the Flash would have readily agreed with his decision, but it still left Cisco with a sour taste. They were *all* his friends. No matter how good the reason, it now came down to him having to seemingly abandon one friend for another, something that went against the grain.

"Just do something!" Cisco muttered to himself. He switched everything over to Caitlin's records and quickly pored over her vitals. Most registered as he had expected, low and slow. One caught his attention, however. The hypothalamus was giving off strong readings. Indeed, its activity appeared to be increasing with each passing moment, something that Cisco had not noticed in previous periods.

Rubbing his chin, Cisco brought up earlier data involving Caitlin's hypothalamus. As the first numbers popped up, he grimaced at the revelation. Caught up in monitoring so many other aspects of metahuman biology, Cisco and the others had not really looked over the hypothalamus as much as they had other parts of the brain.

"Well, we're changing that now," he growled under his breath. The new data gave him a good idea of why the device had begun to fail Caitlin. Cisco's machine had been designed to counter other functions of her brain. He had completely ignored the hypothalamus, which, among other things, controlled many of the very basic functions of the brain. Emotional things. Desires. Simple needs.

Cisco started plugging in numbers, quickly running several scenarios. Unfortunately, none of them showed that reprogramming the device accordingly would compensate for Caitlin's stirring powers.

He peered over his shoulder at the trio... and gritted his teeth as he saw the frost spreading farther. Now it covered the tables, equipment, and floor for more than three yards in any direction. In fact, Cisco could actually see it actively expanding, especially, it seemed, toward him.

"Not good." With the frost to spur him on, Cisco plugged in new numbers and ran more scenarios. All came up as utter failures. The defeats didn't surprise him; Caitlin would have better understood a situation involving the hypothalamus; Cisco was a programmer at heart, not an anatomist.

Still, all his work with Barry had not left him ignorant of the brain and its functions, nor where he might quickly get more necessary knowledge. Cisco called up several pages replete with diagrams. He ran a finger across the screen as he followed the details of one in particular.

"That could be it," he whispered, pulling his collar tight against the cold. "Maybe if I—"

It suddenly sank in that he should not have been so cold.

Cisco leaped away from his station as frost spread rapidly over the spot he had just vacated. It coursed up his chair, covering the piece of furniture seconds later. All along, the change was accompanied by a sinister crackling sound as the frost took hold.

Taking a stapler from the work station, Cisco leaned over and struck the frost all over his seat. The frost gave way with a satisfying crunch. Cisco grinned in satisfaction and moved to sweep the pieces aside.

The shattered frost mended together, quickly growing into one solid mass again.

Growling, he brought the stapler down again. This time, it didn't even crack the frost, and when Cisco raised it again, it was to discover a dent.

He glanced at Caitlin and the others, but saw no

change in any of them. Still, Cisco could not deny what else he was seeing. The frost had spread specifically in *his* direction. Worse, he now saw it moving in a path that would, in seconds, leave him with no path out.

Cisco put aside the useless and now damaged stapler. Grabbing his phone, he skirted around the encroaching frost. He grunted in dismay as it took an immediate turn after him. *It's following!* he realized.

Barreling through the doors, Cisco flattened back against the wall opposite the main lab. For a moment, he stood there catching his breath and silently reminding himself to get back on an exercise regimen should he make it through this alive.

A slight crackling sound arose from the lab, a sound that drew closer to the doors through which he'd just run. Cisco took a look down both ends of the hall, then ran down the one leading to the smaller lab Caitlin had once disappeared into. At the doorway, he paused to listen for anything inside before slipping through.

Compared to the main lab, this one was toasty. Too hot, in fact. Cisco checked the thermostat and discovered the heat not only on, but very high. He had to assume that one of his friends had set it so due to the previous incidents with Caitlin... Perhaps even Caitlin herself in one of her lucid times.

Cisco started to change the temperature, then thought better of it. If, as he feared, the frost was still following after, even a second or two extra might be enough to buy him the time he needed to find an answer.

Darting over to one of the unused stations, Cisco flicked on the computer. The moment it was up, he started calling up the programs and data.

"Come on, come on," he muttered. "Why the heck didn't we upgrade these machines when we did the ones in the main lab? Might as well be running on Commodore 64s..." Despite the overall excellent capability of the computer before him, compared to his usual station things seemed to take forever. Cisco kept eyeing the doorway, watching for telltale signs of the spreading frost.

At last he had everything set up on the screen. Unfortunately, that was the simple part, he knew. Cisco now had to remotely correct for everything he had learned and hope that he could then relay the update to the device.

It was not lost on him that Caitlin had begun reacting to even the slightest surge of the Weather Wizard's power. As he scanned the latest readings, Cisco saw that Mardon had become so inherently bound to the storm— and the weather surrounding Central City in general— that his very life now affected her. Cisco marveled that the Weather Wizard could survive so much power not only coursing through him, but clearly building up. *He should be burning up*, Cisco thought. *He should be a cinder...*

"Oh boy..."

He hoped he was wrong. He prayed he was wrong.

Cisco called up the readings concerning Mardon and studied them with a new, more critical eye.

The Weather Wizard *was* burning up, and at a suddenly accelerating pace.

But that wasn't the half of it, Cisco knew now.

He typed in a few thoughts to verify his worry. Sure enough, there would come a point, at least theoretically, when Mardon's body would not be able to control all this fury. The Weather Wizard would be destroyed—but in perishing would also unleash all that wild, pent-up energy. That would turn Central City's weather truly chaotic. Storms would rage on and on unchecked.

Maybe even *permanently*.

A crackling sound stirred him from his work. He glanced at the doorway.

Frost covered the glass from floor to ceiling.

"Worry about the city later," Cisco berated himself. "You can't do anything to help it if you end up a popsicle!"

He returned to the update. With the data he had drawn from her, Cisco started cobbling together the update. It would not be a pretty piece of programming, but all he needed it to do for the moment was work.

The room started to get cooler despite the hard work of the heater. Another look at the doorway revealed frost creeping over the floor, walls, and ceiling near it. Cisco estimated that at the rate it was spreading, he had at most five minutes left before it reached him.

To his relief, two tests of the update ended positive. Cisco would have liked to have run a couple more tests, but had to hope for the best.

"Time to warm things up." Taking a deep breath, he hit the send button.

Nothing happened.

"Or not." Cisco did yet another check, then hit the button again.

This time, he just caught a glimpse of the update's quickly aborted attempted to upload into the device. Frowning, Cisco checked the link to the device.

As he feared, the problem was on the other end. The mechanism was not receiving the data properly. Cisco had to assume that the frost was affecting the device.

He tried again. For a moment, it looked as if the update would take… but once again failure took over.

"Oh, come on now…" Frustrated, Cisco tried to figure out what to do to overcome the problem. When he had created the device, he had designed it to be very durable. Somehow, he would get it working.

More cracking alerted Cisco to the fact that despite the heat, the frost was rapidly approaching. Cisco swore, then quickly typed in another program. This one allowed him a better chance of operating the mechanism on Caitlin's wrist from this remote location. If he could just activate a couple of emergency programs—

The first went into action. Allowing himself a brief smile, Cisco watched as the device came fully online.

He hit transmit. Again, the newly devised program uploaded.

Setting his hand on the counter next to the computer, Cisco watched impatiently. "Hurry up, hurry up—"

A tremendous chill stung his fingers. With a gasp, Cisco pulled his hand away.

The frost instantly spread over the area where his hand had rested. Cisco shook his hand to bring back the circulation, then peered around and discovered that he was now cut off from the doorway.

"This is not good..." He quickly returned as best he could to the computer. The update had just finished transferring. Cisco eyed the screen anxiously as the mechanism digested the new code.

The moment that was done, Cisco hit restart. He then stood back and pointed his fist to his side and away from the frost.

"Come on vibe powers, Daddy needs a doorway out of here."

Energy danced around his fist, tiny pale lightning that suddenly shot in the direction he pointed. The swirling energy balled together a couple of yards away from him, then began swelling.

"Finally! That's what I'm talking—oh, come on!"

Just as with his attempt to read the toothbrush, his powers abruptly faltered. The breach starting to form collapsed in on itself, the swelling field of energy reducing to a tiny flicker before simply blinking out of existence.

"Still batting zero, Zero," Cisco muttered.

A louder crackling made Cisco look down. All around him, the frost converged.

Cisco tried to back away but his foot would not

leave the floor. To his dismay, he saw that his shoe was also covered with frost.

The computer chimed once. Cisco looked to the screen. A series of new readings crossed it.

He grinned. At the same time, a hint of warmth returned to the room.

Cisco tugged with his leg. His foot came loose when the frost faded away as if never having been there.

The frost swiftly receded until the room was completely free. Cisco rushed to the doorway, then waited as the frost continued its retreat to the main lab.

The moment it pulled back into there, Cisco slipped inside. There, he beheld Caitlin, Iris, and H.R. still frozen in position.

No… Not exactly. Even from a distance, Cisco could see a hint of color in Caitlin's cheeks. He quickly studied the other pair, noticing some color in their faces as well.

"Man, that was close…"

The color faded away again. Cisco felt a new chill in the air.

He swallowed. "Aaaand getting closer yet…"

The Flash began spinning his arms. Faster and faster he spun them, slowing his descent and gaining maneuverability. Struggling to keep what breath he had managed to save, the speedster began pushing himself toward the surface.

All but blind in the dark, he failed to see the heavy

piece of asphalt that had just spilled into the gap. The piece collided hard with him, sending the Flash flailing. He nearly lost his air.

Pushing past, Barry renewed his efforts. Despite his abilities, he still couldn't say for certain where the surface was. Everything around him looked the same.

The water above his head abruptly stirred. Thinking that perhaps the wind was the cause, the Flash moved in that direction. Stirred by his failing breath, he spun his arms as hard as he could—

—and a moment later, burst to the surface.

The storm continued unabated, but the Flash barely noticed. Fighting for air, he slowly pulled himself out of the gap, then lay in a heap by the side as he tried to recuperate.

He pushed himself to his knees. From there, though, he could rise no farther.

Thunder boomed around him. The storm drenched him to the bone, but all the Flash could do was kneel and try to swallow lungfuls of air. He tried his best to keep an eye out for his adversary, but fortunately—or not—the Weather Wizard made no sudden appearance.

Grateful for that small favor but fearful for what it might mean for Joe, Barry pushed himself to his feet. In the distance, he saw the ruined farmhouse, a place where, if possible, the storm appeared even more violent.

"Okay, Mardon..." the speedster muttered. "Let's finally get this over with."

He raced toward the farmhouse.

* * *

Hail rocked what was left of the interior as Joe struggled—this time in vain, he quickly realized— to free himself. He knew that not just he but also the Weather Wizard were in dire danger. The latter was an odd revelation considering that even now Mardon worked to gather more power into himself.

There's got to be a limit to what he can take! The detective could see that the Weather Wizard was already suffering from severe strain, but trying to convince the rogue of the threat to himself was something Joe suspected was approaching impossible. Despite that, though, Joe persisted in trying. He had nothing else to do and there was always that slight chance that he would somehow get through to Mardon.

A barrage of lightning bolts cut through Mardon's silent casting. Hail showered the farmhouse, some of the pieces as large as softballs. Miniature tornadoes popped up in random locations, ripping up old bits of floor, dirt, and other refuse before abruptly fading away. The detective had finally concluded that these were not from some conscious effort by the Weather Wizard. Indeed, he scarcely even seemed to notice them.

If he had appeared haggard when he had first kidnapped Joe, the Weather Wizard now literally looked like death warmed over. He constantly panted from effort. His skin had the appearance of someone who had baked too long in the sun, cracked and dry and flaking. Mardon teetered now and then, but despite Joe's earlier hopes, never actually collapsed. Worst of all, as the detective watched, Mardon fell into more and more obsessive conversations with the figure he called his brother. Joe stared each time in disbelief and concern as the Weather Wizard filled both sides of the arguments, the rogue's voice and facial characteristics shifting completely whenever "Clyde" spoke.

"He's right nearby," Mardon declared as himself. "Right where I predicted he'd be."

"You're going to let him die!" snarled "Clyde" as the Weather Wizard became the younger brother. "He might die!"

"No, he's only being softened up," Mark Mardon returned. The rogue waved his left hand. "There. He'll reach the surface easily, you see?"

"Take him now then," "Clyde" ordered. "He's half-drowned, exhausted… He should be just ripe."

The Weather Wizard shook his head. "No. Almost, but not quite. I need more before we do that."

Joe still had no idea exactly what or who that figure was. He still leaned toward another metahuman masquerading as Clyde Mardon in order to manipulate the Weather Wizard, but as to what end, the detective couldn't say. Whatever the goal was, it was a risky, long-term one, or so Joe thought.

Meanwhile, of the Flash there was still no sign and that bothered Joe very much. It had seemed impossible at first that Barry could have such trouble finding the Weather Wizard even in the chaotic storm. However, more and more Joe became aware of just how thoroughly Mardon had considered his adversary's abilities. Essentially locked up in solitary confinement while incarcerated in Iron Heights, Mark Mardon had clearly spent much time considering every wrong move he had made against the Flash during their previous encounter. Even in his growing madness, those calculations had remained with him.

"Just a minute more," the Weather Wizard murmured. "He's coming. He just can't reach us yet, not until I open the way. He—"

With a horrific moan, Mardon abruptly folded over. The weather outside and in grew worse—much to Joe's amazement, who thought it couldn't get any wilder. Despite the Weather Wizard's predicament, the Flash didn't suddenly rush in and save the day as Joe would have expected.

Part of the reason revealed itself a moment later as the stricken rogue, despite still being doubled over, suddenly said, "Pull yourself together! You want to fail me again? Do you?"

"No… No," the Weather Wizard painfully blurted out. "I won't ever let… you down again, Clyde…"

In a deathly calm tone, the other voice returned, "No… I don't think you will, Mark. Now you take over again. I've kept running boy away from us, but now it's your show again."

"My show…" With great effort, the Weather Wizard managed to straighten. His face returned to normal. "*My* show…"

The air crackled around him. Much to Joe's dismay, Mardon turned to face him.

"Come here, detective."

A gust of wind picked Joe up and threw him toward the Weather Wizard. The law officer landed painfully at the felon's feet.

"Don't try anything stupid and I just *might* not go after your daughter when this is done."

The comment immediately caused Joe to struggle. He tried to roll into his captor, but failed even to accomplish that much.

Mardon laughed, first as himself, then as his brother.

Joe glared at the Weather Wizard, then at the figure behind him. "Your brother likes to let you do the dirty work, Mardon," he burst out, "and likes to stay far away from the danger. What's he got to worry about, Mardon? He's dead, isn't he? Why's he so far away?"

From the shift in the Weather Wizard's expression, it was very evident to the detective that he had hit a raw nerve.

"I've got no reason to be afraid of you," Mardon retorted in his Clyde voice. At the same time, the figure took a menacing stance.

"Easy, Clyde," the Weather Wizard added in his own voice. "All West here can do is bellow."

"Yeah?" "Clyde" interjected. "Let me just remind him of that, though."

The Weather Wizard abruptly kicked Joe hard in the ribs. Joe grunted in pain as the force rolled him over. He had no chance to see if Mardon's mysterious companion had imitated the attack.

"How's that for staying back?" the Clyde voice mocked. "I think I'll give you another so you don't forget—"

"Enough of that!" barked the Weather Wizard. "We may need him able to cry out for help, you know."

"Fat chance," Joe managed. "Not going to help you—"

He screamed as a very brief but also very painful shock from a tiny lightning bolt coursed through him.

"Yes," Mardon replied in a matter-of-fact tone. "You'll cry out if and when we want. You'll do it all and you'll help us put the Flash where we need him when we need him." The Weather Wizard gestured and another wind raised Joe several feet into the air. "You'll do all this so that the Flash can help me bring my brother back."

His face contorted and the Clyde persona took over again. "And then we'll kill you both."

1 7

The Flash felt his strength starting to fail as he raced toward the storm-swept farmhouse; fail not in any normal sense but as it had been doing since the Weather Wizard's manipulations had begun. Barry prayed that he would retain his abilities well enough to rescue Joe and put an end to Mardon's insanity.

"Cisco, do you copy?" Barry called.

Static greeted his question. The Flash called Cisco's name again, but was rewarded with the same lack of response. Barry could only assume that the storm and the struggle in the water hole had ruined their communications equipment again. The speedster would be on his own.

He neared what remained of the front doorway—

A series of lightning bolts struck in front of him, blocking the farmhouse. The Flash grunted in frustration as he veered off. His adversary had become very adept at timing his weather assaults.

Mardon had obviously sensed the Flash earlier and had probably set not only the lightning in motion ahead of time, but very likely other attacks and traps Barry had not noticed. In that manner, the Weather Wizard could be assured that, at the very least, he would be able to keep the Flash off guard at the most crucial of times.

As if to verify the speedster's supposition, beyond the farmhouse he saw another set of bolts rain down on the landscape. Brow suddenly furrowing, the Flash stopped dead in his tracks, then backed up.

More lightning hit just ahead of the path the Flash had been taking. Barry allowed himself a smile for having figured out the Weather Wizard's strategy—

He lost his footing as he stepped back without looking onto ground now covered in hundreds of pieces of hail. The Flash fought in vain to keep his balance and was forced to slow his speed dramatically. Barely had he done so than a new deluge of hail fell down over not just his location, but most of the vicinity too. Ever taking the Flash's swiftness into account, the Weather Wizard battered the entire landscape with the deadly hail. Worse, the lightning assault more than doubled at the same time, creating a nightmare scenario.

Doesn't matter how fast you can run if you have nowhere to run to, the Flash thought, not for the first time. Mardon knew him as few other opponents did and had just the right weapons at his command to make use of that knowledge.

But the Flash had been giving some of the Weather Wizard's potential threats much consideration in turn, especially the hail, which had literally tripped the speedster up more than once. Crouching, he gained back enough of his balance to proceed with his next step. Barry positioned himself and allowed momentum and the slipperiness of the hail to enable him to start spinning in a low circle.

Shifting, Barry spun faster and faster. He extended one hand out, creating a wind effect. The speedster pushed himself, building up the speed of his circle and at the same time causing a wind of his own to pick up.

The wind grew so powerful so quickly that it began to force the hailstorm back. Mounds of deflected hail, some pieces too big to even fit into his palm, began to gather a short distance around him. The general warmth of the region coupled with the heat generated by the Flash began to soften the hail as well.

Continuing to spin, Barry began sending the hail far off in every direction, including some toward the farmhouse. He did his best to see that it didn't travel fast enough to cause possible harm, only annoyance. The Flash couldn't take the chance of injuring Joe in the process.

But he was not done with the hail just yet. The moment a slight break came in the lightning barrages, the Flash stopped spinning and headed to the nearest hail mound. Scooping up an armful of the icy pellets, he pushed on into the ruined farmhouse.

Utter emptiness overwhelmed him. The speedster nearly stopped as he found himself running in blinding whiteness. Barry quickly turned about and returned to the outside, only to find the emptiness spreading there as well.

He now knew it for what it was, an incredibly dense fog. Barry could only shake his head at all the advance preparations the Weather Wizard had put in place for the speedster's arrival. Barry had no doubt that, as with so much before, the fog was yet another scenario Mardon had worked out during his stint in Iron Heights.

While on the one hand, all of these tactics made sense, especially defensively, for some reason they left the Flash warier than ever. For someone seeking vengeance, the Weather Wizard was going out of his way to keep his foe at arm's length. It was almost as if Mardon didn't want to fight the Flash, a peculiar notion contrary to everything Barry had seen of him so far.

What are you up to now, Mardon? the Flash pondered. *Just what do you have in mind?*

He stumbled slightly, this time due to his increasing exhaustion. That reminder of what else was happening to him made the Flash very briefly consider pulling back, but he knew that he could not until he at least had Joe.

"All right, Mardon," the speedster said under his breath. "Let's play things a little differently than we have so far."

Still clutching the armful of hail, Barry made one swift circuit after another around the old farmhouse to judge just how much land Mardon's fog had engulfed. It turned out to be nearly twice what he expected. Still, of the many weapons the Weather Wizard had, fog was one the Flash thought he could use against his foe.

"You like trying to keep others blind?" the Flash whispered. "Let's find out how you fare when you're the one that can't see what's coming at you…"

Taking a deep breath, Barry increased his pace several times over. As he did, he circled the outer edge of the fog. The wind caused by his speed quickly not only matched what was spreading the fog, but overcame it.

With ever-tightening circles, the Flash condensed the fog, pushing it into the farmhouse. He managed this even with most of the hail held in his arms remaining in place.

Finally, when he was nearly at the outskirts of the building itself, the Flash completed one last and very swift circle… then entered.

The fog was now so thick that the speedster could literally not see his hand in front of his face. In the Flash's mind, that likely meant that despite the Weather Wizard's powers, the escaped felon probably couldn't see any better. The only way for Mardon to be able to see his foe now would be to lift the fog. If he did that, then the Flash had him where he wanted him. So near physically, Mardon would stand no chance against Barry's speed.

Yet, thus far, there was no hint that the Weather Wizard intended to withdraw the fog. Remaining on the periphery of the interior, the Flash went from room to room to room, feeling his way along the walls while still balancing his hail in the crook of his other arm.

Still no sign. Mardon was not the type to abandon a plan so easily. He *was*, however, the type willing and able to stand in utter silence, awaiting his opportunity. The Flash needed only one mistake; unfortunately, the same could be said for the Weather Wizard.

Despite the risk, Barry slowed, if only slightly. Now he listened as well as raced. Mardon had to breathe. Joe had to breathe—

There was a very short burst of energy, like a tiny lightning bolt, to his left.

Someone cried out. Barry swore, recognizing Joe's voice.

He turned in the direction of the cry—

And suddenly Clyde Mardon—not Mark—stood right in front of the Flash. Clyde.

Clyde.

The Flash backpedaled. He stared at Clyde, who stood in the speedster's path as a vengeful spirit—

—and then was swallowed up once more by the fog.

"Cisco!" the Flash blurted. "I just saw Clyde! Cisco!"

Not only did Cisco not respond, but too late the Flash realized that he had come to an absolute halt.

The whirlwind formed around him, lifting him two feet in the air and then spinning him toward the nearest intact wall.

Barry hit the wall hard. The remains of his store of hail scattered everywhere. Stunned, he could do nothing as the wind ceased and he dropped hard on the floor.

As he struggled to regain his senses, the Flash saw a form looming over him. He looked up.

The shadowy figure of Clyde Mardon reached for him.

Staring aghast at what was happening with Caitlin and the others, at first Cisco didn't notice the small signal coming from his usual station. However, its incessant beeping finally reminded him of his other important task.

"Barry!" Cisco tapped his headset. "Barry! Do you read me? Barry?"

Static all but deafened him in one ear.

Caitlin stirred. Waves of frost and warmth alternately washed over Cisco, stopping only when Caitlin calmed again.

Swearing quietly, Cisco tried again, "Barry? Dude, come on!"

Once again, static assailed him. Cisco was tempted to tear off the headset and throw it away, but it represented his best chance of reaching his friend.

As the second wave of static rose in intensity, Caitlin stirred once more. The frost surrounding her and her friends took on an ominous deep azure tint.

Cisco rushed to his console and called up the update. He knew that somewhere in his quick patchwork he had made a mistake. The update was functional, but not completely so.

"Come on, where are you?" He surveyed every line, looking for something that didn't fit.

An idea popped into his head. Cisco skimmed over things again, then, shaking his head, once more uploaded everything into the device.

He turned in time to see the mechanism flicker twice. Nodding, Cisco went as close as he could to the frozen trio.

The device flickered once more.

The frost resumed its retreat.

Exhaling, Cisco eyed H.R. and Iris. Like Caitlin, they remained fixed in place. Frowning, Cisco stepped up to the very edge of the frost and studied Iris's face.

She blinked. Only once, but she blinked.

"Iris? Iris, can you hear me?"

Iris blinked again... then began to sway.

Cisco barely moved in time to keep her from collapsing. As Iris fell into his arms, he quickly pulled her away from Caitlin and over to a chair.

"Cisco?" she whispered.

"Easy. Let me get you a coffee."

However, barely had he straightened then H.R. also started teetering. Avoiding the frost again, Cisco came around to the other man just as he slumped.

"Easy there." Cisco helped H.R. to another chair.

"What just happened?"

"Things got... complicated." Cisco returned to Iris. "How are you doing?"

"Good... Except I'm still so very cold."

Cisco's eyes widened. "The coffee! Let me go get it. For you too, H.R.!"

"Do me a favor. Just pour it on top of me."

He brought them both something to drink. As Iris gratefully accepted hers, she asked, "What happened?"

"The frost spread quickly. Neither of you had a chance to even notice before it took you."

"I remember being so cold that everything went numb." Her eyes narrowed. "How long? What happened?"

Cisco gave them a shortened version which still left both staring.

"Barry!" Iris piped up. "What about—"

"Nothing but static on the link, but the system has his vitals still going, although he's clearly getting exhausted. I'm keeping up with both situations as best as can be done, but I need to finish with Caitlin before she has another bad turn." He rubbed his chin. "Not sure what's happening. Just when it seems I've got her back under control, it gets worse again."

"Is it Mardon?" Iris asked.

Cisco blinked. "It's been Mardon for everything else with her. Why not again... and why didn't I just put that together in the first place?"

Cisco rushed back to the console. After calling up the Weather Wizard's readings, he compared them with Caitlin's.

"She's in sync with his activity more than ever," he said to the pair. Straightening, Cisco glanced back at Caitlin. The azure tint had spread over most of the frost covering her body. Cisco had no idea what that meant, but he saw now on the screen that each shift matched some fluctuation in the Weather Wizard's use of his abilities. At first, the information did nothing but verify most of what Cisco had already known or assumed about the links between the two metahumans' abilities, but then something new occurred to him.

He tried the link. "Barry! Can you hear me?"

The static continued. Cisco no longer believed that there was simply something wrong with the equipment yet again. From the wilder and wilder fluctuations in the Weather Wizard's readings, Mardon was up to a major use of his power. It was not only affecting Caitlin, but the connection between Barry and the lab.

Still, what he had just learned gave him hope... Although for it to work, Cisco had to rely on Barry facing off against the escaped felon.

"So much riding on you, buddy," he muttered.

The Flash blinked, unable to believe his eyes. Clyde Mardon loomed over him. Clyde Mardon, whom the speedster knew to be dead.

Then, something even stranger occurred. Clyde Mardon lost all definition. His face distorted, separated. His body broke up into a thousand pieces that swirled around and around before dissipating.

And not even a breath later, the Flash beheld what actually hovered over him.

A whirlwind. A small tornado. It shimmered and shook and when it did the former hints of the solid figure it had once masqueraded as returned. There were even distended portions of the whirlwind where the arms would have been.

There was no ghost. There was no Clyde Mardon back from the dead. There *was*, however, a nearly insane man—in great part stricken with guilt and a need for vengeance—with such power that his very subconscious had pushed together something to match his desire.

The Weather Wizard had displayed no such ability when the Flash had last encountered him. Barry could only imagine that whatever surge of power had enabled Mardon to escape Iron Heights had also been responsible for this bizarre creation.

"Aren't you going to say hello, Flash?" a voice snarled in a good imitation of the dead brother. "You look like you've seen a ghost!"

Had those same words been spoken seconds before, they would have had much more of an effect on the speedster. Now he at least had a fairly good idea who was speaking for the false Clyde.

"It's all over for *you*, Mark Mardon!" the Flash emphasized. "Let me get you some help!"

"My brother's perfectly fine!" the fake Clyde continued.

"And so I'll be, once you've helped bring me back!"

The Flash could scarcely believe it. *That's the point of all this? The Weather Wizard thinks he can bring his brother to life?*

The whirlwind faded into the fog.

"Come on, Flash, get up and fight! We're giving you an opportunity to stop us!"

A gust of wind raised Barry to his feet. The Flash instantly pulled away from the wind, then raced to where the voice had come from.

"That's more like it!" the Weather Wizard added in his normal voice. "Push yourself hard! It's the only way you're going to defeat me… or at least maybe save the damned detective!"

A vaguely human shape materialized in the fog. The Flash closed on it.

He stumbled to a halt as he confronted Joe West. The detective was bound and bruised. He appeared to be unconscious.

"Don't worry, Flash," the Clyde voice commented. "He's not too badly off. We want him to see you go before we take care of him!"

"You've got me here, Mardon!" the speedster called, purposely utilizing the last name so that he would satisfy either personality. "Let West go!"

"We might do that… and we might not. For now, he's got his part to play."

Lightning flashed in front of Barry, forcing him to momentarily shield his eyes.

Too late the Flash realized what the Weather Wizard intended. Still slightly blurry-eyed from the lightning, the Flash nevertheless tried to grab Joe. Unfortunately, he had already vanished. Barry quickly threw himself forward, hoping to catch Joe, but despite his swiftness, he found no trace of the detective.

"Going to have to try a little harder, Flash! Actually, a lot harder."

Barry knew that the Weather Wizard was trying to egg him on, but the exact reason still escaped the speedster. Mardon clearly had so much power at his command; why did he not just use it to get his revenge?

That question sparked a plan. Rather than keep hunting for his opponent, the Flash came to another halt. Crossing his arms, he stood and waited.

It was only moments before the Weather Wizard reacted just as Barry had hoped.

"What's the matter with you? Do what you always do! Run!"

"Move or we'll roast the detective right here and now," the Clyde voice warned.

"I haven't gone anywhere," the Flash pointed out. "I'm right here. In your domain, Mardon. All you have to do is come get me!"

A new wave of hail struck, but again, the speedster stood prepared. He darted around, simultaneously evading hundreds of hard pellets.

Just like that, the hail ceased. The Flash paused again.

"That was pretty close, Mardon," he shouted. "Maybe the next one will get me."

Nothing happened... just as Barry had hoped. Yes, he now had a better grasp on what the Weather Wizard desired. Mardon did not want the Flash dead, at least not immediately. More to the point, the Weather Wizard had some need for the Flash to *keep* moving... but why?

"You're going to pay, Flash," the Clyde voice growled low from Barry's left. "You're going to pay dearly."

The voice came from so close by his ear that Barry reacted despite himself. Moving from spot to spot near where the Clyde voice had spoken, the Flash hunted for the speaker but found nothing.

As he slowed again, the fog crackled with more uncontrolled energy. At the same time, the speedster was overcome with a wave of exhaustion so strong that he couldn't help groaning.

It was another perfect moment for the Weather Wizard to attack, but nothing happened. Barry tried desperately to understand. All Mardon seemed to want of his foe was for the Flash to move, to run.

The Flash did just the opposite, staying where he was and hoping to outdo the Weather Wizard when it came to patience. Barry hoped that Joe would understand why he had not yet been rescued. Unless Mardon accidentally gave the speedster a true opening where rescuing Joe was concerned, the Flash dared not do anything. He had to wait the mad metahuman out.

To his relief, Mardon finally spoke. Anger and

impatience tinged his words. It was clear from the first sound that Barry now faced the Clyde personality.

"You can't stand there forever, Flash! You're a hero, remember? You're supposed to save the day! Well, start with saving yourself!"

Aware of what was likely to come next, the Flash braced himself.

Whirlwinds converged on him from several sides. The Flash immediately reacted... but only enough to evade each one. Whenever there was no imminent threat, he paused again.

The whirlwinds faded, to be replaced by an even thicker fog. Barry held his place, wondering what it presaged.

The roar of thunder erupted directly over him, the actual force of it dropping him to one knee. The Flash clutched his ears and did his best to keep from being deafened.

He eyed the new hail. Gritting his teeth, the Flash uncovered his ears and raced around his location until he had every reasonably solid piece of hail. Then, with the thunder still threatening his eardrums, the speedster took a handful of hail and started throwing.

Had it been a normal person throwing, the results would have been just a few pieces tossed uselessly in various directions. For Barry, though, one handful of hail represented a volley comparable to firing off a machine gun. The Flash tossed piece after piece and when his hand was empty, seized more from those he had gathered. In this way, he cut a line across the fog-smothered room. Barry silently apologized to Joe if some of them caught him, but the speedster didn't throw to kill even though he was quite capable of doing so.

Only when he had emptied his store of hail did the Flash come to a new halt. The moment he did, he noticed that not only had the horrific thunder ceased, but so had much of the rest of the foul weather in and around the farmhouse. Even the fog seemed less obscuring.

Squinting, the Flash sought out any shape. Something at the edge of his vision caught his attention and he raced over to it.

Joe.

At first Barry feared that he had managed to strike down the detective after all, but a swift study showed no hint that any of the hail had hit Joe. In the hope that Joe lay bound on the ground, the speedster had tried to aim high enough so that even if Joe had been sitting up, he would have faced little risk. Any injury Barry noticed now had obviously been dealt in another manner, which meant the Weather Wizard.

Joe was breathing regularly, a discovery that pleased the Flash immensely. What did not please him was the sudden ease with which he had found the detective. There was no hint of a trap on the prone figure, but the Flash couldn't believe Mardon would miss such an opportunity, especially since he wanted both the speedster and the detective dead.

The Flash took hold of Joe and ran.

He knew his mistake the moment he picked up the detective. Barry's inspection of Joe's condition had been necessary before he dared pick him up, but although it had actually taken Barry only two seconds of normal time to do everything, that human hesitation had been all that the Weather Wizard had needed.

The constant drumming sound had nothing to do with thunder this time. It was rain. Rain pouring down so hard it was as if a constant bombardment surrounded the farmhouse.

"No place to go, Flash," Mardon's voice declared over the din. "Unless you want to run in circles."

It's only rain, Barry reminded himself. *Just water…*

Outside, wood cracked.

Tons and tons of rain…

By himself, the Flash might have been able to rush through the torrent outside. Might. The sheer crushing volume of rain cutting off the farmhouse from the outside world made it questionable if even at his swiftest the speedster would have been able to penetrate it.

But with another in tow, Barry doubted he could make it. He didn't worry about himself, only Joe. There was no doubt in the Flash's mind that Joe would not make it through alive.

"Rain, rain, go away," Mardon continued in his Clyde voice. "Well, it all had to come back another day, so why not today?" The laugh that followed had more than a little madness in it.

The Flash took up a defensive posture in front of Joe.

Try as he might, though, he couldn't quite tell where the Weather Wizard's voice came from. The constant booming outside made it remarkable that Mardon could even make himself heard so well.

Blinking, the Flash noted that the fog seemed even thicker, so thick, in fact, that he had to struggle not to cough.

He quickly lost that battle. The first cough opened the floodgate. Behind him, even the unconscious Joe let out an occasional muffled cough.

"All choked up to be reunited with your friend, eh? Imagine how I'll feel when I can finally bring my brother back!"

Fighting another cough, the Flash responded, "That's not your brother, Mardon! That's your own mind! Think about it! You can't seriously—"

Lightning erupted right in front of him. Even with his incredibly quick reflexes, the strike still managed to momentarily wreak havoc with his vision.

"Come on, Flash," the Weather Wizard continued, once more sounding like his normal self. "Don't just stand there and be beaten down like an animal! Fight... Or can you only win when you've got an assassin to back you up?"

Barry tried as quickly as he could to blink away his blindness. Even so, he was not at all surprised when in the midst of the thick, dark fog he beheld an ominous shape surrounded by a fiery glow already nearing him.

"Fight me, Flash," the Weather Wizard intoned as he

coalesced. "Fight me. Give me everything you've got!"

The Flash said nothing, only stared at the monstrous sight of his adversary. He had noticed the telltale signs of stress radiating from Mardon during their previous encounter. Yet what the speedster had seen earlier did not prepare him for the changes he now witnessed in the Weather Wizard.

Mardon's clothes hung limply on his emaciated body. The lightning—for that was what it was—that played around his oncoming figure displayed skin reddened and moist with sweat, not rain. The Weather Wizard's eyes were not only sunken in some, but now also had deep lines that ran underneath them.

Those same eyes rarely blinked as the two men confronted one another. They burned through the Flash as if only half-seeing him and yet Barry knew that he was nearly the entire focus of Mardon's existence.

Near the Weather Wizard's left, a whirlwind roughly the same height as Mardon formed. Immediately, it twisted into a humanoid shape.

"Give *us* everything you've got, I should say," Mardon rasped. "We'll take it all… and we'll take it all *now*."

"Take it all now," he repeated a breath later in the second voice.

The lightning surrounding the Weather Wizard flared. As it did, the whirlwind coalesced more as it drew dust into it to form both body and face.

The brothers Mardon grinned triumphantly at the Flash.

1 8

As he stared at the Weather Wizard and the thing next to the rogue, Barry was reminded that metahumans were not just about their powers, regardless of how astounding those powers could be. They were still men and women, good and evil.

Creatures of emotion.

Barry had his own sins to bear. When he had used his powers to travel back in time and prevent his mother's murder, he had nearly unraveled the fabric of time itself. For a while he had even altered the fates of most of his dearest friends, including Joe. The Flash had finally resorted to going back and letting his mother perish as before so that things could return to as they should have been, and he lived with the guilt to this day.

For all his power, the Weather Wizard couldn't change time as the Flash had. All Mardon could do was grieve and obsess.

Until Iron Heights.

Cisco's brief comments and explanations returned to the Flash, especially that the same technology that had been the basis for the Wizard's Wand had been incorporated in the system designed to keep Mardon's powers under control. As Cisco had intimated, it had instead acted much the way the wand had, magnifying them.

That point Barry had thought he'd appreciated enough at the time, but now he saw that both he and Cisco had so very much underestimated what had happened to the Weather Wizard. Mardon's obsession had fueled his very existence at that point as nothing else could. All that had mattered was what had happened to Clyde. That constant thought, linked to the system, had built up in the elder Mardon until his subconscious had done its best to rectify things.

And so his subconscious had created for him as best it could a new Clyde Mardon utilizing Mark's available abilities. It had drawn from them to at least make a facsimile that, to the Weather Wizard's fevered mind, would pass. It had made Clyde a ghost, a way, no doubt, that had also explained the figure's odd substantiality to the surviving sibling.

"Mardon, that's not your brother. Clyde is dead!"

The Weather Wizard laughed. "Yeah, of course I am. You ought to know: you and the cop. That's the whole point."

Outside, the wind howled wilder, the sky thundered, and the rain continued to come down as if it were stone, not water. The remains of the farmhouse shook violently.

"The detective will be the first to die, speedster," the voice that the Flash identified as Mark answered. "Unless you fight."

The Flash lunged, only to run headlong into a fearsome wall of wind.

"I lay there most of the day and night, Flash," the Weather Wizard growled as Barry fought to escape the wind effect. "Every day so they could keep me from freeing myself. All I thought about was you and that detective... but I especially thought about you. I thought about all your little tricks, all you use. Every time you popped up on the rec room television, I watched every damned fight. I figured out every damn move you made. Just for when we next met."

The Flash continued to struggle against the wind. "Mardon—"

"Fight me!" the Weather Wizard demanded again, refusing to listen to reason. "Fight *us*!"

Another gust of wind struck the Flash from directly behind even as the first gust magnified. Trapped between them, the Flash couldn't even draw a breath.

"Fight us!" Mardon roared in both voices.

The Weather Wizard's readings were all over the chart. Cisco's eyes widened. The upper end of the fluctuations was heading into impossible territory. He couldn't believe that anyone could contain such wildly shifting power and live.

"He's like a living hydrogen bomb waiting to go off," Cisco muttered to himself.

He switched to Caitlin's readings and compared them to the actual storm in progress. The levels differed, but the patterns were identical.

"She's not really looking too well," H.R. announced.

Cisco turned. The blue ice was stronger than ever. "This has gone beyond stirring up her powers. Mardon seems to be trying to maintain and control power on a scale we've never seen in a metahuman and I don't think he can manage that much longer without suffering some consequences."

"Well, that's good, isn't it?" asked Iris.

"Yeah... If he were in the middle of a big, lifeless desert, say on Mars or something. Trust me, no one wants to be anywhere near if he eventually loses it. He'd take everything for miles around."

"Should we warn Barry about that?"

"Yeah, nothing like that's going to even have a chance to happen until I get this recurring communications problem fixed once and for all, and I've tried everything to correct it on our end. Seems the interference must all be originating from Mardon. Right now, I'm more worried about that than what theoretically might happen." Cisco grimaced. "I'm sorry I even brought that up. We need to focus on cutting the interference so that we can give Barry real-time updates on any tricks with the weather Mardon might use. If we can anticipate Mardon's attacks, we have him."

"So what can we do?"

H.R. raised a hand. "Question from the scientifically challenged?"

"Shoot."

"Anything you're trying to do to tamp down Caitlin's power that can be used for him? I mean, their abilities are supposed to overlap in some ways."

Cisco stared.

H.R. made a face. "Sorry. Like I said, scientifically—"

"No! Wait. There could be something in what you're suggesting... but first we've got to get her under control." Cisco eyed Mardon's readings and compared them to the storm's and Caitlin's. "Say, maybe... Iris, you see any slight change when you watch her? Anything?"

After a moment, she answered, "The blue got a little lighter, then a little darker. Just now. I think I saw that happen a few minutes ago."

"Six, to be precise. Same time as the storm and same time as Mardon."

"Same time as what?"

He started typing. "There was nothing wrong with the update. There was just too much of a wall or resistance when I tried to transmit. It's all about timing." Cisco pulled up the program. "Yeah, nothing wrong there, just as I thought."

Iris joined him. "Cisco, please tell us something we can understand."

He pointed at the screen. "See these low points? Caitlin's powers waned briefly then. I'm betting that if I'd transmitted the update then, it would've gone through without a hitch."

"So, are you saying that the correction you made only partially took?"

"Pretty much. Enough so it looked like it was a success. Some of it may even have shut down after initially functioning."

Now H.R. stood with them. "So you're going to send it again?"

"Bingo. All I have to do is wait for a negative fluctuation on her—there! Hang on!"

He hit the send button.

With a beep, the screen changed.

"What is that?" Iris demanded. "What's it doing?"

Cisco didn't turn his gaze from the numbers flashing across the screen. "Its full job this time, I hope."

There came another brief beeping sound.

"Is that it?" she asked. "Has it completely loaded this time?"

"Yeah, but we need a moment to see how it's taking."

Iris returned to Caitlin. "I think the blue ice looks a little paler."

"If I can trust these readings, it should. What we're really waiting for is for it to go away completely. Meanwhile"—he switched screens—"I think I know how I can finally restore contact with Barry for hopefully the last time."

"Same fluctuations?" H.R. asked hopefully.

"That and a strong signal boost at the same time."

"It's almost clear!" Iris shouted suddenly. "Now it's nearly just the frost again!"

Cisco didn't reply this time since he was both busy concentrating on restoring communications and not wanting to splash any cold water on the others' hopes. Until they actually rid Caitlin completely of the frost, the update could not be called a success, only a stalemate. More importantly, none of it would matter for Barry if Cisco had guessed wrong about how to reach him.

What Cisco had purposely not enlightened the others entirely about was that according to all the readings, Barry was growing more and more weary at the same time as the Weather Wizard's attempt to contain a greater and greater amount of energy within him magnified. Mardon was literally feeding off of the Flash, but at the rate he was doing so, what relative stability he still maintained would soon collapse. When that happened, the energies would burst free of their flesh-and-blood container.

And from there they would engulf and destroy Central City and all within it.

This has got to work. Cisco made one last quick study of the low point readings from the Weather Wizard and the storm. As before, by the time those readings were available to him, the window had always passed.

Only by measuring through Caitlin, who still reacted several minutes before the machines could sense the shifts in Mardon, could Cisco hope to do everything he needed to.

There! Cisco pressed the button.

The update loaded as before. Cisco wanted to feel confidence, but he had been confident with the last try and that had proven a bust.

"Come one…" On a secondary screen, he kept an eye on Barry's readings. Some of them were getting worryingly low. Mardon's, meanwhile, were nearly off the charts.

There was a brief ping. Cisco read over the results, then spun to face Caitlin.

"What is it?" Iris asked, new concern crossing her face.

"I don't know. We'll see," was all he dared reply. Not for the first time, Cisco wished that he had Caitlin to check on some of the more medical aspects of the situation. Of course, if she had been able to, they would not be in this mess.

There was no hint of the blue ice anymore, but Cisco dared not hope that this meant it would not return. He gingerly studied her face and hands without touching them, not at all certain that the frost might not still try to spread to him with contact.

Then…

Iris said it first. "I think I see some color in her face."

Cisco leaned close. Sure enough there was a slight hint of pink in Caitlin's cheeks.

"Is that it?" Iris asked. "Is she going to be all right?"

He still wasn't quite ready to say yes or no. Looking up from the unconscious woman, he said, "H.R.! Tell me what the main screen shows."

"Right!" H.R. rushed to the console. Leaning over, he remarked, "Looks like some very small hills and valleys. Does that actually help?"

"Yeah, it does."

"You've got kind of a smile on your face," Iris commented, her eyes hopeful.

"I should probably be more careful about that next time." Still, he couldn't hide his growing optimism, especially when he noticed something else. "Look! The frost covering the device is fading..."

Sure enough, only a very thin layer of frost remained. Cisco finally took a chance and wiped at what was left with the edge of his hand.

The flakes of frost gave way without any repercussions to him. Now he permitted himself a grin.

"Cisco?"

"Just let me check." He quickly typed in the codes enabling him to do a complete diagnostic and scanned everything carefully.

"It's working. Finally, it's working."

Even as he spoke, the rest of the frost covering Caitlin faded away. More color returned to her cheeks. She started to breathe normally.

"Someone get her a coffee or tea," Cisco suggested. "I need to double-check a few more things." Not paying attention as to who, if anybody, obeyed, he went about checking the results from the diagnostics. As he marked off each section, he also took an occasional glimpse at Caitlin's face. By this time, there was nothing there to indicate that she had just been through a hellish transformation.

"All vital signs normal. Looks like the update worked."

Iris returned with coffee. "Will it prevent this from happening again?"

"It should. What we need now, though, is for her to—"

Caitlin let out a small gasp. The trio waited for more, but she merely quieted again.

"Is that bad?"

"No. I don't know. I don't think—"

Caitlin opened her eyes.

"Cisco." She sighed, then noticed Iris. "Iris... I'm sorry. I didn't mean to—"

"Hush. Here." The other woman offered Caitlin a steaming cup of coffee. "I thought you might want something hot."

"I could use that now. Thank you."

Cisco studied her critically. "What's the last thing you remember?"

"Your suggestion that we use my powers to help track the Weather Wizard... Did it at least work?"

"Yes and no..." Cisco stepped back. "Right now, Barry's facing him down, but that's not half of it. I think we've got another, much larger problem with Mardon himself." He started back to the console. "A problem I've got to let Barry know about as soon as I can get into contact with him again…"

Caitlin tried to rise, only to fall back again.

"Keep on there," he called. "Rest up. Now that I think of it, we need you hooked up."

"But I thought you only needed me to locate him. You know where he is, don't you?"

"Oh, yeah, he's on the edge of Central City… which is still a whole city too close!" Cisco began typing. "Come on! This should work now. Barry! Can you hear me?"

Iris and Caitlin looked at one another. H.R. eyed their expressions then said, "Listen, Cisco, I can see we'd all like to know just what new catastrophe we're in the middle of. Care to quickly summarize?"

"You want a quick summary?" Cisco replied, never taking his eyes off the screen. "Whether or not Barry can stop him, Mardon's going to be stopped eventually… or rather, really soon. All that energy he's been gathering? I've done the calculations and boy, was I underestimating the last time! All of this is going to burn him up pretty soon."

"I don't see a downside to that, but I suppose there is one?"

"Yeah, a city-sized one. When that energy's unleashed, at the very least it'll turn the weather here even deadlier."

"And if not the very least?" Caitlin asked.

"Then Mardon will finally get one thing he wanted. No more Central City."

There was something more going on besides the Weather Wizard's obvious insanity. Of that, the Flash was certain. His ability to gather so much power together had not been evident the first time they had faced one another. Worse, gathering that power and controlling it appeared to be different things. If situation was truly as the Flash saw it, Mardon was near to being devoured by the very power he craved.

But before that happened, the Weather Wizard had something else in mind... and if the Flash understood him correctly, it was a plan both outrageous and grief-driven.

The Clyde persona had laid enough hints. Barry had finally put together the puzzle that had been forming since the first confrontation between the rogue and the speedster following the former's escape. Mark Mardon didn't just blame Joe and the Flash for his younger brother's death. He blamed himself as well. Perhaps subconsciously even more. It did not matter at all that he had been lying in a coma. In the Weather Wizard's distraught thoughts, he was still greatly responsible. Because of such thoughts, in his mind, there could only be one solution that would resolve all his turmoil.

Bring Clyde back to life.

It couldn't have been a conscious decision at the

time. Rather, Mardon's subconscious had taken command of the situation and finally determined that the only way to truly make amends would be to accomplish this impossible task. Erase the guilt as if it had never been.

Barry sincerely doubted that there was any method by which Mardon could achieve such a fantastic feat. Yet, in attempting to accomplish it, the Weather Wizard had brought together tremendous forces that should have been kept apart.

And here the Flash now confronted those very forces. The Weather Wizard couldn't have chosen a more deadly attack if he had planned it and yet it was very clear to the speedster that Mardon didn't even realize what was happening. The elder brother didn't look at all healthy. Clearly, whatever he was doing was near to killing him already, but he seemed not to notice.

"I don't want to fight you," the Flash insisted. "Mardon, this isn't your brother. Your brother is gone."

"Dead, maybe, but I'm not gone," mocked the Clyde persona.

"And soon he won't be dead," the Weather Wizard added without pause, "with your help."

The Flash had no idea how he was supposed to help with that and really did not want to know. He suspected that it had something to do with his increasing exhaustion. If so... If he was feeding energy to the Weather Wizard, then to Barry that meant that anything that happened to Central City because of it was in part his doing. Never mind that it was through unwilling means… without the Flash, Mardon would not have been able to become as great a threat as he looked to be.

"He looks rested up enough now, Mark."

The Weather Wizard nodded to himself. "Yeah, I think so too. I think we gave him more than enough of a break."

"Mardon, I don't want to fight you! I want to get you help!"

"You're all the help we need," "Clyde" answered. "And you will fight us, for him."

Too late, the Flash realized what had happened. He spun around, only to find Joe missing.

No, not missing. Floating several feet above him thanks to a subtle wind the Weather Wizard had grown behind the speedster's back.

"Being quick isn't everything," Mardon sneered. "Being smart is."

"And sneaky," the Clyde persona added in a similar tone.

The Flash raced at his adversary. He put a hand on the Weather Wizard.

A tremendous shock sent him reeling.

"Being smart is," repeated Mardon. "I'm more than I ever was before, Flash. This time, I really *am* a god."

Barry rolled aside before the lightning bolt could hit. Jumping to his feet, he used the brief illumination of the bolt to inspect both the vicinity and his opponent.

From the former, he gained little knowledge; the floor of the ruined farmhouse had little to offer other than crumbling refuse.

On the other hand, the Weather Wizard now stood revealed in the bolt's light to be in even more heinous condition than Barry had thought. The Flash noticed that Mardon's body shivered in sync with the electrical surge of the bolt.

"I am the storm," the Weather Wizard remarked coldly. Framed as he was by the fading light of the bolt, he reminded the Flash more of one of the animated dead from one of the television shows. This was no god, save perhaps of some ghoulish underworld.

"Let's try harder now," Mardon ordered, "and let's try expanding our horizons in the process!"

A wind took the Weather Wizard aloft. As he rose, his body glowed from the energy he barely kept checked within him. He spread his arms wide, then looked down at the Flash.

"Maybe he needs more incentive?" came the Clyde voice. "Let's play with the detective…"

With another gust, the Weather Wizard brought Joe toward him. Mardon waved one hand back and forth, the detective's motionless form swinging to match the movement.

"Still out, is he? Guess he's not so strong without a gun to back him up," the Clyde persona commented.

"What do you expect?" Mardon replied. "He's only human, after all."

"Not even really that. Just a cop."

The Flash watched Joe and the Weather Wizard carefully. With Mardon's body virtually untouchable, the speedster had to come up with another way of bringing down the Weather Wizard while keeping Joe from harm.

"Barry…" came Cisco's voice in his ear.

"Gotcha," the Flash muttered, hardly moving his mouth.

"Ah, you're facing Mardon right now. What about Joe?"

"Uh huh."

"Listen, I think—"

Above, the Weather Wizard suddenly gestured.

"Hold that thought, Cisco!"

Joe went flying toward Barry. The speedster attempted to grab him, but the Weather Wizard kept him just out of the Flash's reach.

"You know what I want of you, Flash," Mardon called. "Time to show off! Time to run like your life depends on it… Like his does."

The Flash eyed the farmhouse floor, which had been left half dirt by its destruction. The ground was dry due to the fact that Mark had kept the area around himself clear.

Kneeling, the Flash began digging up loose dirt and tossing it into the air in the direction of his adversary. The speedster moved so quickly that what should have been just a handful of dirt became a vast cloud.

But that was only half of what he planned. The moment he had enough dirt in the air, Barry spun his arm around, making wind that was focused at the Weather Wizard.

The thick cloud of dirt flew.

At the same time, the Flash ran to one of the remaining walls and used his velocity to rush up until he was on the roof. Once there, the Flash rushed along the cracked edge closest to Joe and used momentum to carry him into the air.

He seized the detective and used his remaining momentum to send them both toward another remnant of the roof across from where he had started. His feet barely even touching the weak wood, the Flash carried Joe down to the ground.

However, as he set Joe aside, he was hit by a wall of horizontal rain.

The force sent him crashing into one of the walls, which crumpled from the impact. As he fought to regain his equilibrium, the Flash also tried to see what had happened to Joe.

"It only takes me a glance, a moment now, to set things in motion," the Weather Wizard declared as he dropped down slightly. "A bolt of lightning, a gale, anything I desire, Flash! That, and knowing exactly where you'd pick! I like the dirt, though. That was original, from you…"

Leaping up, Barry returned to Joe. He carried him to the edge of the farmhouse, only to be stopped by the solid wall of torrential rain. Again, the Flash hesitated, not for himself—he was certain that he could get through the harsh downpour fairly unscathed—but he had never carried anyone with him while attempting such a feat.

There was no choice. Barry charged into the rain, his entire body vibrating. Simultaneously, he used his own vibrations to affect Joe's body as well.

As he entered the storm, the Flash felt an oppressive force push against him. Vibrating as he did should have enabled the Flash to evade being touched by even a drop as the water molecules slipped between his own. However, Joe's body had by nature a slightly different vibrancy rate. Barry, more concerned with Joe than himself, did his best to adjust his rate so that Joe received the most benefit. That, unfortunately, meant that with each step the speedster suffered more, something made even worse by his increasing weakness.

Finally, he reached the end of the Weather Wizard's barrier. The rain, although powerful in itself, was nothing compared to what Mardon had created around the farmhouse.

With a gasp, the Flash ceased vibrating. Despite the danger still present, he was forced to set Joe down and take a breath.

Joe moaned.

"Joe!" Barry knelt next to him. "Joe!"

The detective's eyes opened. "Barry?"

"Take it easy. I'll carry you back to the lab—"

Joe shook his head as if trying to clear it. "Listen… Mardon… He's crazy!"

"I know! I've seen him talk as both himself and his brother! Don't worry about that. Let me get you to—"

With a grunt, the Flash doubled over.

"Barry! What's wrong?"

As Joe spoke, Cisco's voice also filled the speedster's ear. "Barry! Do you hear me again? I lost you again, but I've made a correction! We should be good now!"

"Cisco? I'm not… I'm not feeling too well."

"I know! Listen! I don't know exactly what you and Mardon just went through, but it's caused an acceleration in however he's draining you!"

"Tell me about it… My legs feel like lead. I've got to get Joe out of here, though. Then I can deal with Mardon!"

"Barry, I don't think you can face him. That last encounter? Everything doubled. You face him again… Let's put it this way, I might end up being faster than you."

"There's no choice, Cisco!"

"It gets even better. What you're feeding Mardon and what he's gathering… It's going to make him 'explode'. When that happens… no more Central City!"

"No more—?"

"I hate to break in," Joe interjected, unaware of the revelation just revealed to the Flash. "But I'd feel a heck of a lot better if you would at least untie me!"

"Sorry about that." The Flash slipped around to the other side. "I forgot."

Joe glanced up at him. "You don't sound good. How bad are you?"

"I'll be fine if I can just lie down for a century or two—"

Barry's world spun around. Unable to stop himself, he slumped against Joe.

"Barry?" the detective called out in concern.

"Barry!" Cisco called at the same time. "Your readings are sinking fast! You've got to—"

Whatever Cisco prepared to say, it was lost as a tremendous explosion illuminated the sky for as far as the Flash could see. Although nothing physically struck him, the speedster suddenly felt as if his very soul was being torn from his body.

"Barry!" Joe shouted.

The Flash fought to keep himself conscious. In his ear, Cisco also shouted, but Barry couldn't concentrate enough to understand what he said. Barry knew that he had gone through something akin to this before, but now it struck him several times harder. So hard, in fact, that if he had not fallen against Joe, he would have now been face first on the ground.

He fumbled with the detective's bonds, but his fingers kept slipping off. Barry tried to get his hands to obey him, but they refused. He managed one tug, but the effort cost him too much.

The flaring light above grew so intense that even in his awful state, the Flash couldn't help but look up to see the cause.

The Weather Wizard hovered above them, his body not just aglow, but surrounded by crackling lightning erupting from all over his body. Each time the energies around the Weather Wizard flared anew, that feeling that his soul was being wrenched from him increased within the speedster.

Next to Mardon—and glowing with just as much fury—floated the grinning figure of the false Clyde. When the Weather Wizard laughed, he laughed. When the Weather Wizard turned his maddened gaze down at the Flash and Joe, so did the second figure.

The Weather Wizard gestured… and the Flash's world turned upside down.

19

"Barry!" Cisco roared into the mic. There was no reply, not even any static. Cisco knew that he still had a link to Barry and that the only reason that the Flash did not answer was because he could not.

"Cisco?"

He peered at Iris, whose expression more than mirrored his darkening thoughts. Both her father and the man she loved were out there. A moment earlier they had all felt a surge of hope on hearing that Barry had grabbed Joe from the Weather Wizard.

Then Caitlin had groaned and fallen back yet again. Cisco, quickly checking the stats, had discovered an approaching fluctuation more than double any previous. He had instinctively tried to warn Barry, but it was all for nothing.

Too late Cisco realized that he should have been doing something more to help the Flash. Now, though, he feared it might be too late. If Mardon had Barry...

Iris suddenly stood next to him, her expression drawn. "Cisco... What's happening? What's wrong with Barry?"

"Barry's readings are weaker, but still steady enough." It was not a satisfactory answer and he knew it. "And if Barry's alive, so's Joe." There was nothing to back that up either, but it was all Cisco could think to say.

Iris folded her arms tightly across her chest. "What can you do? There's got to be something you can do. Can we help restore Barry's strength somehow?"

"Unfortunately no... at least not directly and not soon enough." He thought quickly. "Still monitoring the fluctuations in the Weather Wizard's readings. There's chance if we catch one of the drops, but..."

"But you need Barry to do something then, don't you?"

Cisco said nothing, instead focusing on the monitor.

A grunting sound made both turn to Caitlin. With H.R. assisting her, Caitlin managed to get up on her elbows.

"I have to go face him," she announced. "I have to go try to stop him. These damned powers should be good for saving my friends at least!"

They all knew what she meant by that. Despite the danger to Barry and her father, Iris shook her head. "No. Not even for them."

"You can't," Cisco added. "You're still susceptible. You'll become Killer Frost. Not Caitlin with her powers. Killer Frost like we always feared, Caitlin."

His monitor beeped. Cisco spun back to it.

Iris joined him. "Is it Barry? Is he fighting back?"

"No. It's Mardon. Everything we've been talking about might just be moot points. I made some calculations earlier and imputed a warning into the system should his readings meet those calculations. They've just done that."

"What calculations?" asked Iris.

Running a hand through his hair, Cisco answered, "Unless Barry stops him very, very soon, it won't matter if Mardon wins. All that power he's gathered is near the tipping point. He's only got minutes before it consumes him and escapes."

"And when that happens," muttered H.R., "Central City will suffer. That's what you were saying earlier was a possibility."

Cisco shook as, for a moment, he saw the future. It was not a true vision, as he sometimes had, but merely a very strong knowledge of the energies in motion. "'Suffer'? If Mardon goes at this point, there won't even *be* a Central City... or, if my new calculations are correct, much else for a hundred miles in any direction."

The incredible weight his body had taken on abruptly left the Flash. He now felt like he weighed nothing, as if he floated free.

Another part of his mind warned him that there was only one reason for that.

Forcing his eyelids open, the Flash saw the approaching figure of the Weather Wizard. After a moment, he realized that it was not Mardon who was approaching him, but rather that the speedster was floating toward his adversary.

The Weather Wizard looked more like a demon than a man. His eyes bulged and his mouth appeared frozen in that great rictus. In contrast, the false Clyde drifted almost serenely and looked far more human even though there was nothing human about him. He stared in the Flash's general direction, but at the moment there was no animation, which the speedster found curious despite his precarious condition.

The next breath later "Clyde" lost cohesion. It was a momentary loss, but enough to give the Flash an idea... assuming he could free himself.

His thoughts turned to Joe. Quickly glancing around, he saw that Joe lay on the ground. The detective appeared to be unconscious.

The speedster refocused on Mardon. "What did you do to him?"

"Don't concern yourself with him. West will get what's coming to him soon enough." The Weather Wizard continued to grin. "Unless you think you've still got what it takes to save him. Want to give it a try?"

The Flash's brow furrowed. Even though his adversary had the upper hand, he was offering the speedster a new opportunity to rescue the detective. *Just what the hell is he up to?*

"Sure," Barry responded. "Give me one more chance."

The Weather Wizard laughed, not a pretty sound to the Flash. Still, just as he hoped, Mardon began to descend, bringing the speedster too.

But more important to Barry, "Clyde" descended with them.

The moment both the Flash and the Weather Wizard touched the ground, the speedster raced forward. As he expected, Mardon already had a wall of hail protecting him from the Flash's swiftness.

Barry veered away from his adversary, instead heading at the false Clyde.

The Flash had counted on a slight hesitation between the moment Mardon had created his own protection and the moment when the Weather Wizard also protected his "brother". With Clyde supposedly a spirit, Barry also thought that Mardon might even believe his adversary unable to inflict any harm at all on the younger brother.

Whichever the case, no hail shielded "Clyde". No hail, no rain, no lightning. Barry raced, assuming he had only a single second before that changed.

A second was all he needed.

Mardon's false brother stood frozen. Yet, as the Flash neared, he noticed that the figure was slightly out of focus. Barry had never noticed such a thing before and wondered about the reason for it.

He grabbed "Clyde"—

—And his hand went straight through him. Momentum kept the speedster stumbling along for several yards.

"Kind of hard to grab a ghost, isn't it?" the Weather Wizard mocked in his "Clyde" voice. "Maybe you should've thought about that when you got me killed!"

"You were never killed because you never lived!" the Flash replied. "Mardon! Can't you see what you're doing! This isn't your brother! This is some construct you've created!"

"Going to have to do better than that, Flash! My brother and I, we're of one mind, you might say!" As always, the changing voice came with a distinct alteration in the expression. The Flash couldn't exactly recall the idiosyncrasies of Clyde Mardon's mannerisms, but had no doubt that this other personality mimicked them perfectly.

In response, the Flash darted back. His target was not the fake Clyde, though, but rather *Joe*. The speedster hoped that the Weather Wizard would remain distracted long enough for the Flash to rescue Joe and get him far away.

But before Barry could reach Joe, the detective shot into the air again, hovering just out of reach.

"Knew you'd try that," false Clyde sneered. "You're staying right here until we're done with you."

The false Clyde form already had a hand stretched toward where the Flash had ended up.

A dust storm engulfed the Flash. Mardon had by

now become expert in calculating where the speedster would have to pause. The Flash expected the Weather Wizard to crow over his success, but Mardon remained oddly silent, leaving only the Clyde persona for Barry to try to deal with... assuming the Flash could escape the dust storm.

Barry quickly discovered that escaping was the least of his troubles. The whirlwind that was the basis of the dust storm kept accelerating. The increased spinning drew up more dirt, which in turn thickened around the speedster's face, and he began coughing as dirt invaded his lungs. He quickly shut his mouth and did his best to hold his breath. The whirlwind pressed at him on all sides in what appeared to be an attempt to either smother or crush the speedster.

In response, the Flash matched the whirlwind's spinning, using the very thing attacking him to magnify his efforts. Faster and faster the Flash spun.

When he knew he spun fast enough, Barry dug one toe into the ground. Then he began kicking the dirt he loosened outward so that it got caught on the edges of the whirlwind and then flew beyond.

A deluge of dirt flew in every direction, including where the Weather Wizard stood.

Mardon—or whichever persona currently controlled him—instinctively ducked the onslaught.

The dust storm faltered.

The Flash burst through the side. As he did, the dust storm lost cohesion.

Without hesitation, the speedster raced through "Clyde", tearing into him.

Barry quickly discovered a thick layer of dust particles and refuse inside. Despite his best efforts, those layers fought to stay together.

Seizing a handful, the Flash continued out the other side of "Clyde", racing to a spot far from the Weather Wizard. There he paused to inspect his prize.

Most of the clump proved to be earth, twigs, and crumbs. Barry tore through the rest, but found nothing out of the ordinary. That left the Flash with only one theory. The clumps had been added to give the false Clyde more substance. It could also be spread and shaped to add some detail to the body. In this manner, it had enabled the "Clyde" to look human from a distance or in the dark.

This verified to the Flash that the conscious Mark Mardon was, ironically, almost as innocent as the rest concerning the Clyde persona. Once more, Barry was reminded of what he and Cisco had discussed about Iron Heights and its experimental devices designed to keep the Weather Wizard nullified. Barry had no doubt now that much of what had changed in Mardon's head had done so while the metahuman had been asleep.

"I've got to get him to understand all this," the speedster muttered to himself. Thus far, Mardon seemed perfectly happy to accept matters as they appeared. And why not? Here Mardon was offered his brother back from the dead.

The inspection had taken no more than the blink of an eye. Abandoning the clump, the Flash returned to his adversary, more determined than ever to at least rescue Joe from what was clearly an insane enemy. So long as Joe remained the Weather Wizard's captive, the Flash's hands were tied.

The Weather Wizard remained protected by a series of storm elements that Barry could not infiltrate without being dangerously slowed. Then, all it would take from Mardon would be an expertly positioned bolt of lightning—

An idea formed. The speedster grunted. *Maybe it'll work. It'll probably be painful, but if it works…*

False Clyde stood ready to face him. Barry decreased his speed just enough to allow the Weather Wizard to be able to better focus on him. The Flash noticed a new shift in Mardon's features and wondered what that might mean.

"That's it, Flash," the Clyde persona urged. "Just keep it up. We're almost there."

False Clyde's voice was extremely calm, a direct contrast to the physical appearance of the Weather Wizard at this moment.

"Almost where?" the Flash countered. "What do you need, Mardon?"

"He just needs you to be you," false Clyde continued. "Can't you feel that? Aren't you ready to sleep? You must be getting tired, hmm?"

The Flash couldn't argue with that. Indeed, Barry

had been trying his best not to think of his growing weariness. Yet there could be no rest, no pause. One misstep might mean catastrophe for not only Joe, but the rest of Central City.

He noticed the subtle shift in the Weather Wizard's expression. Whichever personality controlled him now did not matter. Both had only one thing in mind for the Flash.

That made it no difficult choice when it came to reacting. The Flash turned on his heels just as the landscape before him exploded.

The bolts ravaged the area directly between the Flash and his opponent. Great chunks of earth, some of them massive, flew up into the air.

Twisting around, the Flash leaped atop one and raced up a precarious path toward Joe.

He snagged the still-unconscious detective from where the wind held him, then descended using the now-plummeting fragments from the lightning strike. Barry had banked on both personalities relying on one of the Weather Wizard's favorite weapons.

Alighting on the ground, Barry tried to carry Joe off. However, just as he had become fairly good at calculating his adversary's next move, so too, evidently, had Mardon.

Another powerful wind erupted in front of the Flash: *hurricane wind*.

Barry and Joe flew backward into the air. The powerful gust sent them rushing back to the Weather Wizard.

But Barry had been expecting this from the start. Still holding onto Joe, he turned and with his other hand threw the large rock he had grabbed from the fragments tossed up by the latest lightning.

"Ungh!" Mardon toppled back as the rock hit him squarely on the forehead, dropping hard on the ground.

The wind ceased. Clutching Joe with both hands now, the Flash braced himself for the collision with the ground.

It proved to be a softer landing than Barry expected. He was briefly jolted, but otherwise didn't suffer.

His first action was to quickly inspect Joe again. Finding nothing more amiss, the speedster turned.

Mark Mardon still lay unconscious. The storm continued to rage around them, although the Flash noted the unnerving fact that the region around the Weather Wizard—a region that still encompassed Barry and Joe—continued to be free of direct rainfall. While certainly welcome in one way, the fact that this element of the Weather Wizard's power continued to manifest itself was somewhat unnerving.

But not nearly as unnerving as belatedly noticing that the ominous figure of "Clyde" stared at him.

Just your imagination, Barry finally told himself. *Without Mardon, that thing is nothing. Nothing.*

This was his chance. The Flash pulled out a pair of the special cuffs designed specifically for holding metahumans. He reached for his fallen foe—

False Clyde transformed, losing all evidence of a

human shape and becoming another whirlwind. That revelation in itself didn't entirely surprise the Flash after his previous encounter with the false brother, but what happened next did.

The whirlwind faded away—only to re-form directly in front of the Flash.

More unnerving yet, in that same instant it returned to the semblance of Clyde Mardon... and grinned evilly at the speedster.

Uh oh... was as far as Barry got.

The rumble of thunder was so sudden and so intense that the Flash's instinctive response was to cover his ears. However, that did little to protect him against the quake created by the ear-splitting sound. Rocked by it, the speedster lost his footing.

It took him only a moment to regain it, but in that short space of time "Clyde" had swollen in size. The animated whirlwind—the Flash could think of it as nothing else— continued to wear the guise of Clyde Mardon, but a guise more and more distorted as the whirlwind grew. Yet always the eyes remained consistently on Barry, eyes that were and were not human.

"You'll pay for killing me!" False Clyde roared... only, as before, the true origin of the voice belonged with the Weather Wizard.

The Weather Wizard, by all estimations, was still very, very unconscious. Yet his mouth moved and words spilled forth. Somewhat slurred words, but words with meaning nonetheless.

"You'll pay for killing me," repeated "Clyde", the distorted figure acting out the words with a threatening stance.

The Flash tried to go around the false Clyde in order to reach the Weather Wizard. If Barry could reach Mardon, there was a good chance that he could get the unconscious rogue to dismiss this manifestation of what had to be Mardon's subconscious as affected by the system set up at Iron Heights.

But as swiftly as the Flash moved, "Clyde" moved even quicker. He not only blocked the speedster again, but with him came a rush of wind and a brief barrage of lightning that kept the Flash at bay.

And all the while, all very evident to Barry, was the fact that the storm, rather than abating, had started to grow stronger again. Stronger and more violent. The Flash heard the renewed thunder and saw bolt after bolt strike within Central City. There was nothing natural about it either, nothing that did not make him think that it was due to his fallen adversary. Even unconscious, the Weather Wizard had reached the point where his very existence meant danger to anyone around him.

Out of desperation, he shouted as loud as he could: "Mardon! Wake up! You don't want this! This isn't Clyde: Clyde is dead!"

The Weather Wizard stirred, but did not wake.

"Clyde", on the other hand, reacted by pointing one hand at the Flash. The speedster immediately dodged... only to see nothing happen.

A moment later, the hailstorm struck him from behind.

"Aaargh!" The force with which it hit threw the Flash forward. As usual, the padded suit protected him to a point, but not enough to keep him from collapsing to the ground, stunned and pained.

"I am *alive!*" the false Clyde declared to the Flash, his words slurred as they erupted from the Weather Wizard's slack mouth.

The storm surged, growing especially violent around them. The more violent the storm, the more distorted "Clyde" became. His body rippled and stretched. Now and then, pieces—a leg, an arm, his head—would briefly give way to swirling winds in which the fragments of body would spin about before reconstructing.

"I am alive..." continued the phantasm. "I am alive... which is more than you'll be able to say for much longer..."

2 0

It had been a struggle feigning unconsciousness for even the past couple of minutes, but somehow Joe had managed. It had been bad enough waking in the middle of the air in the midst of what had turned out to be a fight between Barry and the Weather Wizard, but at least twice Joe had nearly been knocked back into oblivion thanks to Mardon's purposely reckless handling of the detective.

Joe began to wonder if it had been at all worth it to be awake. Not only was he drenched—the Weather Wizard had not bothered to extend his protection to where he had finally dumped him—but he couldn't undo his bonds, which meant that he couldn't do anything to help Barry.

There's got to be some way out of this, Joe thought with much frustration. If not for him than at least for Barry. The world needed Barry. Iris needed Barry. It was not that his daughter was not strong, but in finding

Barry—and he finding her—a part of Iris Joe had never seen had awakened. A wonderful part that he knew he wanted—no, *needed*—to remain with her when fate finally did take him from her.

But that was for another time. Now Joe had to find some way to at least loosen his bonds.

Barely had he thought it than the ropes did indeed loosen. Joe marveled at this miracle until a familiar voice whispered in his ear.

"Just relax," Wally murmured. "Don't know what he did with these, but I'll get them undone soon enough, I swear."

"Get out of here," Joe muttered back. "Go on!"

"Not until you're safe. Now hold still." Wally tugged at the bonds. "And just in case, knowing you, I brought some extra insurance."

"Wally—"

"Quiet now. This guy has a thing with knots that being super swift isn't helping with much."

Joe let out a low growl, but said nothing more. Instead, Joe started praying that Wally would either figure out the Weather Wizard's knots or finally have the good sense to leave.

Lightning flared, lightning so obviously nearby that it could only have been summoned by Mardon. The lightning continued unabated for several seconds, further fueling Joe's concerns for Barry.

"Wally… What's happening? Can you see Barry? Is he all right?"

"Almost got it. Hang on. I'll seeee—aaaargh!"

Joe felt as well as heard the titanic explosion as another bolt hit just beyond where he lay. Not only did the lightning bring down his son, but it also threw him past the detective. Joe could do nothing as it happened save pray Wally would be all right. He silently cursed at the Weather Wizard, cursed at his own carelessness, and even cursed the damned ropes.

He felt the ropes loosen more.

Joe made no sound or movement that could be noticed by anyone. He gingerly felt the ropes to verify that Wally had managed to indeed slightly undo some of them.

Good man! Joe thought to his son. He tried to think optimistically about Wally even though there had been no sound since the lightning bolt. What he would do if he freed himself, the detective couldn't say. Over the course of his career, he had many times been forced to improvise on the job. He would do so now, whatever it took.

He shifted slightly… and stared. Wally was out of his sight, but something he had clearly dropped when he was hit lay just out of arm's reach.

And just in case, knowing you, I brought some extra insurance, Wally had said.

Joe smiled grimly, thinking in great part of Wally's potential sacrifice. Wally had indeed thought ahead. The odds were still against the detective, but they had just gotten a whole lot better…

* * *

At first the Flash had not quite understood what had happened. Although facing Barry, the false Clyde had suddenly apparently unleashed elements of the storm on something else nearby.

No. Not something. Someone.

"Joe!" the speedster blurted. The foul weather had prevented him from seeing exactly where Joe had been deposited, but Barr0y had no idea who or what else would have been targeted by the Weather Wizard's power.

The very thought that a helpless captive would still suffer the rogue's fury enraged the Flash. He wanted to race past his foe and see to Joe, but he knew that was probably just what Mardon wanted.

Mardon. Barry had faced a variety of bizarre adversaries, but nothing like what stood before him. The Weather Wizard lay unconscious, yet some part of his consciousness not only functioned, but even seemed attuned to what was happening around them.

Even now, "Clyde" kept watch on the Flash. The murky, sometimes distorted figure made no move, no sound. The only time he had shifted since responding to the speedster with his outburst about being alive had been when Barry quickly regained his footing after the trick with the hail. The false Clyde had instantly adjusted his stance and the surrounding weather had darkened dangerously.

It's as if Mardon himself stood before me, eyes wide open, mind still in tune with the entire storm—

Could it be? The Flash raised one hand.

"Clyde" instantly shifted.

"Uh oh."

The Flash moved just in time. Five, ten, twenty bolts left the area where he had been standing a charred ruin. Even as swift as the Flash was, the bolts had come exceedingly close to hitting him. It was almost as if the Weather Wizard had a better sense of what was happening now than when conscious.

But that's impossible… Isn't it?

"Cisco, you hear me?"

"I do. Listen, Mardon's getting entirely unstable! If you can't quickly convince him of the danger he represents to himself much less us, he could literally explode—"

"Cisco, hang on! How're his readings right now?"

"Going through the roof! He's one step from going nuke!"

The Flash frowned. "Cisco, he's unconscious. I repeat. Mark Mardon is unconscious, but, if anything, he seems to still know what's going on and is reacting through 'Clyde' and the storm itself!"

"Barry, that's crazy!"

"I know, but how else to explain what's going on? Cisco, 'Clyde' is just standing there, almost as if he won't do a thing unless I do!"

There was an uncomfortable moment of quiet on the other end, then… "Wish it was that simple! We've got a big problem! It doesn't matter if Mardon's unconscious or not! Looks like whatever he was doing to draw out power from both you and storm are still going on, but at an accelerating pace!"

"What's that mean?"

"It means that we don't even have a temporary reprieve going on! It's eating Mardon up and when his body can't contain it anymore, there goes everything. At best, we've got a few hours."

"At worst?" asked the Flash.

"We may not finish this conversation. Our best bet is to somehow get Mardon to let it go willingly."

The speedster eyed the Weather Wizard's limp form. "I'll have to try to wake Mardon up. I hit him pretty hard. At the time, I thought I *wanted* him out for the count."

"Do whatever you can, buddy."

"Yeah." The Flash stared at Mark Mardon. "I'm going to try something."

Cisco went silent again. The Flash took a deep breath, then moved one step forward.

As he expected, "Clyde" reacted instantly. It was almost as if in this state Mardon's mind worked faster, without distractions.

"Easy, Clyde. I only want to talk."

No new barrage struck Barry. Instead, "Forget it, Flash. Maybe you can plead for your life or that of your buddy. We might show a little mercy." The false Clyde grinned darkly. "Just a little."

The Flash noted a bit less slurring in the words. What that meant, he couldn't say just yet. "I'm not thinking about us. I'm thinking of your brother. He's not well."

"My brother's nearly a god… and when he restores me to full life, he'll actually be one!"

It's like talking to a living person, the Flash couldn't help thinking. The schism in Mardon's mind was so strong that the second personality—clearly born from the combination of Mardon's incredible guilt and the untested system Iron Heights had thought would nullify his powers, not magnify them—had grown dominant enough to exist almost separately.

The sky rumbled ominously. There was that too, Barry realized. So long as the Weather Wizard remained bound to the storm, feeding on its energies, then the Clyde persona also had those energies to feed upon.

This is madness! Yet the Flash realized that his only chance remained in trying to reach Mardon through "Clyde". Worse, if Cisco was correct—and Barry had no doubt that he was—then the window was quickly closing. Mardon would perish, but he would take all of Central City and much beyond with him.

Taking another deep breath, the Flash continued. "Clyde, I really need to speak with Mark. I'm not trying to pull a trick here. It really is about Mark's life."

"Clyde" shimmered. His expression grew slack. Barry realized suddenly that "Clyde" looked like an animatronic suddenly shut off. The Flash was tempted to see if he could reach Mardon's body, but then a semblance of life returned to "Clyde" and the chance passed.

"Mark can't talk. You hit him damn hard. Another

thing I owe you for, Flash. Almost as bad as helping me get killed."

As the figure glared at him, the speedster couldn't help thinking how used to the bizarre situation he had already become. Mark Mardon continued to be the actual source of "Clyde's" voice, but at times it was easy not to notice that, even despite the slurring.

Still, for all "Clyde" seemed more and more alive, the Flash knew that the truth was otherwise. "If you're here in front of me, that means that you should be able to reach him, Clyde. Do it."

To his dismay, the figure laughed. At the same time, various parts of the false Clyde also fragmented again. "You're a fool, Flash, but then, so is my brother. He's all broken up over his guilt, just like he should be. Only, he thinks he can actually bring me back from the dead, can you believe it?"

Something's not right here, Barry noted with growing concern. *Why is he talking like that?* "Listen, Clyde. Mark is going to die very soon if we don't help him—"

The murky figure smiled more widely... too wide, in fact, for a true human being. "Sure. That's been the idea all the time."

The Flash stood stunned. After a moment, he managed, "What do you mean?"

"Mark's been living with the guilt since he woke up. When we were young, he swore he'd protect me. He swore no one would touch me. He let me down. Now he'll never let me down again."

"Cisco, you guys getting this?" Barry whispered.

"Yeah. Talk about creepy…"

To "Clyde", the Flash responded, "Mark couldn't help what happened. He was in a coma. From the same accident that gave both of you your powers."

"He should've been there! He should've been there to keep me from doing *anything* that could have led me to getting killed! He knows that! He was supposed to be there! He was supposed to keep me safe!"

"Sounds like Mardon's got some big brother guilt issues," Cisco ventured.

"Really big," Barry murmured. He continued to glance at the Weather Wizard. Mardon showed no sign of stirring. The Flash wondered if there was more to it than a lucky strike by him. The Clyde persona seemed a far more dominant one than Mardon's own and if the constant rants about the elder brother's failure to protect the younger were any clue, Mark Mardon had been carrying around a tremendous burden. So tremendous, in fact, that a part of him had secretly believed he needed to face the ultimate punishment for that failure. "Got an idea, though."

"Well, that's more than we've got here. Go with it."

"You know that's not fair, Clyde," the Flash finally answered. "Besides, if he dies, you die with him."

"But I'm already dead… No… I'm alive."

Ah! The Flash had wondered if he had noticed a potential conflict within the Weather Wizard's mind. Mark Mardon was evidently willing to die to assuage his guilt. Yet the persona he had created of his brother had shown an insistent desire for life. The speedster wondered just how strong that second desire was. It was also based on the elder sibling's guilt, and past encounters had shown the Weather Wizard himself fearful of losing Clyde again.

"But you're only alive as long as Mark is," the Flash dared say.

"But he'll make me live again... No..." For the first time that the Flash could recall, a look of absolute confusion crossed "Clyde's" shadowy features. "No... I failed him. I deserve to die..."

"You hear that?" Cisco asked in Barry's ear. "He's talking like he's Mark Mardon now."

"Yeah. Maybe that part of him is waking up. We need that."

"I failed him... No... I will live... No... We are all guilty..."

The storm shifted along with the voice, rain and wind blowing wildly. The Flash noticed a couple of specks of rain on the other metahuman. Up until now, the Weather Wizard had had instinctive control over the elements. This was the first hint that his control was slipping.

"This may be our one chance," Cisco suggested. "If we can get him to the lab, we might be able to bring this to a safe conclusion."

"Agreed."

"Just watch it, though. His readings are still off the

charts. Mardon may look unconscious, but his body is still churning with power nearly ready to burst free."

Barry eyed the Weather Wizard. His body glowed faintly, but otherwise looked normal. Still, Barry trusted Cisco's information.

"We can help you," the Flash offered carefully. "We can bring Mark to a place where he can be helped—"

"'Helped'? Iron Heights… they said it was best for me… for him…" A new volley of thunder punctuated the last statement. The false Clyde's features turned more shadowy and less human. "Help… Iron Heights *helped*… We'll die before we go back there…"

"You better move, Barry!" Cisco suddenly warned.

The Flash had no idea what his friend had noticed in all the readings to issue such a dire warning, but knew better than to ignore it. He darted away from where he stood—

And not even a breath later, lightning ravaged the spot.

"We'll never return to Iron Heights!" the Clyde persona roared through the Weather Wizard's mouth. "Never!"

Wind, rain, and hail struck wherever the Flash paused. Try as he might, the speedster could not get close enough to grab Mardon's still body.

Then, a gold-clad form materialized next to Mardon. Wally, eyes on "Clyde", reached down and took hold of the unconscious rogue.

A wind swept past Wally and scooped up the

Weather Wizard before he could tighten his grip enough. Mardon's body went flying high into the air.

"No Iron Heights... No..." Mardon's Clyde persona insisted to no one in particular. He rose several feet in the air. "No Iron Heights ever again..."

Wally appeared next to the Flash. "Sorry! I thought for sure that I could grab Mardon and get out of there before I was noticed."

"You might've had a chance if it'd been Mardon himself, but even I'm not fast enough to keep up with thought itself!"

They split up just as a tornado nearly caught them both. The two speedsters met a short distance away.

"What did you mean by that and how's he striking so near to us?"

"This is Mardon's subconscious attacking us. It's pure thought! Maybe full of emotion, but still—watch it!"

He grabbed Wally and dragged him off as hail falling as hard as if shot from a thousand rifles decimated their new location. The entire landscape had been turned into a ruin akin to a war zone.

"What do we do?" Wally asked the moment they paused again.

"We're beyond trying to reason with him! We need to come at him from different directions at the same time! Follow my lead!"

As they split up, the two speedsters veered away from their adversary and then back again. Rain battered their paths, meaning they could slip at a vital moment. Despite the danger, the Flash had to slow down somewhat. He saw that Wally had had to do the same.

The two crossed paths, then kept going. The false Clyde floated in a circle above them, eyes seeming ever more attuned to Barry's route. That suited the Flash just fine. While he appreciated Wally's aid, Barry's preference would have been for Wally to take his father and go.

Thinking of Joe, the Flash peered around. There was no sign of the detective, which gave Barry the hope that Joe was at least safe.

As the Flash came around the Weather Wizard and his guardian, he darted in. Naturally, the storm's fury suddenly focused on him. The Flash braced himself for the worst.

Rain, thunder, lightning, hail, wind… the entirety of the storm's power fell upon the Flash. He dodged when he could, raced faster when that was possible, and prayed he would be able to suffer the rest long enough.

Wally suddenly rushed up onto the farmhouse roof. In one hand, he held a long metal pole.

Come on, Wally! Let's see how your aim is!

Wally readied the pole like a javelin—

"Clyde" changed, his form immediately reshaping so that instead of facing the Flash he faced Wally. Barry felt an abrupt shift in the wind and rain toward the other speedster and knew that the lightning and hail would quickly follow.

The shift in the wind was so immediate that it caught Wally off guard. He fought to retain his balance just as lightning crackled in the sky above him.

But in the midst of the accompanying thunder there came a single sharp crack all too familiar to Barry and yet startling because of its very existence at this moment.

False Clyde shifted again, this time to face away from both speedsters. For the first time, the Flash saw a glimpse of fear in the murky figure's expression. "Clyde's" body lost cohesion, with parts becoming the swirling winds of a tornado.

At that point Wally threw. His aim was good. The makeshift lance headed directly for the twisted form.

Seemingly ignorant of the pole's very existence, "Clyde" darted closer to Mardon's floating figure. The pole passed harmlessly by.

The false Clyde and the Weather Wizard suddenly dropped several feet lower. Simultaneously, there was a second sharp crack, the source of which Barry finally located.

Visible only in the brief illumination from the lightning, Joe West knelt ready to fire again despite the downpour. While the Flash was happy to see Joe free, the gun startled him. Barry had assumed the detective to be unarmed.

Wally. He must've brought it just in case for his father.

There was no time to worry anymore, about either father or son, for "Clyde" then chose to rise higher in the air, taking the Weather Wizard with him.

"No…" The Flash quickly looked around, but the tallest structure nearby was the farmhouse. Wally already stood there, clearly trying to do the same thing on Barry's mind.

Wally backed up as far as he could, then raced forward.

"Don't do it, Wally!" the Flash called uselessly, his shout drowned out by the weather.

The moment he reached the edge of the roof, Wally leaped. With momentum only a speedster could produce, he soared up into the air.

Wally reached the Weather Wizard, seizing the floating body by the leg.

The Flash expected both to fall, but the wind keeping Mardon aloft proved strong enough that although they did descend, it was at a rate slow enough to prevent any real harm to either man.

"Clever, Wally," the Flash said with a brief smile.

But suddenly both Wally and the Weather Wizard spun in a circle. Mardon's body spun faster and faster. Wally tried to hold on, but his grip slipped even as the Flash raced toward them.

Wally dropped. Mardon's body ceased spinning, then rose up once more.

The Flash looked around. Wally was too far up to land safely and the Flash knew he couldn't catch someone from so high up. Barry needed something better.

The Flash raced from the ruined farmhouse and down the road to the nearest functioning farm.

As he hoped, this time of year the crops were near harvesting. With a silent apology to the farmer, the Flash raced along, gathering stalk after stalk in his arms. Each time he had an armful, he carried it back to the site of the struggle.

A moment later, Wally landed… on a heaping pile of soft vegetation so high, it completely cushioned his fall.

The Flash rushed up to the top. "Are you all right?"

Eyeing the pile, Wally nodded. "I am thanks to you! And here I thought *I* was the clever one for knowing that the thing with Mardon would never let him fall to his death. I figured we'd drop slow enough—but then the spinning started."

"Are you all right up there?" shouted Joe from the darkness below.

"I'll take care of him," Wally told the Flash. "You get after Mardon. We can't let him get away, not if he's as dangerous as Cisco explained!"

Barry didn't argue. He moved to Joe.

"You two be careful, all right?"

"We will," Joe began. "But you—"

But the Flash had already raced away, following the trail left by the false Clyde and the Weather Wizard. High in the sky, he caught a glimpse of the pair continuing to ascend as they headed in the direction of Central City. As the Flash picked up the pace, he tried his best to keep both in sight. That proved harder and harder, with only the continuous lightning giving him any real view of either.

The night erupted into blazing daylight so intense that the Flash had to avert his gaze.

When he looked again, it was to find no sign of the Weather Wizard and "Clyde". The Flash inspected the darkening sky to no avail.

"No…" The Flash searched desperately, but again came up with nothing. The storm had swallowed up the Weather Wizard. "Cisco! Where's Mardon? I can't locate him!"

"Hang on!" There was a moment of quiet, then, "I can't find him either. The storm's reached a new level of craziness! The energy fluctuations are like nothing I've ever seen!"

And they're going to get a lot, lot worse if we don't locate Mardon quickly! Barry thought. He continued his search of the heavens. *But what can we do?*

The storm rumbled as if mocking his question. What could they do? If they failed to find Mardon, then all that remained for all of them to do… was simply *die*.

Barry and Wally covered the city several times, but could find no trace of the Weather Wizard. Cisco ran program after program, only to come up short each time.

And, meanwhile, the storm somehow continued to grow more frightening. The incessant torrent of rain shifted to an incredibly thick fog that left Central City paralyzed as never before.

The two speedsters managed to get Joe and themselves to the lab. There, somewhat bedraggled, the trio tried to recuperate.

Iris brought her father a cup of coffee and a hug. The hug was accompanied by a hard punch to the shoulder.

"What was that for?" demanded Joe.

"Next time, don't take such chances!" She turned on her brother and Barry. "You don't go out there again, you understand me, Wally?"

He gave a noncommittal grunt which seemed to satisfy her.

That left Iris and Barry staring at each other in such a way that the rest quickly left them alone on one side of the lab.

"I'm so glad you're all right," Iris told him.

"You're not going to punch me now, are you?"

That briefly brought a smile to her face. Then, "Thank you also for all you've done for Dad."

"Joe's pretty capable himself," Barry responded, "and Wally's getting better and better with his abilities."

"I agree on both counts, but where would both of them be without you, Barry?" She shifted position. "I know I've gotten on your case about Dad, but I think it's fair to say that it had as much to do with you as it did him or Wally." Iris put a hand on his shoulder. "I couldn't imagine what would happen without you."

"I'm being careful... but I can't give this up, Iris. Not just for my sake, but for everyone who has ever or will ever need my help. Especially not now."

"I know that more than ever. I wondered if I could handle that... and while I may not like it at times, nothing is going to separate me from you!"

Iris leaned forward and kissed him. Barry returned the kiss, then pulled back without warning.

"Did I do something?" a startled Iris immediately asked.

"No. I was just reminded how quickly I'd better get out there. The storm's hitting Central City like never before. I won't just be trying to find Mardon; there are people out there who won't realize that things are getting worse."

She nodded. "I understand and appreciate that. Just be careful. Please."

"I will." Before she could say more, Barry shifted over to Cisco, who was in a quiet but intense conversation with Caitlin. They both straightened when they realized that he was with them.

"You're getting ready to go out there, aren't you?" Caitlin asked anxiously.

"I have to. Mardon's a literal bomb!"

"Wally's been itching to go out too," Cisco interjected. "Joe and I managed to convince him to wait until you decided to as well. Guess he'll be happy."

"Before Wally and I leave, any progress on locating Mardon?"

"We may have figured out how to do it," Caitlin piped up. "We were just discussing the details."

"We can feed you the info while you're out there," added Cisco.

Wally suddenly stood next to Barry. "Tell me you're ready to go out."

"Ready as ever."

Wally smiled grimly. "Then let's go."

Barry nodded to Caitlin and Cisco, then looked over his shoulder at Iris. She gave him an encouraging if somewhat nervous smile.

He smiled back... and then, to the eyes of everyone else, vanished.

* * *

"Guess it's time to go," Wally remarked just before he too, vanished.

Caitlin instantly turned to Cisco. "I know you've still got a few qualms, but it'll be okay. We've done this before and now we know everything should be safe. You've made all the corrections needed."

"Everything *should* be okay, but that's what I thought before and look what happened!"

"I'm still getting headaches at odd intervals. I think they match actions by the Weather Wizard. The only thing is, because of the device, I don't even notice them at first. We need me to be as sensitive to them as possible! Do it, Cisco. We don't have any choice, not if Mardon's as near to disaster as we think!"

Cisco grunted. "All right… but at the first sign of trouble, I cut it off. We'll find some other way then. I swear."

Caitlin nodded solemnly, but said nothing.

"Talk to me, Wally," the Flash called on the private link.

"I'm uptown. You?"

"Near the stadium. Be wary. This fog is so thick you could run into a lamp and not realize it until you're dead."

Wally grunted. "Tell me about it. I feel like I'm moving at normal speed. Whoa!"

"What is it?"

"Accident! I'll deal with it."

Barry said nothing more. He had already helped a woman who had nearly fallen to her death by missing a step. Now, in addition to the heavy fog, the Flash noticed the rain picking up again. This time, though, there was a strong, chilly wind too.

"Cisco, talk to me."

"Go ahead."

"Is it getting a lot colder?" Barry asked.

"Is King Shark one ugly dude?" Cisco retorted. "Man, it's dropped more than fifteen degrees in the last five minutes."

"Mardon... Somehow."

"Looks like it. Might help us narrow down where he is. We need a break. We're nearly out of time... if we aren't already."

Barry dodged a dog in his path. He had moved so fast that the animal had not even noticed his presence. "You may be right. There's definitely something in the air. Something building rapidly."

"How are you feeling? Readings put you about seventy-eight percent. You've dropped only one since you left, but that's still quicker than it should be."

"I'm feeling well enough," the speedster remarked, abruptly turning back. "Just find Mardon for me," he added as he scooped up the bedraggled dog, clearly a stray. "That's all I ask."

"Will do." A pause. "They've just upped the State of Emergency! Mayor's office is asking everyone to get off the streets and for every available first responder, police included, to go on active duty until further notice! We're hitting critical, Barry! Central City can't take much more of this!"

The Flash dropped off the stray at a shelter and moved on. By that time, the temperature had dropped much more. A simple pass by a bank revealed the actual additional drop to be another fifteen degrees.

It's coming to a head, the Flash knew. *The storm's getting too chaotic! All these abrupt changes are having repercussions…*

Without warning, the Flash found himself sliding along at a breakneck pace despite his boots. He immediately dropped down and used his hands to slow his speed. Despite that, he still collided with a wall at enough of a speed to feel it in his bones.

Biting back a moan, he reached out to Wally. "Can you hear me?"

"I hear you!"

"Watch out! Fog and rain turning into the slickest ice I've ever seen! I think I slid a mile. Thankfully, there was no traffic because of the storm."

"I got you, man! The accident I helped? Turns out to be because of a patch of ice too! Believe me, I'm glad to keep moving! No word from the lab?"

"None. Hang on and let me check! Cisco, you and Caitlin make a decision yet?"

"We're about ready to start!"

"Great, because it's just dropped another six degrees!"

The Flash cut communications as something vaguely seen in the fog caught his attention. A few steps later, he came across the car that had evidently careened into a building. Despite extensive damage to the front especially, the engine continued to run. Meanwhile, a large, sinister puddle underneath gave every indication that the vehicle was leaking badly. Meanwhile, electrical wiring broken free from the building by the crash hovered dangerously near the puddle, that situation made worse by the occasional spark.

Ever aware of the imminent threat, the Flash rushed up to the vehicle and discovered two unconscious passengers in the front and a child sprawled in the back. Barry reached for the driver side passenger door, only to recoil just as his fingertips were about to touch the metal. A cautious check revealed exactly what he had assumed. Somewhere, a loose wire was touching the car in such a manner that a good charge was going through it.

Gritting his teeth, the Flash grabbed the door handle again. Pulling the door open as swiftly as he could, he pulled the young girl free, carried her to a safe location, then returned. He opened the front passenger door, removed the man from there, and brought him to the girl.

With one last effort, Barry sped to the driver's side and removed the mother. He carried her to the others, then looked back to the car. In all, he had taken far less than a second.

The car exploded as somewhere on or near the vehicle the electricity and the leaking fluids met.

The Flash located an EMT crew five blocks away and informed them of the family. That done, he returned to his search.

"How about it, Cisco? Anything?"

Barry waited, but Cisco said nothing. The Flash almost asked again, then decided that he would be disturbing their effort. Cisco and Caitlin had something unusual in mind, of that he was certain. He just hoped whatever they attempted would work.

"Do it, Cisco," Caitlin ordered from the platform. "I'm ready. Do it!"

"What can we do to help?" Iris asked, H.R. nodding behind her. Beyond them, Joe West said nothing, the detective having fallen asleep from exhaustion only a minute or two before.

"Just hope it all works out." Cisco attached the electrodes.

Caitlin smiled confidently. "I'll be fine, everyone. I promise!"

Cisco nodded, then returned to the console. "Okay! Got all the storm readings running through the program. Got you hooked into them for real-time comparison. Got the system ready to mark any subtle change." He looked back at her. "And we've got your instincts."

"If I feel the slightest change, you'll know."

"All right then." Cisco punched in a final couple of numbers. "Here we go!"

No sooner had he spoken than the entire building trembled from a loud rumble.

"What? Does he have the power to create earthquakes now?" H.R. asked as everyone clutched something solid.

"That's… *thunder*," Iris breathed.

"But that's about a hundred times worse than anything he's done before!"

"Two hundred and twelve times worse, according to the computer," Cisco reported. "If his influence on the storm is this powerful now, we're in real deep!"

"I'm confused," H.R. interjected. "With all that, shouldn't we be able to trace him?"

Cisco eyed the screen. "Actually, all this uptick in the violent weather is just confusing the situation. Caitlin and I are hoping to use her to fine-tune matters, so to speak."

"Okay, if you say so."

Iris rubbed her chin in thought. "Cisco, tell me again why we can't use the wand."

"My fault really. Through channels, I provided them with the tech the wand is based on so that they could utilize it to keep Mardon under control. What I didn't expect was for some other geniuses to create a device they could implant in his head and actually get a court order to do it. Mardon's on the same wavelength, so to speak. We pull out the wand, he's just as likely to seize control of it with a thought and use it to focus his power. Like that thing in his head has been letting him do all along it seems."

"So the implant is why he's so powerful?"

"Yep!"

"If it's the same as the wand, isn't there a way to shut it down?"

Cisco mulled the idea. "Theoretically we could…" After a moment's more thought, though, he shook his head. "All that power around him is causing too much interference. What's worse is that whoever made it upgraded the design, hence the fact that it's now not just drawing together the elements of the storm, but also the energies that make a metahuman what they are. That's why Barry's losing so much so fast. We'd need to get really damned close."

"How close?"

"Very," interjected Caitlin. "And since the Weather Wizard won't come to us, we'd also need to devise a device that could transmit the signal strongly enough no matter where we find him."

"It'd have to be a special sort of transmission device," Cisco went on. "Something as complex as—" He slapped himself on the forehead. "As Barry's com device! Cisco, you are the greatest—*ignoramus*, that is! You couldn't think of that sooner?"

Iris brightened. "Is that possible?"

"It should be…" Caitlin said. She leaned back again. "But that means we need to get started with me, Cisco. Right now."

He gave her an apologetic smile. "Already have."

"Oh." She frowned. "Sorry."

At that moment, the building shook again.

Caitlin gasped. Cisco and the others—with the exception of Joe, who did not even stir—looked at her. Caitlin touched her left temple. Her hand shook slightly.

"Cisco… It's Mardon! He's doing something! I can sense it!"

"Already?" he studied the data. "Are you sure? I don't see any change."

Iris peered closely at her friend. "She's reacting to something. Find it or stop."

"But I don't—wait. Let me refine the measurements, get more minute changes." Cisco quickly typed. "There. Damn! You're right!"

Caitlin now had fingers to both temples. "Nice… to know."

"This is good. This is very good." More typing, then a pause.

When Cisco did not continue, Iris finally asked, "Did it change again?"

"No… but there's something new that doesn't make sense. Wait. Let me adjust for…"

Fingers pressed against her temples, Caitlin bent forward. "It's getting worse…"

Iris looked vexed. "Cisco, I'm not going to let her go through this again!"

"Got it!" he declared. Spinning to face her, Cisco held up a small mechanism like an electronic car key.

He pressed a button on it. It made a brief beeping sound, accompanied by two flashes of the tiny red light on the front end.

Caitlin gasped, then sat back, her expression relieved.

"What did you just do?" she asked.

"Iris had it right, Caitlin," Cisco said. "I cobbled this together for emergencies. I swore, one way or another, I wouldn't let anything happen again."

"But the data you needed—"

"Already there and ready for Barry."

"So you know where he can find the Weather Wizard?"

Cisco pocketed the small mechanism, then swung back to his computer. "Yeah… and where he is right now you wouldn't believe…"

The Flash circled around again. The elements of the storm continued to shift, but thus far he had been successful in not running afoul of them. The temperature remained far below normal, but was at least above freezing.

Ironically, it was now the thunder that was the greatest threat, its intensity so tremendous that it cracked buildings, smashed windows and set off alarms.

Barry had handled matters as well as he could, and from an occasional response from Wally he knew that Iris's brother had everything well in hand.

His communications crackled. "Cisco here! Got it!"

"Finally! Go ahead!"

Cisco gave him the address. The Flash frowned. "You're joking!"

"At a time like this? Not even me! Well… not much actually, but not now."

"Okay! Heading right there!"

"Listen! One more thing! We think we've got an idea about Mardon, but you'll have to get awfully close!"

"I'll hug him if that's needed! Tell me." After Cisco gave him an abbreviated version, he asked, "Are you sure? We've had a lot of trouble keeping communications functioning!"

"We'll make it work, buddy!"

"All right! Let's do it then!"

"You got it!" Cisco cut the connection.

The Flash raced on. It took him hardly a thought to reach the outskirts of the location. For some reason he was not entirely surprised by where the Weather Wizard could be found. There, though, the Flash paused, well aware of a thousand potential threats that existed nowhere else.

Iron Heights stood an even more ominous structure in the midst of the wild storm, especially with the ruined section where the Weather Wizard had been kept a stark reminder of the type of prisoners housed here. The Flash prayed that neither of Mardon's personas would think of unleashing them.

Wally had given him a vivid description of the fight with Mardon, so it didn't surprise the Flash that the area had been cleared of much of the heavy stone. Still, it was a strong reminder of just how powerful the Weather Wizard had become. Barry knew that he should have told Wally to join him, but after what had happened to him at the hands of the Weather Wizard, he preferred to deal with Mardon by himself. It was bad enough Iris had to fear for her father; Barry didn't want to risk Wally as well if he could help it. He understood that he was taking a risk, but refused to change his mind.

Seeing nothing, the speedster ran over to the cell. Iron Heights remained active elsewhere, so searchlights sometimes crossed the area; the Flash made certain to stay out of any of the lit regions as he inspected the place for any clues. Cisco had detected the Weather Wizard in the vicinity and Barry had every faith in his friend's calculations.

Yet not only was there no sign of Mardon but there was also no hint that he had even been back to Iron Heights since being confronted by Wally. The Flash darted back and forth around the area, inspecting the ground wherever he paused. Despite a thorough look, the speedster found nothing, not even the wires and assembly that should have been there.

"Come on, Mardon…" he muttered. "We're wasting valuable time! Show yourself!"

But the only reply Barry received was a howl of wind and more deafening thunder.

The Flash studied every part of the prison not currently in use but again came up empty.

"Cisco?"

"Go ahead!"

"Any change in that location?"

"No. Wait…" After a brief pause, Cisco returned. "He's definitely there! Based on what I've got coming in from you, you should be almost standing face to face with—"

A wrenching noise was the Flash's only warning. Even with that and his speed, he barely evaded the heavy steel beam suddenly ripped by a gale-force wind and tossed his way.

The beam crashed on the spot where the speedster had just stood. Barry paused several yards away, trying to spot his adversary.

More thunder shook Iron Heights. This time it was accompanied by lightning, some of which struck close. Distracted by the lightning and unable to hear because of the thunder, the Flash failed to notice the concrete block soaring at him from behind. Only a chance turn saved him from a direct blow. As it was, the strike knocked him off his feet and might have crushed his shoulder if not for the padded suit. The Flash tumbled forward, ending up on his back.

"He's here!" Barry warned Cisco.

"I was just about to warn you! Readings on him flaring higher than ever," Cisco responded. "It's like he's a bomb about to blow!"

"Great! I haven't actually seen him yet, but I'm under attack! He's pulling up every piece he didn't manage to throw at Wally and he's using the storm to distract—"

This time, the Flash saw the attack coming… mainly because it was coming from every direction.

Small but powerful whirlwinds carried heavy refuse from the damaged penitentiary toward the speedster. The Flash turned in a quick circle. The attack was coming from all sides. Mardon—whether of his own mind or that which thought itself Clyde—had again been calculating a trap taking Barry's speed into account.

But still there was no actual sign of the Weather Wizard. The Flash would have expected him to be present in order to savor the death of one of those he considered Clyde's murderers.

"Got a problem," Cisco warned.

"I think I already see it."

"I'm talking about you. You left here up to about eighty-two percent ability. You're now down to seventy-six, five points of that down since you got to Iron Heights."

The Flash had not had a moment to consider his own situation, but now made aware of it by Cisco, he realized that he did feel slightly more tired. Until now, he had chalked anything to being struck. "How fast am I draining?"

"Too fast. It's accelerating. You're down another point already since I told you."

"Great." The Flash kept an eye on the circling whirlwinds and their missiles. Something did not seem right, but he couldn't yet put a finger on it. "Cisco—"

The whirlwinds converged on him, the air now filled with scores of spinning, deadly objects of massive size.

Barry moved. As the first piece of debris neared him, he took a running start toward it. Calculating its trajectory, the Flash jumped.

He landed atop the piece, then held on as he and it soared around the whirlwind. As it neared another good-sized fragment, the Flash jumped.

From his new perch, Barry tried to judge where next to leap. With any luck, he hoped to escape the ring of whirlwinds soon—

As quickly as they had formed, the powerful winds died.

The Flash found himself dropping earthward. Quickly adjusting, he readied himself for a leap toward safer footing—

The whirlwinds returned. The unexpected shift sent the Flash stumbling off.

For a moment, he plunged toward the ground. A sudden swelling of the whirlwind caught the Flash and sent him spinning around with the refuse.

Out of the corner of his eye, the speedster caught glimpses of the other whirlwinds as the automated searchlights of Iron Heights briefly touched on them. To his surprise, the other tornadoes again ceased. Only the one in which the Flash flew continued on.

More lightning then revealed that the remaining whirlwind was also *moving*. Barry watched as the landscape below him shifted back to that of downtown.

What's he up to? Barry wondered as he tried to maintain his equilibrium. The Weather Wizard had already had ample opportunity to kill him. Why not simply do it? He recalled some of the comments by both personalities, comments urging the Flash to stronger effort. That and the draining the Flash suffered even now meant that whatever Mardon desired, he still needed his adversary alive—

A crackle of lightning lit Central City as bright as day. The whirlwind ceased.

The Flash instinctively twisted around. He managed to get his feet on a plunging piece of wall. From there he leaped to a girder and then across its length before jumping to a nearby rooftop.

As the speedster paused, he heard the multiple crashes of the refuse from Iron Heights below him. Peering down, the Flash breathed a sigh of relief that the streets in the vicinity looked absolutely empty due to the increased instability of the storm.

Another crackle of lightning swept over Central City again… but this time its fantastic illumination did not fade.

Startled, the Flash looked up to see why… only to discover that it was no longer lightning keeping the city aglow.

It was a single distant figure high above all but the tallest buildings… A single figure that had to be the Weather Wizard aglow like a sun.

2 2

Caitlin eyed Cisco's efforts with an expression of both concern and hope across her face. "Are you sure we shouldn't wait a little longer?"

"No. The coordinates I gave Barry should've been right on the mark. We need to finish with you so that you'll never have to go through this again. Then we can work on the com link for Barry."

"But won't this always happen when the Weather Wizard's active?"

Cisco said nothing. Instead, he made a few more programming adjustments, then stepped back.

"Is that it?" asked Iris.

"That should be. Honest. I swear this time. Maybe."

"Oh!" Caitlin gingerly touched her forehead. "It's… It's out of there."

The others looked puzzled, Cisco finally asking, "What is?"

"I didn't even really know it until now. All this time

it's as if something was sitting on my mind, pressing down on it... but not now. Not anymore."

Cisco did a calculation. "Since shortly after they last locked Mardon up and started using that last system to keep him in check?"

"Yes... Yes, that would be it."

"Yeah, that's probably when it started making changes in him... Which reminds me, gotta go. Barry's been awfully quiet the last couple minutes."

"Barry..." Iris murmured. She turned after Cisco but did not leave Caitlin's side.

Caitlin touched her hand. "Go. I know you want to be near in case there's something to hear. I'll be fine."

"If she needs something, I can get it," offered H.R.

"Thank you." Iris hurried to Cisco.

H.R. studied Caitlin. "Are you sure you're all right?"

She leaned back. "As well as we all are right now. You know what will happen if Barry can't stop Mardon."

He nodded. "Yep. We all go together."

Caitlin nodded and closed her eyes.

The Flash eyed the tiny figure. He had always been impressed by Mardon being able to use the wind to fly, but he had never believed the Weather Wizard capable of hovering so high.

He waited a moment to try to judge what Mardon might do next, then realized that it was *his* move to make. The whirlwind had not stopped randomly. The

Weather Wizard wanted the Flash to come to him. Again, Mardon was pushing the speedster to exert himself. The Flash could only assume that it helped the other metahuman drain him faster.

And for what? Barry wondered. The Weather Wizard's plan to bring his brother back from the dead was a mad fantasy. Mardon could not possibly succeed—

But that, the Flash realized, didn't matter. What mattered was that Mardon believed he could.

The Flash focused on the buildings around him, judging their distances and heights.

He darted off, heading toward one of the tallest buildings in the area. Zipping through the entrance, the Flash soared up the eighty floors to the roof in less than a second.

But there he stumbled. His breath escaped him. The Flash was unable to stop himself as he fell to his knees on the roof.

"Barry!" Cisco called. "Barry! You just dropped to sixty-five percent! Are you all right?"

"Just need—just need to catch my breath. I felt that, Cisco. I felt that drop."

"Listen! If you keep up at that rate, you'll only have a few minutes before you're helpless. Wait there. We're going to have to tell Wally to get over."

"No! You need Wally. If I fail, he's going to have to get you out of Central City before it's too late. Speaking of which, how's the other plan going?"

"Still on it. Should be workable any moment!"

"I'm counting on that!"

His breathing normal again, the Flash renewed his search for Mardon. He saw the distant figure and swore. The Weather Wizard had shifted position.

The Flash studied the building closest to where his adversary floated. He made a new judgment call based on what he saw, then, without hesitation, descended the skyscraper.

"Wake up," croaked a strange voice. "He's coming up for us, Mark. Just as we wanted…"

"Clyde?" the Weather Wizard managed. He didn't notice that both his voice and that of his brother sounded much alike. "What did you say?" A howling wind rose, smothering other sounds. Although he didn't sense it, the wind rose and fell and rose with his racing heartbeat.

"The Flash. He's coming for us. It's time. It's all got to end here, remember?"

Mark slowly opened his eyes. It didn't surprise him to see that he was floating high in the sky. Nor was it any shock that he glowed like the sun in the midst of the violent storm. It all felt very natural. "If the Flash is on his way, shouldn't he be here already?"

"Funny. You were always the funny one, Mark. Of course it's a lot easier to be funny when you're alive."

The Weather Wizard winced. "I'm going to change that, Clyde. I'm ready. I'll bring you back or—"

"Or die trying?" his brother finished.

The Weather Wizard turned his gaze in the direction he believed the voice was coming from. Out of the corner of his eye, he briefly glimpsed a whirling form filled with dust and other minute refuse. However, by the time Mark finished turning, it was to find Clyde patiently watching him.

"He's coming," Clyde reminded the Weather Wizard.

"The Flash…" As he looked down, Mark rubbed the spot where he had been hit. His eyes narrowed in utter hatred. "I can feel him. He's feeding me just like the storm is."

"Why don't we greet him, Mark?"

"Why don't we?"

A simple thought was all the Weather Wizard needed to make the wind drop him to a lower level. Now he skirted the top of the nearest building, waiting.

It was not a long wait. A blur suddenly formed on the roof of the nearby skyscraper. It paused, finally coalescing into that very familiar, hated red costume.

"The Flash…" the Weather Wizard muttered.

"Mardon, I'm going to try one last time to make you see sense!" the speedster called from the skyscraper roof. "You won't be able to bring your brother back! All you'll do is kill yourself and probably most of this city too!"

"He's lying to you, Mark."

"Of course he is." To the speedster, the Weather Wizard declared, "If I have to take the entire city with me, I will, Flash! It'll be worth it to make Clyde live again!"

The Flash looked frustrated. "Mardon, have you

really ever looked at him close? You saw me run through him! He's not real! Your power and your pained mind made him—*it*—in your brother's image! That's not Clyde and it's not Clyde's ghost! All you have floating next to you is whirlwind full of loose debris your subconscious has formed into something that looks vaguely like your brother!"

"No!" The Weather Wizard sent a massive gust of wind toward the Flash, who quickly shifted to the other side of the roof where he had some protection.

"Don't just kill him. Not yet."

Breathing heavily, Mark looked at his brother and hesitated. For just the briefest of moments, he thought that he saw something other than Clyde. Something... not real.

Then Clyde became Clyde again. Guilt filled the Weather Wizard. He shook his head, and eyed his brother grimly. "Let's get this done."

Clyde said nothing, answering only with a smile that, had he paid any attention, the Weather Wizard might have realized was a mirror image of his own.

The Flash kept himself pressed against the protection the rooftop provided. As he waited out the gale, he activated his communications device. "Cisco? Does it work yet?"

"You are good to go, dude... Once you get close enough!"

"Just leave it to me!"

Three bolts of lightning struck the building next to where the Flash stood.

"Did something unusual just happen?" Cisco asked.

Barry snorted. "Define unusual."

"Yeah. Sorry. I keep forgetting what kind of lives we have now. We *really* need to come up with a new word. Anything *different* from what we'd expect from our *unfair weather* friend?"

"Nothing physical, unless you mean the enhanced wind."

"No, I have that. Did he cast anything?"

The Flash considered. "Can't think of anything. I tried again to make him realize that Clyde was dead and that all he had next to him was some self-made construct of wind and dust and—"

"Wait! Did he react?"

"He still is! The wind!"

Cisco made a clicking sound. "Still hasn't tried to kill you? I mean at this moment."

"If looks could've done it, he would've… That was just before he created the wind. You should've seen his face…" The Flash considered. "It was almost as if just for a second, he finally believed me!"

"That's got to be it! There was a marked fluctuation at that point. Things dropped down to less-than catastrophic!"

Barry took a peek around the corner just in time to see the Weather Wizard beginning to approach. "Cisco, if what you're saying is true, I've got an idea: one I need to try quickly. Mardon looks nearly burned out. He can't last much longer—"

"That's part of our problem, yeah."

"But listen. I think it's also giving us our best chance. Mardon's straining to control everything. It's been taxing on his mind. I think he may actually be becoming more susceptible to hearing the truth. It might also let me get near enough for you to send the signal."

"You're going to try to beat him by forcing the *truth* on him? Dude, you're the fastest runner alive, not the fastest shrink! I don't—"

"Just trust me… and pray!"

"Listen, Barry—"

But the Flash had no more time. He dodged around the other side of the roof and came around while the Weather Wizard seemingly hovered in place due to the Flash's speed.

"Going to take a couple of big chances here, Cisco," he called as he paused just enough to measure distances.

"Just what do you—" was as far as Cisco got.

The Flash took a few steps back, then ran off the building.

Now having to trust to momentum, he lost some of his speed advantage. The Weather Wizard began to move forward as if through tar. Slowly, Mardon turned toward him, the rogue's eyes rising in rage.

Barry reached out and, praying he had made the right calculation, attempted to seize "Clyde".

The murky figure did not react, just as the Flash had hoped. More to his relief was the fact that as he and his target came together strong winds seemed to pop out of nowhere and keep the speedster from plunging into the city.

Despite their abrupt appearance, the Flash had calculated their presence from the start. If "Clyde" was essentially a construct of wind, it had to be a strong one to maintain any substance for so long.

"Clyde!" the Weather Wizard roared.

"Do you see now, Mardon? Do you see the truth?" the Flash shouted as he sought to balance.

With "Clyde" no longer in human form, the whirlwind from which he had been created now expanded to several times its original size. The Flash kept himself just off the center, using the spin to create an area of near stability for him.

"What's going on there, Barry?" Cisco shouted. "Mardon's readings have suddenly gotten even crazier, believe it or not!"

The speedster had no chance to reply. He and the whirlwind began dropping. At first, Barry feared he would plummet to his death, but the descent abruptly slowed.

The reason floated above. The Weather Wizard wore a murderous expression as he descended after the Flash.

"You're trying to take him from me again!" Mardon cried. "I won't let you do it! I won't fail him again!"

"I'll take you with me!" The Weather Wizard added

in his "Clyde" voice. "You, him, and everything! I'll take everything with me!"

"Are you listening to that, Mark Mardon?" The Flash asked. "Are you listening to *yourself*? You can't bring him back! All you can do is destroy yourself and everything around you!"

"Lies! I can do this!" The Weather Wizard twisted in midair. As he did, the whirlwind that had been "Clyde" began to condense once more. "I just needed enough power!"

"It won't be enough, Mardon! It'll never be enough! Your brother is dead. We didn't want it to happen, but he forced it! This isn't even his ghost, just you trying to make him exist through your own voice!"

"You're not making any sense," the Weather Wizard retorted.

The Flash might have thought he was getting nowhere if not for the brief glimpse of uncertainty he caught in his adversary's face. Barry knew that he remained in a precarious position. Right now, he hovered high in the sky, held up only by the powerful whirlwind the Weather Wizard believed to be his brother. If the Flash convinced Mardon of the truth, the speedster had very limited options as to what to do if the Weather Wizard abruptly dismissed the whirlwind.

Mardon continued to hover a short distance above him, the glow radiating from him adding an even more monstrous aspect to the already twisted figure. The Weather Wizard looked like nothing less than a nightmare version of himself, a cadaverous ghoul someone had set on fire. Barry hazarded a guess that Mardon was literally skin and bones and that he had lost at least a quarter of his mass since he had escaped Iron Heights. His lips had curled back from his teeth and his hair stuck out wildly in every direction. The ever-growing contrast to what Mark Mardon had once looked like was an unnerving reminder of just how close the situation was to culminating in utter destruction.

"He's trying to make you turn from me, Mark!" the Clyde voice suddenly warned Mardon. "He's trying to kill me again and you're letting him!"

Mad as the declaration was, it had some effect on the Weather Wizard. The whirlwind condensed more, almost trapping the Flash within it.

Then, to the speedster's surprise, Mardon bent over as if struck in the gut. Tightly clutching his sides, the Weather Wizard shrieked in agony.

A *ripple* spread across Central City. The Flash could describe it no other way. A ripple. As it crossed over the city, street lamps in many places blew out. The ground shook as if from an earthquake. The wind was so strong that the heavy sheets of rain now fell nearly sideways. Lightning played everywhere.

And the whirlwind that had been "Clyde" exploded in every direction, leaving the Flash suddenly in the air with nothing to keep him from dropping to his death.

Yet, nearly as quickly, the whirlwind re-formed into something vaguely humanoid. The Flash barely had time to drop before one large appendage stretched forth and enveloped him.

A guttural sound erupted from it—or rather from the Weather Wizard, who still provided a voice of sorts for it. The appendage rose, taking the Flash with it.

"You can't take him from me!" the Weather Wizard shouted as something brought the Flash toward him. He had managed to straighten, but just barely from what the Flash could see. Mardon was still clearly very much in pain. "I won't—I won't—"

The Flash glanced down. Their shifting position had put him close to a rooftop. If he dropped now, he could land safely.

"Flash…"

It was not that Mardon had called his name that surprised the speedster so much as the tone he now used. The Flash looked at his adversary.

Without warning, an awful paleness had replaced the burned look of the Weather Wizard's skin. Barry noticed Mardon shiver.

"Flash… I'm… It's not well… It's…" He looked just past the speedster. "Clyde… No… You're gone… I—"

The Weather Wizard shivered again… and dropped like a rock.

2 3

At the same that Mardon began falling, so too did the Flash start to drop. As he had planned, he landed barely a moment later on the rooftop he had been studying.

No sooner had he regained his balance than he raced from the edge of the roof and leaped toward the next building, a smaller one by some ten floors. From there, the Flash jumped to another, smaller structure and from that to a smaller yet.

All the while, he kept watch on Mardon's plummeting body. A part of Barry—a great part, he had to admit—was sorely tempted to let the Weather Wizard fall to his death. Certainly Mardon would have done nothing to save the Flash under the same circumstances. But even now Barry couldn't simply let Mardon perish. The Flash leapt across one more building, then noted the Weather Wizard's current location. Mardon had dropped nearly three-quarters of the way down. The Flash had to catch him now.

The speedster leaped. If he had everything calculated correctly, he would be able to catch hold of Mardon and use momentum to carry them easily to the rooftop across from him.

As the Flash jumped, time began to catch up. Mardon's body started to slip lower. That suited the Flash just fine as it set the Weather Wizard to be at the correct height for the plan.

But then a fearsome gust of wind caught the speedster unawares. As it tossed him toward the side of a building, the Flash thought he glimpsed a hulking form several stories high.

Barry rolled onto the rooftop for which he had already been aiming, the added momentum from the wind threatening to send him slipping off the other side. He turned around to see Mardon's body nearing the street level.

But a rush of wind underneath pushed the Weather Wizard's body up just a few feet from disaster.

The Flash started down after Mardon... only to be struck by yet another burst of wind. The speedster went crashing through an office window.

As he pushed himself up, he beheld an even greater monstrosity than before. The false Clyde now stretched larger than ever, a huge tornadic shape lacking all but the most vague human traits shifting through the street, ripping up mailboxes, benches, huge cement planters, and adding them to the already massive collection swirling within it, heading toward the Flash with malevolent purpose.

The speedster peered up at it, then back at the Weather Wizard. Mardon knelt on the street, once more his arms tightly wrapped around his sides. He remained as pale as earlier and his hollow eyes stared ahead as if not really seeing anything.

The Flash started toward the Weather Wizard, only to find the unsettling tornado somehow directly in his path.

He looked back behind him and verified that it was indeed the very same behemoth. Barry frowned. "Cisco!"

"Go ahead!"

"Cisco, are you reading anything in front of me? Something really, really large?"

After a moment, Cisco replied, "This is weird, man. I've got Mardon in front of you *and*… another Mardon? What've you got going on there? He hasn't developed the power to clone himself now, has he? I mean, that's not fair. One power to a metahuman, that's the rule!"

"Remember 'Clyde'? He's a lot bigger and no longer masked! He's a whirlwind, a huge tornado, Cisco! A tornado on the hunt for me, apparently!"

"Well, as awful as it sounds, you must've gotten through to Mardon at least some! His subconscious is focused on you specifically now! It's bought us a slight reprieve and may be the key to ending this!"

"If we still have enough time. Mardon looks like he's about gone and—"

The Flash shifted out of the way just before a mailbox hit where he had been standing. However, as he came to a halt in a spot he felt was at least a momentarily safe one, he was overcome by a new wave of exhaustion.

"Barry! You just slipped below fifty percent!"

"I can feel it…" It was now a race against time in more ways than one. The Flash warily eyed the massive tornado as it moved in his direction: one extension of the funnel swept up a car someone had abandoned and tossed it the Flash's way. It should have been a simple task for Barry to evade such a missile, but as the speedster moved, every muscle in his body stiffened. He was able to keep moving, yet at a pace that made him feel as if he stood still.

By the time the car crashed into his previous location, the Flash had barely moved far enough away. His reflexes were slowing.

"I'm getting some bad fluctuations from you!" Cisco cut in.

"I'm sure! Listen, I've got to try something. This can't go on!"

He did not wait for Cisco to reply. Instead, he raced past the swiping limb of the tornado figure and headed directly for the Weather Wizard.

The moment he came within earshot, the Flash called out: "Mardon! Listen to me! I know what it's like to lose a loved one! To lose someone that was a part of yourse—"

A lightning bolt struck just yards from the Flash. Even despite the debilitating effects of what the

Weather Wizard was doing to him, the Flash still managed to back out of range before it actually hit. Despite his success, the speedster knew he couldn't keep this up much longer.

"Dude, be careful!" Cisco reported, as if on cue. "You're down to forty-six!"

"Do—do me a favor! When I get down to twenty-five, let me know! Nothing before!"

"Your choice!"

"Listen, I think I'm onto something. Mardon looks like he's in a coma, but when I started talking about losing someone, the weather got even more violent right around him! I think if I keep pressing him on this, it could break the impasse—"

"Or break you. That drop happened as a result of that last little stunt! Barry—"

Whatever Cisco said next was lost to the Flash as he dodged another heavy piece of refuse thrown at him by the whirlwind. It became readily apparent that it too was seeking to keep the speedster from reaching Mardon.

The Flash hesitated. With his abilities weakened, the sinister construct and the protective barricade of weather surrounding Mardon were nearly more than he could handle. He watched both situations, hoping for a gap of even a single second. A golden streak ran by, crossing paths with the whirlwind a moment later.

"Cisco filled me in, man!" Wally called over the link. "Do whatever you need to do! I'll keep old Windy here occupied long enough!"

Barry wanted to reprimand Cisco for drawing in Iris's brother, but knew that he needed Wally right now. "Just be careful!"

"Aren't I always?"

The Flash refrained from answering, instead eyeing the Weather Wizard. The path to Mardon appeared momentarily clear.

Barry ran. The moment he was again close enough, he paused and called out, "Mardon! I know the pain! I've lost someone near to me too! I did something to try to bring them back, but it only ended up creating disaster on a scale you can't imagine! That's all that's going to happen here! Countless lives will be lost and for nothing! Clyde is gone and there's nothing that can be done to change that!"

To the Flash's surprise, the area around the Weather Wizard remained subdued. The speedster wasn't certain whether this was due to a trap set for him or because his words had actually penetrated Mardon's fevered mind.

The Weather Wizard looked up.

Barry shivered. Mardon still looked as if he had just risen from the grave himself. His gaze would not quite focus and he wheezed. He seemed as if he was either in a trance or halfway to a coma.

What's happening to him? the Flash wondered.

Then, the bloodshot eyes opening wider, the Weather Wizard stared at his adversary. "All gone. It'd never work. You were right."

"Mardon, listen. No one could appreciate what you

were going through unless they'd suffered through it too. Clyde's not coming back. You have to accept it…"

"Accept it… Never worked…"

The Flash continued to watch warily. "Maybe we're safe here, Cisco."

"Maybe… But he's still burning off the charts, Barry. If he should lose it completely at this point, then it's bye-bye everything. We need to shut down that thing in his head.'

"Hold on, Cisco." The Flash watched the Weather Wizard through narrowed eyes. A subtle change had come over Mardon's expression, one that disturbed the speedster. "I think—"

The Weather Wizard rose, a scene that reminded Barry of a zombie movie. Mardon swayed back and forth and twice the Flash expected him to collapse.

"Clyde's not… coming back. He's dead, Flash, and you and I know that. How do we know that? Because we made sure he was dead, didn't we, Flash? You and the detective, but me too. I let him die."

The Flash took a quick glance at where Wally was. Wally continued to keep ahead of the animated tornado, which looked as if it were starting to lose form.

Returning his full attention to the Weather Wizard, the speedster said, "It's time to put an end to this, Mardon. Just come with me—"

Mardon cocked his head in clear bewilderment. "'Come with you'? Why? It doesn't matter where we go! Clyde's gone from everywhere!"

The illumination surrounding the Weather Wizard's body grew stronger.

"Barry, his readings are taking off!"

"Get ready to hit that button, Cisco!" The Flash moved in at a speed against which the Weather Wizard could do nothing, but the moment the Flash reached the edge of the illumination, he was flung back like a rag doll. He collided with a huge storefront window, which shattered, and he fell into the store, momentarily stunned.

As he stirred, Cisco's voice shouted in his ear. "You've got to get out of there, Barry! You've just dropped to twenty-four percent! You can't keep this up!"

"I've got... Got to!" Still, he understood Cisco's concern the moment he tried to stand. If not for a nearby table to lean on, his initial attempt would have seen him back on the floor. The Flash inhaled deeply, then pushed himself out of the store.

The Weather Wizard stood where the Flash had last left him, his hands stretched high. His eyes were shut in concentration.

From the Flash's left came a loud crash. Zipping toward it, Barry found Wally still trying to harass the whirlwind. The crash had been the sound of a bus being thrown across the street at the spot where the other speedster had been standing.

Wally saw the Flash and vanished, reappearing beside him.

"Are you all right?" he asked. "You look almost as pale as Mardon!"

"I'll be fine."

"If you say so." Wally looked doubtful. "What's happening with him?"

"The Weather Wizard's about to destroy everything, including himself."

Wally made a face. "Great. And what do we do?"

"First, I need you to keep an eye on that thing." He gestured to the whirlwind. "Will you?"

"Sure, no problem. It looks friendly. What else?"

"I haven't heard anything more from Mardon's Clyde persona, but if that whirlwind still exists, the other personality does too, deep down. Just make sure you steer clear of it. Don't try anything tricky."

"I wouldn't know just what trick to use on it anyway."

The Flash nodded. "I have an idea, if it comes to it. First, though, I've got to see to Mardon. Maybe we can still avoid a full catastrophe."

"Maybe."

Barry had no better answer. He nodded to Wally, then rushed away.

The Weather Wizard stood seemingly frozen in place, only the crackle of energy around him showing any change. Now it flared brighter, stronger.

The Flash did not hesitate. At the very least, he had to try to break Mardon's concentration. There was one simple way to attempt that.

Accelerating, the Flash threw himself directly at the Weather Wizard.

He did so well aware that it might not be possible to penetrate the forces surrounding his adversary. Barry only hoped to distract the Weather Wizard, even if it meant the speedster bouncing off.

Closer and closer he got. When he passed the point where the weather had tried to block him and nothing happened, the Flash prepared himself for the collision with Mardon.

"Now, Cisco!" he shouted.

"We're on it!"

An explosion of energy marked the impact. The Weather Wizard let out a grunt as the speedster barreled directly into his midsection. Still grappling, both men went flying.

They crashed into a plant display from the city's recent beautification project. The energy loosed by the men's collision sent plants, concrete planters, and benches scattering everywhere.

A second burst threw the Flash from atop his foe. Barry flew a few feet in the air—at which point a massive gust of wind plucked him up.

No, not just any gust of wind, the speedster saw... but rather the "hand" of the gargantuan whirlwind Mardon had used to recreate his brother.

Barry had no idea what had happened to Wally and could only pray that he was all right. There was nothing but static in Barry's earpiece, which likely meant that the energies unleashed during the collision had ruined it. That left the Flash almost entirely on his own.

The swirling air drew the Flash higher and higher. A shift in its direction sent the speedster facing the whirlwind.

There, for a single moment, Barry thought he once again beheld the murky features of Clyde Mardon. The Flash's view changed before he could verify his impression. The wind turned again, sending the Flash flying across the street. He grimaced as the wall of an office building quickly filled his gaze. A hand pulled him to safety just a few yards from what would have been a very painful collision. Wally helped the Flash to his feet just as both heard a horrific wrenching noise.

"I don't like the sound of that," Wally muttered.

"No."

They looked in the direction of the noise.

A mass of girders, bricks, cement, and more, clearly torn from the side of some building, came flying at the pair.

"Split up!" ordered the Flash.

A girder barreled through where Wally had stood, the long, heavy piece burying half its length in another building. A two-ton piece of masonry rolled over the location where the Flash had just been standing.

Another girder crashed just inches from where he moved to after that, but by then the Flash had managed to move further away.

The bombardment spread rapidly over not only the location where the two had initially stood, but an area reaching far ahead. It was clear to the Flash that even now there was no lack of cunning on the part of the Weather Wizard despite the turmoil going through his mind. Chunks of debris wreaked havoc over the center of Central City: all to try to kill the two speedsters. Several pieces from what the Flash determined was a sidewalk shot just above them, battering a nearby building like a volley of heavy cannons. This sent a shower of deadly fragments and glass raining down on the duo. The Flash and Wally raced into the ruined building, locating the offices struck by the concrete. Together, the pair pulled several shocked innocents free, carrying them to safety in seconds. But even as they did so, more makeshift missiles assailed them. Another huge piece of concrete came down just in front of Wally, who barely avoided running right into it, but in veering off left Barry's line of sight. Unfortunately, the Flash couldn't check on his friend, evading those missiles sent after him fully demanding his attention.

Barry's body screamed for rest, but he tried to ignore both the screams and the memory of the last update Cisco had given him concerning his capabilities. The physical stresses the Flash felt were evidence enough that he was fast approaching the zero mark and yet not for a moment was surrendering to his pain an option he considered. Still, the Flash knew he couldn't keep retreating. That meant turning into the onslaught. Hoping that Wally wasn't planning the same suicidal tactic, the Flash chose the narrowness of the street to enable him to leap to the side, run up the wall of one building, and use it to arc around back toward the center without actually treading the street for some distance.

It was a tactic that saved him at least once; the street now a ruin from so many gigantic missiles. Gaping holes and upturned sections of concrete marked the once neat street. A crushed water main left a good portion of the street flooded.

Finally alighting back on one of the more serviceable parts of the street, the Flash picked up speed as best he could as he headed back to the Weather Wizard.

Another girder crashed into a storefront far to his right. The Flash adjusted his route. Fast as he was, he could now run at only a fraction of his optimum speed. He prayed this would be swift enough.

The hulking form of the tornado briefly filled the Flash's vision, then vanished behind him. Ahead, the speedster saw the fiery illumination that marked where Mardon had to be. He found the Weather Wizard pushing himself to his feet with jerky movements that added to Mardon's zombie-like appearance. The Weather Wizard was even more on his last legs than the Flash. It amazed Barry that the man could stand at all.

It turned out that not only could Mardon stand, but he still retained some of his faculties. Brooding eyes fixed on the Flash.

"Ungh!" Out of nowhere, a massive funnel cloud swept into the Flash and threw him into a wall. Barry managed to brace himself enough to avoid much injury, but the collision still left him shaking his head.

He looked up to see what appeared to be the same enormous whirlwind, save that to have reached the Flash then it would have had to teleport—

No, the speedster realized. *Something even faster. It moved as quick as thought!* A creation of the Weather Wizard's mind as well as of his powers, it made sense that it could be moved from one spot to another at Mardon's whim. The Flash just wished he had fully appreciated that before now.

Dust and rubble filled the hulking figure. Now and then enough pieces gathered around the "head" to form a vague semblance of a human face. Clyde Mardon's.

Mardon's obsession with Clyde is my best chance, the Flash concluded. *It may be the driving force behind all the Weather Wizard's done here, but it also keeps distracting him. If I can just make use of that distraction…*

Caitlin's voice came over the com. "It's done!"

"Then why does he still look like that?"

"He's still got what he gathered! Cisco is—"

Jumping to his feet, the Flash kept one eye on the whirlwind while closing as best he could on the Weather Wizard. Even now, the other metahuman was a danger.

"You've got to listen to me, Mardon!" Barry shouted. "All you're doing here is killing yourself! You need to stop before it's too late! I want to help you!"

"And you know what I want?" the Weather Wizard growled in his Clyde persona. "I want you to shut up!" Simultaneously, the whirlwind tried to snatch up the speedster.

Barry dodged the attack, then said, "Look at this, Mardon! Look! This is nothing but a creation of your powers!"

Bracing himself, the Flash suddenly turned and headed toward the whirlwind. As he neared, he ducked down and turned in the opposite direction of the whirlwind's natural spin. Keeping as low as he could, the Flash cut a tight circle around the whirlwind's base.

The counter wind created a disruption in the giant whirlwind. It lost cohesion, then fragmented.

The Flash felt the elements attempting to re-form. He looked over at Mardon and saw the Weather Wizard gaping at what was happening. Mardon could now see "Clyde" for what he actually was.

Barry had not wanted to do it this way. The strain he felt almost made him trip. If Cisco was taking readings, Barry felt certain that by now they had to be in the single digits. Yet still he pushed on. Then, as abruptly as he had started, the speedster broke off from his attack on the whirlwind. Not only could he not continue it at that moment, but as he had eyed Mardon again, the Flash saw his effort take effect.

The Weather Wizard had shut his mouth tight. Eyes narrowed to slits met those of the Flash.

"It's as I said, Mardon," the Flash continued as he neared. "Clyde is truly gone. I'm sorry, but that's the truth. There's only you and your guilt giving this thing any resemblance to him!"

Mardon stared at the speedster a moment and then a single word escaped his lips.

"Clyde…"

The name was followed by a guttural scream. The storm rumbled. Taking a look at the whirlwind, the Flash saw it had no semblance of anything human any more.

That's it then, Barry thought. Unlike the Flash's previous attempt to talk with Mardon, this time there would be no return of the Clyde persona. Disrupting the towering figure had finally proven once and for all that there was no Clyde and never had been.

But without the false hope of bringing his brother back, Mardon slipped again into his dark guilt. The Flash had given that some thought too. He would have to bluff Mardon.

"You damned…" the Weather Wizard growled as the two faced one another. "You took him from me not once but twice, damn you!"

"There was nothing to take, Mardon. Give up now!"

The Weather Wizard crackled with energy again. "You've taken *everything* from me! Everything! Well, I'll do you that favor in spades! I'll take everything important to you with me! You think your friend the detective is safe? His daughter?" Mardon's unearthly glow grew almost blinding. "I'll take them all from you!"

Despite the dire warning, the Flash held firm. He could not allow the Weather Wizard to know just how near to collapse he was.

"Listen to me, Mardon. It doesn't have to be this way. I know the awful pain of losing a loved one! I did some terrible things while I was grieving! It didn't help though. They were still gone…"

"Gone…" The Weather Wizard laughed abruptly. "Truth be told, I can't go on one way or the other, Flash, but it'll be a pleasure to take you, the detective, and everything else in this damned city with me! Then there can finally be—finally be—"

Mardon flared brighter. The Flash almost started forward, but knew he had to stay where he was.

"Can't… Can't seem to be able to contain it anymore anyway," Mardon managed. "Be a pleasure to let it loose on Central City…"

This is it, Barry told himself. To the Weather Wizard, he said, "Go ahead then, Mardon. I tried to do what I could for you. It's not worth it to me or anyone else anymore."

Mardon shook his head in an obvious attempt to clear it. "What're you talking about? Why aren't you begging?"

The Flash shrugged. "I can't touch you and I can't move a city. I'll just be satisfied to get everyone out. That's good enough for me."

"You… You're not making any sense. You… You're going to move all the people? That's impossible, even for you!"

"No. I did it last time, during the tidal wave," the Flash bluffed. "Turns out I didn't need to, but I don't like to take chances."

"You're lying!"

"You know what I do, Mardon. You know what I'm capable of. A city can be rebuilt. There'll be a lot to work with, but that's minor."

The Weather Wizard clutched his head. "That's not possible," he repeated to himself. He doubled over, shrieking. The Flash wanted to help, but forced himself to stay still.

"Can't control it anymore! Damn you... I won't go without taking you and West with me!"

With a final monstrous shriek, the Weather Wizard stretched both hands as high as possible. From his fingertips shot streams of energy that spiraled into the cloud-enshrouded heavens. Mardon's shriek continued unabated as energy poured from him.

Now the Flash wanted to help the Weather Wizard, but dared not. He watched, helpless, as the powers once held in check by Mardon now poured out with such force that the Weather Wizard could not have stopped the process even had he wanted to.

Central City blazed bright as the energy poured out. The stress proved to be too much for Mardon, who fell to one knee.

The whirlwind lost any traces of its semblance to Clyde Mardon. It began shifting back and forth, tearing apart more of the vicinity in the process.

Barry looked from the whirlwind to Mardon and back again, abruptly aware that the constant physical drain that he had been suffering had made him ignore one possible solution to the towering menace before him.

He turned and raced toward the tornado. As he neared, he repeated the steps he had previously taken against it. Faster and faster the Flash raced around the tornado in the opposing direction. He made the circle tighter and tighter with each turn, fighting against the natural spin of the tornado.

The reverse circle finally had its desired effect. The strain proved too much for the tornado. With what almost sounded like a loud sigh, the last of the huge whirlwind broke apart and died as a shower of refuse hit the area.

Returning his attention to Mardon, the Flash froze in shock. Mardon remained on one knee, his hands clamped to his head, his skull glowing.

Finally, there came one last monstrous burst of energy into the storm above. The sky turned an unsettling black and crimson, as if the heavens had grown molten.

A brief gasp escaped the Weather Wizard. He shook. His hands dropped to his sides.

He collapsed forward and would have struck the concrete face first if he'd not been caught at the last moment by the Flash.

The wind howled, sounding not a little like the frustrated voice of Clyde Mardon...

2 4

The sky cleared the next day. As if trapped on Noah's Ark for forty days and forty nights, far more than the usual crowds of people found reason to be outside. Repair crews were out in force too. The Flash had saved Central City from much destruction, but there was still a lot to replace, especially in the city center. Casualties had been light, but there *had* been casualties. How many of those could be blamed on the Weather Wizard and how many had simply been from the original storm was still a matter of conjecture.

Barry met Iris outside the main lab. Inside, Cisco and Caitlin were at work going over the still-comatose Weather Wizard. Mardon had not moved since collapsing.

The signal the team had sent had worked, greatly reducing the danger Mardon had represented. Barry's other efforts had taken care of the rest.

"Have you been in the lab all night?" she asked, concerned.

"I needed to be there just in case he woke up. Wally was here too."

"He promised he wouldn't come back to the lab after we got Dad home!"

Barry rubbed the back of his head. "Yeah… Joe's been back already too. He's going to help make arrangements when it comes to officially putting Mardon back into custody."

Iris sighed. "I give up. It just proves I came to the right conclusion after all."

"What does that mean?"

"It means that after all this I realize that there are some things I have to learn to live with. I still don't like the fact that Dad, you, or Wally have to risk yourselves so."

"You don't always live the quietest life," he countered.

"Don't even try to compare! As I was saying, despite that I can't imagine what the world would be like if there weren't those like you risking yourselves to keep madmen like Mark Mardon under control. Yes, it scares me, but it also makes me so damned proud of all of you. You save so many people…"

She leaned forward and kissed him.

"I'm glad to see you're not angry with me anymore," Barry murmured after they separated.

"Just… keep doing all you can to stay safe when you're out there."

"Hey, I've got you to come back to. That's all the impetus I need."

H.R. chose that moment to step out of the lab. He looked embarrassed to come across them as they were. "Sorry! Cisco sent me out to get you, Barry. I think they're finishing up with him."

"Has he woken?"

"Not so far and if we're lucky he'll wait. Joe's champing at the bit. He wants to get Mardon secured."

"Oh, does he say just where? Iron Heights is still in pieces."

H.R. shrugged.

"We'd better get inside," Iris said. "It may take all of us to convince him otherwise."

As they entered the lab, they saw Cisco and Caitlin studying a screen while Joe stood near the Weather Wizard's prone body, the detective looking ready to tackle the rogue should he wake. However, Mardon remained motionless on the platform.

"What's the verdict, Cisco?"

"Well, first of all, he's going to need a rigorous program of fluids. It seems like he hasn't had a drop of water in a week. I've seen juicier mummies."

"That sounds awful," Caitlin muttered. "I know it's Mardon, but still…"

"He also looks as if he hasn't eaten for days. Don't know how true that is, but according to records, he's several pounds lighter than he should be."

Barry studied the still form. "All important, but what about his powers? That's the most critical factor, especially before we can trust him to any prison."

Cisco tapped the screen. "Well, to put it plainly, he's shut down completely. All the readings are way down in the normal area. However that system augmented his mind, it seems it was wearing off for a while anyway. That's why everything was going terminal!" He leaned back. "Now, according to everything I've got on hand, he's back to the way he was before… or will be whenever he wakes up. I'd say his hallucinations about Clyde will be pretty much gone too. Yeah, he'll be just your ordinary villainous master of weather again. Nothing special!"

"So, if what you're saying is true," Barry responded, "then Caitlin won't be—"

"I'm free of him," she happily told them. "For the same reason, yes. I won't have to worry anymore."

"Great… But next time I want to be in the know too! You're my friend as well, Caitlin!"

"I know, Barry… I'm sorry."

"Don't you apologize, Caitlin," Iris put in.

Joe cleared his throat. "So, does that mean he can finally be shipped out?"

Cisco exhaled. "Yep. We just need to make sure he ends up somewhere where they can handle his normal powers."

"'Normal powers'," the detective grunted. "Isn't that called an oxymoron or something?"

"Not anymore."

"Well, Iron Heights still has a special hospital. It'll hold him in this condition and with those other injuries he has, they should have time to fix up something proper."

Barry stepped to the side. "Sounds like it's time for me."

Even as he spoke, he switched from his street clothes to his uniform. To the others, it was as if Barry vanished and the Flash stood in his place.

"So he's okay for this?" the speedster asked.

"With you?" Cisco nodded. "Yes."

"All right." The Flash picked up Mardon... and vanished.

The warden was among those who met the Flash at Iron Heights, quickly assuring him that the Weather Wizard would be secured properly.

"He's not the only one of his kind here, after all," the man said blithely, perhaps not realizing he was talking to one of Mardon's "kind". He guided the Flash into the prison hospital so that the speedster could see the precautions being made. "The implant will be removed later today and all will be well."

Barry silently watched as they prepared the Weather Wizard, hooking him into several machines and strapping him in so that, supposedly, his powers would be of no use if and when he woke.

Several thoughts stirred in the Flash's mind as he observed everything. Again he sympathized with Mardon's loss and the deep effect it had had on the man, however ruthless the Weather Wizard was otherwise. Clyde had been the only thing of value to his older brother. Thinking of his own losses—especially his mother—the Flash wondered if there was any way he could still someday help Mardon cope with these things. It was worth a thought, he decided.

Perhaps.

Once he was satisfied, the Flash thanked his host and sped off. More than ever Barry looked forward to being alone with Iris, being alone with the woman he loved, and just, at least for a time, feeling human.

The storm filled his world, raging in sync with his fury. The storm and he were one, powerful gods and yet ineffectual at the same time.

Once, this same storm had raged under the influence of another: his brother. Clyde was gone though. Now the storm raged in his own image, in that of Mark Mardon, the Weather Wizard.

And that storm raged around one hated image, that of the Flash and Joe West standing and mocking him. The storm assailed it, beat at it… but to no avail. Yet Mardon continued to guide its efforts to destroy the image. Even in his subconscious, the Weather Wizard knew his efforts had thus far come to nothing, but still he pounded at the image. Pounded at it with his full fury no matter how impotently those blows landed.

Impotently… At least for now.

ACKNOWLEDGEMENTS

With thanks to Cat Camacho and Steve Saffel.

ABOUT THE AUTHOR

Richard Knaak worked as a warehouseman, résumé writer, and office clerk before becoming a full-time freelance writer. He is the bestselling author of the *Dragonlance*, *Dragonrealm*, *Diablo*, and *Warcraft* novels, as well as originals such as *Dutchman*, *Ruby Flames*, and *Beastmaster: Myth*.